CASSIUS COX

Living Is Losing

First edition

ISBN: 978-1-8384450-1-0

Proofreading by Laura Joyce
Cover art by VeryMuchSo.Agency

This book was professionally typeset on Reedsy.
Find out more at reedsy.com

Contents

II   Part Two

III   Part Three

Prologue

He looked in the mirror, smiled, and felt proud. He'd achieved so much. Today was a great day. Soundproofing the basement had gone exactly to plan. Up until now, the basement had only been used for storage. There was no handle on the inside of the door and, once locked, there would be no escape. There were no windows. No exit points. Just four dark walls. It was the perfect room for the job at hand. It was big, big enough, measuring in at twelve by eighteen feet. The single bed fitted perfectly.

I

Part One

Chapter 1

'Grief is the price we pay for love'
Colin Murray Parkes

Jack

June 11th – 2 pm

Thirteen-year-old Jack Stone gazed across the water before deciding not to go in. On a scorching hot June summer's day, it was tempting, inviting even. The water that filled the old brickworks would be cold but welcoming in this heat. A gentle breeze swept across the lake causing a ripple on the surface. There were not many challenges Jack would back out of but when it came to water his choice was made easier. He couldn't swim far and hated deep water. He would not be attempting the challenge set before him by his friends. This one was a step too far.

Not all of Jack's friends shared his fear.

Shawn and Martin were the first to go in. They made their way to the island in the middle of the lake. Both were confident swimmers and had the added bravery of youth.

They were almost halfway across when, as if in slow motion and completely out of character, Sam, Jack's older brother, walked past him. As Sam stepped into the lake, Jack noticed a cloud of muddy water come to the surface. Sam had not once indicated he was going in when the friends were first daring each other. Now, he simply set off, as if on autopilot, to catch up with his two equally dauntless friends.

Horror filled Jack's body. A sickening feeling brewed up from within. 'Where 'ya going, Sam? You won't make that,' Jack said, half-heartedly. He was confused at his brother's decision to go in. He didn't want to come across like he was telling a sixteen-year-old what to do, especially in front of any of their friends, but felt he had to say something. He was thinking about what their mum and dad would say. They would go mad if they knew.

Neither brother was a strong swimmer. They'd never had lessons. Swimming wasn't an interest in their family. Their experience was limited to what they had learned from rare swimming trips at school, or the odd dip in the sea with their family on days out to the south coast of England.

While Jack stood helplessly watching, he was hoping and praying that his brother's confidence and bravery would be rewarded.

Lee was the only other friend who didn't go in. Jack looked back at Lee and froze. Was he thinking the same thing, that the other would make Sam stop?

Jack was a month away from his fourteenth birthday and before this day he wanted so much to grow up quickly. He wanted to be like his big brother, but standing on the bank of this lake, he had never felt so young.

Shawn was near to the safety of the island. He was strong. He might be only fifteen, but he had the body and strength of an adult. Martin started to struggle. He'd stopped moving forward. Jack watched him treading water. He heard him gasp, 'Shawn, I can't make it, please...' This was all he said. He probably couldn't catch his breath to say anything more.

Jack watched as Sam caught up with Martin. He heard Sam call out, 'Get on me.' Sam wanted to help him but as he tried to swim with Martin hanging onto him, the enormity that he couldn't do it must have hit him.

'Get off, Martin, I can't,' he begged. 'Martin, get off.'

Jack could see that Martin couldn't get any further without help. He couldn't let go. Self-preservation had set in for them both. They started thrashing hard against each other. They both went under the water. They reappeared, gulping for valuable air as they panicked. Their lives were being pulled away from them.

Jack was paralysed with fear, then he managed to take a few steps forward. He was in the water, but his body was in shock. Blind terror gripped him. 'Help him,' he screamed, but his words didn't come out with any volume.

Shawn was standing on the small island. He must have regained some energy because, bravely, he made his way back. He managed to get a hold of one of the friends.

From the view Jack had, he couldn't tell what was going on. Arms were flying about in a sickening attempt to save their own lives. Jack was trying to make some sense of the events that were unfolding in front of him, but he had never experienced such a gut-wrenching pain inside himself. This wasn't real. This couldn't be happening. It couldn't. This sort of tragedy only happened to others. It happened in films or to faceless strangers in the newspaper.

'Sam,' Jack shouted, cupping his hands around his mouth. 'Just keep going. Please. Keep going.' Unsettling panic was clear in Jack's voice as his screams grew louder.

Lee clutched him. 'Someone's gone under.'

'Who is it?'

'I can't tell.'

From Jack's viewpoint, all three boys looked as though they were struggling against each other, fighting for their lives. Two of them managed to carry on forward, one was pulling the other along. The last of the three was getting nowhere, struggling in one spot.

'Lee, please go in,' pleaded Jack.

'I can't. I won't make it. You go,' Lee replied, with fear in his eyes.

'I won't make that. He's gonna go under.' Jack's tears were running down his cheeks as he screamed out for help. He was feeling light-headed and unsure of what to do. He ran to another part of the lake to see if he could get nearer. Maybe he could swim across from a shorter distance. He ran across the uneven terrain not taking his eyes off the lake. Suddenly he stopped in his tracks as he spotted one of them going under again. He still didn't know who it was. An arm came back up and then slowly went back down, the forearm disappearing. Then the hand. Finally, the fingers.

Jack's scream was haunting. 'Nooo.' But no-one came. Nobody helped.

He could see two of them on the island holding each other. They were crying out loud in distress, both looking in the direction of where the body had disappeared. The water went back to how it had been, calm and still with the breeze sweeping across. It was so peaceful; despite the horror it had just inflicted.

Jack felt hazy. His vision was blurred. He rubbed his eyes

and took one more look at the island. Now he could see who had gone under.

'I never had any friends later on like the ones I had when I was twelve. Jesus, did anyone?'
Stephen King

June 11th – 9 AM

'That's bloody hot, stop it.' Jack said as he wiped himself down.

'Course it's hot, it's tea. Lee's just called. We're going out,' Sam said as he flicked more tea at his little brother before walking out of the bedroom.

'Out where? What time is it?'

Sam answered as he walked down the stairs, 'It's time to go, that's what time it is. We're going for a ride, grab ya' rucksack.'

Jack pulled the curtain back, just enough to see it was a nice day, he mumbled to himself, 'right, let's go.' He got up and dressed. He thought about brushing his teeth but chose not to and joined his brother downstairs.

'Put them in,' Sam said as he put them in himself, two giant bottles of diluted orange squash.

Jack took it off his back and felt the weight, 'Sod that, I ain't carrying them.'

'Give it here, what's wrong with you? Need to get you in the gym, build you up a bit,' Sam said as he flexed his bicep and laughed at his little brother.

'Yeah, whatever. Where are we going anyway?'

Sam picked out a few packets of crisps from the cupboard and two Snickers bars from the fridge, 'Up Anstie Lane to Coldharbour, down to Ockley to do a bit of strawberry picking, and then across to Newdigate. And then home.'

'Does mum know?' Jack asked.

She appeared in the doorway, 'Does mum know what?'

'We're going on a bike ride...with Skins, Dummy, and Parky.'

She folded her arms and repeated what Jack just said, 'Skins, Dummy, and Parky!'

'Lee Skinner, Shawn Dunmall, and Martin Parker in your language mum.'

'Why didn't you just call them that in the first place? They have Christian names for a reason.' She unfolded her arms, reached for the kettle, and started filling it up.

'Is that other kid going? The one from Willow Close, the one who looks like he needs a good bath and a smack in the ear.'

Both the boys started laughing, 'No mum. He hasn't got a bike.'

'Plus, he's too fat and won't make it,' Sam said as he held his arms out around his waist to exaggerate how fat he is.

Their mum tried not to laugh and slapped Sam's shoulder, 'Sam, that's not nice. I am glad he isn't going, I'm not sure about him. What have I always told you?'

'We know mum, show me your friends and I'll show you your future, you say it all the time.' Sam said as he raised his eyebrows.

'It's true, trust me. Your dad had some awful friends when he was young, he ended up in all kinds of trouble. Once he got away from them, he was a nice boy. And then he got me,' she smiled as she lightly flicked the switch on the kettle.'

'It's just the five of us, we'll be careful. And I promise we'll be home before dark.'

She pointed a teaspoon at Sam, 'Just stick together, and no showing off. Once one of you does something silly, you'll all do it.'

The boys replied at the same time with sarcasm, 'Yes mum.'

Sam punched Jack on the arm, 'Come on Shorty, let's go.'

Jack pretended it didn't hurt, 'Is that all you've got? Felt like a flea bite.'

Sam laughed as he brushed past his mum, ''Right, we better go, love ya' mum.'

They closed the door behind them and got their bikes from the shed.

They didn't have far to go, Lee lived next door. Jack opened the gate and there he was sitting on his bike.

'What the hell is that piece of shit?' Jack said looking at Lee, and then at his brother.

Lee rolled his eyes, 'It's all I've got. It's my sister's old one.'

Sam tilted his head to read what was on the bike, 'Raleigh Budgie, are you sure? You'll look simple riding that.' The brothers could not stop laughing.

'Piss off you two, my bike has punctures and the only other bike in the shed is my dad's. He'll bloody kill me if I touch that.'

'Don't be a pussy, just go and get it,' Sam said.

Lee nodded, 'No way, José, we are not talking about a simple telling off here. It's a proper expensive mountain bike, carbon frame, full suspension, disc brakes, the lot. If I take it, he will spark me out. Cold.'

Sam looked at Jack, and then back at Lee, 'Just go and get it.

You ain't gonna keep up with us on your pink Rayleigh Budgie. So, go get the bike and hurry up before your dad comes out. We will be out the back waiting. Hurry up.'

The brothers waited. The gate flew open, Lee came out, red in the face but laughing on his dad's bike, 'Go, go, go. He'll bloody kill me.'

The boys rode off at speed and headed for Martin's house.

Jack, Sam, and Lee pulled up outside Martin's house. Shawn was already there, helping Martin pump his tyres up.

'Here they are, Bradley Wiggins and Chris Hoy,' Sam joked.

'You're joking, I'm gonna struggle getting up Anstie Lane today,' Martin said.

Sam went and patted him on the back, 'I'll give you a little push if you're struggling.'

'I'll make it, don't worry about me.' Martin stood up, grabbed a bottle of squash, and walked behind Sam.

'Here you go mate, stick that in there.' Martin undid the rucksack and put it in.

Sam stopped smiling, 'Cheers mate, put a couple of bricks in while ya' there.'

Martin laughed, 'Come on, you're a big boy, you can take it.'

Jack grinned, 'Serves you right.'

'Shut it shorty,' Sam replied to his brother.

'Martin, what is that on your head?' Lee asked.

'It's a helmet, Lee. Mum said I have to wear it.'

Lee's smile was slowly building, 'Up to you. But you look a right dick.'

'When one of you lot come off and crack your head open, we'll see who's laughing.'

Lee looked over to Jack, 'Why would he be laughing if we cracked our head open? Sounds a bit sick to me. Martin, you need help.'

Martin nodded, 'You know that's not what I meant...anyway, I'm wearing it so shut up.'

Jack watched Shawn finish pumping the tyres, then gave him a fist pump, 'Are we ready to go?'

'Yep, he's all good now,' Shawn replied.

'Good luck keeping up with me on this thing, c'mon, let's go benders,' Lee said as he attempted to pull a wheelie and rode off.

'He such a dick,' Sam said as they got on their bikes and followed.

'That's a lovely hand signal you've done there, Martin,' Sam said with just the right amount of sarcasm.

'Passed my cycling proficiency with flying colours, bet you lot didn't?' Martin replied.

They turned left and headed up Moorhurst Lane.

'Crashed on mine. That arse of a teacher got in my way. Mrs. Westgate, she put her arm out and I crashed into the bloody sign, completely her fault.' Lee said.

'So, you didn't see her standing there with her massive hi-vis coat? She wasn't exactly small, was she? she was so big planes going into Gatwick tried to land on her.'

The lads laughed. All apart from Lee.

'Yeah, whatever. I don't need to know the poxy hand signals anyway, it's a bit square. I just let rulebook Martin lead the way.'

'Piss off Lee,' Martin replied.

The road ahead was covered by shade from giant trees that

went on for miles. 'Mind that corner, it's a sharp one, cars come around there bloody quick. Keep to the left.' Jack shouted.

'Now who's being a rulebook?' Martin said.

'Just get over to the left ya' knobhead or you'll get knocked off.'

As Jack said that a white van came around the corner, narrowly missing Sam. The driver sounded his horn blaming the lads.

'Sam, what did I just say, be careful.'

'Calm down, I had it covered.' Sam looked at Jack with raised eyebrows knowing that was a close one.

They carried on to the top of Moorhurst, and once at the top they turned onto Anstie Lane. The boys were ready for the challenge. It was a comfortable start but once they hit the max 22% incline, it got the legs burning. There were no more jokes and no talk of any kind until they hit the top.

Lee made it first, 'bloody love this bike, what a piece of kit. I struggled at first but once I put it in granny gear, I pissed it.'

Jack pulled up next. 'Good for you, I'm breathing out of my backside. I'm stopping here for a bit,' he said as he parked his bike against the fence and took in the view across the Surrey Hills and into London, 'I'll never get bored of that view.'

Sam pulled up next to him, 'Right, one of you lot can carry these drinks. I'd have beaten Lee if I didn't have twelve stone on my back.'

Jack laughed, 'Yeah right. Give me the bag, I need a drink. That'll help lighten the load. You were so slow, looked like you were pedalling through treacle.'

Martin came in next. Followed by Shawn, between deep breaths he spoke, 'The next bit to Ockley is mostly downhill, reckon I weigh the most, so I'll smash you lot on that. No more of this uphill crap, this isn't the Tour de France.'

'Tour de dickhead more like,' Lee said looking round the group with a grin.

Lee took his t-shirt off, 'Time to get some sun on this work of art,' he said as he flexed his small but growing muscles.

Jack spat out his drink laughing at Lee, 'Look at you, it's like looking at Arnold Schwarzenegger himself.'

'Might see some birds, gotta let them see the goods, show 'em the whole thing,' Lee said as he raised his arms.

Jack pointed at Lee, 'Oh yeah, they will be throwing themselves at you. But I'm pretty sure Ockley isn't full of birds. Fields and cow shit, yes; girls, no.'

'Well, we can't all have a girlfriend at school, can we? How is Kirsten?'

Jack stopped laughing, 'She's not my girlfriend so stop talking about her.'

Lee grinned and poked Jack, 'Then you won't mind if I ask her out then? I'd love to get hold of her.'

'You dare, leave her alone.' Jack said putting his finger in Lee's face.

Lee held his hands up, 'Point proved. Just ask her out, you big pussy.'

Jack shrugged, 'I might. One day.'

'She's a good-looking girl, you need to get in there quick before one of the others asks her out. My dad says time waits for no man. So, get in there, she might let you touch her...'

Jack pushed Lee before he could finish, 'Shut it, now.'

'Come on you two, let's go,' Sam said as he took his shirt off. One by one all the lads took their t-shirts off, they were all sweating loads in the eighty-degree heat.

'That's right, take the piss, then you all copy me,' Lee said.

As Sam got on to his bike he looked back at Lee, 'That maybe so, but I look better doing it.'

'He's got a point, you can't argue with that Arnie,' Martin said followed by his best Arnold Schwarzenegger impression, 'I'll be back. Get to the chopper'

Lee shook his head, 'Dicks. All of ya'.'

A quick look out to the road, no cars coming, they flew out on to the main road. Cranked their gears up and pedalled hard. They flew past The Plough pub and headed downhill. Jack's bike had a digital speedometer, he could see the speed they reached as they went down the steepest hill into Ockley, twenty-nine miles per hour, his handlebars started shaking so he gently pulled on both brake levers. His speed dropped gradually to twenty-two miles per hour. Lee overtook him, 'Pussy, leave the brakes alone,' he shouted.

Jack could tell Sam, Martin and Shawn hadn't touched their brakes once, he could see them trying to go faster than they already were, all three of them were crouched down in what they thought was the most aerodynamic position possible. Jack was worried that one puncture, one large stone in the road, and they would crash for sure, and it would be a serious crash. He decided not to say anything, if he did they would mock him, plus he knew they wouldn't slow down even if he told them to. He couldn't wait for them all to be safe at the bottom.

The sign in front of them said pick your own strawberries. They threw their bikes down in a heap on the roadside and headed in. Apart from Lee who gently put his dad's bike against a fence where he could see it at all times.

'Look at the size of this one,' Sam said as he threw it at Shawn hitting him in the back.

Shawn turned around, 'who did that?'

Sam pointed at Lee. Before Lee could deny the accusation, Shawn took the juiciest strawberry he could find from his basket and threw it. Lee wasn't quick enough to move, it hit him in the forehead, exploding red juice into his eyes.

Jack fell to his knees laughing, he couldn't get his breath he was laughing so hard.

'Funny is it?' Lee said. He took out three strawberries and pushed them into the back of Jack's head. His hair turned red, 'That's for being a West Ham fan.'

'You prick, I'll have wasps chasing me everywhere now.' Jack got up to his feet and threw one back at Lee.

'I'm having some of this,' Martin said as he threw one hitting Shawn in the chest.

The boys heard shouting in the distance. It gradually got close enough for them to hear.

'You lot. That's enough. You are paying for all of those, the ones you've thrown, the ones you've eaten, and the ones you take home,' the lady said.

She had her hands on her hips and her teeth were showing.

Lee nudged Jack, 'She looks happy, don't fancy yours much.'

Jack sniggered, 'Shut up, Lee.'

'Alright love calm down. We'll pay on our way out,' Lee said.

She walked up to Lee, 'I know you will. Bloody fools. Hurry up and go.'

Sam came forward, 'We are very sorry. We'll come over now and pay.'

She tutted, turned her back, and walked back to the farm

shop. As she walked away Lee walked behind her mimicking her walk with his hands on his hips. She suddenly stopped and turned around. Lee stopped and looked in the air like he wasn't up to anything.

'Just hurry up and go,' she said.

The boys paid for the strawberries, including the extra charge that the lady had put on to satisfy her fury. They then stood out by their bikes eating their prize. Lee walked in front of them all and said, 'look at this, she didn't find these,' as he pulled open his shorts and pulled out handfuls of strawberries, 'Silly cow didn't check there did she?'

'Neither would I,' Shawn said as he pretended to be sick.

'At least you've got plenty of room in there,' Sam said laughing.

'Anyone want one?' Lee said as he waved them in the lads' faces.

'Piss off, not where they've been, they've touched your maggot,' Jack said.

Lee smiled as he carried on getting bits of strawberry out of his shorts, 'Bigger than yours.' He waved his little finger at Jack.

Sam got on to his bike, 'Come on you lot, let's get to the old brickworks, wash this sticky shit off.'

They headed along Coles Lane, across to the village of Capel, and then into Newdigate.

Once they arrived, they could see there were lots of people already swimming in the water. The bit they normally went to was only around fifteen meters to the island. But that was packed with other kids.

'Let's go around the other side, there's no one around there,' Sam said as he waved the gang to follow him.

Jack did not move. He looked out to the water feeling nervous.

Sam patted him on the back, 'Come on bruv, let's go.'

Chapter 2

'No one ever told me that grief felt like fear.'
C.S. Lewis

Jack

Jack's mum, Liz, decided not to go. She said she wanted to remember her beautiful son the way she last saw him. Remember the final hug he gave her that morning and his last words, 'Love ya', Mum,' as he left their garden, closing the gate behind him.

Jack entered the funeral home with his father, Ken. They were taken through to the room where Sam's body lay. There it was, the heavy wooden coffin with a padded white velvet material that encased Sam's body, a sheet covering him up to his chest. Jack moved slowly forward taking in that smell, the smell of embalming chemicals. A smell he would never forget.

'Dad, that doesn't look like Sam,' he said, turning to his father for answers. 'He looks cold, Dad. He looks cold.'

Jack felt his dad's grip on his hand tighten but his father had no words of comfort for him. There were none. He wondered if his dad was regretting the decision to let him come to the funeral home. The police had advised it was sometimes a good idea for older children to go, especially in Jack's situation. Being that Jack's last memory of Sam was traumatic, they suggested it would be good for him to see Sam at rest. Jack's mum had disagreed, saying Jack was too young.

Jack touched Sam's chest. It felt like stone, cold, and hard. He started to cry and leant forward to kiss his brother on the forehead. He turned and caught the pained look on his dad's face. He looked broken. Jack looked back at his brother and could hear his dad whispering to Mr Sherlock, the owner of the funeral home. 'He shouldn't have to do this, not at his age. I can't do this.'

Jack watched Mr Sherlock comforting his dad.

Jack wanted to grab Sam and take him home. He couldn't bear to be parted from him. The thought of leaving him alone in that coffin, in this cold room, made him panic. His breathing became fast and he couldn't get enough air. 'Dad,' he said, 'we can't go. We can't leave him.' He knew it would be the last time he would ever see his brother again.

'We have to, son. It's time. Let Sam rest,' said his dad. 'We have to go. We'll get through this together. Sam will always be with you. You know that, don't you? He's with you in here.' Jack's dad touched Jack on his heart. 'He'll be with you forever.'

Jack didn't reply.

Sam's funeral took place two weeks after his death. The church was full. Shawn, Lee, and Martin were given seats near the front. It would be the first time the boys had met up since that day. The gang was back together, but they were missing one piece of their puzzle.

Jack looked at his friends. Lee was looking down, clearly distraught but no tears. Martin and Shawn were both crying uncontrollably and being comforted by their parents.

Shawn caught Jack's gaze. 'You OK?' he mouthed. Jack shrugged.

'Sorry,' Shawn mouthed next.

Jack didn't understand. He didn't think Shawn needed to be sorry. Jack blamed no one. No one except himself.

Large numbers of pupils from Sam's school were there. Some knew him. Some didn't. Jack thought that, like him, it would be their first experience of loss. Sam dying affected them all and they must have felt they needed to be there. He wondered if some of them were trying to imagine what he was going through and thanking God it wasn't them, sitting there at the front, heartbroken and destroyed by grief.

During the first hymn, Make Me a Channel of Your Peace, Jack felt panicky. The lyrics didn't make sense to him. 'In dying we are born to eternal life.' He'd had enough. He looked around the church, at the stained-glass windows that were full of colour. Jesus on the cross overlooked them all. Jack was scared to be in there. The ceiling was so high, with huge dark oak beams covered in cobwebs. In front of Jack, a cushion was hanging. He tapped it gently, over and over with his fist. If there was a God, why would this happen?

He touched his mother's arm. 'I want to leave. I've got to go,' he said. 'I can't do it, and everyone's staring at me.'

His mother held his hand tightly. 'It won't be much longer. We can go soon,' she whispered.

Jack didn't want to be there a minute longer. He felt like he was at a circus, and he was the main act. He could feel all eyes on him. He received the same look from everyone. He noticed people would tilt their heads slightly and look at him in pity, or was it blame? He wasn't sure.

As Sam's coffin went beyond the curtains *You'll Never Walk Alone* played. Part of the song triggered a specific memory of Sam, his chest tightened. He had been afraid of the dark when he was younger and would often jump out of his bed and hop in with his big brother. Sam used to call him silly and tell him, 'Get in your bed and don't be a baby.' But Sam would always relent and let Jack have his way. He always did. He looked after him. He loved him, his little brother. Jack would sometimes feel Sam give him a brotherly hug once he thought he'd gone back to sleep.

He sat listening to the words about walking alone. It was exactly how he felt. He was now walking alone. He no longer had his big brother, his hero. His dad was alone too. Jack envied his strength as he stood to thank everyone for coming to the funeral. He'd shake their hand and say the same thing over and over.

It wasn't until that evening that Jack heard his dad cry. His parents were in the front room with the door closed but Jack could hear them from where he stood in the hallway. He heard his father asking 'Why, why did it happen to them? ' His mother was going through poignant moments they'd all shared: holding Sam as a baby, helping him take his first steps, watching their father hold the back of Sam's bike seat and then letting go for the first time as Sam rode unaided. Sam had no idea that his dad had let go. He'd thought he was still there until he looked around and his dad was behind him fading away into the distance. He was riding a bike, by himself.

Liz chuckled and repeated what Sam said on that day. 'Daddy, I'm doing it. I'm doing it. Look at me.'

They talked about how they had been looking forward to teaching Sam how to drive a car next year, but now that had been cruelly snatched away. The comment that broke his mother was the mention of not getting to see Sam married or having children. She cried uncontrollably then. Jack had heard more than he could take, it was too painful.

He went to his bedroom alone.

Chapter 3

'No man chooses evil because it is evil; he only mistakes it for happiness, the good he seeks.'
Mary Wollstonecraft

David

David also lived in Dorking but had never met Jack. He was slightly older and had had a very different upbringing, mollycoddled by his mum. He had heard about the drowning of the boy in the local lake, everybody in town had, but he didn't know Jack.

He always felt different, abnormal even, but he accepted it. He didn't have friends and didn't want them.

His dad questioned him many times when he'd caught him looking at images on his computer, but he'd deny they were his and then delete them. His mum would choose not to believe the hearsay. She would defend him against the world. Accusations going back to school days were ignored, she would blame anyone, even the teachers for picking on *her boy.*

If anyone would question or accuse her David of anything, she would shut them out of her life, and that included her own family.

David's auntie brought her son, Bertie, around most weeks. She would let him play with his big cousin, David. David would always insist on the door being closed. And for a long time, no-one in the family thought anything of it, until his dad walked in on them.

David was seventeen. His cousin seven. They shared a love of gaming, but Bertie had to earn his right to play. 'If you touch me, you can have a go,' said David.

Bertie hesitated. 'Not this again. This is silly.'

David watched his cousin thinking about what to do.

'OK, touch you where?' said Bertie.

'Only on my tummy, to start with,' said David.

'I'll do it, but I want a long time on the game.'

David smiled as he lifted his shirt and felt his cousin's warm hand press on to his skin.

Bertie was loving playing on the computer, he was laughing and shouting in frustration when his character died.

'My turn now.' David snatched the controller.

Bertie got upset. 'No. I want one more go. Please.'

David rubbed his chin in an exaggerated fashion. 'One more go. But you have to touch me again.'

'I don't want to,' said Bertie, his bottom lip quivering.

David shrugged his shoulders. 'No problem. You can watch me play. Come on, out of the seat.'

'OK, where?' Bertie replied.

'I'll show you.' David undid the string on his tracksuit bottoms and pulled them down.

The door opened and David's dad entered the room. He covered his mouth in shock, but his tone of voice was friendly as he spoke to his nephew. 'Bertie, please go downstairs. I just need to have a chat with David.' He took Bertie's hand

24

and led him out of the room.

David followed and watched as his dad stopped at the top of the stairs. His father thought no-one else was listening and bent down to Bertie's eye level. 'Bertie, please don't tell your mum about the game, just say you played on the computer. And if you do that, you can go to the kitchen and help yourself to the chocolate tin.'

David smiled. His dad was protecting him, again.

He carried on watching as Bertie grinned. 'And a fizzy drink?'

'Yes. And a fizzy drink There are cans in the fridge. You know the chocolate tin I mean, don't you?'

'Of course I do.' Bertie smiled and ran downstairs.

Unaware David was watching, his dad walked back into the bedroom. David jumped back to his seat and started playing his game, laughing with his back to his dad.

'Look at me,' his dad said.

No response.

His voice grew louder. 'I said look at me. Now, or I'll pull the bloody plug out.'

David slowly turned around in his chair keeping the smile on his face. 'What?'

At that moment he saw the hatred in his dad's eyes. He'd never seen it before.

'What. Is that all you can say?' his dad said. His face was red.

'Chill out, Dad. It was just a game. Look at you, all red like a tomato. You'll have a heart attack if you're not careful.' He swung back around on his chair and picked up the controller.

David felt his chair being yanked around until he was facing his dad who was spitting with anger.

25

'He's a little boy, only seven years old. He was touching you. Do you understand what will happen to you? Prison, that's what. They'll call you a paedophile, the lowest of the low.'

David pushed his dad away. 'I'm not one of those. It was just a game.' He sat back down and carried on with his game.

'You're my son and I love you, but I have limits. I will not protect you forever, not if that's what you are. Your mother can't see it. She doesn't believe me when I say what I think you might be, but I promise you, I'll happily lock you up myself if that's what you are. She hasn't got long left and I don't want her going knowing that about you.'

David's smile had gone as he turned and stood face to face with his Dad. 'Just leave me alone. There's nothing wrong with me. Maybe you're the weird one for thinking such things. I was just trying to make Bertie happy.'

His dad raised his hand. David flinched and put his arms up to defend himself. But nothing came of it. When David lowered his hands, he saw tears run down his dad's face. Then he watched him as he left the room.

When Bertie's mum walked into the kitchen to wash up her cup before they left to go home, she caught her Bertie going into the chocolate tin. 'You should ask your Auntie before you help yourself to her chocolate.'

Bertie smiled at his mum. 'It's OK. Uncle said I could. But only if I didn't tell you about the game I played.'

She grinned. 'Did he now? I think you should tell me about the game.' She turned the tap on and started rinsing her cup, smiling at the thought of them all having fun together.

'David said I had to touch him if I wanted to go on the game. I don't like touching him, it's...'

She dropped the cup into the sink. There was a smash as the china cup broke into pieces.

Her sister came running in. 'Are you all right? What happened?'

She made Bertie repeat himself, but her sister wouldn't listen. Their row was heated and a lot of opinions on David were given.

Her sister threw them both out, disgusted that she would believe her seven-year-old son over her David. Bertie looked back at his Auntie, not realizing he wouldn't see her again.

Chapter 4

*'It takes courage to grow up and turn out to be who you really
are.'*

e.e cummings

Jack

Life had to move on, but Jack had not; the days and weeks
were hard. Jack handled his grief by spending hours at night
tormenting himself. He would play the music that reminded
him of his brother and, as the music played, he would look
at the same old photos over and over again. Photos of them
together. He felt that if he didn't cry every day then he didn't
care enough. The guilt was crippling. He played this music
until late at night and would cry himself to sleep. Every
morning he would wake, open his eyes, and hope that it
wasn't real. Dreams of Sam being alive felt so vivid that some
mornings Jack would wake and wish he hadn't. He'd wish he
didn't have to wake up ever again. Thoughts of suicide were
creeping in, but no thoughts on how to do it yet. He hadn't
got that far.

Sam's hair gel, a can of Lynx deodorant and some cheap
aftershave were all still in the same spot. Sam's hairbrush still

had strands of his hair attached to the bristles. Jack couldn't bring himself to throw any of it out.

Jack turned as his mother entered his room. She always said he got his blue eyes from her, and like his, hers too were bloodshot from another night of crying. He could see that his Mum was losing weight. She had hardly eaten since losing her Sam. She was already slightly built and couldn't afford to lose much more without becoming unwell. Her beautiful blonde hair, usually kept perfect, was being neglected and she hadn't used any makeup since the funeral.

'Jack, can I move Sam's clothes out of your room?' she asked.

Jack's response was immediate. 'NO! Leave them alone.' His eyes filled with tears again. He hadn't meant to shout at his Mum and instantly regretted it.

He felt her hand gently touch his shoulder. 'It's all right, Jack. We can leave them here. I just thought...' Jack waited, but Liz didn't end the sentence.

As she left, he felt bad and hated the thought of upsetting her. Creeping out of his room, he looked into hers. She was curled up on her bed. He couldn't make it better for her. He didn't know how.

He would hear his parents arguing. The suggestion of counselling for him came up regularly. His mother was pushing for it saying it was the only way Jack could start to feel better, but Jack had told her he wouldn't go, and he couldn't be forced.

His father, a well-built man from years of manual work and going to the gym, was old school and not one for talking about emotions. He refused to push Jack into going. He'd aged since losing Sam. He looked tired and his hair was greying. Jack heard him say that he'd been through enough, that he didn't need therapy. The police advised that counselling would be a good thing, but his father had said it had been wrong to take Jack to the funeral home. That decision had been based on their opinion and he didn't want to make a wrong decision again.

Jack had the dilemma of when to go back to school. The thought of this made him physically sick. He didn't want to go back as he knew all eyes would be on him again, just like at the funeral. He missed his friends. He even missed certain teachers. He also wished he could see Kirsten again. He liked her. He could talk to her and not feel awkward like he did with other girls. He'd been close to asking her to be his girlfriend, but the fear of rejection scared him. If she said no, would the friendship be over? And now their relationship was another victim of that day. Something else that had suffered.

Kirsten had the most stunning, kind eyes. During class, when she looked at him, she made him feel that he was the only person in the room, despite what was going on around them at that time. She was the one girl he'd always felt comfortable around. He didn't need to show off or be scared to say the wrong thing. He'd love to talk to her now, but he couldn't.

Jack had noticed she was at the funeral, but he didn't get the chance to be near her. He wanted to thank her for being there, he wanted to say so much, talk to her the way he couldn't to anyone else. Kirsten didn't know Sam very well, so Jack knew she was there for him. Her being there was the one bright light on the darkest of days.

The school had put Sam's name on a plaque and planted a tree in his memory. Shawn had told him that the plaque was on the wall as they entered the playground. Jack knew he would have to see this every day once he returned. They invited the family into school on the day the tree was planted but Jack didn't go. The thought of being stared at by the other pupils was too much. His parents went. They told him they felt they should, and that it was a kind gesture by the school.

'Do you want to go back to school yet?' his mother would often ask.

'No...one day. But not yet.' Always the same reply.

'When you're ready, you let us know.' His mother would smile, and Jack knew this meant he didn't have to.

He'd stay at home in the day and be alone reading or watching films, but he'd started to meet his friends off the school bus. His closest friends all lived in the same quiet village of Beare Green. The bus would pull in around 4 pm and Jack would be there waiting. Most days were the same. The four friends would chat about how school was going, then Jack would build up enough confidence to ask how Kirsten was. The three of them would look at each other and grin. Jack would blush and tell them to piss off.

They'd talk about football and how crap their teams were doing. They all supported different teams and would mock each other if they lost.

The subject they rarely brought up was Sam.

Jack started looking forward to his daily meet with the lads. His confidence was steadily building, and he felt he might try school soon. But then that confidence was rocked. He was waiting as usual for his friends to get off the bus. He looked past the other pupils and saw Martin was crying and being comforted by Shawn. Jack could see the indignation in Lee's eyes. He felt uncomfortable inside, and his eyes widened. This feeling was new, a fit of uncontrollable anger was desperate

31

to come out.

Jack went to Lee first. 'What's happened?'

He could tell Lee didn't want to tell him. Lee wouldn't look him in the eye.

Jack pulled on Lee's jumper. 'Tell me, now.'

'That fucking divvy kid asked Martin if it was true that we'd pushed Sam in the water. He asked if it was a prank that went wrong. He said we did it.'

Jack saw Shawn shake his head at Lee in disappointment. 'I told you not to mention it to Jack,' he said.

A red mist descended over Jack. He'd never felt like wanting to hurt someone before. He did now.

'Who said it? What kid?'

'There he is,' said Lee.

Daniel King, a weaselly looking boy with crooked teeth and a lazy eye. He didn't stand a chance as Jack ran at him and, like a pack of wolves, his friends followed. They all gave chase, closing in on their prey. Daniel was running but he wasn't quick. Shawn followed them all and was pulling Jack back by his T-shirt. 'Don't do it mate.'

Lee and Martin caught Daniel and held him as he fought to get away. Shawn stood in front of Jack. 'Don't, Jack. Daniel's a gobby little shit, I know he is, but don't hurt him.'

The old Jack would have stopped, he'd have listened to Shawn. The old Jack would have thought about this first and acted in the correct way later, but things had changed. Jack had changed.

Daniel kept saying he was sorry. 'I didn't mean it. It's what they were all saying at school. It wasn't just me. I didn't mean it. I was asking, that's all.'

Lee and Martin held an arm each. 'Go on, do him, Jack. If

you smack him hard enough maybe it will put his eye straight,' Lee said, goading him on.

Ken had taught Jack how to throw a punch, but Jack had never hit another human, only a punchbag.

He planted his feet and threw a jab to Daniel's nose, followed by an overhand right. Martin and Lee flinched at the sound of fist hitting jaw, bone against bone.

Jack felt instant relief at taking out his pain and anger on this boy.

Daniel was on the ground, curled up into a ball, crying and bleeding heavily from his nose. 'Please stop. I didn't mean it. I want to go home.'

Shawn stepped in and pushed Jack away. 'Enough. That's enough. Let him go.' Shawn was in front of Jack staring hard into his eyes. 'You're my best friend but, Jack, just look at yourself.'

Jack stared down at his fists and saw the blood that covered his knuckles. He was unsure if it was his blood or Daniel's. It didn't matter. He took another look at Daniel and then at Shawn and said, 'Fuck him,' as he walked away.

Shawn pointed down at Daniel. 'This isn't right, Jack. Look at him.'

Jack didn't listen and carried on walking.

Shawn turned his attention to the other two. 'Bloody idiots. Go home. You've done enough.'

'He deserved it. The little prick,' said Lee.

Shawn pointed at Lee. 'Go home now. Martin, take him home.'

Martin listened and led Lee away.

Lee knew Shawn was serious. Shawn was tall and strong, stronger than Lee, and he knew it. Lee had no choice but to walk away.

Shawn helped Daniel to his feet. He then straightened Daniel's collar and handed him his school bag, checking his injuries as he did so.

'Please don't tell anyone. Jack isn't back to his old self yet. It's not like him, you know that. He didn't mean it. You know he wouldn't normally do that, don't you?'

Daniel shook his head and pointed to his nose. 'My face. He's an animal. He's not right in the head. Just get off and leave me alone.'

That evening the doorbell rang, followed by a hard, double knock. Liz answered the door.

'Mrs Stone, please can I come in?'

Liz paused before replying. 'Err, yes but what's happened?' Awful memories came rushing back, memories of that day. The day the police had told her about Sam.

'I'm PC Mason. There's been an incident involving Jack. Is he here?'

'He came home earlier but went straight to his room. What do you want with him?'

'Four boys, including your Jack, were involved in assaulting another pupil after leaving the school bus.

'Who? What four boys?'

The policeman took out his notepad, 'Jack Stone, Lee Skinner, Martin Parker and Shawn Dunmall. The other boy, Daniel King has sustained serious injuries. His parents don't want to press charges. They know what you and your whole family have been through recently. To be honest, I'm not sure I'd be so kind. We're aware Daniel may have provoked them, we know what he said, but that doesn't mean Jack and his friends can use violence.'

Liz noticed PC Mason looking past her, probably to see if there was any sign of Jack.

He continued. 'Daniel has admitted he said some painful lies and he's sorry, but I've seen the lad. He has a broken nose and is very shaken.'

Liz was shocked. Her son didn't assault people. He was a gentle lad. He wouldn't do that. She turned to Ken who was in the background listening. Before Liz could reply, Ken came forward.

'I'm sorry, officer. I really hope the boy is all right. This won't happen again. I'll talk to Jack. I promise this isn't how we do things in this family. Jack knows violence doesn't solve anything but he's angry at the world and it sounds like this Daniel said some bad things. Kids can be so cruel.'

PC Mason went to reply but Ken cut him off. 'I'll talk to Jack about other ways to deal with these situations Leave it with me.'

Liz was nervous, despite Ken being polite she knew when he was getting angry. He'd stop blinking and stare intently. She was hoping the officer would believe Ken and leave.

Liz smiled at the officer.

Ken continued. 'Listen, you know what the boy said to Jack. I'm not going to apologise for my son's actions. Are they pressing charges or not?'

Liz rubbed her forehead. 'Ken, please don't.'

Before Ken could reply to Liz the officer spoke. 'Don't worry, Mrs Stone. I'll leave. You've all been through enough. Just doing my job, Mr Stone. I understand you're upset. I can't begin to imagine what you're going through, but Jack can't go around being violent. That's not a path he wants to go down.'

Liz reached for Ken's hand and squeezed.

'I'll talk to him, I'm sorry if I was rude.'

The officer nodded, thanked them for their time and left.

Once the front door was closed, Liz spoke to Ken. 'I can't deal with this. You need to talk with Jack.'

He touched her arm. 'I'll talk to him, Liz, but that kid should have kept his mouth shut. I'd have done the same thing as Jack. You know Daniel's family. Soap-dodging arseholes, the lot of 'em.'

Liz managed a weak smile. 'I know you would have. That's the problem. That's not my Jack.'

'I'm glad Jack hit him, and I hope it hurt. Have you seen how ugly he is? Probably did him a favour. If his father comes around here...'

'Enough,' Liz shouted. She'd heard enough. 'Don't, Ken. No more violence. No wonder Jack hit him. He wants to be like you. You need to make this right, tell Jack it's not the way to behave.'

She heard Ken sigh and exhale heavily. 'I'll talk to him. But we need to help him control his grief. He's bound to be angry. He's a boy, and boys fight. Maybe he should go boxing like I did. There's a good club in the town with a coach I know. Pete.'

Liz stood in front of Ken. 'No. No way. You know my feelings on that. Boxing was something you did. They're not like you.' She paused. 'I mean, Jack isn't like you. He can use his brain, not have it beaten in,' she shouted.

'Boxing never did me any harm. It taught me respect. How many street fights did I have once I started boxing?' Liz didn't answer so he continued. 'None. That's how many. It will do him good, give him confidence and show him he doesn't need to fight outside of the gym.'

Liz leaned against the table, her head and shoulders drooped. 'No. He's my son and I say no. I've lost one son already. I can't lose another. I won't.' She was in tears. She felt Ken move closer. He was right behind her, but he didn't comfort her. She wasn't sure she wanted him to. Nothing could ease her pain. Only one thing would make things better and he couldn't give her that. No one could.

Ken made his way to Jack's room and pushed the door open. He could see Jack was asleep. His eyes were puffy and red, from crying. Music was playing. Music from Jack's playlist. Ken picked up Jack's smartphone to see which song was playing. 'One More Light' by Linkin Park.

He could see blood on a T-shirt on the floor. He picked it up and scanned the room - Sam's old deodorant, Sam's hairbrush, and his photos. He took in all the memories and then stared down at Jack, knowing he couldn't take away his pain. The empty feeling in Ken's chest felt sickening. He tried to compose himself but couldn't get his breath. Inside he was screaming, asking himself the same question. Why? A photo of him and Sam was in front of him. Sam looked so happy and full of life. Ken held the photo and sank to the floor.

More painful months went by for Jack and his family. Jack had not returned to school. Instead, he would spend his days at home watching films. The Rocky films were his favourite choice. Watching Rocky reminded him of happier times. His dad loved these films and would put them on all the time. As the boys got older, Sam, Jack and their dad would watch them together. By the time the film finished the boys would have boxing gloves on, recreating the fight scenes. Their father would be the ref. He would count to ten whilst one of the boys pretended to be knocked out. Their mother would smile and say, 'It'll end in tears.' She was usually right.

Films helped Jack get through the hardest of days. Escapism was better than listening to the painful thoughts in his head. He couldn't handle the silence. His thoughts were becoming too dark.

He felt close to his dad when they bonded whilst watching films. He'd get excited when his father dug out his old DVDs and show him past fights of the greats like Mike Tyson, Muhammed Ali, and Joe Frazier. He would educate Jack on the great British fighters he loved like Nigel Benn, Chris Eubank, Steve Collins, Prince Naseem Hamed, Joe Calzaghe, and Ricky Hatton. Jack asked hundreds of questions. His passion for the sport was obvious and he knew his dad loved doing this with him.

Jack would ask him to rewind clips and demonstrate the punch combinations. He loved how animated his father would get. 'See, Jack. Look how he threw that shot,' and then he would get Jack to copy it. Or he would say, 'Come on, I'll show you in the garden.' They had a punching bag out there. His dad would correct his stance until it was perfect. He'd show him how to generate power through his legs. Other times they'd simply train, taking it in turns hitting the heavy bag or doing press-ups, sit-ups, and pull-ups. They didn't talk much during these workouts, but it was quality time together. Jack would sometimes catch his mother watching from the door. She'd smile and he knew she was happy for them, but he felt she was growing further away from them both.

Night-time was the hardest. He still found sleeping hard. Every time he closed his eyes, he'd see Sam going under the water. He'd start to cry and the more he cried the more he felt he deserved this pain. He was crying when he heard a noise at his door. He froze and stayed silent. He didn't reach for the handle, instead he put his ear against the door. He could hear his mother crying on the other side. Had she been listening to him? Why couldn't she bring herself to come in? Jack's hand hovered above the handle. He desperately wanted to open the door. He wanted to hold his mum. And he wanted to be held.

Chapter 5

'Anger is just a cowardly extension of sadness. It's a lot easier to be angry at someone than it is to tell them you're hurt.'
Tom Gates

Jack

Liz was sleeping in a separate room to Ken. The last few years had been hard on them both. The glue holding them together was Jack, and she knew he was living in his own painful world, a world of anger, grief, and confusion. When Liz and Ken did speak, it was about Jack. They were both worried about his behaviour. He was their why, their reason for pushing forward with life, but neither of them wanted to come down hard on him when he needed it.

Liz knew Jack wasn't being guided in right and wrong. He was doing as he pleased and was coming in at all hours. She didn't want to take the risk of being the disciplinarian, the fear of upsetting and pushing him further away was too strong. She knew Ken probably felt the same way. They both wanted to be the good guy.

Liz still wanted Jack to have counselling, but Ken didn't agree and wanted him to find a focus in life, he thought that focus could be boxing.

'I'm off out Mum,' Jack shouted, and made a quick exit before she could ask where he was going.

Jack, Shawn, Martin, and Lee had been using alcohol more and more. It started with cheap cider and weak beer over in the local park. Any chance they had to get hold of some booze they would take it. They'd ask the older lads locally to get it for them which would normally mean losing a can or two, but it was worth it. They agreed that was a fair price to pay. Jack's anger was especially bad when he was drunk. The boys would start out having fun, but then things would turn sour. The alcohol would often trigger them into bringing up Sam's name. They would talk about what could have been done differently on that day, but they normally stopped short of blaming each other.

They'd started early that night, and the alcohol had kicked in. Jack noticed Lee's eyes were heavy. He could feel Lee was about to say something upsetting, and he did. 'I miss him... do ya' think we'd still be sitting around here getting pissed if Sam was alive?'

'Let's change the subject,' Shawn said. Jack knew Shawn's intentions were good. He'd noticed him look over in Lee's direction as he made the comment.

Lee often brought the subject of Sam up. He couldn't help himself. Jack wasn't surprised.

'If I want to talk about him, I will. Sam was my best friend. I'll never forget him. I don't think you realise how close we were. I'll never get that back, that friendship. We should have saved him,' Lee said.

Jack, blaming himself, didn't know if Lee was directing that last comment at him. Did Lee blame him too?

Jack felt uneasy as he watched Lee pace about. He could feel himself go tense and started digging his nails into the palm of his hand as he made a fist.

Jack knew Shawn was also getting frustrated and the more Lee spoke, the worse it got. Lee turned his resentment towards Shawn.

'Take that shitty look off ya' face, Shawn. If I want to talk about Sam I will.' Lee pointed to himself and continued. 'Sam was my best friend...mine. Why did it have to be him?'

Shawn being singled out like this was adding to Jack's anger. He knew Shawn would let Lee get away with it. Jack was ready to erupt when Shawn put his arm across Jack and spoke. 'It didn't have to be any of us, Lee. I hate that Sam has gone. We all hate it. But we can't change it. I don't want to talk about it. None of us do.'

Jack stayed where he was and watched as Shawn nodded in his direction. Jack gave a nod back and was hoping Lee would take the hint to shut up. Jack was no longer in control over his temper. He knew the warning signs, but he couldn't stop himself. Suddenly, he lunged at Lee. 'Shut the fuck up. He was my brother, not just my friend. *My* brother. If Shawn says to leave it, fucking leave it.'

He was squeezing Lee's neck with his left hand. His right hand was still a fist and, knuckles turning white, it took everything in him not to throw the punch. He couldn't do it. Lee was his friend. He was one of them.

Struggling to breathe, Lee said, 'Do it Jack. I don't care. Just fucking do it.'

Shawn and Martin broke them apart and Jack felt Shawn's hand on his chest. It helped. Jack let go and turned his back on Lee. Shawn followed him.

Martin put his arm around Lee and walked him away. 'He doesn't mean it. Neither of you do.'

'The wrong brother died. He's an arsehole,' Lee said.

'Don't say that, Lee. Never say that again. You don't mean it.'

Lee shrugged like he didn't care.

'It's just the drink talking, don't say that again.'

'I'm sorry, mate, but he doesn't get to be the only one grieving. It's not all about him,' Lee said. 'Everyone worries about Jack, poor little Jack. We were all there that day. Every day I regret not jumping in that water. I hate myself for not trying.'

Martin pacified Lee. 'Come on, mate, I'll walk home with you. Or stay at mine if you want?'

The following morning Jack called Lee. They both apologised. The apologies got easier each time this happened. They both agreed that it was just the booze talking and arranged to meet up later as normal.

At seventeen years old, the friends were nearly entering adulthood. They all had fake IDs and were going into any pub that would let them in. Jack's body was changing. He wasn't tall, but he was stocky with powerful shoulders, a mixture of being naturally strong and from his training with Ken in the garden at home. The hours and hours on the heavy bag had paid off. It added to his confidence if there was a fight to be had. No one intimidated him. He wasn't scared, not because he thought he was some hard man, but because he didn't fear being hurt. Or worse, he didn't care. He got into fights regularly and didn't always come away the winner. It wasn't the winning and losing. He just wanted to fight. Shawn had stopped more than one fight from happening, but he couldn't stop them all. When Jack would go into a rage after one too many pints, it would start. This was happening too much and those closest to Jack were getting tired of it. The excuse of grieving had grown old. It had to stop before he went too far but no one could get through to him.

Closing time and the bell had rung for last orders ten minutes before. Jack was necking his last drink and any others he could find before the door security threw him out. He heard Lee shout, 'Mine sweep'. They both went around finishing any unfinished drinks left by other patrons. The security on the door knew Jack and his mates by now.

'Come on, pissheads. Go home.'

Jack stumbled out of the bar and Lee followed. Shawn and Martin were already waiting outside.

Worse for wear, Jack dropped his wallet whilst fumbling around for money. He wanted to get a takeaway on the way home. Picking up the loose coins, he awkwardly put them back into his pocket. The wallet in his hand still had several notes hanging from it.

'Nice one, dick head.'

The comment came from in the distance, followed by group laughter.

A gang of lads carried on talking in their huddle. Jack was feeling uneasy. He squinted and tried to focus on them but couldn't. Tired and hungry, he was about to leave. He knew he should. It would be the right thing to do. But he couldn't. He didn't want to do the right thing.

He looked back at the pub door. Security were now inside, and the door shut.

'Oi, Knobhead, what did you say?'

No reply, so Jack moved closer and tried again. 'Ladies. How are you?' he said sarcastically as he looked them all up and down.

He had got their full attention. 'What did you say? I dropped my wallet and one of you said something.'

'We didn't say anything. Go home, mate,' was the reply from one of them.

Jack could feel rain. He looked up at the streetlight and could see it.

'C'mon, who said it? Was it you with the long wiggy hair,' Jack said as he pointed out the tall good-looking lad with shoulder-length hair.

The biggest of the group smiled and stepped forward.

'Here we go,' Jack said. He was excited. Turning, he could see Lee was now behind him laughing.

'Go home mate. You're pissed up. We don't want any trouble. We laughed at how pissed you are, that's all. Let's leave it,' the lad said, as he backed away from Jack.

Jack nodded. His face was now serious. 'No one's going home, and no one is leaving anything.' He put his wallet in his jeans and then took off his watch and handed it to Lee.

'Take this please. It was Sam's.'

Lee took it and put it in his pocket.

'Thank you, Lee.' Jack said and gave a false smile.

Jack beckoned the big lad back over, needing him closer. When he came Jack whispered in his ear, 'Are you ready?'

He laughed at Jack as he towered above him. 'Fuck you. Look at the size of y...'

45

Before he finished the word, Jack powered forward and up with his head. A sickening head butt to the nose. Blood instantly spilled. The lad fell back, clutching his face. Despite the blood pouring down into his mouth and the obvious pain, he came back at Jack, raging.

'You little bastard.'

A left hook from Jack sent him crashing to the floor, his head missing the kerb by inches. This time he wasn't coming back. He lay there, hurt but conscious.

Jack looked at his left hand, then grinned at Lee. 'Ouch! That really hurt.'

Lee was laughing. 'Not as much as it hurt him.' He pointed to the bloodied lad on the wet concrete.

Before the rest of the group had a chance to help their friend, Jack stepped forward full of confidence. 'I'm about to close my eyes and, when I do, just go for it.' He wanted to feel something, anything, even if it was the pain. This wasn't going to be a normal fight for him. Normally he'd win or lose and go home happy but tonight he wanted more. This pain inside was getting worse. He no longer cared if he lived or died. He'd thought about suicide many times but never got past just thinking about it. Maybe this was the way. Suicide by another's hands, being beaten up for being an arsehole.

The group of lads didn't come any further forward. Jack noticed Shawn hadn't intervened. He'd stayed further back with Martin. Shawn always stopped him. Why not tonight?

Jack shouted to him. 'Oi Shawn, I'm gonna give 'em until the count of ten. If by then they haven't knocked me out or killed me, I'm going to fight back. And if they go down, I'll carry on. If they ask me to stop, I won't. What do you reckon Shawn? Sound fair?'

Shawn shrugged his shoulders. 'I honestly don't care, Jack.'

'They started it. We finish it. It's how it goes.' Jack pointed to the lad on the floor covered in blood. 'Here we go. My eyes are closed.' He put his arms out pretending to be blind and started feeling out for what was in front of him. Lee was laughing even more now. Jack opened one eye to have a look as one of the group came forward. Lee stepped in. He stopped laughing and said, 'Don't...just don't.'

Jack could hear footsteps behind him and, turning, saw Shawn running at him. Shawn grabbed him by the back of his shirt. 'I'm done with this. Done with you. You're an animal. No one cares if you think you're tough anymore.'

Jack laughed. 'I don't think I'm tough. I just don't care. There's a difference.'

'It's all an excuse. You're taking out your pain on anyone and everyone...it's not their fault Sam's gone.'

Jack went nose to nose with Shawn. 'What the fuck did you just say? Say his name again, I dare you.'

Jack was taken aback that Shawn didn't move an inch but stood strong. 'I'm not scared of you, Jack. I'm the only one that will tell you how it is. I'm saying it coz...'

'Coz what?'

'Because I care, you stupid prick. Just fucking stop.'

Seeing Shawn's eyes filling with tears made Jack feel ashamed.

'I can't do this anymore,' Shawn said.

Martin and Lee got between the friends. Jack's eyes softened like someone had just flicked a switch. The violence had stopped. Shawn saying he cared was disarming. Jack needed violence He wanted fuel for his fire. Love weakened him. He couldn't deal with it. He'd never hurt Shawn.

47

Shawn moved closer and put his hand on Jack's shoulder. 'Jack, I miss Sam so much. I'm sorry I couldn't save him. He was your brother but you're like a brother to me. I don't want to lose you as well. You've changed. I miss Sam, but I miss you just as much.'

Like a badly wounded lion, Jack had no fight left inside. It was time to get away. More feelings of guilt and shame washed over him as he looked behind at the group of lads helping up their friend. He backed away from Shawn. 'I'm going home,' was all he could manage. He walked off alone.

Lee went to go with him. Jack heard Shawn say, 'Leave him, Lee. Let him go. Only he can change this.'

Jack arrived home, drunk and feeling ashamed of himself. Silence greeted him. On the kitchen work surface, Ken's car keys glistened from a brilliant moonlight shining through the window. He knew instantly where he was going and why he was going there.

Before leaving he wanted more alcohol. He couldn't do this sober. He clearly wasn't sober but that was not what his brain was telling him. There were no beers in the fridge or the kitchen cupboards. No alcohol anywhere. He went to the dining room, knowing there was always a stash of Christmas booze in his mum's cabinet. Opening the glass door, he saw an array of treasure. Snowball, a mixture of Advocaat and lemonade. He tutted to himself. 'Fuck that.'

Moving the Snowball to one side, Jack knocked over several small bottles of tonic water. That left Baileys or Pernod. 'That'll do nicely,' he said, grabbing the Pernod. The label said 68% Alc./Vol. That would have the desired effect.

Jack sat in the driver's seat and moved it slightly forward so that he could reach the pedals comfortably.

As he started the engine, Ken's music was playing. Jack turned it up. Ken always had soul music playing. 'O-O-h Child' by The Five Stairsteps. He drove forward, narrowly missing Mr Carter's car from next door.

As he drove, he took large swigs of Pernod. His vision, already blurry, was made worse by the rain hitting the windscreen. He blinked hard and rubbed his eyes. Tears began to flow. The onset of grief was overwhelming, but it felt different from before. It was time to let go. Sam wouldn't mind. Something was changing inside. He'd had enough of being angry. He'd had enough of the pain. He had to end it.

Chapter 6

'It is one thing to show your child the way, and a harder thing to then stand out of it.'
Robert Brault

David

His son was closer to his wife than to him, she could see no bad in their only child, and he knew it. All the signs were there. It was clear David had issues, but all the time his mother was around he was protected. Losing her had been a significant moment in his life, he no longer had the security of her unconditional love.

He felt lost without his wife, and raising David alone petrified him. Troubled teen was a term perfectly written for his son.

Since her diagnosis, two years before she died, he never accepted she would have to leave them. Her final words to him had been, 'you must protect David, no matter what he does, no matter what people say he has done, please protect him.'

Now she was gone, he wanted to honour her dying wish, but wasn't sure he could. Does a parent stick up for their child no matter what? Surely there's a limit? He decided to focus his time on preventing David doing anything bad. Prevention was better than cure. If he could change his son's thoughts, maybe he could be normal.

Whatever the cost, he wanted the best help he could get. He researched psychotherapists. The mental health hospital in Tadworth had several, all highly recommended. He advised the hospital that David was only nineteen and had suffered a traumatic loss. He also reluctantly told them about what he suspected David was capable of.

Chapter 7

'I would feel real trapped in this life if I didn't know I could commit suicide at any time.'
Hunter S Thompson

Jack

The sun had risen, blinding rays shone through the dusty car windscreen. Birds seemed like they were competing to see which of them could sing the loudest. After such a traumatic night, this was a beautiful start to the day. Jack was parked outside the quarry entrance. Two signs on the fence read, 'Danger. Keep out' and 'Danger. Deep water'. These signs had not been there in the summer when Sam died. They were put up one week after the tragedy. Jack sat there staring at the signs wondering why a teenager had to die for that to happen. Would they have stopped five teenage boys from being adventurous on that day? He concluded probably not.

Jack had driven there with thoughts of suicide, convinced the quarry would be a fitting place to end it all.

On arriving, he'd carried on drinking, asking himself over and over, what would be the best way to commit suicide?

Jack wasn't thinking about the physical pain. That wasn't a problem. Pain was temporary. He wanted to limit the amount of people affected by his actions.

He had not slept. He looked out and could see the morning dew shining on the grass. Dark thoughts had plagued him all night. Constant thoughts of suicide, but how best to do it? If he slit his wrists here, who would find him? What would that do to that person? He pictured a lonely old lady walking her dog stumbling across him. The poor lady, another life potentially ruined.

What would his mum and dad do if he killed himself? Would they both want to live? The guilt was overwhelming. He was angry with his own parents. Their crime was loving him. He resented being born. If they had not given him a life, he wouldn't have this pain. He was blaming them. If it wasn't for them, he could end it all.

Thinking of all the famous people that had committed suicide over the years he admired them. They weren't cowardly, as some would say. He thought they were brave for having the strength to go through with it.

He had come up with a plan. It would have to be for another day, not for there and then. He decided he'd post a letter to the police. It would describe where his body would be and what it would look like. He would ask the police to only send officers who were seasoned in finding dead bodies.

If he posted it with a first-class stamp, it would arrive the following day. He could lie in a sleeping bag and cut his wrists. He'd be found by the police and not a dog walker or kids out exploring. The letter would have a map showing where to find him. He knew the perfect spot. There was a woodland area, out the back of their village. He and Sam used to play there. Some of his fondest memories were in those woods. He, Sam and the others would play soldiers there, pretending they were in the army carrying out missions. They'd make their weapons and use small apples for ammunition. They loved apple hopping. This involved sticking an apple at the tip of a long flexible stick and then flicking their arms forward. The apple would fly off dangerously quickly. In the fields close by, there was a battered, unused barn they used for target practise.

The barn would be perfect. No one would go in there. Jack could die alone.

His note to the police would end, 'I'm so sorry but I couldn't think of a better way.'

This was the plan, his best idea. How else could you kill yourself? Jack remembered newspaper reports he'd read, about parents killing their children before they killed themselves. Was that why they killed their children? To save them from living without a parent? To save them grieving? To prevent them living alone in this shitty, selfish world? Who knows what goes through people's minds when they are feeling so desperate?

The guilt kicked back in, stronger than ever. Jack felt weak for thinking in such a way. He couldn't do it to his parents, or to his friends. He wanted to fight this. For Sam. He was letting down Sam. He should live for him. Sam would have been strong, made something of his life. Jack should do the same.

Angry and confused, he started punching the steering wheel in a rage. He held his hand down on the car horn, screaming in pain as he did so. Getting out of the car, he picked up a rock and threw it at the sign. He ran towards it. Screamed and punched it. Split it in half.

He was exhausted. His knuckles bleeding. Old wounds reopened.

This was it. Jack's rock bottom. He couldn't kill himself. He had to move forward. But if he was going to live, he needed help. He knew that now. He couldn't do it alone.

Last night could not happen again. The vicious street fight had to be his last. He was putting his friends in danger. And the drink driving disgusted him. He was ashamed.

He looked at the time. It had gone 7am. 'Shit.' He needed to get home.

Aware he was probably still over the legal limit to drive; he locked the car and walked the three-mile journey home.

His parents were still sleeping. A huge relief. Waiting patiently for them to come downstairs, he started practising in his head, rehearsing what he was going to say to them.

For a long time, Jack's family had stopped talking about Sam. No pictures of him were on view in the house. It was too painful. If his name was brought up, even a happy memory, they would shut down, and change the subject.

Jack was nervous. He had to talk to them, but he wasn't sure what their reactions would be.

His mum was up first. She looked surprised to find Jack sitting in the kitchen.

'Are you all right? I didn't hear you come in last night.'

'I'm OK, Mum. Is Dad awake? Can I talk to you both?'

As she left the room, Liz saw the blood on Jack's hands. Tears sprang to her eyes and, putting a clenched fist to her mouth, she ran up the stairs to Ken's room.

'Ken. Ken. Wake up.' She shook her husband. 'I think Jack's

done something bad. Get up.' Together, they made their way downstairs.

Liz stared at her son. Something had changed. She knew from the look in his eyes that the old Jack was coming back. He was still in there. She had missed him so much. But what had it taken for him to return?

Ken went to speak but she touched his arm to stop him. 'Let Jack speak.'

The warmth of her husband's skin, the feeling of strength it gave her, felt so good. They'd not touched in such a long while. She smiled at Ken and waited for Jack to speak.

'Mum, I think I need help. I'd like to talk to someone. Someone who can help me, ya' know, a counsellor or whatever. I don't want to be like this anymore.'

Liz could see that Ken was still tired. She watched him rub his eyes. 'Be like what, son?' he asked.

'So unhappy. So bloody miserable. I don't want to have those thoughts anymore.'

'What thoughts?' Liz said, as she squeezed Ken's arm.

'Yes, what thoughts?' Ken repeated.

Liz knew what Jack was trying to say but hoped it wasn't true.

'Of being with Sam, I wanted to go... to... you know... kill myself. I wanted to do it last night. But I don't think I want to die. It was just thoughts.'

As if praying, Liz clasped her hands up to her mouth. Tears ran down her face, blinding her. She felt Ken put his arm around her.

She brushed away the tears and looked at her son. 'Oh Jack, I'm so sorry,' she said, moving towards him.

For once, he didn't step away from her. He didn't shut down.

She knew he wanted her, his mum. He wanted to be in her arms.

Liz held him tightly, whispering, 'It's going to be all right. We'll do whatever it takes.'

Ken hadn't joined in. He'd stayed where he was. Liz heard him say, 'Son, we both want what is best for you. All we want is for you to find happiness again.'

Liz slowly let go of Jack who looked at his father.

'I thought you both blamed me. I thought you wished it had been me, not Sam.'

For Liz, the pain was gut wrenching. She couldn't find any words. She saw Ken's body posture change. He suddenly stooped, his body shrinking in front of her as she looked desperately for answers from him.

'No. No. No, Jack. We love you both. We loved you and Sam both the same. And we know it wasn't your fault.' Ken said. He was shaking, his eyes wide.

Liz could see that he too was trying to make sense of it all. He straightened and composed himself enough to continue. 'I don't know what made Sam think he could swim that far. We'll never know. The police told us it was over ninety metres to that island. Sam hadn't swum close to fifty in his life before that day. It wasn't your fault. Sam made that decision.'

Liz was hurt that Jack thought they blamed him. Why would he think they would prefer Sam alive over him? It had not crossed her mind. But she couldn't dwell on it. They all had to move forward together and find a way to help Jack and to reassure him they loved him.

'I'll call the doctor and get an appointment, first thing tomorrow,' Liz said. It was what she wanted. She'd wanted Jack to get professional help since Sam had died. She was anxious but happy.

'Mum, there's one more thing,' Jack said.

'Yes, what is it?'

'I want to box. I want to join a boxing club. Dad's old club.'

'If that's what you want.' Liz paused. She could see Ken smiling. Wagging a finger at him she said, 'You can stop grinning. And you.' She said, pointing at Jack. 'Just don't expect me to come and watch.' She meant it. She would never watch her son fight.

Ken hugged her. 'I'll keep him safe. I promise.'

Liz hung onto him. It had been a long time since that had happened.

'Umm, Dad? Seeing that you're in a good mood and we all agree we want to help each other, we don't want to be mad at each other, do we?' Jack bit his lip.

'What have you done?' asked Liz.

'Well, I might have taken Dad's car out last night. And I might have left it somewhere.'

'You what?' Ken snapped.

Liz intervened. 'Ken, it's just a car. We'll go and collect it.'

Ken had his arm around Liz's shoulder. She squeezed it as he began to speak.

'You're a lucky boy. Lucky you have a lovely mum who won't let me strangle you,' said Ken.

And then something happened that hadn't been heard for a long time. They all laughed together.

Chapter 8

'A father is a man who expects his son to be as good a man as he meant to be.'
Frank A. Clark

David

He looked at his son, regretting the hatred he felt for him at times. How could he hate his own son? Especially since the loss of his wife. He'd promised his wife he would keep going for the sake of David. He knew deep down he loved his son and he wanted to help him. It was the right way to respect the wishes of his beloved wife.

He thought about going to the police for help, but they would probably put David on some sort of register which would affect him for life. If he did that, David would no longer be able to work with him. It wouldn't be possible in their line of work. And he knew no one else would employ his son.

His only option was counselling. If his son could openly talk to someone and not be judged, then maybe he could see what he felt for children was wrong.

As a father, he was lost. Even when she was alive, his wife wouldn't talk about it. And this wasn't the sort of conversation he could have with his mates at the pub. 'Oh, by the way, I think my son is a paedo... My round. What are you having?' Or, 'Do you think children are born bad or made bad? Because my boy is a massive wrongun who likes small boys. Another pint anyone? Short maybe?'

'Where are you going, Dad? You've missed the turning.'

He and David had got into the car as they normally did each day when they went to work but, after the first roundabout, David had known they were heading elsewhere.

'Nothing to worry about, son. We're going to see someone. I'll tell you once we're there.'

He saw David raise his eyebrows. 'OK. Whatever. Can we stop at one of the garages and get a coffee?'

He smiled. 'On the way back, David. No problem.'

As they arrived David started to fidget in his seat. 'Blimey, Dad, someone's got too much money. This house is massive. Who lives here?'

He parked the car and switched off the engine. Taking a sharp intake of breath, he looked lovingly at his boy. 'This isn't a house. It's a hospital.'

'Are you all right, Dad? Is there something wrong with you?'

'Nothing wrong with me, son. We're here for you.'

His reactions were lightning quick as he saw David grab the door handle, pull it and throw open the door. He grabbed his son's arm. 'Stay here and listen to me. Please.'

He saw David take a glance at what could be freedom, then change his mind.

'No. Fuck this, Dad. I'm not going in there. What sort of bloody hospital is it? A looney bin?'

'Close the door. Now.'

David did as he was told, and he let go of his son's arm. He could see the fear in his son's eyes. He looked like he did as a toddler, wide eyed and scared, needing his parents' protection. He put his hand on David's shoulder. 'You know I love you more than anything in this world. Since your mother passed away. you're all I have. Please do this for me. It's only one hour, once a week. Just talk to them. Tell them what you're thinking.'

David started to cry. 'I won't do it again, Dad. I promise. I'll never touch a boy again. I won't go near them. I'll get a girlfriend...and be normal.'

He pulled his son into his chest. 'I don't want you to get a girlfriend unless that's what you want. I don't care if you are gay, bisexual or whatever. I just want you happy. And I want you safe. If you find children attractive, we need to find out why...and make it stop. I don't know how but we'll do it together.'

David held onto him and screamed out in pain. 'I can't help it. I don't want to feel like this. I hate myself.'

He felt sick hearing his son say it. He knew it was true, but hearing his boy say it out loud was a knife to his chest. But this was his son, and he was going to help him.

'It's all right, David. You can't help what you feel. But you can help how you act and what you do about it. You can learn not to act on it. We all have dark thoughts, but we know when it's not right to act on them. Over the years I was attracted to other women, but I chose not to be unfaithful to your mother. These are the choices we make that change our lives. Do you understand?'

David sat back in his chair and looked at him. 'I understand. I'll do it. I'll talk to them. I'll do it for you...and for Mum.'

'She'd be so proud of you.'

They sat in silence for several minutes.

'Do you think Mum knew?'

He knew his wife had but he shook his head. 'No. She loved you more than anything in the world. She only saw the good in you, as she did in everyone.'

David smiled. 'I miss her every day.'

He could feel tears forming and wanted to change the subject. 'Right. Let's go inside. We've got about ten minutes until your appointment. We'd better go and find out where we have to go.'

They stepped out of the car and headed towards reception.

'Dad, were you really never unfaithful to Mum?'

Without blinking or any change in his facial expression he looked across at David. 'Of course not.'

David smiled. 'I like that.'

He put his arm around his son. 'Let's go in.'

After a short wait in reception, they were shown the way to a small office. He knew he'd have to leave his son at the door.

He opened the door and ushered David inside. A woman sat at a desk. She gave them a friendly smile.

'Nice to meet you, David. I'm Dr Roisin Kelly.'

He closed the door quietly and returned to the waiting room.

Chapter 9

'Unexpressed emotions will never die. They are buried alive and will come forth later in uglier ways'

Jack

Jack had a preconception of what this hospital was going to be like. Their family doctor had referred him to Ramsden House in Surrey. A hospital for people with various mental health problems, including rehabilitation for those with drink and drug related issues, specialist assessment and care for individuals with eating disorders, and treatment for depression.

He knew his friends would call it a nuthouse or a loony-bin but felt he had to tell them he was starting treatment. They deserved to know after what they had witnessed recently. First, he had to apologise.

Shawn first. He seemed pleased to see Jack. 'Hi. Are you OK? I wasn't so sure you'd go straight home last night. I hoped you would.'

'Yeah, I went straight home,' Jack lied. He didn't feel the need to tell Shawn he'd been to the lake. He couldn't tell him he was going to end it all.

'I came to say sorry. I can't keep putting you and the lads

through this. What I did to the bloke last night was disgusting. I hate the person I've become. I'm gonna get some help. 'I've promised mum I'll do it for her.' Another little lie. He knew he wanted the help more for himself, but he couldn't bring himself to admit that to Shawn.

'That's good. I think that's right, you know, to do it for your mum. Nothing wrong with doing it for yourself too,' Shawn said, with a grin.

Jack smiled back at his friend. 'I might not be around much whilst this is going on. I can't go out drinking and all that.'

Shawn frowned. 'Jack, we don't have to drink to see each other. Just make sure you keep in touch. We can go for a coffee or whatever you want. Our friendship is built on more than just going out and getting wasted.'

'Can you let the other two know? If I tell 'em, they'll only take the piss. Lee will have visions of me being in somewhere that resembles *One Flew Over the Cuckoo's Nest*. He'll think it's like that. You know he will.' They both laughed.

'I'll tell them. They'll be fine. They'll take the piss. Of course, they will. But that's only right. You wouldn't want them any other way, would you?'

Jack nodded and smiled. As he was about to leave, he turned and said, 'One more thing. Mum's agreed I can try boxing. I'm gonna join up, give it a go. Dad says it'll get my aggression out.'

'I think your dad's right. It could be good for you. I think you should have done that a long time ago. It's not too late though. It's never too late, Jack. I think you could be whatever you want to be.'

Jack smiled and his eyes softened. 'I don't know about that, but thanks.' He started walking home.

Shawn called out. 'Time to start living for you, Jack.'

Jack didn't turn around because he was welling up. He threw up a hand to wave goodbye.

Giant leafy oaks lined the hospital drive. Gravel kicked up, hitting the bottom of the car. Jack opened the window, tipped his head slightly, and looked up to the highest branches. He took in the smell. It was so fresh, and the air was so clean. The gated drive and giant trees made him feel like he was entering a fortress.

The building itself was an old Victorian House, formerly Priory Sturt Grange House, beautifully painted white, with immaculately kept flowerbeds.

Jack momentarily smiled to himself. He remembered his conversation with Shawn about going into a nuthouse. He'd been visualising crazy patients throwing their pills at each other or rubbing food into their hair while dancing naked to classical music.

After they parked the car, they made their way into the hospital. A security room to the left as they entered had eight monitors. They had the whole place secure. No one was running off without being spotted and no one was coming in who shouldn't.

Jack and his dad were asked to take a seat in the waiting room.

'Bloody hell Jack. Look at this,' his dad said as he pointed to the free tea and coffee which you could help yourself to, using the posh china cups and saucers.

Jack laughed and peered around to make sure no one heard. Patients and staff were walking around, and he was pleasantly surprised that there was nothing scary about the place. All the patients he had seen so far appeared normal. From their appearance Jack assumed they were from all walks of life. Some appeared wealthy, probably paying for themselves, some not so well off who had most likely been placed in there through their healthcare insurance. Jack was from the latter. He qualified under his dad's healthcare insurance. Prior to Jack needing treatment, his dad had always moaned to his bosses that the insurance was a waste of money and he'd rather have extra pay added to his salary.

Jack looked up as he was taking a sip of his coffee. He noticed a girl walking down the corridor. She looked upset and her clothes were hanging off her tiny frame. He checked himself for rudely staring. He wanted to ask if she was all right, but she wasn't looking for any conversation. She had her head down and was in her own world.

Jack was called for his appointment.

'Good luck, champ,' his dad said. 'I'll be here when you come out. I'm going nowhere. We'll ring your mum on the way home.'

A member of staff led Jack into a dimly lit office. It was small but immaculate. He looked at a bookcase that was full of highly intellectual-looking books he'd never heard of. Two chairs were facing each other either side of an impressive antique desk. On the desk was a gold lamp and a single gold pen, resting in its holder. A striking conker-brown Chesterfield leather sofa stood below the window.

Nerves were kicking in. Was it too late to back out? Jack wasn't sure, but he thought about it. Darkness had begun to fall outside. It wasn't late but a heavy rain was coming. The room was lit by a single table lamp which gave a relaxed atmosphere. The rain started gently tapping on the window. Something outside caught Jack's attention. A solitary robin, sitting on a tiny branch enjoying his freedom. Jack wished he could trade places.

He didn't feel like talking, but he was starting to enjoy the feeling of just being. He couldn't remember the last time he'd sat in silence with no TV or music in the background to help kill the dark thoughts in his mind. He took in his surroundings and started to feel calm and, most of all, safe. He wanted to do nothing but enjoy the peacefulness in his head.

An attractive lady, tall and slim with straight red hair, entered the room. She had piercing green eyes and was wearing bold scarlet lipstick. Although twice Jack's age, he immediately felt an attraction to her. He was expecting a male, middle-aged, professor type, sporting thick-rimmed glasses and a big bushy beard, wearing a tweed jacket with leather elbow patches. She wasn't like that.

She introduced herself as Dr Roisin Kelly. Her Irish accent was soft. She asked Jack to call her Roisin, saying it would help make their sessions more personal. Therapy ground rules were set. Roisin explained that timekeeping and notice periods for cancellations were important. She clarified that everything Jack spoke about was safe with her. It would go no further. There would only be one reason she would have to break this rule and that was if she felt someone was in danger. Jack understood and nodded.

She smiled. Her smile changed her whole appearance. She was clearly a beautiful lady, but she also initially looked professional and hard. Her smile was warm, homely and, Jack felt, genuine.

'Now that we have got that part out of the way, we can talk

about you, Jack. Please tell me a bit about yourself,' Roisin said.

Jack was nervous and slightly intimidated by her presence.

'Not much to tell,' he said. Seconds past before he continued, 'I live at home with mum and dad. I'm not in school. I left. And I haven't got a job.'

For a while, he was silent again but so was Roisin. He raised his eyebrows and felt he had to carry on.

'I like being with my friends. I like drinking with them. It's fun but sometimes I get into trouble. I upset people and I don't like it.'

Roisin nodded.

'I don't like hurting anyone. Especially the people I love.' He was looking down at his feet, feeling ashamed about his recent behaviour.

Again, there was a long silence. This was frustrating Jack. He felt like he had to say more. The silence made him uncomfortable.

'I just want to be normal. Happy, I suppose.'

'I'm sure you don't mean to hurt anyone. And you do deserve to be happy. Everyone does. But normal? I don't think you need to be normal. I'm not sure there is a normal. But you can be happy,' Roisin said, as a tiny crease appeared at the side of her eyes as she smiled.

The session flew by as they continued talking about Jack's parents, about his friends and his thoughts on what would make him happy. Jack watched Roisin steal a glance at her watch. Their time was nearly up. Jack didn't think she'd said much, and he had not mentioned Sam yet. He'd expected to by now.

Jack noticed Roisin refer to her notes several times. She

must know what had happened in Jack's past so why hadn't she asked about Sam?

He sat through the next silence, waiting for Roisin to speak first.

'You've talked a lot about your parents. Do you have any other family members?'

Jack bit his lip. He knew this was it. He'd have to open up about Sam. He wanted to. He trusted Roisin.

'My brother, Sam,' he said. He saw her look at her watch again. This time she was less subtle.

'Time is nearly up. We have to leave it there for today,' she said.

Jack frowned. He wanted to talk. He was ready.

'Please could you do something for me. Next time you come, could you bring a few photos of Sam, or of you and Sam?'

'Err...I suppose so.' He started biting his lip again, nervous at the thought of taking the photos out of the house. Frustrated their time was up, he let out a deep sigh as he stood to leave.

'Thank you for coming to see me today, Jack. It was lovely to meet you. I'll see you on Friday at 4 pm.'

Jack thanked Roisin and went back to his dad in the waiting room.

'Good stuff this.' His dad was wide-eyed. He raised his cup to Jack. 'This is my third.' He placed the cup down on the coffee table so that he could put his arm around Jack.

'I'm proud of you champ. Are we good to go? Tell me all about it in the car,' he said as he led Jack out of the building.

Once in the car, Jack rang his mother and told her all about his session with Roisin, leaving out the fact of how attractive she was.

That night in his bedroom, he felt a sense of achievement and, resting his head on his pillow, he allowed himself a smile. He was exhausted. He thought about his mum's reaction, how she'd told him she was proud of him for going. He was proud of himself too. Part one of rebuilding his life had started. Part two would begin tomorrow. He gave in to his tiredness and let himself fall asleep.

Pete's Gym was on an industrial estate just outside Dorking, Surrey. The small town wasn't known for producing boxers. It was predominately middle class, very conservative and full of restaurants, pubs and antique shops.

The gym was a large metal warehouse, not pretty from the outside, but inside it was a boxer's dream.

'I trained at Pete's old gym when it was at a small village hall,' Jack's father had told him. 'Pete's come a long way since then.'

Jack had listened in on his dad's phone call with Pete. His dad had asked if Jack could give boxing a go, hit the bags and see what he was capable of.

'He might only be joining for fitness purposes,' he said. 'I'm not sure sparring would be a good idea. I don't know if Jack has it in him to be punched back. It isn't for everyone.'

Jack heard Pete assure Ken he would do right by his son. He gave him the timetable and asked for one thing in return, for him to be on time.

Jack asked his friends if they wanted to go with him. He knew it would be less daunting having a friend with him, safety in numbers. Lee was interested and said he would try it. Shawn wasn't, telling Jack that getting his head punched regularly didn't appeal in the slightest, and Martin was set on joining the police force so wouldn't have the time.

The following evening, Jack, his dad and Lee arrived at the gym ten minutes early. They pulled open the metal door and stepped in. It was raining outside but hadn't felt that heavy. Once inside the warehouse it sounded like they were under siege. The corrugated roof amplified the sound of every drop.

Dumbfounded, Jack took in the sound as he scanned the whole building, his mouth open. A huge picture of Muhammad Ali was above him. Above Ali was a quote. 'The fight is won and lost far away from witnesses, behind the lines, in the gym and out there on the road, long before I dance under those lights.' On another wall was a giant picture of Mike Tyson. Above Tyson was his famous quote. 'Everybody has a plan until they get punched in the mouth.' Two legends of boxing, two very different quotes.

The smell of leather, sweat, and deodorant greeted them. Half a dozen fighters were wrapping their hands in long bandages. Others were helping to set up the equipment. They looked disciplined, focused but friendly as one by one they gave Jack a welcoming nod.

Pete approached the boys. 'You must be Jack. You're the spit of your dad. He was stocky like you, could punch a bit as well. I'm coach Pete, Pete Huntley.'

Jack could feel himself begin to grin. He felt proud as he looked across at his dad. Jack was the same as any other boy. He liked hearing he was like his father.

'And you must be Lee. Nice to meet you both,' Pete said, winking at Lee.

Pete pointed beyond the boxing ring. 'You can put your bags in the changing room. Everything's safe round here. No need to lock it away. I'll get one of the boys to help wrap your hands.'

Pete showed Jack his fist and spoke again. 'Your hands are your tools. A good workman always looks after his tools. Without them, you can't go to work.'

Jack saw his dad smile. He whispered into Jack's ear, 'He said the same thing to me on my first day.'

'Thank you, Pete,' Jack said.

At six o'clock on the button Pete turned to the rest of the gym and shouted, 'Right you lot, warm up.' He scrolled through his phone and must have pressed play because classical music suddenly filled the gym. 'Bach's Mass in B Minor. BWV 232: *Kyrie Eleison*,' announced Pete.

Jack had never heard music like this. Along with the bullet sounding raindrops hitting the roof, the music was powerful and uplifting. It felt right. Jack's chest was pumping, hairs on his arms stood up. He felt something he hadn't for a long time: he felt alive. Lee seemed equally excited.

Mark, a fighter who was shadow boxing and stretching out his arms, called across to them. 'Pete always plays this music, just for the warm-up. Once we're ready to go, we can put our music on.'

All the boxers started to jog around the gym. One of the senior fighters shouted instructions. 'Right hand,' and they would touch the floor with their right hand. Then the same with the left. Then heel kicks while still jogging. They would have to kick their backsides with their heels. The warmup continued with running sideways, running backwards, punching the air whilst running and some shadow boxing. Jack and Lee kept up the best they could. They would have to get used to them all.

Ten minutes had passed and warm up was over. 'Get your gloves on, boys,' Pete said, then looking at Mark, he said, 'All yours.'

Mark grinned and pressed play. '99 Problems' by Jay-Z blew out of the speakers.

Jack and Lee smiled with excitement. The music and the atmosphere made them feel as if they belonged.

The two newbies were advised to hit the heavy bags while Pete got started on the mitts with his regular fighters. Jack watched in awe. He was shocked. Considering Pete's age, he was so fast. He moved around like someone in his twenties.

Another man was coaching. He was a few years older than Jack, not very athletic in appearance and he didn't hand out too many smiles. His shoulder length hair had been tied back. He had the boys doing the basics, stressing to Jack and Lee how important it was that they always use the correct boxing stance. Just as Jack's dad had previously taught him, their feet had to be apart for balance. He explained that if they stood square on, they would have no balance. He asked Jack to face him, he then gently pushed his chest. Jack took a step backwards.

'See? You moved. Now stand feet apart, slightly bend your knees and face side on.'

Jack did as he was instructed to. Again, the coach pushed Jack's chest. This time Jack didn't move an inch. He remained solid. Such a simple instruction had given him an obvious and clear benefit. The coach established both Jack and Lee were orthodox which meant they were both right-handed, therefore as boxers they led with their left hand.

'Nice,' he said. 'Now get your gloves up, protect your face and start throwing left jabs. But keep that right hand nailed to your chin. Once you start sparring that will protect you so get used to it now.' The boys did as they were asked. Again, Jack thought the coach looked pleased.

Near the end of the session, the coach asked Jack and Lee to face each other and lightly throw jabs. He demonstrated and explained that a jab was a straight punch thrown with your lead hand, you didn't load up on it, you threw it out with speed. 'It's more of a range finder although, if thrown effectively, a jab can cause damage once a few of them land,' he said.

These were not heavy punches that were going to hurt but it was exciting for the boys to throw their first punches at each other.

'Having a punch thrown at your face isn't for everyone. This is not an easy sport. If it were, more people would do it,' their new coach told them.

Jack and Lee found hitting each other awkward. They were purposely throwing their punches short or wide, but when they did connect, they'd grimace and apologise.

'Stop apologising. You're here to hit each other. You'll be apologising all bloody night.'

They shrugged their shoulders and carried on. The coach was watching them closely, his head bobbing from side to side, watching each punch and when a punch landed, he would say, 'Nice. Great jab.'

Jack wanted to impress him. He started to up his power on his punches. Ego and testosterone were kicking in.

'Time,' Pete shouted. Time was up.

Jack was disappointed it was over but exhilarated from the experience.

Jack saw Pete and his fellow coach compare notes on the

session while he and the other boxers all put the equipment away. Everyone did it without being asked to, the same as earlier. The respect in this gym was clear to see.

The boys thanked Pete and left the gym. Jack's dad was waiting outside. They jumped in the car full of excitement. Endorphin levels flying high.

'Dad, it was amazing, you should have seen us.'

'What about that shot I caught you with?' Lee said, smirking.

'Yeah, right. What about the one I caught you with?'

'Glad you enjoyed it, boys. Fancy going again then?'

'Bloody right we do,' Jack said. He was so happy. His dad looked across at him and smiled.

'Thanks for taking us, Mr Stone,' said Lee.

'Yeah, thanks, Dad,' Jack said.

He shared a glance with his dad that felt special. A simple moment, but one he felt he wouldn't forget.

Chapter 10

'The world is a dangerous place to live; not because of the people who are evil, but because of the people who do nothing about it.'
Albert Einstein

David

'Hello David, how are you?'

David sat down without looking at Roisin and replied, 'OK.'

Their first session had gone well. He'd been very open and friendly, and Roisin felt he was a good person behind the thoughts he was having.

She leaned in slightly so that she could see his face. 'Just OK?'

David shrugged his shoulders. 'Yeah. Do you want me to do cartwheels and clap for you? I can if you like.'

Roisin leant back and looked away. Something in David's eyes unnerved her. 'That won't be necessary, I'm just con-cerned about how you feel.'

He stuck his tongue between his teeth and stared at her. 'I find this all a bit much. All this with you and every other arsehole finding out about my life. Nosey, that's what it is. I know nothing about you. What if I asked you a million questions? You'd get pissed off, wouldn't you?'

'I'm not the one requiring help at this stage in my life. I'm here to help you…if you'll let me? I want to help but I'm feeling some anger and resentment from you. Is that just towards me? Have I upset you?'

Roisin watched carefully as he let out a huge sigh and stared hard at her.

'I haven't decided,' he said.

Roisin started reading through his notes to avoid eye contact. She was about to speak when David sat upright, folded his arms and leaned towards her.

'I've decided. It is you. You've upset me. You're pissing me off.'

She felt more discomfort as he looked her up and down.

'Little Miss Perfect with your posh clothes, your flashy pens and your judgmental green eyes.'

Roisin put her notes back on the table. She decided to challenge him but was scared this could go wrong. 'I'm not here to judge you, David. I'm here to listen. And I'd rather you refrain from using bad language in our sessions.'

David laughed. 'Bad language. You think pissing is a bad word. How about cunt, fuck or arse? They are bad words.'

She raised her voice. 'That's enough. I'll ask you to leave if you don't stop.'

He laughed again. 'Calm down. I won't swear anymore. I wouldn't want to upset you, would I?'

'I think you do want to. I think you'd like to upset me. Last time you came here you were polite and wanted my help. You looked frightened. This time you are angry and rude. What's happened since we last saw each other?'

'Nothing,' he snapped back.

During a brief silence, Roisin thought about his behaviour. 'David, have you ever been assessed for anything other than depression?'

He shot her an aggressive look. 'Like what? No. I bloody haven't. Have you?'

'You seem so different to our last meeting. I want to understand why, that's all.'

Roisin was distracted by David's foot. He'd raised it up on to its toes and was tapping his heel to the floor.

'Do you think I have a split personality? Bipolar or some other mental disease. My dad said he thinks I have. But he can be a pain in the arse, just like you at times.'

'David, last warning. Do not insult me or swear again.'

'Then don't make out I'm mental. There's nothing wrong with me. I don't torture animals, I don't lick windows and I don't throw my own shit at people, do I?' He smiled at her and continued, 'See, I'm perfectly normal. All that's happened is I've decided I like who I am. Everyone wants me to change. I don't want to. If I like something, I can't help that, can I?'

She looked at him closely. He was still smiling. 'I'm not saying you're mental. I wanted to be sure you are not suffering from any other diagnosis. Your change in attitude since last time is so vast, I have to ask the question.'

Roisin took in what he had said about liking something and not being able to help it. 'What do you like?' she asked.

His grin grew bigger. 'Oh, you know what I like. That's why I'm here. I like boys. Little boys.'

Roisin felt anxious but didn't want him to know it. She knew that was what he wanted. 'We talked about this. What you like and what you do are two different things. I have to ask you... are you thinking of acting on your thoughts?'

His grin had gone. 'If I tell you, will you have me arrested?'

She nodded. 'I can't have you arrested for saying you might do something. If I feel someone is in danger or if you tell me you have done something illegal, I'll have no choice but to tell the police.'

'I do want to, but I don't have anyone in mind.'

Roisin wasn't sure how to play this.

He pointed at her. 'You're a pretty lady, an eight out of ten. Maybe nine for older men. I bet you like big six-foot tall men with broad shoulders and perfect teeth. Nothing wrong with that. That's what you're attracted to. You can't help it. Well, I can't help being attracted to boys. What's the difference?' He held out his palms and shrugged his shoulders.

Roisin felt anger towards David but remained professional. 'What I'm attracted to isn't your concern, but let's say I am attracted to a certain type of person, it would be consensual, between two adults. They would have to like me, and I would have to like them. It would be our choice, as adults.'

She continued and made sure she held his stare. 'You are talking about children. They are at an age where they don't know about such things, and nor should they. What you are interested in doing is illegal and immoral. And you know it. Yet you tell me you are still thinking about doing it. I find that worrying.'

He shrugged. 'Maybe so. But if no one finds out, who's really getting hurt?' Another cocky grin appeared, and she knew it was for her sake.

Roisin's anger grew to disgust, and she felt herself losing her professionalism. '*They* are getting hurt. The children. It will affect them for the rest of their lives. You have to understand that. It will shape how they are as adults and

79

potentially ruin their lives. I need you to acknowledge that before we continue.'

David sat in silence. Roisin waited for his answer.

A minute went by before he replied, 'I will acknowledge it. But I don't agree with it.'

Roisin felt this was a good time to stop. She was drained. There were five minutes left but she'd had enough. Her dislike for the young man opposite her was profound.

Chapter 11

'Our greatest glory is, not in never falling, but in rising every time we fall.'
Oliver Goldsmith

Jack

He heard Roisin's voice. 'Come in, Jack.'

He pushed the door and peered around. 'Hello.'

Jack sat down, adjusted his shirt, pulling it over the top of his jeans. He was ready to go, envelope in hand containing five precious photos. He held them up. 'I brought these with me, like you asked.'

'That's great, shall we start? Can you tell me a bit about the photos?'

Jack spread them out evenly on the desk and felt a pain in his chest, so he took a deep breath to compose himself. He exhaled and then pointed. 'That's Sam, my brother.' Wiping his eyes before tears arrived, he didn't know what to say next.

'It's all right, Jack. Continue when you're ready.'

He nodded. 'Sam was sixteen.'

There was silence again. He knew Roisin was waiting for him to go on. He looked out of the window, then back at her.

'He died four years ago.'

Another few seconds of silence. This time Roisin spoke. 'I'm so sorry. That must have been very hard for you.'

Jack stared down at his feet. 'He drowned. We were at a lake with our friends. We'd been out cycling and wanted to go for a swim. We were so hot. The weather was boiling. There's an old brickworks in Newdigate, the village next to ours. Lots of kids used to go there in the summer. We'd been before.'

'So, you were with him when he drowned?'

'I was there but I didn't go in. I wanted to but I can't swim very far. I should have tried but I couldn't do it.' He bit his lip and rolled his head from side to side to release the tension. His hands were beginning to shake so he clenched them into fists. His jaw clamped shut and he bit down, trying to control his emotions.

'It's fine, Jack. You're doing well. Tell me what you are thinking?'

Jack watched her inch closer whilst reassuring him.

'It shouldn't have been Sam. I wish it had been me. If I had died it would have been better,' he said.

'Better for who?' asked Roisin.

'For mum and dad.' He paused, put his hands over his face and rubbed his eyes. 'And for Sam. He could have handled this. I can't do it.'

More silence, more pain building in his chest. He pushed his shoulders back to release the pressure.

'Jack, what you witnessed was traumatic. Being here now, talking to me, shows bravery. I can't say how Sam would have handled this but I think you should give yourself some credit.'

He couldn't look Roisin in the eye. He went red. Being complimented made him uncomfortable. He sat back in his seat and folded his arms. 'Credit? I don't deserve credit. I didn't try to save him. I'm a coward. How do I tell my Mum I didn't try to save my brother?'

Thoughts about hurting himself were creeping back in.

'Jack, what are you thinking? Please be honest with me. I want you to trust me. If you say it out loud, I can help you deal with the thoughts you are having.'

He slowly lifted his gaze to meet hers.

'When I think of that day, I only see two things.' He stood up and put his hands on his head. He didn't want to say it. He wanted to leave.

'Tell me, Jack.'

'I see Sam's hand going under the water. When I close my eyes at night, I see it, over and over. It's there all of the time.' Jack let out a huge breath. 'I can't do this.'

'What is the other thing? You said there were two things in your head.'

'I see me dying. When the time is right, I'm going to. I can't yet. My parents have been through too much.'

Jack stayed silent. He hadn't admitted that he still wanted to commit suicide. He felt ashamed for saying it out loud. He was exhausted, mentally drained.

He wasn't sure how much time they had left when he saw Roisin check her watch.

'Jack, I want to thank you for being so honest with me, I'm sure you haven't spoken about that terrible day very often since it happened. I appreciate how hard it must be for you.'

Jack didn't reply. He didn't want any more sympathy, not from anyone.

'What happened to Sam was a tragic accident. You and Sam were so young. Accident is the keyword here. It was an accident. You didn't cause it to happen. Can you picture yourself at thirteen? You were a boy.'

Jack stayed silent but registered what Roisin said.

'You were a child. I can see from your photos that Sam is a lot bigger than you. And you've told me you couldn't swim very far. I don't think you could have saved Sam. I'm so sorry.'

Jack's heart was thumping. His head pounded. He stood up and shouted, 'I should have died trying.'

He noticed Roisin was pushing her chair slightly backwards using her feet. He didn't mean to upset her or scare her. He sank back in his chair, put his head in his hands, and cried.

'I'm so sorry. I'm sorry.'

Roisin inched forward. She put her hand on his arm.

'You've nothing to be sorry for. Maybe I pushed you too far. Let's stop for today. We've only got two or three minutes left anyway. Next time I see you, can we carry on from here? But only if you're ready to. If you need to talk to me before then, you can ring me here at the hospital. They will put you through to me.'

Jack wiped his tears. 'I'll be OK. Sorry I shouted. You know I would never hurt you, don't you?'

'Of course. I know you weren't shouting at me. It's fine.' She stood, eye level with Jack and gave him a warm smile, 'Can I ask you to do something?'

Jack didn't answer, but he nodded.

'I'd like you to look up the word 'accident' in the dictionary.'

Jack shrugged. He didn't see what good it would do, but he agreed to do it.

Once their session finished he felt tired and sombre as he met his dad back in the reception area.

'What happened?' his dad asked.

'Sorry Dad. I just want to go home.'

They walked to the car in silence.

He didn't talk in the car. He stared out of the window for the entire journey and, once home, went straight to his room and cried himself to sleep.

Several hours later he woke and remembered what Roisin had asked him to do. He opened his laptop and Googled 'definition of accident'.

Noun, an unfortunate incident that happens unexpectedly and unintentionally, typically resulting in damage or injury, an event that happens by chance or that is without apparent or deliberate cause.

Chapter 12

'A person who has nothing to lose will help you lose everything you ever worked for.'
Mike Tyson

Jack

Three days later, Jack and Lee arrived for their next session. They completed their warmup, put their wraps on, and the music was pumping. Jack and Lee were left to hit the heavy bags and work on what they did last time. The regular fighters looked tense. Pete called them into the ring, two at a time for sparring. If Pete thought they were looking sharp and holding their own, they would stay in for another round with a new opponent. Respect was a must. No power shots. No mocking your opponent.

Jack and Lee were watching the sparring. 'Don't fancy that yet, Jack,' Lee said.

'I do,' Jack said and grinned.

Jack was still feeling uneasy from his session with Roisin and wanted to let his anger out.

He'd been on the heavy bags for over ten minutes, and neither Pete nor his son had come over to check on them. Jack got upset. The more anger he felt, the harder he hit that bag. He had a natural right hook with good power. When he hit that bag, it let out a loud bang. Jack had caught Pete's attention.

Pete instructed his son to take sparring alone, and he came over to Jack.

'You OK, lad?' he asked.

'Yeah,' Jack said, but he didn't look at Pete as he said it.

'Slow it down, less anger in that punch, boxing isn't about fighting angry. Having a hard punch is good, that's either in you or it's not, but having control is more important,' said Pete.

'OK,' Jack said. He calmed down and accepted what Pete was saying, but he wanted more. Punching bags wasn't enough.

'When can I do that?' He pointed at the boxers sparring.

'You wanna go in there? You sure?' Pete asked.

Pete thought about it for a moment. He thought about what Ken said, that Jack might only be here for fitness training, not sparring. Jack had that look; Pete had seen it before. He was going in.

'You got a gumshield?'

'Yes sir,' Jack smiled, revealing it was already in his mouth.

'Let's go.' Pete waved Jack over to the boxing ring.

'Careful, mate,' warned Lee.

Pete went over a few ring rules while tightening up the straps on Jack's head guard. Jack agreed to obey them all.

Jack punched his gloves together. He was pumped up with excitement. He was nervous, not because he would get hurt, he was nervous because this was his chance to shine.

Pete shouted, 'Let's go,' and the fighters met in the middle of the ring. His first sparring partner was Justin. He was skinny and quick. Jack started well and held his own, but he couldn't catch Justin with a clean shot. Jack was not covering up. He was being picked off by his slick opponent. Jack enjoyed the feeling of being hit. He felt like he deserved it. He kept his guard low to take in more punches. A stiff jab caught him on the nose. He had a copper taste in his mouth and knew it was his blood. He liked it and knew he was in a real fight.

He threw a left hook, catching Justin hard and knocking him into the ropes. Justin covered up and so Jack stopped throwing back. Jack showed control and stepped back.

Pete's son shouted, 'Why are you stopping?'

Jack was confused. He didn't want to hurt Justin any further. The fight was over and there was nothing to be gained by beating him even more.

Pete called out, 'Time.' The fighters stopped. Jack went back to his corner. Justin walked back eyes wide and unsteady on his legs.

'Put your gloves up and defend yourself at all times. You did well, but not being hit is more important than hitting your opponent. Have you watched Floyd Mayweather? The guy still looks twenty-one. He hardly gets hit. His defence is amazing, watch some footage of his fights. Now, do one more round for me.' He called over Nick, another of his boxers. Nick was well built, not an inch of fat on him, and heavier than Jack. Pete had decided Jack should be in with heavier fighters because of his punching power. The two touched gloves in the middle of the ring, and it was on. Nick threw a jab that hit Jack's forehead. Jack felt that shot. His head jolted back, but he still went forward unfazed. Nick landed an uppercut, this shot came up through Jack's guard and landed under his chin. 'That's for Justin.'

'Go easy, Nick, no need for that,' Pete shouted. Throwing heavy uppercuts at a new boxer was not on in any gym.

Jack was hurt. He opened his jaw wide to help ease the pain. He knew Nick was trying to show Jack who he was, but he also remembered Pete's warnings. This was supposed to be light sparring. A couple more of Nick's big shots landed. Jack had had enough. He shook his head. 'Fuck this.' He couldn't match Nick for skill, so he was going to fight back the only way he knew. In anger.

Jack waited for Nick to come in close again, and he threw back with full power. He landed a right hook low into Nick's ribs. Nick went down, unable to get a breath.

'Time, that's enough, both of you,' shouted Pete. His son jumped in the ring heading towards Nick. Jack gave him a long stare as he walked by, 'That's what you wanted, wasn't it?'

Pete's son smiled as he helped Nick, 'You started that Nick, that uppercut was unnecessary.'

'Jack, get over here. Come with me,' Pete said.

Jack followed Pete to his tiny office. There wasn't much furniture, just a tired old chair and a desk, a dozen pictures of fighters, past and present covered the walls.

'The idea in sparring is to learn, not to hurt each other,' Pete said.

'He was trying to hurt me, so I thought I could throw back.'

'But you did it with anger. We'll work on that.'

'So, you'll still train me? You'll train me to compete?'

'Yeah, I'll train you. You're not just here to get fit. I can see that. But if I'm going to do this, I need you fully committed. No drinking. No drugs. No fighting outside of the gym, my fighters don't fight on the street. And no shagging about. You kids these days, you get about. I need you healthy. It's no good

89

getting STDs, keep it in your pants. Fast women have been the downfall of many a good fighter in my gym. Find yourself a good lady and stick with her.'

Jack laughed. 'Pete, I promise I'll take it seriously. I won't let you down.'

Pete's son came into the office. He pointed at Jack. 'Dad, I like him. He can stay.'

'I'm glad you like him; you're going to help me train him. Control his temper, and we'll be OK.'

'No problem,' his son said.

'Now take Jack and show him a few combos.'

Jack followed his son back into the main gym.

He was excited at the thought of training for some real fights. He tapped Pete's son on the shoulder. 'By the way, what's your name? Your dad hasn't told me. I should have asked by now, sorry about that.'

He smiled at Jack. 'That's OK. I'm David.'

Chapter 13

'If you're going through hell, keep going.'
Winston Churchill

'Jack, please come in. How are you?' Roisin asked.

'I'm fine.'

'I know our last session was hard for you. Therapy can take time to work. You may find you'll feel worse before you start to feel better. We're opening up a lot of emotions and I know how hard it must be for you. It will get easier to talk about in time but if you're finding it too hard please tell me and we can pause and take a different approach.'

Jack sat down and gave Roisin a warm smile.

'How have you felt since our last appointment?' she asked.

Jack looked past Roisin and out of the window. It was raining again. He thought back to last night when he was crying alone.

'I still feel empty and question why I'm here. Please don't think I mean here with you. I mean here at all.'

'And does anything make you feel better?' Roisin asked.

'Getting drunk helps me to forget. But I know that's not good. It's escapism isn't it?'

Roisin nodded but remained silent.

Jack looked out of the window again. The rain had slowed down.

'I get these thoughts that suicide would be so easy, and drinking makes it feel achievable.' He tapped his temple hard twice. 'It would be a release from this darkness in my head.'

Roisin left one of her long silences. He knew she was waiting for him to elaborate.

'I'm bored with myself. I must be so miserable to be around. I feel sorry for my friends having to put up with me. I look for reasons to get in trouble and I hate myself for it. I want to change. I want to be a better person. Like I was when...' Jack stopped talking and stared out of the window again.

'When what, Jack? Please say it?'

Jack shook his head, refusing to speak.

'All right. You don't have to. Tell me something that you think could make you happy?'

Jack looked at Roisin and shrugged. 'Nothing.' He held out his palms in submission. 'I'll be honest with you. I sat at home last night and cried for hours, and I wasn't crying about my brother. I was shaking uncontrollably and looking pathetic. I wanted out. I thought of my parents and my friends and wondered how they could be so happy. I got angry with them, jealous maybe... How horrible is that?' Jack let out a sigh. 'Even if you gave me a million pounds, a Ferrari and a beautiful girlfriend, I wouldn't even flinch. It wouldn't mean anything. I feel so empty. I can't see a way out of this. I don't even know if I want a way out.'

Roisin looked deep into Jack's eyes. She moved forward in her chair. 'Can you see that it won't always be like this? There will come a time when you're happy again. I want to help you get through this dark time. I haven't got a million pounds, a Ferrari or a girlfriend for you.' She smiled at Jack and he allowed himself a grin back at her.

Roisin continued. 'It may take time but if you trust me and keep being honest like you just were, I will do my best to help you.'

Jack looked up in despair 'But how?'

'Jack, do you know what made me happy today?'

He shook his head.

'You. When you entered my room, you smiled. You, or anyone, has that power to make another human happy. It doesn't have to be money or material objects.'

Jack rubbed his eyes, but he wouldn't give in to the tears approaching.

'The pain I see in you is hard to witness but that smile... When you smile it brings me joy. Internally, you are fighting your own demons and life has kicked you hard, but you are still here and you still have it in you to give me a smile every time you see me.'

Jack went red and couldn't look Roisin in the eye. They were both silent and Jack thought back to what simple memories he had that could make him smile.

'Sam and I had a play fight. I was six, maybe seven years old and he hit me in the stomach. Took the wind clean out of me. I couldn't get a breath. He rubbed my back and kept saying, 'Sorry, don't tell mum.' Once I could breathe, he smiled at me and said, 'Thank God you're OK.''

Tears filled Jack's eyes. 'I'll never forget how he looked at me. Maybe part of it was relief for him but I could also see how much he cared for me and, at that moment, I knew just how much.'

Looking out of the window Jack noticed how sunny it had

become. He was surprised when he looked back at Roisin to see that her eyes were glazed. He felt she truly was listening and cared about what he told her.

'Jack, please believe me, there will be more moments like that in your life. Hopefully not from being punched, but precious moments that money cannot buy. It could come from your parents, a best friend or even your own children one day.'

Jack smiled through his tears. 'Thank you, Roisin.'

'You don't need to thank me.'

'But you make me feel a better person than I am.'

'That's not me. You're doing that yourself. You are a good person. One day you won't feel the need to punish yourself anymore. You'll begin to open yourself up to the good in your past and the good you deserve in your future.'

A minute of silence passed, and Jack noticed it was now bright sunshine outside.

'Now can we carry on from where we left off on our last session?'

Jack nodded but the smile had gone as he knew what he was about to discuss.

'It will be all right, Jack. Stop if you need to.' She paused, crossed her legs the opposite way and continued. 'We ended our last session at a very traumatic point. Where Sam sadly passed away. Do you mind talking about what happened afterwards?'

'After? I'm not sure where to start.'

Jack watched Roisin refer to her notes. 'Were your parents at the lake?'

Jack was quiet while he stalled for time then, taking in a deep breath, he started. 'I think I blacked out for a bit. I remember shouting. I was screaming. Once I realised it was Sam who drowned I kept screaming. I went down on my knees, and then I'm not sure...' Roisin stayed silent.

'The next thing I remember was a policeman helping me up. He walked me to a police car away from the lake. There's a car park at the entrance and as I was getting into the car, I could see my three friends, Shawn, Lee, and Martin. They all had their parents with them. I didn't understand why mine weren't there. They were all staring at me. I'd never felt so alone. I felt they all blamed me.' Jack paused and exhaled.

'You can do this, Jack. Please continue.'

'A female police officer sat with me in the back of the car and they took me home. As we drove into Beare Green - that's the village where I live - my mum drove past and saw me in a police car. I'm not sure where she was going, I've never asked, probably to my Nan's or something. I watched as she turned her car around and followed us back to the house. I kept looking at her from the back window. When we pulled up, my mum came straight over. She didn't cuddle me or hold me. She shouted at me. 'What have you done now?' She looked furious. Then she said, 'And where is your brother?'

Jack took another deep breath. Remembering his mum's look of fear was a painful memory.

'The police didn't tell my mum at that point. They asked her if we could all go inside. I think she knew something had happened to Sam. I can't forget the look on her face. I'll never forget it. We all sat down. The policeman told her that Sam was missing in the lake. He didn't say he was dead because they hadn't recovered his body. They didn't find Sam's body until the next day.' Jack paused while he thought about that. It horrified him that Sam was alone in the water all night.

He felt tense and was clenching his fists the same way he

had the last time he'd got upset in Roisin's office.

'Do you want to stop for a while?' she asked.

Jack thought about it for a moment and shook his head. 'My mum didn't come to me. I was on the other sofa with the policeman. She stayed with the police lady. Mum was screaming. Although it sounded more than a scream. It was a noise I'd never heard before. Sort of like an animal. She was begging them to tell her it wasn't true. Begging me to say it wasn't true.'

Another silence. Jack wiped his tears on his sleeve. Roisin looked down at her desk. A gold-plated metal box held her tissues. She picked out two and passed them to Jack.

He wiped his eye and carried on. 'The policeman took me into the kitchen. I can't remember what he said. He was talking about my Dad, asking where he was. It goes a bit hazy again here. The next thing I remember was I was in bed and my Dad was holding me. I must have blacked out again.'

Jack stopped. Remembering his mum's pain was too much.

'Can I get you a drink, Jack? We can have a break.'

'No thanks, but I think I'd like to stop now.'

Roisin moved forward, 'Of course we can stop. You've done so well. Thank you for telling me. It can't have been easy. I do believe the more we talk, the easier you will find it to talk about Sam. And in time you will talk more about the good times and you'll smile about your memories with your brother.'

Jack had relaxed his fists. His hands were curled half open in his lap. He gave Roisin a broken smile.

Chapter 14

'Boxing is the only sport you can get your brain shook, your money took and your name in the undertaker book.'
Joe Frazier

Jack was enjoying the sparring sessions and was holding his own against other fighters in the club. He admired Lee for still coming with him even though it wasn't coming as naturally to him.

Jack was hungry to learn and wanted take in every single detail of Pete's training. Pete would shout, 'Get it right from the start. Practice does not make perfect. That saying is bullshit. Practice makes permanent. If you practice it wrong, it will stay wrong, so get it right.'

If Jack threw a sloppy jab in sparring, Pete would make him stop. He would jump through the ropes and shout, 'As you throw the jab, hold your right hand tight to the side of your face. He might throw a counter shot. Your face needs to be protected.'

Jack would get frustrated with himself but knew that getting it right would pay off. Pete would show him combinations. They'd work on his strengths and even harder on his weaknesses. He didn't have a vast reach, but he had power. Pete would make him practice moving in close on his opponent. He'd remind all his fighters about head movement. Mike Tyson was his go-to for this. Tyson would bob side to side to avoid being hit when coming in close. Most of Tyson's opponents were bigger than him so he needed to be in range to fire his shots off.

Pete would demonstrate they could go for the body with a left hook once they were in close. Jack tried to perfect this in sparring. When it came off, his opponent would often be bent over, wincing in pain. A correctly placed body shot could stop anyone.

In sparring, if a fighter looked in pain, Jack would always stop to let his opponent recover but he would grow in confidence knowing that if he pulled this shot off in a competitive fight, it could be over. In sparring, they used 16oz gloves which had lots of padding. The punches would still hurt but not as much. The combination of these gloves and the padded headguards prevented the fighters from getting cut or seriously hurt. In a professional competitive fight, they used 10oz gloves. Jack knew he could be effective wearing those.

If the opponent didn't stay down from the body shot, they planned to use the uppercut next. Pete told Jack that a hard uppercut after a body shot and then going for the body with a left hook would be a dangerous combination from him. Either of those punches could stop someone.

With excitement in his voice, Pete would shout out, 'That's your combination, son. That will stop them.'

Jack was now jogging four miles every morning and training at the gym three days a week. His fitness was improving and so was his speed. His power was that of a much heavier fighter.

Pete and David could see real potential. They were both excited but before they went to the next level, Pete needed to make a call.

'Hi, Ken. Is it a good time to talk?'

'No problem, Pete. How are you?

'I'm good, thank you. I'd like a chat about your boy. He's got it, you know. He could be something. I mean, really something.'

After a brief silence Ken replied, 'I knew he was doing well. Jack told me about the sessions. He said the sparring was tough, but he felt he was doing good. He loves it. I haven't told his Mum yet, about the sparring that is. She worries.'

'Oh, he's more than good. Tell Mum the opposition is more at risk than Jack is.' Pete laughed.

'I trust you, Pete, I know you won't let him get hurt or push him too early.'

Pete did a victory clench with his fist and mouthed, 'Yes!'

'So, it's all right with you if I push things on, train him more often, start looking into getting Jack some fights? Nothing heavy, some three rounders. Head guards, large gloves. We'll go from there.'

'If Jack's happy, I'm in. I just want him happy. Let's do it,' Ken said.

Pete was ecstatic. He couldn't wait to tell David. Pete had dreamed of finding a fighter like this, at this age. He'd had good fighters in the gym before, but he believed Jack was the one.

Chapter 15

'Truth and untruth often co-exist; good and evil are often found together.'
Mahatma Gandhi

Monday 10 am

Roisin never knew which David would turn up. She hoped it was the one who wanted to change. She said hello and asked David how he was.

'I'm doing well. I'm a bit stressed out but I'm working hard to make the changes we've talked about. I haven't gone near any schools, any playgrounds or been on any illegal websites.'

The thought of him visiting these places disgusted her but she smiled the best she could. She was genuinely pleased he was trying so hard. 'That's good, David. You should be immensely proud of yourself. I know it's not easy for you.'

He nodded but didn't reply.

'Would you like to tell me what is stressing you?'

She watched him tapping his fingers on his thigh while he thought about the question.

'My dad. I love my dad, and since mum died, we've become so close.' David stopped talking.

Roisin frowned. 'It's good that you've become close, isn't it?'

He nodded. 'It is but now he's found a new plaything. He's less interested in me these days and more interested in his new boy.'

'New boy. What do you mean?'

David's finger tapping was getting faster. He was doing it with both hands and his tone of voice was becoming sarcastic. 'At work. In the gym. He has a new fighter he's fascinated by. It's all he talks about. Jack this and Jack that.'

Roisin thought about Jack, her patient. He was the only Jack she knew. But she then dismissed the thought of it being him.

'It's natural to be jealous. He's your father. You want his attention, there's nothing wrong with that. I don't think we ever stop wanting the attention of our parents. And especially so with boys and their fathers.'

He stopped tapping. 'I'm not jealous. I just think he should calm down a bit. He's saying Jack will be a title contender. And I can see how dad wants that so badly. He'd love to train a champion. And it certainly wasn't going to happen with me. I wasn't good enough and he knew it.'

'Did you try boxing?' Roisin asked.

'Yeah, but dad said I wouldn't make it because I didn't like getting hit. I used to lose my temper when I got hurt. I lost control and wrestled a fighter to the ground once and kicked him in the face. That was enough for dad, so he's trained me to be a coach.'

Roisin could see the disappointment on his face. 'Do you enjoy coaching the other fighters?'

He bit down on his tongue and then answered with more disdain, 'I suppose so. I don't train any little boys, only over sixteens. That's dad's rule. So, you can take the police off speed dial. There's no kiddie fiddling going on.'

'I wasn't meaning anything like that David. I just wanted to know if you enjoy coaching. It's important to be happy and enjoy what you do.'

'I'm incredibly happy, thank you.'

More sarcasm. Roisin left a silence so that he would calm down. She'd seen the signs of his oncoming anger before.

'I do enjoy it. And I think I'm good at it. But I'm different to dad. He likes skilled fighters. I like real fighters. The type who want to knock people out and finish someone.'

Roisin had no answer for that so asked, 'Could you work together with your father and this new fighter? It could be a good way of bonding with him.'

'I want to. But Jack pays more attention to dad. He puts up with me but I'm not sure he likes me.'

Roisin wasn't surprised to hear that.

'See how it goes. Be there for your dad. Help him. I'm sure he'd be grateful for your help.'

'I'm not so sure. But we'll see.'

Wednesday 4 pm

Jack sat in his usual seat. He felt comfortable in front of Roisin. As hard as their conversations were, Jack loved being in her company. He was relaxed and ready to talk.

Roisin sat back, pen in hand, note pad on her lap and crossed one leg over the other. 'We had another tough session last time. How did you feel afterwards?' she asked.

'I was tired. I slept for hours when I got home but I was fine.'

'Can I ask you about your parents?'

Jack nodded.

'Do you go home and tell your parents what we've spoken about?'

Jack shook his head. 'Not the tough bits. I don't like upsetting them. They've been through so much.'

'I don't know your parents, but I think they might like to hear how you're doing. I think it would help you. Is this something you could try?'

'I could. I'd find it difficult. We don't really do feelings in my house. We all love each other but it's not said out loud.'

'You could instigate it and then they might do the same. From what you've told me about your parents, they want the best for you. They sound like they're being supportive and if they thought you were happy being open with them, they might open up to you.'

Jack thought about it and didn't think it would hurt to try.

'Just something to think about. You don't have to do that straight away but in time you might feel able to.' Roisin went back to her notes and twiddled her pen between her fingers.

Jack was looking at her, in awe. Once he realised he was staring, he looked out of the window instead. He started thinking how nice it must be, to be like her. She appeared so well organised. Jack assumed she had it all figured out. She was smart and beautiful. He truly trusted her and had never respected anyone in such a way.

'I have my first proper fight soon, at boxing,' he said.

He noticed a different facial expression on Roisin, one he had not seen before. Her normal smile had turned to a frown.

'Are you OK?' Jack asked.

'Boxing? You'll ruin your good looks doing that,' she said.

Jack felt his face burning. 'I really enjoy it. And I believe it helps.'

'Helps in what way?'

'I feel alive in the gym. I feel happy. I think I could do well, maybe achieve something.'

Roisin smiled. 'That's good, Jack. I tell you what, if you fight for the world title, I'll come and watch.'

'I'd like that.' Jack was excited at the idea. He'd love to show Roisin he was good at something. And for the first time in a long time, he didn't doubt himself. He believed he could go all the way in boxing.

Roisin smiled. 'We have a deal, I'll come to your fight. I've never been to a boxing match before, or any fight come to think of it.'

'You will one day,' he said and grinned.

II

Part Two

Chapter 16

'Service to others is the rent you pay for your room in heaven.'
Muhammed Ali

Jack had progressed through the amateur ranks and made a name for himself locally. He didn't necessarily have the right attributes for an amateur as it was all about scoring points. You would earn points per shot that landed on your opponent. Jack didn't throw a great volume of punches but what he did throw had bad intentions. He wanted to stop his opposition, get the knock-out. Once he stepped through those ropes a switch would go off in his mind. Mentally, he would go into a dark place. He would use the painful memories of Sam drowning and the years of grieving to psych himself up, ready for battle. He knocked out a lot of fighters, but he also lost a few amateur fights on points. He was typically losing to tall, thin fighters with long arms, opponents who had better speed and superior footwork.

Another amateur fight, another win. The fights were coming in regularly and Jack was improving every time. He felt he'd reached a point where he needed pushing on, a real test.

It came on Monday morning when he received a phone call

from Pete saying he needed to see him at his office. Jack rarely considered good news could come his way. For him, the glass was always half empty. He hoped he hadn't done something to upset Pete. Throwing on some clothes he went straight to the gym.

Pete was waiting for him and got straight to the point. 'Where do you want to go with this? You have options, real options. You could stay amateur and aim to try out for Great Britain Boxing, Team GB. If it paid off, you would have the Olympic dream, but that would take a long time and it doesn't suit your current fighting style.'

'I'd still be with you, right?' Jack asked. He felt Pete was uncomfortable as he wasn't looking him in the eye.

Pete continued. 'I don't want to hold you back from that. I'm not saying I want you to leave me, but I want to do what's right for you.'

It had never crossed Jack's mind to leave Pete. 'What's the other option?' he asked.

'We could make you some real money going pro. Go for those belts.'

Jack couldn't hide his grin. 'I like the sound of that.'

'Are you sure? The Olympics is a special place to be. You'd get the country's best coaches, the best equipment. And a steady income.'

Jack didn't need to think. 'But I've got you and this place.' His open hand indicated the gym. 'You gave me my chance. I'm not going anywhere else. I wouldn't make the next Olympics as there isn't time, and then I'd be waiting for the next one. It could be five or six years in total. I'd be getting on a bit. We could put in all the hard work and not even qualify. Let's go pro'.'

Jack loved seeing Pete's smile.

'Cassius Clay won the Olympics. A lot of fighters dream about it.' Pete said.

Jack came straight back at him. 'I'm staying with you. Mike Tyson didn't go, and he did OK. Nigel Benn, Chris Eubank, Ricky Hatton, they all had amazing careers without the Olympics.'

'I love your enthusiasm and knowledge of past boxers.' Pete beamed at Jack. 'What do you want from boxing?'

Jack thought carefully before answering. 'At night, when I allow myself to dream, I'm holding those belts. Those belts would look pretty, wouldn't they?' He laughed.

'Yes, they would.'

Jack was now serious. 'Pete, I don't want fame. That doesn't interest me. I'd like to give my family options. Hopefully I could do that with money. Help mum and dad pay the house off early. No one in my family has ever had money. I'm not saying money is everything but if a few quid can help my parents, I'm happy. What about you?'

'Me?!'

Jack shrugged. 'Yeah, you. What do you dream of?'

'No one's ever asked me what I want.'

'You must have dreams. What would make you happy?'

Pete thought about it. 'If David and I could coach a fighter to a world title, I'd die happy.'

'Let's do it then. We both know what we want so let's do it together.' Jack clapped his hands. 'And I'll buy you a decent car. That piece of crap out there isn't safe.'

Pete laughed. 'I'll hold you to that.'

Wednesday 10 am

She opened the door and called David through.

'How's your week been, David?'

'Fine.'

'Just fine?' she asked.

'Well, nothing's changed. I'm still being a good boy. I'm helping dad with the coaching and that's about it. I've not acted on my thoughts.'

Roisin dreaded their sessions. She couldn't build anything close to a decent relationship with David. His only smile was a sarcastic one. This was their final session, and she was pleased in one way but nervous in another because she didn't feel they'd made enough progress and he was still a potential risk.

'Can I ask if you are sure this is to be our final session?'

His grin was the usual one. 'Are you scared I'm still a paedo and you haven't cured me?'

She looked at him and changed her mind. She was glad it was the final session. He didn't want to be helped. Some people were just bad. These were not thoughts she could express out loud. It would be highly unprofessional but, at that moment, it was how she felt.

'That is not what I was thinking. I just feel we have more to talk about.'

He was still smiling when he replied, 'I'm afraid, Roisin, we are definitely done. I don't want to be here anymore. My dad is probably paying you a small fortune to talk to me, and what's he getting out of it? A son who still wants to touch boys.' His laughter grew louder, slightly manic.

'David don't talk to me like that. I show you respect, please do the same for me.'

'You show me respect? Really? You think so. By listening to me moan about my crappy life and how I like boys.' He stopped laughing. He stopped smiling.

'Roisin, you show me nothing. You've taught me nothing. You haven't changed a goddamn thing.'

He stood up, and Roisin was convinced he was going to do something to her. She pushed her chair back to create space between them.

It made him laugh. 'Sit still. I'm not going to touch you.' Taking a step towards her, he bent down and whispered, 'I don't like women. Remember? It's boys I like.'

Roisin felt cold. 'Get out. You disgust me.' She stood up but, before she could say anything, he'd opened the door and left.

She went to the door and leaned against it to stop him coming back in. She clasped a hand over her mouth and tried to compose herself. He was out of her life forever, but she worried about whoever's life he would enter next and contemplated calling the police. But what could she tell them? She had nothing. There was no individual in danger. Not yet.

Wednesday 4 pm

Jack had mixed emotions about finishing his treatment with Roisin. He felt better mentally and knew he could move forward with his life with the tools she had given him, but he was upset at the thought of not seeing her again. He felt close to her and didn't like the idea of a life without her in it.

He entered Rosin's office for what he assumed would be the final time. Before sitting down, he gave her a card and a gift and smiled when she said thank you.

'What are these for?' Roisin asked.

'Just to say thank you,' Jack said. He took his seat and looked at Roisin's eyes. They were bloodshot. 'Are you all

111

right, Roisin? Has something happened? We can rearrange the appointment if you don't feel great.'

Jack thought Roisin was going to tell him something. Her look was serious as she turned to him but turned to a gentle smile.

'Thank you, Jack. I'm a little tired.' She held up her gift. 'Can I open this now?'

Jack didn't want her to. He was embarrassed but he nodded.

Roisin opened the card and Jack watched her read the words he had written. '*Thank you for changing my life, I'll never forget you.*'

'Thank you, Jack. You know, you can tell me these things that you've written in here.' She held up the card.

'I just wanted get you something to remember me by.'

'That's nice and I'm grateful, but part of what we have achieved together is you opening up to people, being honest with how you feel. Would you find it hard to say this to me?' She pointed to the words in the card.

Jack thought about it. 'Yes. I'd find it hard and a bit embarrassing but that's not to say I don't mean it.'

'I know you mean it, Jack. But I'm thinking about you. When you leave here, I'd like for you to tell people how you feel. Whether it's good or bad. If someone close to you upsets you, tell them. If you don't, they won't know how upset you are, and it can lead to something far greater. And the same with telling someone how much you like them or how grateful you are. You should let them know. They would appreciate it.'

'I'll try. I will,' Jack said.

'You really didn't need to buy me anything but thank you.' Roisin unwrapped her gift. It was a small pendant, a gold four leaf clover.

'You don't have to wear it. It's just a little something. My mum helped me choose it. I wasn't sure what to get you, so I asked her to help me find something nice, and Irish.'

'It's lovely, Jack. Thank you, and please thank your mum.'

Jack waited as she put the wrapping paper in the bin under her desk and placed the pendant back in its box.

'You know this isn't goodbye, right? You can contact me if you feel you need to see me again. I think you'll be fine. You'll go on to have an amazing life but if times get hard and you feel you need to see me, please call.'

'I will. I promise. I'm scared though.'

'What are you scared of?'

'Of not having someone to talk to, like we do.'

'Like I said earlier, you can be more open with those around you. You'll be surprised how friends will listen and how they'll then open up to you. We all walk around with doubts and worries on our minds but when we share those feelings, it feels better. Talking is powerful. Words mean so much. Words can do a lot of damage, but they can also do so much good.'

'I'm not sure my friends are ready for my issues.'

'You'd be surprised. Try it. You'll find they have plenty of issues of their own.'

Jack nodded. 'Do you have any? Issues that is. I can't see it.'

'Why would I not have issues?'

Jack raised his hand. 'Look at you. You're perfect. You always know what to say.'

He noticed she was blushing. She pushed her hair behind her ear.

'Sorry, I didn't mean to embarrass you.'

'We all have plenty of issues, and a past. That's how I got into this profession. My husband will gladly tell you I'm far from perfect.'

Jack raised his eyebrows. 'Nope, not having it.'

Roisin laughed. 'Before you go today, I'd like to thank you too.'

'Really, what for?'

'For trusting me and being honest. From the very first session you've been open with me. I've always felt you wanted to help yourself. Despite how low you felt, even when you were at your lowest, you fought to get better. You're a fighter. You wouldn't give in. And I'm grateful to have been part of your journey.'

Jack raised his eyebrows again and took in what Roisin said. He became emotional and could feel tears surfacing.

'I'll always trust you, Roisin. You're someone who sees the good in everyone. I think that's special. People normally look for the bad, but not you.' Jack stood up as he started to feel a single tear run down his cheek.

'I'd better go. I've got training tonight.'

'But we've got twenty minutes left. You don't have to rush off.'

'I think I should.'

'If you're sure. Take care, Jack.' She held out her hand.

'Thank you.' Jack put his hand in hers. Then he broke down in tears and was pleasantly surprised when Roisin moved forward and held him.

Chapter 17

Jack had turned pro. It was his fulltime job and he loved it. He still had time for his friends but couldn't always do what they were doing. With his strict training regime and diet plan it could be quite a lonely existence, but he was more than happy to live that way because he could see a future in the sport. He stayed especially close to Shawn. Shawn had gone on to college to study business and finance. Jack had joked about him being his manager when he made it big. Now, the more he said it, the more he could see it becoming a reality. Shawn had loved the idea, but Jack knew his friend wasn't sure it could happen. He promised Shawn that one day it would happen.

Now the dream was on. Jack turning pro was the first step to it becoming real. He agreed with Pete that, as his head coach, he would get ten percent of any fight purse. It was then up to Pete how he was going to split that with David.

Lee was still training with Jack. He was fighting in the amateurs but not looking like he'd get to a professional standard. He was financially safe with a steady income and

Jack knew boxing would never be a career for him. Lee's path was to help in his father's family business. Boxing wasn't his way out like it was for so many others.

Martin was five weeks into his training with the Met Police. Jack, Shawn, and Lee mocked him about his career choice. They told him he'd have to leave the gang for his police friends and that he would change too much and become too square, too boring. It was just friendly banter, but they expected him to find it hard balancing a life in the force with hanging out with them. Jack and the others knew Martin wouldn't change towards them and secretly they were proud of him, but they couldn't tell him that. It's not what men did. Martin had never opened up to them about how he felt. He'd never spoken about how that day affected him, but Jack knew he had a burning desire to help people, and it was because of that day at the lake. It was his way of dealing with it and Jack accepted that. If Martin could help save lives, he hoped it would help him feel better.

Jack's first fight as a pro was against a slightly older man. He looked tough and had a career record of five wins and three losses.

Jack sat in the changing room, preparing mentally for the fight. He had put together a few songs that reminded him of Sam. He listened to them while warming up, hitting the pads with David.

The music and thoughts of Sam would transform Jack so that he was ready to fight anyone. The fire was lit within. As the fight time approached Jack was near to crying but held it back. Pete would regularly warn him about getting too emotional before the fight. He said it was wasted energy.

Jack had his dad by his side. He always said he wanted to be in his corner for every fight. His mum wouldn't watch. She hadn't seen any of his amateur fights. Instead, she would stay at home and read to take her mind off it. She'd only relax once she got the call. The first thing Jack did after a fight was to call her. He never missed.

'You've got this.' His dad's hand was on Jack's boxing glove.

Jack didn't reply. He was taking deep breaths, knowing what his dad was thinking – that he was getting too emotional and was struggling to hold off his aggression until he was in the ring. Somehow, his father always seemed to know when he was thinking about Sam.

He finally raised his head as Shawn approached him.

'Jack, I've got a present for you.'

'What present?'

Shawn handed him a large flat box.

Jack opened it. Inside was a pair of shiny black boxing shorts. On one leg was a badge for Pete's Boxing Gym. On the other leg, a sponsor's name. Lee's family's business, South East Tree Surgeons, had paid for the shorts and a bit extra towards Jack's other costs. There was a small British flag on the back. And on the gold coloured waistline was the name Sam, in capital letters.

Jack nodded. 'Perfect,' was all he said before jumping up to hug Shawn. 'Let's do this for Sam,' he said.

Shawn squeezed him tightly. 'Yes. For Sam.'

Jack turned to ask Pete, 'Is it time?'

'It is. Let's go.'

His walk out music was something the friends had grown up listening to together. It was blasting out, 'Ill Manors (The Prodigy Remix)' by Plan B.

His friends and family cheered him on as he walked to the ring. Not a huge crowd but around eight hundred local fight fans, all ready to go.

As Jack stood in his corner his opponent, Justin 'The Hammer' Woodrow, made his entrance to huge applause. He was a popular fighter. He loved to brawl and always went for the knock-out. The fans loved him. He jumped through the ropes, full of confidence. Then he smiled at Jack. It was unnerving but, Jack told himself, probably just bravado and done to intimidate him.

'Don't worry, son. No matter what anyone says, every fighter gets nervous,' said Pete. 'Whether it's your first fight or your fiftieth, it's always the same. He's as worried as you are.'

The ref called them to the centre of the ring and gave his final instructions.

'Remember what I said earlier in the changing rooms, no using the head, no low blows, no rabbit punches and if I say break, you break.' He then asked them to fight clean, touch gloves, and go back to their corners.

Woodrow wouldn't touch gloves. He just turned his back.

The bell went for the first round. Jack could no longer hear the crowd. His own heavy breathing through his gum shield filled his ears. His opponent came out like a bull on steroids and threw an almighty right hook. Jack's guard was up. The power knocked him back against the ropes. The crowd went mad thinking Woodrow had Jack in trouble. He followed this up with a flurry of blows to Jack's body and head. Jack protected himself well. He took most of the punches on his arms. This went on for over thirty seconds. Jack looked through the small gap in his guard, right into the face of the man in front of him and noticed Woodrow was breathing extremely hard. He had used up too much energy. There was still over two minutes of the round to go.

Looking for an opening, Jack threw his first punch, a stiff hard jab through his opponent's defence. It sent him four or five steps backward. The Hammer look confused at the power of the shot. It was only a jab. Jack went towards him and feigned another left jab, which made The Hammer put his gloves up to his face. In one fluid motion, Jack bent his knees, rotated his upper body to the left, then rolled his body back to the right, throwing a crushing left that landed in the solar plexus, right in the pit of the stomach of his tired opponent. Jack didn't need to use the uppercut to finish the combination. Justin 'The Hammer' Woodrow was down, and he wasn't getting up.

Before the ref got to a full ten count, his corner men, knowing it was all over, were jumping into the ring to help their fighter up. Jack stepped forward to help Woodrow too and thank him for the fight. He won and should have been celebrating but he felt slightly uncomfortable seeing this man still wincing in pain. The corner men appreciated Jack's concern and wished him luck for the future. They complimented Jack on his body shot and let him know their fighter probably had a couple of broken ribs. The crowd was happy with what they saw. They didn't care that the fight was over quickly. They simply liked to see a fight finish with a knockout or stoppage. Jack had gained some new fans.

'That was great. You've made an old man very proud.' It was Pete, speaking softly. He hugged Jack, who could tell his coach was excited but knew he wouldn't fully celebrate while the other fighter was still hurt.

A month later and the next fight lasted a little longer. Pete asked Jack to start getting some rounds under his belt. He explained this was essential for his career. He would eventually have to step up in class, and those fights would be going into the later rounds.

It lasted for two. Jack worked on his defence in the first round and then decided in the second that the time was right for a knock-out. His opponent, Jeremy Williams, was another decent British fighter but he couldn't take the power of the shot Jack delivered.

Over the next eight months Jack won four more fights all by way of knock-out. He was making headlines within the boxing community. His boxing record was now six wins, no draws, no losses. His seventh fight was coming up. It would be against an older guy, thirty-six years old. He'd had a good career but was known as a journeyman fighter. These fighters were hard as nails. All good, but they never had what it took to make it to the next level. They were happy fighting once a month, giving the crowd a good show and taking home a few quid.

Jack made his entrance to the ring and stood there waiting for his opponent to enter the ring. Ricky 'Psycho' Parsons came through the ropes. At the weigh-in Parsons had kept his tracksuit on. Jack hadn't been able to see how well built he was, but it was a different story on fight night.

'Bloody hell, Pete, this bloke's massive. He didn't look like that at the weigh-in.' Parson's body had muscle on top of muscle.

'Don't worry, son. He might look like a hard nut, but this

isn't a street fight. It's boxing. He's probably juiced up. He'll be out of breath in no time. Use your ability and don't, under any circumstances, get involved in a brawl. Box him at distance and keep on the move. One solid overhand right from this guy and your career moves backwards a year. Use your speed. You can dance around this old man all night. And for Christ's sake, keep those gloves up. Now go out there and have some fun.'

'Fun!' Jack said, with raised eyebrows.

They came to the centre of the ring. Parsons looked Jack up and down. He saw the name on his shorts. 'Sam, who's that, your boyfriend?'

In an instant, Jack's mood changed. He was caught in Parson's trap. He let Parsons get to him and now he wanted violence. Jack went forward, nose to nose with him. 'Don't say that. Don't mention his name again. If you do, I'll break ya' nose, and then ya ribs.'

The Psycho tried hitting Jack there and then, but they were separated by the ref.

Pete got hold of Jack. 'Ignore him. It's what he wants. You should have said nothing.'

'Fuck that, Pete. I'm happy to give him what he wants.'.

'Jack, listen to me. He's an arsehole. Don't let someone like him ruin your career. Beat him the right way, in the boxing ring using your skill. Beat him within the rules. That's how to win. After tonight you'll never see him again.'

David moved forward and whispered to Jack, 'Ignore my dad. Kill this motherfucker.'

Jack grinned, revealing his black gumshield and nodded.

The bell rang. Jack rushed out to the middle of the ring. No jab. His first shot was an overhand right that landed on the top of Parson's head. He went down.

Once he got back up, he was unsteady on his legs. Jack turned to his corner and smiled. He thought he had him beat so, instead of getting ready to follow it up, he stepped back and put his arms on the top ropes.

'What are you doing, Jack? Don't get cocky. Use your boxing,' Pete shouted.

Jack had Sam on his mind. He wanted to make this bastard suffer. Parsons took his eight-count from the ref, then came back towards Jack.

Landing a clean right cross that buckled The Psycho's knees, Jack stepped back again and smiled at him. He was waiting for Parsons to recover but only enough so that he could punish him even more with the next onslaught. Jack threw a left jab, followed by a cruel uppercut. If Parson's mouth had been closed, this shot would not have been so damaging but he was suffering and gasping for air. His mouth was wide open at the time and Jack knew it. In training, Pete had always told Jack to keep his mouth closed tight on his gumshield. If you got punched in the jaw when your mouth was wide open, the jaw could easily be broken. And that's what happened to Parsons.

Jack stopped thinking about Sam and calmed down. He looked over at Pete and finally took in his instructions.

'That's enough. He's done,' Pete said.

'Fucking finish him, Jack,' shouted David.

Pete grabbed hold of his son. 'What's wrong with you? Shut up.'

Jack wanted the ref to step in and stop the fight. He didn't want to hurt this man any longer. In his head, the fight was over. The red mist had cleared. He shouted, 'C'mon ref. He's hurt. Stop the fight.'

Because Parsons didn't go down from the shot, the ref decided he could fight on. While Jack was pleading with the ref to stop it, Parsons came forward and landed a good shot on Jack's nose. He didn't go down, but he did stumble. There was a ringing noise in his head and lights flashed before his eyes. He was in pain and shook his head to clear it. He couldn't breathe through his nose and knew it was broken. He had to finish this.

Parsons was on him again, but Jack held him tight and kept hold of him until his head felt clear.

Whilst holding Parsons, Jack started talking to him. 'You should have stayed down.' He then stepped back and threw a jab and an overhand right. Parsons was leaning on the ropes. He wouldn't go down. He even smiled at Jack.

'You hit like a bitch,' he shouted and waved Jack in.

'End it. Knock this prick out,' shouted David.

Jack threw a flurry of shots to the ribs and the head and didn't stop until the ref physically pushed him off.

The Psycho went down on his knees. He was wincing. No more gamesmanship. No more smiling. He was busted up. The ref finally waved the fight off.

David shouted at him. 'Are you happy now? You should have stopped that after the first knock down.' The ref ignored him and helped Parsons to his feet.

Jack had won.

Pete stepped into the ring. 'You may have won, but the way you did it wasn't right. You were like a wild animal. You should've stuck to the game plan. You have the skill and the power, but you've got that temper. It's gonna cost you big one day.'

Jack apologised but Pete walked away.

'I fucking loved that. What a fight,' David said, with a huge grin.

Parsons had just finished being checked over by the ringside doctor. He walked towards Jack who was ready to defend himself. He thought he was coming back for more but, to Jack's amazement, he shook hands and, in the politest British accent, said, 'Lovely fight, young man. You'll go a long way. That body shot was crippling. What a shot. Whoever you hit with that won't get up. I've been in with them all and I've never been hit like that in the ribs. Best of luck in your career. If I can help in any way, please let me know. If you need a sparring partner, give me a shout. I also do a bit of door work and security so if you need any of that, I'm your man.' After shaking hands with the rest of Jack's team he walked away.

Jack was perplexed. He looked at David. 'Can you believe that?'

David laughed. 'I like him. Why do you think he's called The Psycho?'

It was Jack's seventh straight win. The prize money was getting bigger. He was starting to earn some money from the sport. Nothing life-changing yet but it was becoming a possibility.

The following week they were back in training. 'Jack, come in for a minute. I've got someone I'd like you to meet,' said David.

Jack exhaled and stopped punching the heavy bag. He removed his gloves, grabbed his towel and wiped his face. As he walked into Pete's office, he saw a man sitting down holding some paperwork. Jack watched as the man placed the paper down and held out his hand to shake Jack's.

'I'm a bit sweaty, sorry,' Jack said as he carried on toweling himself down.

'I'm Roy Hardy. How are you Jack?'

Jack took in the red bow tie and double cuff shirt before answering. 'I'm well, thank you.'

Pete was sitting at his desk. 'Sit down, Jack. Roy's come in for a chat about your career going forward.'

Jack rubbed the back of his neck and stared at Pete. 'Think I'll give my dad a ring before this sort of thing happens.'

Roy leaned towards him. 'It's nothing like that Jack. It's just a chat. I've talked to Pete and he's got your best interests at heart, trust me. He's already warned me twice not to try anything dodgy with you. And I won't. This is just a straight up chat about how I can help you.' Roy moved back in his seat, smiled at Jack and then at Pete.

'He's a good egg, Jack. David knows him well and has assured me it's all in your interest,' Pete said.

'With all due respect I'd still rather my dad was here. I just want to fight. My dad is the one to work anything else.'

'That's fine. You haven't got to sign a thing today. Just a quick chat and then when you and your dad are ready, we can talk about contracts,' Roy said.

David moved forward and ruffled Jack's hair. 'You're a cautious one, aren't you? But you'll soon see Roy's a nice fella.'

Jack touched his hair and shot David a fake smile. 'Let me call dad and get him to come down here.'

It took Ken ten minutes to get to the gym. He walked in, smiling nervously. He didn't introduce himself to Roy, instead he spoke to Pete. 'You should have called me first, Pete.' He pointed at Roy. 'This isn't cool.'

'It's my fault, Ken. My old man didn't know he was coming in. I sprung it on him. I thought I was helping out,' said David.

Ken nodded. 'That's fine, David. Just...in future give me a call and I'll sit in with Jack on these sorts of things. He's too young to be making these decisions alone.'

'You're right, Ken. My apologies,' said Pete.

Ken winked at Pete. 'It's forgotten.' He then turned to face Roy. 'Hello, mate. I'm Ken. Are you a promoter, manager or what?' He leant forward and shook his hand.

'I'm a manager. Got a few years in the boxing game and know all the contacts in British boxing. I can get your son decent fights. And decent money. I can also help with selling merchandise and get Jack some sponsors. That way he can just concentrate on training and fighting. The money can take care of itself.'

'That all sounds good to me, Dad,' Jack said.

Roy continued. 'It's all on percentages. You don't pay me a thing. If I make you money, I take fifteen percent. If I don't, I take nothing.'

'Let's look at the paperwork. I assume that's what's in front of you?'

Jack stood up. 'Dad, I'll leave it to you. I only want to commit to one year at a time. Shawn will be my manager when the time's right. I need to get back out there, still got twenty minutes to do on the heavy bag. I'm happy if you are, Dad, but one year only.'

'You sure, son? You don't want to read the paperwork?'

'Nah, it's all good. As long as it's one year. Other than that, you know what's best for me.'

'Good boy, Jack,' said David.

Jack gave David another fake smile and once out of Pete's office muttered to himself. 'Boy. Who's he calling boy?' He took his anger out on the punch bag.

'You don't look happy.' It was Lee. 'Is it something to do with that weird looking dude in the office? What's with that bow tie? Looks like a nonce.'

Jack laughed. 'He wants to manage me.'

'You sure that's all he wants? He's proper weird.'

'He's all right. Just eccentric I think.'

'You hope.' Lee laughed and jabbed Jack in the stomach.

Jack laughed too before pushing Lee away. 'Get back to training you.' He looked into the office feeling uneasy as he watched his dad reading the paperwork.

Chapter 18

'When I saw you, I fell in love, and you smiled because you knew.'
Arrigo Boito

'Are you training next Saturday? Have you got anything on?'

Jack swapped his phone to his left hand before answering. 'Not on the weekend. I've got an easy couple of weeks then it's back into full training for my next fight.'

'That's the correct answer. We're all going out. Martin, Lee, you and yours truly,' said Shawn.

'Sounds good, but where?'

'We're going to a party at The Jolly Butchers.'

'You must be j...'

Shawn interrupted. 'I know it's not the best pub in the world, but she'll be there.'

Jack knew who Shawn meant but played it cool and replied, 'Who is she?'

'You know exactly who I mean. Now, go out and get yourself some decent clothes. Don't turn up in a bloody tracksuit. Get your hair cut, put on a bit of smell-nice and look the part.'

Shawn hung up before Jack had a chance to ask how he knew Kirsten would be there. He rang him back.

'How do you know she'll be there?' he asked.

'She? Who is she?' Shawn laughed.

'Piss off. Just answer the question.' There was no more playing it cool. He needed details.

'It was on one of those groups on Facebook. I got an invite to a party. Before I accepted, I looked at who was going. I didn't want to go if it was full of knobs. And there she was. Kirsten Kenward. And when I think of Kirsten, I think of you. Check your bloody Facebook. You're on there too. You're invited,' Shawn said. Then he hung up again.

Jack opened Facebook, looked at the invite and pressed on the tick. He was now going. While he was on there, he checked Kirsten's profile. She hadn't changed - same infectious smile, same amazing blue eyes. Jack thumped the air.

The 'Add Friend' box was staring him in the face. Before he had any more time to think about it, he pressed it. His heart was racing. What if she didn't want to be friends? What if she had a boyfriend?

Within seconds a notification came up. 'Friend request accepted'. Jack smiled. He was so happy. He told himself it wouldn't matter if she did have a boyfriend. It would be lovely to see her again. He was trying to kid himself. He went back into her profile. It didn't say married. That was good. It didn't say she was in a relationship. Perfect. He went into her photos, checking if there was any sign of a boyfriend in there. There were lots of pictures, all of Kirsten out having fun. But no pictures of her cuddling up with some horrible bloke who clearly wouldn't be good enough for her.

She looked so happy. Jack smiled again. He was pleased for her. Then he panicked. What if she knew he was looking at her pictures? He didn't want to be a stalker. He closed her profile down and quickly Googled, 'Can someone tell if you are looking at their profile pictures on Facebook.'

Google gave Jack the answer he hoped for. No. Exhaling a sigh of relief, he put his phone down and imagined seeing Kirsten at the party. A few minutes later his phone lit up. A red square with a number one in it appeared in the corner of the Facebook messenger app. He opened it.

Three words. 'How are you?' followed by three x's.

Three words that made Jack's heart pound. He could see who it was from, but he double-checked anyway.

Jack's mum walked into the room.

'What are you up to? What's that smile for?'

Jack played it down. 'It's nothing, Mum. Nothing.'

'Don't give me that. A mother knows her son. Who are you talking to? Who is it?'

Jack had no choice but to come clean. 'It's a message from Kirsten, a girl I used to go to school with.'

His mum came closer to look at Jack's phone. 'I remember her. She's a lovely looking girl. What does she say?'

'Blooming nosy, you are.' Jack showed her his phone.

Mis mother read the message. 'She likes you and, if you like her, you'd better reply.'

'She's probably just being polite, Mum. I sent her a friend request.'

'When did you send it?'

'Five minutes ago.'

'Well, I can tell you now, she likes you. She's already sent you a message, after five minutes of getting a friend request. And three kisses. You don't send three kisses. Two maybe, but not three.' His mum winked at him and shouted through to his dad. 'Ken, if a girl sent you a message and ended it with three kisses, what does that mean?'

'She wants it,' his dad replied. They could hear him laughing at his own joke.

'Ken, don't be so crude. It doesn't mean that. But it means she likes you. Now phone the poor girl or send a message or whatever it is you do these days. Just get on with it.'

Jack smiled at his mum and gave her a peck on the cheek. 'Thanks, Mum.'

His mother went into the kitchen. He heard her say, 'He's going to be OK.'

Jack stood up and went closer to the door.

'He is. We'll all be OK.' That was his dad.

He heard a slight thud and guessed what it was. His mum had probably picked up a tea towel and given his dad a swipe.

'Oi, what was that for?'

'She wants it...stupid man.'

He heard them both laugh.

As Jack went up to his bedroom he and Kirsten continued talking on messenger.

'I'm OK, thanks. How r u? x' Jack typed. He waited anxiously for a reply. Within seconds he got one.

'I'm very well. How is ur boxing going? xx'

Jack started replying and then wondered how she knew he was boxing. He changed his reply. 'How did u no I box? xx'

The answer didn't come back quite as quickly this time. Jack smiled. She must have been looking at his Facebook pictures.

'A friend told me xx'

Jack's smile widened and being a gentleman, he accepted her white lie. What else could he do? He'd been looking through all her pictures. More than once.

'It's going well. Maybe come watch me fight soon? xx'

'I'd like that xx'

'R u going 2 the party next Saturday? xx' He knew she was but asked anyway.

'Yes. Wud u like 2 walk in together. I don't want 2 walk in alone xx'

Jack wasn't expecting that. Another massive smile to himself.

'Yes. I'd love that. meet u outside. In the carpark at 7.30 xx'

'OK xxx'

Three kisses again. Jack was beyond happy. He was excited and unsure how they had set up a date so quickly. They'd not seen each other since they were so young and now they were meeting up to enter a party together. That was third or fourth date behaviour.

'Can't wait xxx' He couldn't help himself. He had to send the three kisses but wasn't sure he should have. Did boys send three kisses? He had no idea.

'xxxx' From Kirsten.

'Yes, get in,' he said, falling back on to his bed. He hadn't felt this happy in years. He wasn't sure he'd ever felt like this. It was a new feeling. And he loved it.

Over the next week, Jack and Kirsten continued talking via messenger. They had established early on that neither was seeing anyone else. They talked about life after school. Jack talked about boxing. Kirsten talked about her work within the National Health Service. She was studying to become a midwife.

Jack already knew how he felt about Kirsten but was petrified in case he messed things up. What if she didn't fancy him and she just wanted to be friends? He decided he'd take that.

Having her in his life was what he wanted, and he'd take anything she offered.

Saturday evening finally arrived. Jack's phone rang. It was Shawn. Jack hadn't told his friends he was going in with Kirsten. He knew they would give him hell for dropping his mates for a girl. Those were the rules with a group of male friends. Even if you are happy for your friend, you still give them abuse. It's a form of affection. Or just the male way of showing emotion to each other.

Jack answered his phone. 'I'll meet you in there. I'm running a bit late.'

'You're never late. Is something wrong?' Shawn asked.

'Nope. Perfectly good. Meet you there. Get the beers ready.'

Jack arrived outside the pub ten minutes early. New shirt on, hair freshly cut, and swimming in Hugo Boss aftershave, he waited nervously.

A car approached, coming to a stop next to Jack. Blinded by the headlights, he tried looking inside. He couldn't make out who it was and then, there she was. That smile, those eyes. Even better than the photos. Jack didn't notice who was driving the car. He didn't care. The window came down, and Kirsten's Dad said hello.

Jack composed himself. 'Hello, Mr. Kenward.'

Kirsten said goodbye to her Dad, encouraging him to go. He offered to pick her up later and drove away.

They were alone.

Pushing her long dark hair to one side, Kirsten said, 'Hello you.'

Jack had never felt this way before. When Kirsten looked at

him, he felt he was the only person that mattered in the world to her. To feel that important to another human is special and he already knew he never wanted it to stop.

He hadn't planned his first words. He felt like he'd never been away from her. Like he already knew everything about her.

'Hello you,' was all he could say.

They stared hard into each other's eyes and Jack knew everything was as he hoped it would be.

He was overwhelmed when Kirsten, who was the braver of the two, said, 'Come here,' and held him. She smelled amazing. They held each other so tight. At that moment, Jack started regretting not getting in touch with Kirsten years ago. All those wasted years. But probably for the best. He was a vastly different person in his late teens. Kirsten may have grown tired of the old Jack, his drinking, and fighting. It wouldn't have been fair on her.

Holding her, Jack felt safe. This feeling was truly a gift.

'We'd better go and say hello to everyone,' Kirsten said.

Jack pulled back, only slightly. He didn't want to let go.

'I suppose so.'

Slowly, they let go of one another and walked towards the pub door.

A few feet from the door, Kirsten reached forward and held Jack's hand.

He never wanted to let go.

Chapter 19

'To be free from evil thoughts is God's best gift.'

Walking through the playground alone he didn't feel uncomfortable. He knew he had to look like he fitted in, just like any one of the many dads there on that day. He didn't stare too long and didn't focus on any one child. He simply walked through, taking in all the exits and working out how long the children were out of sight of their parents. He was shocked but happy to see the number of parents who would rather be on their phones than watch their children play. They'd look up every now and then, mostly when their child called them, wanting their parent's attention when they did something good or brave.

'Mummy, watch me go down the slide.' Mum would look up from her phone and say, 'Wonderful, darling. You're so clever.' And then back to social media.

There were no cameras at the park. The nearest CCTV was at the football stadium but that was a hundred metres away. He'd worked out he could get to the playground without being seen by those.

During the time it took a parent to check how many likes they had on Facebook, he calculated he could get a child out of the playground and into one of the many alleyways just outside the park. The easiest target would be a boy playing alone. There were plenty of them, all lost in their own little world. It would be easy to gain their trust, take interest in what they were doing and convince them he had a better game for them, with him.

It was time to move on. A moody looking mother on her own was staring at him. He did his best to walk away without causing any more suspicion. He pretended to wave at someone who was out of sight. The moody looking mother fell for it and went back to her child, and then to her phone.

Chapter 20

'You always gain by giving love.'
Reese Witherspoon

They had arranged to meet the following day. Jack didn't have a plan on where to go and he didn't care, just as long as he got to be in Kirsten's company. He thought the previous evening had been amazing, but he hadn't got to be alone with her as much as he'd wanted.

He sat in his car outside Kirsten's house and fidgeted in his seat. He took a quick look in the mirror planning what to say. He didn't know who would be in and was worried whether her parents would like him, or not. Perhaps they wouldn't want their daughter dating a fighter. They might think he was some sort of thug.

He rang the doorbell and took two steps back. Putting his hand in his pockets he looked down to check his fly. Relieved it wasn't open he took his hands out again. He felt as if he had forgotten how to stand without looking awkward, and then Kirsten opened the door. She smiled and asked him to go in. He wanted to tell her how stunning she was, but her mum appeared behind her.

'Hello Jack. I'm Carol, Kirsten's mum. How are you?' She gave Jack the warmest of smiles, relieving his fears and making him feel welcome. He thought about saying something cheesy or funny but calmed himself and settled for, 'Hello Mrs. Kenward. I'm fine thank you.'

'Thank you for getting Kirsten home safely last night. It sounded like you all had fun. Kirsten didn't stop talking when she got in. Your name came up a lot.' Kirsten's mum raised an eyebrow and smiled.

Kirsten was blushing. 'Goodbye, Mum. You've said enough.'

Her mum looked at Jack and they both laughed.

'I'll leave you to it, bossy. I know when I'm not wanted. Lovely to meet you, Jack.'

'Dad will come and say hello later, he's waiting for half time.' Kirsten grinned and shook her head.

'That's fair enough. If I weren't here with you, I'd be watching the game.'

'Are you a Chelsea fan too?' Kirsten asked.

'Err, no, West Ham.' Jack widened his eyes pretending to be shocked. 'Don't tell him yet. Can we wait until about the fifth date for that?'

Kirsten laughed. 'Fifth date, eh?'

Jack blushed. 'Actually, we'll leave it until the tenth.'

She smiled. 'Deal! He's pretty passionate about Chelsea. Perhaps we should leave it until after we're married.'

Jack liked her answer. 'I can live with that.'

'Shall we go out for a drive? We could grab a coffee some-where.'

'Sounds great. Did you want to go to a pub? We could find a quiet one.'

'I was thinking we could get a drink from somewhere and

stay in the car. Just us.'

'I know where we can go.'

The petrol station in town had a coffee machine. Jack went in and got himself a large Americano and Kirsten a large hot chocolate with added caramel. Jack kept looking out to the car, excited every time he caught sight of Kirsten waiting for him.

Back in the car, Jack placed the drinks in the cup holders and, from his pocket, produced several different bars of chocolate. 'I wasn't sure what you liked so I got a few.'

'Any chocolate is good with me,' she said.

He started the engine, checked the mirror and, looking across at Kirsten, reached across and touched her hand. 'Are you all right?'

The look in her eyes told him all he needed to know.

They stopped at a viewpoint in Coldharbour, near Leith Hill. The view there, across the Surrey Hills, was beautiful. It was early evening and still light enough to see far into the distance. Jack told her how he jogged up there regularly and said on a clear day he loved the view of London and that Wembley Stadium, Canary Wharf, and the Shard were all visible.

They talked about Jack's boxing and his upcoming fight and about Kirsten's job as a midwife. He loved how her eyes lit up when she talked so passionately about helping families bring new life into the world.

Kirsten reached for Jack's hand and held it. It was slightly awkward with the handbrake in between them.

Kirsten looked directly into his eyes. 'Shall we jump in the back? Much more room.'

Jack was pleasantly surprised. He'd been thinking of suggesting the same thing but wasn't confident enough to instigate it himself. The radio was on and he turned the volume to low before getting out to open the passenger door. He then opened the back door for Kirsten to get in. She shifted halfway along the seat. When Jack got in, they were close enough for their legs to touch. With more confidence now he took Kirsten's hand in his, leaned towards her and whispered, 'You look gorgeous.'

Kirsten pushed her hair behind her ear and tilted her head. 'Thank you.'

'I didn't get a chance to say that earlier, your mum was there.'

'You look great too.' She leaned against Jack and kissed his cheek.

He edged closer still. They both stared into each other's eyes and when the time felt perfect, he kissed her.

'I'm not going to say what I want to say, it's the wrong moment, but this feels right, so right.' Kirsten's voice was husky.

Jack kissed her and stroked her hair from her face. 'I know. I feel it too.'

Chapter 21

'The two most important days in your life are the day you are born and the day you find out why.'

Averaging a fight every three months, Jack now had a perfect record of fourteen wins and no losses. All future fights were going to be a big step up in class and he would need more time off between each one to recover. One loss at this stage of his career would put him back to the bottom of the ladder.

Roy arrived at the gym just as he always did on a Friday afternoon. David would always greet him first and make him a cup of tea.

Jack was on the speedbag, his session nearly finished. He felt a tap on his shoulder. 'Jack, can you come in the office for a bit?' David said.

'No problem, I'll be five minutes.'

David left him to it and returned to Roy.

Friday was always a good day at the gym. The fighters had another good week of training in the bag, and they could often look forward to a weekend of a bit more rest and time with the family. This Friday was no different with Roy and David having their usual friendly but close to the mark banter.

'Jack, good to see you, how's it going? Feeling strong, ready for your next fight?' Roy asked.

Jack took a seat next to Roy, 'It's going well. Plenty to improve on but Pete and David and pushing me hard,' Jack looked at David and smiled.

Roy nodded with a grin, 'that's good. I like to hear that. We've only got about a month left on the current contract so I wondered if we could sit down with you and your dad and iron out the next one?'

Jack's knee started bouncing, 'I'm not sure what we are doing going forward. Remember I said that Shawn would take over my management when the time was right?'

Roy shot David a concerned look and then back at Jack, 'What are you talking about. We have had a couple of amazing years. I've got you good fights, I've looked after you.'

'You've been great Roy. But I said from the beginning, about Shawn. Nothing's changed. I'm grateful to you and all you've done but Shawn was always going to be my manager when he was ready.'

Roy edged closer to Jack, 'I don't think you understand what that means Jack. You can't just dump me like this, that doesn't happen to me, I've worked fucking hard for you.'

'He has Jack, you're being unfair here.' David said.

Jack folded his arms and sat upright, he pointed at David, 'You, keep out of this. You're my coach, that's all.' He then pointed at Roy, 'And you, don't make out you do this all for me, you haven't been working for free. You've made good money out of me, I'm the one in the ring getting punched in the head. And now it's time to move on. I was straight with you from the beginning and I'm being straight now. This is our last contract. Shawn takes over next month.'

Roy stood over Jack and put his finger in Jack's face, 'You little shit. You think you can just get rid of me when you are about to make some real money, I don't think so. I will fucking sue. I will take whatever I can from your future earnings.'

Jack stood and went nose to nose with Roy, 'You point that finger at me again and I'll snap it off and put it up his arse.' Jack pointed at David. 'Both of you know we should be having this conversation with my dad and Pete here. But you thought you could get around me by doing it with just me. I'm going to walk out of here before I do something that gets me in trouble... and you in hospital,' he jabbed Roy's chest.

Roy stumbled back, 'You'll regret this Jack. No one gets the better of me, do you understand what I'm saying?'

Jack stopped at the door, 'Roy, don't threaten me, it's not a good idea. David, you need to get hold of him now, he's your mate so shut him up.' Jack walked out of the office and over to his gym bag. He found his phone and called his dad.

David poked head his out of the office, 'Come on Jack, don't do this. Come back and talk to us.

Jack didn't turn around.

It had been a week since Roy had gone from the team, it was time to move forward. David wasn't happy but his dad made him keep quiet and accept Jack's decision.

Jack was standing next to Pete in the gym when a call came through from Chris Bowman, a tough, no nonsense northerner. Chris had been born in Manchester and was a former fighter whose career had been cut short due to injury, so he'd decided to become a boxing promoter. He looked after his fighters and wasn't one who bled them dry and dropped them once they lost a fight. It wasn't all about the money. For Chris, it was about the journey with the fighter. Shawn had shopped around, but liked what Chris had to say, he felt Chris was a genuine guy who had Jack's interests at heart, so he was now their promoter.

'Hi Pete. It's Chris here.'

'Chris, how's things going?' Pete replied, beckoning to Jack to come closer so that he could listen in.

'Are you sitting down?'

'No, and I don't want to. I won't get back up. Go on Chris, hit me with it.' Pete put his hand over the phone and whispered to Jack. 'Sounds like we're getting a big fight next.'

'We've got the British title fight. They feel Jack has earned a shot,' Chris said.

This was something Jack and Pete had dreamed of. The British title winner would come away with The Lord Lonsdale Challenge Belt, commonly known as the Lonsdale Belt, the oldest championship belt in British professional boxing, first awarded in November 1909.

Jack grasped his coach's arm.

'Is he ready? That's all I need to know,' Chris asked.

'He's more than ready. I reckon the timing's right. I thought he was ready three or four fights ago. He's definitely ready now.'

Jack nodded, gave a wide smile and gripped Pete's arm harder.

'Good. Let's make it happen. You ring Jack, give him the news. I'll ring Shawn and sort out the finances.'

Pete was about to put down the phone when he heard Chris say, 'Oh Pete?'

'Yeah, I'm still here.'

'Well done. You and Jack both deserve this.'

Pete dropped onto a chair. He gave a half shrug and grinned. 'You deserve this title shot. One of my fighters, fighting for the Lonsdale Belt.'

Jack sat down to face him. 'You should feel proud of yourself too.' His hands were shaking. There was only one person he wanted to share his news with, but he had to wait. Kirsten was working a long night shift at the hospital.

Kirsten had moved into Jack's house with his parents. Money had been slowly building from his fights but not enough to get their own place.

Jack waited until Kirsten came home from work. When he heard the key turn in the lock, he jumped up to put the kettle on.

'Cup of tea, beautiful?' he shouted.

'That would be lovely,' she said as she walked into the kitchen, leaned in and kissed Jack's cheek.

He was trying not to laugh from excitement.

'What's up? I know that cheeky look,' Kirsten said.

'I don't know what you're talking about.' A huge smile broke through that Jack couldn't control. He placed his hand on Kirsten's shoulders. 'We did it. We got the fight. I'm fighting for the British title. It's going to be at the York Hall, London. I've always wanted to fight there. Pete's so excited.'

Kirsten jumped on Jack, wrapping her arms around his shoulders and her legs around his waist.

'You deserve this, Jack. I love you. You know that don't you? I'm so proud of you.'

'I love you too.' He paused and then said, 'The money's not bad either.'

Her feet were now back on the ground. 'Go on,' she said.

So far, Jack's biggest payday was ten thousand pounds. But it never went very far. He had lots of outgoings. Paying Pete, Shawn and Ken came first. Then there was the nutrition which wasn't cheap. There were sparring partners to pay. After all that it didn't leave much, and even then, he still had tax to pay.

Jack paused a bit longer for maximum effect.

'Shawn reckons, with the ticket sales, sponsors, the Sky TV money, and advertising, I'll clear over a hundred thousand. And that's after tax. Not bad for thirty-six minutes work is it?' he joked. 'And that's after Pete gets his ten grand, and Shawn and dad take their bit.'

Kirsten looked at him in shock. He kissed her forehead. 'Start searching for a house, beautiful. We've got a nice deposit coming.'

He held her tight and when he went to break away, she wouldn't let him. He tilted his head to look down at her and could see she was crying. 'Hey you, what are the tears for? This is good news.'

'I know and I am happy. These are happy tears. You told me this would happen, that you'd be a champion and make money and I always believed in you. But now it's happening I'm so happy for you. You deserve it.'

He cupped her face. 'It's happening to us, not just me. This is for both of us.'

'Follow me upstairs,' she said.

Jack forgot about the tea and did as he was told.

The following morning Jack sat across from his dad, having breakfast. He'd told him about the fight, and, in his own way, his dad had said he was proud of him.

Jack watched as his father poured a second cup of tea and stirred three giant spoons of sugars into it.

'You want some tea with that cup of sugar?' Jack said.

His dad ignored the comment. 'This fight is going to be hard. He's a good fighter. We'll need top sparring partners. I'll talk to Pete today.'

Jack reached for the milk to top up his cereal. 'Dad, sparring partners at this level aren't cheap. I haven't won the belt yet. Money's a bit tight.'

'That's why I've transferred some money to Shawn today. He's sorting it.'

Jack was confused. 'Where have you got it from? I'm not spending yours and mum's money.'

'It's your money. That money you've been paying me to help manage you. Did you honestly think I'd keep it? Take money off my own son? No chance. I've been saving it for you. And now you need it.'

Jack couldn't believe his dad had done that for him but, before he could protest again, his dad continued. 'Don't argue with me. It's done. You may be the future British champion, a tough guy boxer, but in this house you're still my little boy. I'll still slap you if you don't do as I say.'

'Give ya dad a hug then,' his mum shouted from the kitchen. Jack realised she'd been listening the whole time.

His mum cried happy tears as Jack hugged his dad who didn't get up but, with a tear in his eye, he patted Jack's arm that was wrapped around him.

Jack had three months to train for the biggest night of his life. He allowed himself one day off a week. Sunday was always rest and recovery. His diet was strict. No processed foods, no sweets, no crisps, no alcohol. Lean meats only, tons of vegetables and litre after litre of water. His biggest treat was his morning coffee. He kicked the day off at 5 am with a large cup, followed by a six-mile jog. Training at the gym with David and Pete would start at 11 am.

David was becoming closer to Jack. They both shared a love of boxing. It was the only thing they had in common. They'd talk for hours about the fighters of yesteryear. They would watch hours of footage of old fights and how the boxer used to train. If any of what they saw was something they liked, they'd bring it into their next training session. They didn't always agree with each other. David was aggressive as a coach. He wanted power and knockouts. Jack would often stop arguments between David and his dad. Pete was the opposite, being all about the sweet science of boxing.

Six weeks into a full training camp and all was going to plan. The sparring was getting heavier. Jack was on target with his weight. He felt unstoppable.

Dinner time was difficult. He was tired of the same old food but knew it was the right thing to do if he wanted to be at his best. Some nights he'd be eating alone as Kirsten was on shift at the hospital. Not this night. Jack walked in from training and the house was in complete darkness. Confused, he turned on the lights as he came through the front door.

'Turn that light off,' he heard Kirsten say.

'But I can't see bugger all. What are you up to? Are we hiding from someone?'

'Just shut up and come into the dining room. I'm just lighting the candles.'

He walked in and there she was smiling at him. 'Your parents have given the house to us for the night. They've gone out to the cinema.'

She was wearing a black dress, cut high above the knees. Her high heels gave her legs a gorgeous shape. Jack looked her up and down. His heart rate sped up. 'Wow, you look... I'm not hungry. Can we go upstairs?'

'You like what you see then?' She gave him a twirl.

'You could say that.' He laughed. 'It's going to be a shame to ruin it.'

'Behave you, I've cooked. We're having a nice meal together, like proper adults.'

Candlelight was flickering, causing shadows to dance around the ceiling.

Dinner was perfectly laid out. It was still a healthy meal, white meat and veg but the way she'd presented it was perfect and a welcome treat for Jack. There was a small gift next to his plate.

'What's this? It's not my birthday,' he said.

'Sit down and open it. I hope you like it.'

'What is it? You know I don't like surprises. We should be saving money, not spending it.'

Jack removed the bow and undid the wrapping paper, being careful not to rip it. He could see she had wrapped it carefully. Inside was a small box. His first thought was a watch. He'd always wanted a Rolex Submariner, but it couldn't be. They cost thousands.

'No, it's not the Rolex,' said Kirsten. She could read Jack so well.

He smiled as he took the lid off the box. And there it was. A piece of thin white plastic with a small window in the middle, and on that small window were two bold vertical lines. Two lines that would change Jack's life forever.

'It's not... You're not...'

Jack was wide-eyed. 'You can't be, I've been training so hard. We haven't done much of that... I mean, when?'

'That night, you know. The night you told me you were fighting for the title.'

'Oh, that night,' Jack allowed himself a few seconds to remember just how good the sex was that night. Then he was back to reality and thoughts on being a dad.

'But we didn't want kids yet. We talked about this.' Jack said, holding up the pregnancy test stick.

Kirsten touched her stomach. 'Jack, I'm afraid you don't get to send this back. This is happening. We did this.'

'I don't know what to say.'

Kirsten knelt by his chair. 'You could tell me you love me. And that it's going to be OK. That would be a good start.'

Jack smiled. 'Of course, I love you. And it will be OK, but I'm scared. Scared I'll be a terrible dad. Scared, I can't protect him. What if something happened to him?'

'For a start, it might be a girl so less of the him. And we've spoken about this before. Not everyone is going to leave you, Jack. What happened with Sam was so awful. I understand why you're worried. I get it. You took a chance on loving me and I'm not going anywhere. You won't lose me or the baby. Our baby will be the luckiest baby ever to be born and do you know why?' She grabbed Jack's hand and put it on her stomach. 'This baby has you for a father. That's why.'

Jack squirmed in his seat, uncomfortable with the compliment. 'This baby is lucky having you, not me. I'm lucky having you. Without you I'm a different person. I like me now that

I'm with you.' They kissed and Jack could feel himself welling up inside. 'I can't believe I'm going to be a dad. This changes everything. For the better. Definitely for the better. I love you so much, Kirsten.' He hugged her and squeezed her tight. 'Thank you.'

'What are you thanking me for?'

'For being you.' He felt so content having her in his arms. He kissed her again. You're going to have to marry me now, you know that don't you?'

She kept her head against his chest. 'One day,' she said.

Chapter 22

'I'm a competitor and a very proud man. If a guy beats me once,
he'll have to do it again to make me believe him.'
Sugar Ray Leonard

Jack was on target to make weight. He'd trained so hard that he wasn't far off what he needed to be for the fight. He still had two days to go until the big weigh-in. The weight cut was the hardest part for some fighters and often they'd have to lose as much as a stone in the final few days, wearing sweat suits on treadmills and in saunas, dangerously dehydrating the body. Stress caused by another letter from Roy helped with the weight cut. Jack and Shawn knew Roy couldn't win in court as Jack had fulfilled his contract and been fair all along. But it still left a bitter taste that Roy was so angry.

The fight was at middleweight. Jack needed to weigh a maximum of 11 stone 6lbs. He had stopped heavy training a week before. The hard training and hours of sparring were all in the bank. Eleven weeks of hard work had paid off. He was now only doing light pad work, stretching and short runs to tick over. His body needed to be free from injury and at its peak on fight night.

The weigh-in was the day before the fight. This was also going to be where he'd meet his opponent, the current British champ, James Carrick. A hard-punching, ginger-haired fighter from Liverpool. He had a huge following from his hometown, and even the blue half supported him.

Jack arrived at the weigh-in to be greeted by hundreds of fight fans, more than there had been at some of his previous fights. Fans from the north of England always got behind their fighters who were often down to earth, working-class lads. The fans felt like they knew James, he was one of them.

Jack walked out on to the scales to a chorus of boos. Followed by chants of, 'Who are ya?' It was unnerving but he took it well, waving to the crowd and thanking them for coming along. The fight official read out Jack's weight. 'Eleven stone, six pounds.' Perfect. Relief for Jack, he could now eat and drink what he needed to feel strong again. He put his tracksuit back on and watched Carrick get on the scales. The crowd cheered, singing their own version of the song to the tune of Winter Wonderland. 'There's only one James Carrick,' echoed around the room.

Jack watched as Carrick, who was on fine form, played to the crowd. He was confident rather than cocky and he didn't slag Jack off directly. Instead, he was encouraging the crowd to sing louder.

When they had to face off, Jack was called in by Chris, the promoter. He was ready for the stare down. They were nose to nose. Jack looked hard into Carrick's eyes, desperately trying not to blink or show any weakness. It was going on for too long. He had to get himself into that dark place to continue. A place he didn't want to be.

He then said two words to Carrick. 'Thank you.'

Carrick frowned. 'Thank you for what?'

Jack didn't reply.

'C'mon Jack, let's get some fluids in you. Let's go,' David said as he tried to pull Jack away.

Carrick broke away from the stare first but played it down with more geeing up of the crowd, sending them into a frenzy.

As they walked away, David asked Jack, 'What were you thanking him for?'

In a calm voice and with no change in his expression Jack said, 'For his title. I've got him. I could see it in his eyes.' He then turned to Pete who was looking grim and said, 'I'm good. I'm calm and ready to go.'

'Your eyes changed up there. I was worried you were getting upset, going somewhere not nice in your head.' Pete tapped Jack's temple. 'If it works for you, I'm happy. Go where you need to. It scares me at times but it's what separates you from the others.'

David patted his dad's back. 'I like it. He needs it. If he's gonna fuck up this Carrick, he needs to get dark. This is his toughest fight. He'll be fine. He's got the best coach in the game.'

'Honestly, I feel great,' Jack said.

David put his arm back around Pete. 'Dad, you worry too much, it's all going

to work out. You'll see. And anyway, you've got me to look out for him.'

Jack looked at Pete and noticed the uncomfortable expression on his face as he nodded to his son.

Chapter 23

'When life hits you pretty hard, you can go into a dark corner.'
Sylvester Stallone

On the night of the fight, Kirsten stayed at home with Liz. Three months pregnant, she knew Jack didn't want her in amongst a hostile crowd. He was so scared something could go wrong and his worrying was starting to rub off on Kirsten. She knew Jack saw the danger in any situation. He never wanted to lose anyone he loved again, and, under his influence, Kirsten was now starting to see the world differently. She agreed to watch from home and was downstairs alone while Liz was up in her room. Kirsten popped up with a cup of tea for Liz and found her relaxing, reading a book.

'Are you sure you won't come down to watch the fight, Liz?'

'No. Not for me, love. I've got my distraction right here.' She raised her book and continued, 'Jack will ring me when he's done. Thanks for the tea.'

Kirsten understood and didn't ask twice.

York Hall, Bethnal Green, London. The undercard fights had all gone ahead as planned. Jack was up next. He'd had his hands wrapped in front of Carrick's head coach. His coach was happy and signed off to say so. Pete had done the same in Carrick's dressing room. Jack then warmed up as he normally would, some pad work and stretches. He looked down at Sam's name on the waistband and closed his eyes for a few seconds. He felt fully fit and ready to go. But something was missing. He didn't feel the usual fire in his belly. It had normally kicked in by now. He didn't panic and assumed it would come when he needed it most. From within the changing room, he could feel the atmosphere. The music was so loud. 'Sweet Caroline' by Neil Diamond was playing and the crowd was going crazy all singing along.

Jack was ready to go. Behind him were his dad, Pete, David and Shawn. They all made their way out of the dressing room into the corridor.

A member of security approached them.

'It's time, Jack. Time to head out to the ring.'

Jack looked at his team. 'Anyone fancy a British title?' As he said it, he could hear his walk out music start. The same song as normal, 'Ill Manors' by Plan B (The Prodigy Remix).

The team was fired up. 'I love this shit,' David said.

Jack headed slowly for the ring. Most of the crowd was against him but he ignored them. His mind was elsewhere. He could only think that at that moment he'd rather be anywhere else as long as it was with Kirsten.

Kirsten was at home anxiously watching her Jack, live on Sky Sports, walking out amongst the hostile crowd. It hurt to hear so many people booing him. She was thinking, if only they knew him the way I do they wouldn't do that. She was upsetting herself and with the baby in mind, she was worried about getting too upset. She turned the television off and went upstairs.

She knocked on the door and heard, 'Come in,' from Liz.

Poking her head round the door, she asked, 'I don't suppose you have a spare book?'

Liz smiled. 'It's horrible, isn't it? Come here and sit with me until it's over. I've got the perfect book for you.' She reached over to her bedside table and then handed Kirsten 'One Day' by David Nicholls.

Jack waited patiently for Carrick to enter the arena. His walkout music of choice was Liverpool Football Club's adopted anthem, 'You'll never Walk Alone' by Gerry and The Pacemakers. As soon as it started playing, Jack got tense. He looked across to Shawn and started punching his gloves together whilst pacing back and forth. He felt like a caged animal waiting for meat to be thrown into his cage. Memories of Sam's funeral came flooding back. He instantly felt like that thirteen-year-old scared little boy. The pain of that day felt so fresh. Only one person could make him feel better, and she was at home.

'Jack, I'm sorry, I had no idea Carrick was coming out to that song,' Shawn said.

Jack felt mentally gone inside. Tears started to fall. His chest felt tight and vision blurry.

'I don't want to fight. I don't feel right,' he said.

'You'll be with Kirsten later. Just get this out the way. You've done this plenty of times before. This is what you do. You're a fighter, Jack. Get the job done like you always do, and we'll go home.'

'I'm not feeling it. For the first time, I don't want it.' Jack said. 'Dad, I can't.'

'You're gonna be a dad soon. It changes you inside. Maybe it's that. You're no longer living just for you. You're living for them. When you were born, I felt the same. But it doesn't need to change you. Instead, you do things for them, for Kirsten and your baby. You have the chance to give your family everything. Fighting is your gift. Use it,' his dad said.

Jack thought about it. Kirsten being pregnant had clearly changed his thought processes. He couldn't be reckless anymore. For the first time in years, he wanted to be alive. He was scared to die. He couldn't tap into that angry state of mind that had served him so well in the boxing ring. He was scared. If he died his baby would grow up without him.

'Jack, you're a good enough fighter to win this title with skill alone. You don't always need anger. Use what Pete and David have taught you. You can do this.'

Jack didn't feel any better, but he tried to reassure himself and his dad that he'd be OK. 'Yeah, I'll be fine. It's just a fight. Let's get it over and done with. Let's finish it early.'

'That's my boy. Go and do what you do.'

Jack watched him father re-join the rest of the team.

The ring announcer gave the introductions. Both men headed to the middle of the ring and the ref gave his commands. Complete respect was shown and both fighters touched gloves.

'I don't like that. This is all too friendly,' David said to Jack as they walked back to the corner. 'I prefer it when you're fighting some horrible gobshite. It's what gets you fired up. This soppy bastard is gonna have you hugging him soon.'

Jack was getting his final tactical advice from Pete. 'Use the first round to feel him out. Throw your jabs. Give him a few hard shots but save your engine. He won't go down easy. This could be a long night.'

Jack bit down on his gumshield as the bell sounded. He stepped out to meet Carrick in the centre of the ring.

Both fighters were landing their jabs, but both were being careful. If they went for a power shot and over extended, they could get caught with a counter punch. Both fighters had one-punch knockout power.

The first round ended even. The fighters gave a sportsmanship fist pump to each other at the end of the round.

The second and third rounds were the same. Carrick may have edged the third. They tapped gloves at the end of the round again.

As Jack sat down on his stool for his one minute's rest, David spoke. 'Fuck all that nice shit. That's what he wants. At some point, he's going to open up on you and you won't expect it. He's playing mind games. He knows you can be a vicious bastard so he's trying to disarm you with kindness. Kindness doesn't win fights. Punching him in the face does. Do it to him first. Fuck him. You can be nice to him after the fight. Not now.'

Pete agreed. 'He's right this time. I don't want you going crazy, but you've shown him enough respect. A little too much. It's time to hurt him.'

'You tell me to control my emotions. That's what I'm doing. Now you're telling me to hurt him. Make your mind up.'

'You're doing great. But every fight is different. What we need now is the Jack who finishes it. Carrick is no joke. He's crafty. He'll beat you on points fighting his fight. He's the champ for a reason and he will get the nod if this goes to points. He knows it. To beat a champ on points you have to beat him convincingly. You watch what happens when you land a heavy shot. He won't be nice then, he'll come for you. Try it for me.'

'Fuck it. I will, if that's what you want.'

Pete put Jack's gumshield back in and he rushed back out.

Round four. Jack walked towards Carrick. Carrick reached a glove out to touch Jack's. 'Nah, lets fight,' Jack said. He didn't return the gesture of touching Carrick's glove. He had to try Pete's advice, so he threw a jab and loaded up on an overhand right. Carrick caught it on his guard, but it hurt. Jack watched as Carrick changed his posture. He was coming for blood.

'You soft prick,' Carrick said. He threw a screw-shot through Jack's guard, followed by a heavy right hand that hit Jack on the side of the head. He'd been hit harder than that before, but it was right on the temple. Jack's legs buckled. He touched down on the canvas with his glove. The ref jumped in between the fighters and gave Jack an eight-count, the first of his pro career.

'I'm OK,' Jack said to the ref. 'Let me fight.'

The ref let him continue.

Jack looked at his corner and saw the pained expression on their faces.

The fourth round finished. That was a 10-8 round in favour of Carrick because of the knockdown. Jack took his seat.

David slapped Jack across the face. 'Right. You listen to me. I don't give a flying fuck if you've got your missus pregnant. I couldn't give a bollocks. But what I do care about is winning this fight.'

Jack was furious. He knew his dad had told them.

'Don't look at your dad. Look at me. My dad and I have put our hearts and souls into training you. And you're gonna fuck it up over getting a bird up the duff.'

David talking about Kirsten in that way felt like having a knife twisted in his stomach. Jack jumped up from his stool and put his gloved hand under David's neck.

'You ever talk about Kirsten like that again, I'll kill you.' Jack was spitting as he shouted. His dad jumped up on to the ring and pushed Jack off as the ref approached.

'What's going on? Any more of that and I'm stopping the fight. Do you all understand?'

'It's OK. We're OK,' David assured the ref.

'I thought that went well,' Jack heard David say to his dad.

Jack turned and faced his team. He pointed at David. 'I'll see you after the fight.'

'Rather you than me,' Pete said to David.

Jack's face was red as he rolled his head trying to clear the built-up tension. He was now desperate for round five to start. Full of fury, he was back in that dark place he needed to be.

A double jab landed from Carrick. Jack landed a left hook followed by a single jab, then a right cross. Carrick was unsteady but still throwing shots. Jack was walking through anything that Carrick threw. Every time he was hit it was more fuel for his fire. He wanted to be hit. They traded blow for blow. Neither man would go backward, only forward giving and taking punishment.

For the next three rounds, they went to war. They were both tired but going toe to toe. Round nine. Jack looked across at Carrick. For the first time in the fight, he could see his opponent was breathing hard. He was also blinking a lot and didn't look comfortable. He felt something inside Carrick had broken.

At the start of the next round, Jack threw a straight jab and Carrick stumbled on to the ropes. He'd taken a hundred of these shots tonight and hadn't flinched but this one affected him. The fight had left him. His hands dropped dangerously low. His face was no longer protected. Jack landed a right hand, straight down the middle. Carrick's whole body shut down. He was out. He fell forward and was unconscious before he hit the ground. His head violently bounced off the canvas. There was no need for a ten count from the ref. He put Carrick into the recovery position and tried hard to remove his gumshield, trying desperately to make it easier for him to breathe.

Jack stepped back while the doctor ran in to help the ref. The crowd was silent. An eerie silence. They knew Carrick was hurt.

Jack was now calm and disturbed at the sight of Carrick lying there motionless. Any thought of becoming British Champion had long gone. He had just won the British middleweight title, The Lonsdale Belt, but all he wanted was for Carrick to move.

Just as the paramedics were about to give Carrick oxygen, his arm raised, letting everyone know he was conscious. The crowd applauded. Jack was relieved and walked over to Carrick's coach and wished them all well and told them he hoped Carrick wasn't seriously hurt, apologising for what had happened. Their coach replied, 'There's no need to apologise. We'll take care of him.'

Jack walked over and reached down and held Carrick's glove. Carrick managed a wink. The paramedics decided to take him to the hospital just in case he had any brain injuries.

The ref announced Jack Stone was the new British champion. He was given the prestigious Lonsdale belt. His team didn't jump up and down. They didn't celebrate. That would wait until Carrick was given the all-clear.

David apologised to Jack and explained why he said what he

did. He hadn't meant it. Pete and his Dad had agreed he needed to wind Jack up to get him in the right head space for the fight. Jack accepted it was the right thing to do but suggested David shouldn't do it again and to never talk about Kirsten like that again.

Back in the changing room he sat with the belt lying across his knees. He wondered what Sam would have said, how proud Sam would have been that his annoying little brother had won the British title.

'You've made us all proud. British champ. No-one can take that away from you. You've won the British title. Henry Cooper, Lennox Lewis, Ricky Hatton have all been where you are now. I love you, son. I'm so proud,' said his dad.

'Thanks, Dad.'

Pete came over and sat with Jack. 'You did it. I knew you would. I'm proud to have you fight out of my gym. If it's all right with you, we'll get a picture up on the wall of you holding the belt. But first, let's have a few days off then, next week, come into the gym and we'll see what's next. Go and spend some time with your girl. And congratulations on the baby.'

'Thank you, Pete.'

Jack rang his mum as usual. She put him on the loudspeaker so that Kirsten could hear. They were so happy for him. He explained that Carrick was injured, and no-one was celebrating until they knew he was all right. He told them both he loved them and said he'd be home late, possibly not until the morning.

'Why did you tell your mum and Kirsten you'd be so late? We'll be home in a couple of hours. It isn't that far from here. This time of night, just over an hour with no traffic,' his dad said.

'We're not going home,' said Jack. 'We're going to the hospital.'

Chapter 24

'I don't like this man. I must get to know him better.'
Abraham Lincoln

St George's Hospital, Blackshaw Road, Tooting. Jack and his team entered through accident and emergency, straight through the giant sliding doors. With no idea which ward Carrick would be on, they approached the receptionist. She peered over her thick-rimmed bright red glasses and told them all to take a seat adding, when she had the time, she would make a call and see if she could find out where Mr Carrick was.

Jack looked up as the doors opened and Martin and Lee walked in. They'd been at all of Jack's fights and at the end of title fight he'd suggested they come to the hospital to help give lifts to any of the team who wanted to go home.

Jack greeted his friends and then turned his attention back to the receptionist. She didn't look rushed off her feet and he felt she was letting them know who was in charge by delaying making any calls. He, along with his team and friends, was getting impatient but watching David get all worked up was keeping Jack entertained. A huge vein on David's neck bulged as his temper grew. Jack tried to calm him, reasoning that she had probably been dealing with drunks all night.

Jack was looking around the waiting room, people watching mostly. Anything to take his mind off David being impatient. He could hear a lady behind him calling for her son. The annoyance in her voice became more apparent, 'Josh, come and sit down.'

Jack watched her son run past him, then go over to the vending machine and push the glass, 'Josh, get back here, now' she shouted. He then jumped up on to the metal chairs and started jumping between the empty seats.

Jack felt his knee being tapped, it was Lee, 'He's a little shit, isn't he? Next time he runs past, I'm sticking my leg out,' Lee said.

'You were no different at his age, you were the biggest shit of the lot,' Shawn said. Jack started laughing.

Lee pointed at the kid, 'I was nothing like that, bloody cheek.'

'Wasn't he Jack? Always doing something to annoy others.'

Jack grinned, 'I'm not getting involved.'

'Yeah, you were. Proper pain in the arse. And you were a bit of a thief,' Martin said.

Lee stood up, 'Oh great, you as well. Bloody thief, load of bollocks.'

Jack gave Lee a slight nod, 'I have to back the boys up here. What about Faisal's shop?'

Lee smiled, 'Come on, he deserved it. He used to buy cans of coke in large packs, and on the can it said not to be sold separately. And then he'd put a massive mark up on them and do exactly that. He was the thief. So, sod him, I did take the odd bit here and there, level the playing field, that's all.'

'And that time he caught you in the chest freezer,' Shawn said, and then he started laughing so hard, he couldn't carry on with the story.

Jack took over, 'You were actually in the chest freezer,' Jack joined in laughing with Shawn.

Lee wasn't smiling, 'I was in the sodding freezer coz you tipped me in there. I was trying to get a Calippo. Old Penfold always put 'em in the bottom, so I was reaching in, and the next thing, Shawn threw me in.'

They were laughing, Jack stopped briefly. 'It was Sam. Sam threw you in there.'

Lee was now smiling, 'After all these years I thought it was Shawn.'

Shawn was still laughing hard, 'Stop, my stomach hurts.'

'But he did look like Penfold didn't he? He was five feet tall at most, bald head and wore those little round glasses,' Lee said.

'And what was it you shouted at him when he was trying to get you out of the freezer?' Martin asked.

Jack pointed at Martin, 'I remember exactly what Lee said to him, he said, get off me you bender, go back to Danger Mouse.'

Shawn got up and walked away, 'I can't, I'm going to wet myself, stop it.'

Even Pete and David were smiling at the story.

The laughing died down as they looked at each other, 'I miss those days,' Lee said.

'Best days of our lives,' Martin said.

Twenty minutes later the receptionist called out, 'Mr Stone.'

Jack and his dad both looked up.

'Just him, the other fighter. He can go up and see Mr

167

Carrick.' She was pointing at Jack who got up and followed the directions she gave him.

As he approached the ward, he could see a lady he recognised. He'd seen her at the weigh-in. It was Carrick's wife. Jack was nervous that she would be angry with him, but he couldn't back out. She'd seen him. As he approached, she didn't move and showed no emotion.

Once he was near to her, she stood up.

Jack nervously spoke first. 'Hello, Mrs Carrick. Is he OK?'

She put her arms around him and kissed Jack's cheek. 'Thank you for coming. The doctors are with him. He's had a scan. Would you sit with me, please? I hate hospitals.'

'I would like that,' he said, pleasantly surprised. She showed kindness and warmth even though he was the one who had put her husband in this state.

Together they sat patiently waiting.

She held Jack's hand and only said one more sentence until the doctor came, an hour later.

'I don't blame you, Jack. I married a fighter. That could have been you in there and your girlfriend could be in my seat.'

Jack didn't reply. He felt there was nothing he could say.

After an hour of silence, Jack's phone beeped twice. He reached into his pocket and read the text from his dad. David is going to end up being arrested. We will head home. Martin and Lee will wait for you downstairs. Jack tried not to smile and was relieved they were taking David home.

When the doctor eventually came over, he asked to see Mrs Carrick alone. She was visibly shaking.

'I'll be right here, don't worry. I'm not going anywhere,' Jack said.

The doctor took her to see her husband and another hour passed before she returned.

'He's going to be fine. No brain damage. He's just a bit roughed up.'

'I'm so pleased. Please tell your husband I'm glad he's all right. If there's anything I can do, just call me.' He got up and was preparing to leave.

'You can tell him yourself. He wants to see you.'

Jack was surprised. And nervous. He walked into Carrick's room and was taken aback by his opponent's appearance. His forehead was swollen which made both eyes look as though they were closed.

'Is that you, Jack? Hope I didn't hurt you too bad,' Carrick joked.

Jack moved closer. 'Oh, you hurt me. That shot in the first, on the side of my head, my legs were like jelly. I don't remember much after that.'

In a thick Scouse accent, Carrick replied, 'Shame you didn't stay down. Bastard.'

Jack smiled and pulled a chair closer to Carrick's bedside.

'Heard ya gonna be OK. That's good. You had us scared.'

'Of course, I'm going to be OK. Bit of concussion and a burst eardrum. Bit of time off, maybe. I'll be back.'

Jack thought about how he might be thinking differently if he were lying there.

'I think we both left a piece of us in that ring tonight,' Jack said.

Carrick stopped joking. 'I think you're right. The crowd loves it. We love it. But too many fights like that and it will be short careers for both of us.' After an awkward silence, he continued. 'But you. You keep going, lad. You've got it in you.

Go and get that world title. Two, three years, I reckon you'll do it.'

Jack shrugged, made uneasy by the compliment. 'Who knows. I'll try to. That's the one we all want. What about you? You can still do it too.'

Carrick looked at him. 'I know. And I will. I'll get there one day. I'm not stopping until I do. It's a shame the two best middleweights in the world are both British.'

Jack nodded in agreement.

'But you'll get there first, Jack. And when you do, promise me something?'

Jack moved in even closer. 'Anything. Just ask.'

Carrick removed the oxygen tubes from his nose and leaned into Jack, and grinned. 'I want the re-match.'

'You're in a hospital bed and you want to arrange our re-match. You're a lunatic.' Jack was laughing but composed himself when he could see that Carrick was deadly serious.

'OK, I'll make a deal with ya. You get yourself well, then agree it all with your lovely wife... and if I get a world title, I'll give you the re-match. We'll do it in Liverpool. Are you a red or a blue?'

'Red of course.' Carrick said.

'Anfield it is then, 'Jack said.

'Yes, get in there, lad. I knew you were a good man. Now you go home to your family. Send the Missus back in, would you?'

Jack shook Carrick's hand gently. 'I'm glad you're OK.' He felt emotional as he held Carrick's hand tight. 'You take care.'

Two working-class men, from different parts of the country. Both sharing one dream.

Chapter 25

'We can't solve problems by using the same kind of thinking we used when we created them.'

Driving himself back through the giant oaks, Jack felt different to the last time he'd been there. Gravel flicking on to his own car this time, not his dad's.

He was anxious but excited. He'd missed her. She'd helped him when he was at his lowest.

'Please come in, Jack,' Roisin said.

'Thank you.'

They both sat down, same chairs as before. The office hadn't changed. Jack, however, had. He had been in his late teens the last time he'd sat there.

'How are you?' Jack asked.

'I'm very well, thank you. But I'm concerned to hear how you are. I was a little surprised you booked an appointment. I'm happy to see you. But part of me hoped I wouldn't need to see you again.'

Jack moved uncomfortably in his seat, looking down at his feet.

'I don't mean I don't want to see you. I just hoped your life was going well. And that you wouldn't need me.'

'My life is going well. I have a beautiful girlfriend. She's pregnant. And I'm the British champion. It couldn't be any better.'

'Congratulations, Jack. And well done on winning. I watched the fight.' She raised her eyebrows and smiled.

Jack grinned and sat up straight. He couldn't hide how proud he felt that Roisin had watched him. He'd hoped she had.

'I haven't forgotten my promise. If you fight for a world title, I'll be there.'

Jack was now glad he'd come for the appointment.

'Did you think I'd forget?' Roisin said.

'No. I just wasn't sure you'd want to.'

Roisin smiled and changed the subject. 'It's been over five years since I last saw you. Can I ask what's made you come back?'

Jack started tapping his fingers on the desk, biting his bottom lip.

'I had a wobble, just before my fight. I was scared. I'm never scared. I can't have that happen again. Not in the ring. I can't be a fighter if I feel that way.'

Roisin twiddled her gold pen between thumb and forefinger.

'Was there a trigger? Did someone say something or do something you didn't like?'

'It was partly the song. His walkout song reminded me of Sam. That didn't help. But it was before that. Normally I walk out to my fight fully pumped and I'm ready to take on anyone. No fear. No negative thoughts.'

'What do you think it is, Jack? Have you spoken to anyone else about this, to your parents or your girlfriend?'

'Kirsten thinks the same as my dad. They think it's because

I'm about to become a father... that I've changed. That I'm scared something will happen.'

'They could be right. What do you think?'

'I think I'm simply scared. I didn't want to get hurt.'

'There's nothing wrong with being scared. Especially in your chosen career. I'd be scared.'

Pointing at his chest, he said, 'I can't be scared. I need that rage inside.'

Roisin put her pen down.

'What if you don't? It could be you don't need to fight anymore.'

Jack nodded his head, 'No... I still want to. It's what I'm good at. It's all I'm good at.'

'Well, if you do decide you still want to be a fighter, you'll need to find what works for you. Find your reason to fight. You don't need rage and anger for that.'

'I'm not so sure.'

'Jack, you're allowed to be happy. Allow yourself to be happy. Don't fight it.'

'I feel guilty. I know that sounds silly. When I feel happy, I feel something bad will follow.'

'I don't think that's how life works. Life just happens. Everyone will have their share of bad and good times. Hopefully, we get more of the good. You've met Kirsten, your career is going great, and you'll soon be a father. This is your good time. You deserve it. Accept it and enjoy it. Then I think you'll know what you are fighting for.'

Jack nodded but didn't reply.

'And if you decide fighting isn't for you, it wouldn't mean you failed. You find another career. You could do anything you want to, be anything you want. Kirsten and the baby would love you for who you are, not what you are.'

'I suppose so.'

'Don't decide right now. When you're feeling anxious, try talking it through with Kirsten. Enjoy this time in your life. And when you're ready, decide what you want.'

Jack exhaled. He felt the anxiety had left him. He smiled at Roisin.

'And if you need to see me again, you can. Take it a day at a time. Don't be hard on yourself. A lot of our thoughts are temporary. Some days you may feel scared and, if you do, who cares? Allow yourself to be scared. It's perfectly normal. Even for a fighter.'

As Jack walked back to his car, he felt relaxed. All he wanted was to be home with Kirsten and talk to her about their future together.

Chapter 26

'I train the same way as I've always trained, even before I was champion. That's the difference, I train like a challenger.'
Joe Calzaghe

Jack had his next fight planned. He had to defend his belt within a set time period, or it could be taken away from him. He didn't feel a fighter could call himself the British champion without defending the belt. He wanted to get this one out of the way before the baby was born. That gave them just over five months, Jack wanted the fight within four, in case the baby came early. Afterwards he could take time off and be with Kirsten and the baby.

His opponent was Greg Fry. A good fighter but not on the level of Jack's last opponent, Carrick. Chris, Shawn, and Pete suggested Jack have a well-deserved, so-called, easier fight. The beating he took from Carrick was damaging and, ideally, a long lay-off would have been preferred.

Greg Fry was from Wales and would bring a huge following. It would be good for ticket sales and TV ratings. He was a quick fighter but didn't have the power to seriously trouble Jack.

Training camp went well with no injuries. Weight was not a

problem. When Jack wasn't training, Kirsten and Jack were preparing their new home. They stayed in their hometown of Dorking, putting a large deposit down on a three-bed house with a nice garden. They both wanted to be near their families, feeling it was important that both sets of grandparents got to see their grandchild.

Fight night came round quickly. Walking out to the ring, Jack was ready to go. He had his reason to fight. His baby was being born soon and the idea of having time off with Kirsten and the baby was all he wanted. Jack had spoken with her earlier that day, she had the unfortunate pleasure of letting Jack know that they'd received another legal letter from Roy Hardy. Roy was trying to sue them for all of Jack's future earnings within the boxing ring. Jack's response was as usual, 'Burn it. He can't do a thing to us.'

'You OK?' Pete asked.

'I'm good. I fancy an early night,' Jack said.

'Well, you know what to do then.' Pete put his hand on Jack's back. 'You've got this, son. Get in close, break his body and his head will follow.'

David was behind Pete and Jack listening to Pete's advice. Jack looked back at him and noticed him moving his head side to side. Jack thought about including him in the talk, but Pete carried on talking.

Jack looked down to ringside, and there he was sitting in the front row, Roy Hardy. He had his red bow tie on and was waving a small Welsh flag. Jack smiled and nodded in his direction, but nothing came back, nothing but a dirty look and followed by exaggerated cheering from the overweight ex-manager.

The fight was about to start. The last instructions were given. The bell rang.

David shouted out from the corner, 'Let's have an early night, Jack. Put him away. There's no overtime being paid here. If you can knock him out, fucking knock him out.'

Jack nodded and headed out to the middle of the ring.

Fry looked the part. A huge red dragon on his shorts and he was covered head to toe in tattoos. He threw lightning quick double jabs. They were firing out, back and forth like pistons. The jabs were only hitting Jack's defence though. Jack felt confident he could unload when he wanted to. He wanted Fry to throw a power punch before he committed himself.

More double jabs and then a right hand. Jack wasn't worried. That wasn't going to put him to sleep anytime soon. After the next double jab, Jack moved in close and threw a left to the body and then backed off. He waited for Fry to throw his double jab and then moved in close again. Same shot to the body. Fry was wincing in agony. Jack followed up with a right hook to the side of Fry's head. It landed perfectly. The fans ringside heard the sickening thud. Fry went down. He was brave. He wanted to stand up. The army of Welsh fans was begging him to fight on, but his legs wouldn't let him. He was stumbling on his feet and the ref called it off.

Jack went straight to Fry and held him up until he was safe to stand unaided.

Jack and his team celebrated together, all staying in the same hotel in Cardiff. They didn't want to go out to any busy nightclubs and pubs in the city centre. They knew Cardiff was well known for a good night out, but Jack and his team didn't fancy upsetting Fry's fans. Pete had warned Jack that no Englishman wants an army of Welsh fans after him, not late on a Saturday night in Cardiff.

They sat at the hotel bar. They could have driven home that night, but Jack wanted a night out with the lads. Just a few beers and some good old-fashioned banter with his team. He knew this would be his last night out for a long time. Kirsten and the baby were his priority going forward.

'Is that the British champ sitting over there?' The shouting came from behind Jack and his team.

Jack knew that voice. He turned around, hoping he was right. A huge grin lit up his face.

'Lee! About time you turned up,' Jack said as he embraced his friend.

Martin was with him. They'd been ringside thanks to Jack, but they'd had a hard job getting out of the arena.

'Right, boys, let's get on it. Jägerbombs all round,' David shouted.

'Oh God, here we go.' Jack knew this was going to be a late night.

Jack, Lee, Shawn and Martin reminisced about their child-hood days. They talked boxing and discussed Jack becoming a dad. They also cracked jokes at Martin's expense.

'So, PC Parker, you arrested anyone yet?' Lee asked, giving Martin a gentle nudge.

'Of course I have. Mainly pissed up arseholes like you,' he replied.

'Well said, Martin. You can do us all a favour and arrest him now,' said Shawn.

Lee grinned. 'I'm a well-behaved boy these days. Not been in any trouble for years. Jack calming down was the best thing to happen to all of us.'

'Don't put it all on me. You were a dickhead just as much as I was. We just needed to grow up a bit,' said Jack as he jabbed Lee gently in the stomach.

Jack noticed his dad was looking a bit solemn. 'Anything wrong, Dad?'

'Yeah, c'mon Ken, get another Jäger inside you,' David said.

Jack's dad raised his drink. 'I'm perfectly fine. It makes me happy seeing you boys together. You've all come a long way. You've been through a lot and it could have gone very wrong for every one of you. But you've come through it and you're all finding your place in life. You should all be proud.' Welling up, he gave a smile.

Jack gave his dad a smile. 'I can tell you've had a drink, getting a bit emotional on us.'

'Shut it, you,' his dad said and gave Jack a wink.

The friends went silent. They all knew what Ken was saying. They were all thinking about that day. Thinking of Sam and what they'd been through. Jack's dad was right. They had come a long way.

'Let's raise our glasses and make a toast,' Martin said.

They all picked up another Jäger bomb from the bar.

'To Sam. And to the future,' Martin said as he waved his drink in the air.

They all raised their drinks, then downed them in one.

Jack went over and hugged his dad. 'Thank you, Dad, love you.'

'This is all getting a bit gay round here. More drinks please, barman,' David shouted.

Jack moved towards David. 'Come on, mate. Don't say that. It's not on.'

179

'What? Gay? I can't say gay. I don't mean actual gay; I mean it in the other way.'

Jack was uncomfortable but smiled hoping it would calm David down. 'C'mon, just don't say it. It's not cool.'

David touched Jack's chest. 'Well stop acting gay and then I won't say it anymore.' He smirked and pointed at them all. 'You lot need to lighten up.'

Jack looked at Pete for guidance. Lowering himself off his bar stool, Pete raised his arm. 'That's me off to bed. I'm too old for this. I'll leave it to you youngsters.'

David squinted his eyes. His legs wobbled as he poked his dad in the chest. 'Not good enough for you, eh? Maybe if Jack made a joke, you'd laugh, or if Jack asked you to stay with us, you'd do it.'

Pete frowned. 'What are you on about, boy? Don't be silly. I'm off to bed. And maybe you should go as well.'

'Bollocks to that. I'm going nowhere. I'm staying out with golden boy over here.' David grabbed Jack round his collar and pulled him closer.

Jack wasn't laughing. No one was. He gripped David's hand, squeezed it and removed it saying, 'Maybe we should all go to bed. We need to drive home early tomorrow. Come on, David.'

'Fuck you. He calls you son, fucking son. He did it earlier in the ring. I've sacrificed a lot for you. Do you know that? Including my dad. He worries more about you than he does me. You're not going to tell me what to do. In front of my dad, you think you can boss me about. Fuck. That.'

Pete raised his voice. 'Enough, boy. That's enough. You're embarrassing yourself. Go to bed.' He walked away.

'David, I like you. But you're a shitty drunk. Get some water inside ya and go to bed. We can all forget about this by the morning,' said Jack.

'Fuck off Jack. You're a jumped-up little prick. Look what you did with my mate Roy. Used him. Used him to make money and then fucked him off.'

Jack bit his lip, then spoke, 'You need to shut up, now. I did right by Roy and was nothing but honest with him from the beginning.'

'But he was bit odd, wasn't he? A bow tie. Looked more like a paedo magician.' Lee said before laughing.

David threw a punch, catching Jack on the ear. Jack didn't move. He was angry but composed. Lee got hold of David before he could throw another then turned to Jack. 'I'll take him to bed. Don't hit him. He isn't worth it.'

Jack caught Shawn and Martin looking at each other, both with raised eyebrows.

'Never thought I'd see Lee stopping a fight,' Shawn said.

'Get off me, you prick.' David elbowed Lee in the face. Lee fell to the floor. Blood spilling onto the carpet. David then squared up to Jack. They were nose to nose.

'OK. Do him, Jack. Fucking end him,' Lee said as he held his nose to stop the blood pouring out any further.

As they stepped forward to help, Martin and Shawn couldn't help but smile. 'And he's back,' Martin said.

Jack pushed forward into David's face and put his hands round his neck. 'Hitting me wasn't a problem. For the sake of your dad, that punch was free. But now you've hit my friend. I can't let that go.'

The barman pointed his phone at them.

'Jack, no. Don't do it.' Shawn jumped in between them and led Jack away.

'Martin, get that idiot out of here,' Shawn said pointing at

David.

As Shawn led Jack toward the hotel staircase, Lee followed, squeezing his nose to stop the blood gushing out and complaining, 'He elbowed me in the nose. That bloody hurt. What an arsehole.'

The staircase was their only choice. They couldn't wait for the lift as the barman was still filming them, waiting for his social media gold. This was going to be all over Facebook, Twitter and Instagram by the morning.

They got to their floor and headed down the corridor. As they walked past the lifts a ping sounded and the doors opened. It was Martin, Ken, and Jack's manager, Chris. Just behind them, feeling sorry for himself and unsteady on his feet, was David.

'Fuck that,' Jack said and jumping through the group he punched David on the nose. David fell back into the lift and lay their unconscious.

The lift doors tried to close but were repeatedly hitting David's body.

'Please clear the doors. Please clear the doors,' droned the automatic voice.

Lee was laughing. 'Love it, Jack, you legend.' He leaned over David. 'Not nice being hit in the nose is it, arsehole?'

Shawn stepped in. 'Lee, get to bed. We need to make sure he's all right. Jack, you go with him before anyone turns up.'

'Nah. Bollocks. Throw his legs in and leave the prick in there. Let him go up and down all night.' Lee said, laughing even harder than before.

Shawn caught hold of David's left leg. 'Chris, get his other one.'

They started dragging him out. The lift opposite pinged.

The door opened. It was a young couple heading back to their room. The lads all turned around. No one knew how to explain this one.

Chris did a bad impersonation of a drunk having a swig out of a glass and said, 'Few too many for this one. We're getting him to bed.'

The couple looked concerned, even more so when the lift doors closed again, this time on David's head.

'Please clear the doors. Please clear the doors.'

'Shit. Pull him out,' Shawn said as they dragged him clear.

'Fucking brilliant.' Lee was holding his stomach laughing. 'Jack, I'm gonna piss myself. I've missed coming out with you.'

David's eyes opened but he didn't get up. The lift doors hitting him brought him round. The couple looked worried but obviously wanted no part of it. They walked on to their room, occasionally glancing back.

They helped David get to his feet. Once they got to his room, Shawn propped him against the wall while he opened the door. 'You'll be OK. You've just had a few too many, that's all. Let's get you to bed.'

'I'll stay with him, just in case,' said Shawn.

'You're a good mate, Shawn,' Jack said.

'All part of the job. I think.'

'But this isn't your job, Shawn,' said Ken. 'This is you being Jack's friend. He needs you. He'll always need you.'

Chapter 27

'There is no such thing as a perfect parent. So just be a real one.'
Sue Atkins

The pizza was ordered and was already late. The perk of not being in a training camp was Jack could eat what he liked. He hadn't had a takeaway pizza for months.

'Jack, can you get the car keys ready?' Kirsten shouted.

Jack was in the kitchen, preparing drinks. 'No problem. You want me to go down and pick the pizza up? Probably a good idea, I'm bloody starving.'

'Not exactly, Jack. We need to go to the hospital. Now.'

Jack stopped in his tracks. 'Shit. I'll get the bag.' He ran into the front room and grabbed their baby bag; the one Kirsten had prepared two months before.

'What else do we need? The pizza, it's going to arrive, and we won't be here.'

'Sod the bloody pizza. I'm having a baby. They're late anyway. Bastards. I was starving too.' Jack raised an eyebrow at Kirsten as she rarely swore. She managed a weak smile until another contraction kicked in.

Jack comforted her, squeezing her hand. Once the contraction finished, she was ready to walk to the car. The nearest hospital was twenty minutes away. The first set of traffic lights they encountered were at red.

'Don't think so, mate,' Jack said as he drove straight through. He was feeling very proud of himself.

Kirsten tutted. One hand was on her bump and the other was holding the handle above the door. 'Men! You never grow up, do you? You didn't need to run a red light.'

'I know. But it was fun. We have the perfect excuse. No-one is going to nick me in this situation.'

Jack dropped Kirsten off at the entrance doors of the hospital and went to park the car. He left it unlocked and didn't check if he needed a parking ticket. Running flat out, he got back to Kirsten just as she started another contraction.

'I'll grab a wheelchair. Wait there.'

'I'm not going in a bloody wheelchair. I'm not disabled. I'm pregnant.'

Jack tried not to laugh.

The contraction finished, and they made it to the maternity ward. They were given their room. As they walked in, Jack noticed there was just a bed. No chair. Where would he sit? He was tired and disappointed but couldn't moan.

'Are you OK? Can I get you anything?' Jack asked.

'Cup of tea would be good.'

'Good shout. I wonder if they'll do me a coffee,' Jack said.

'You are unbelievable. They are not waitresses, they're midwives. You go and get it.'

'Right, Yes, of course. I'll go. Don't you go having the baby without me.' He kissed Kirsten on the forehead and went off to find a cup of tea. And a coffee if they had one. A second later he poked his head back into the room and said, 'I love you.'

Kirsten smiled. 'I love you too.'

On his return, he comforted her through the many contractions. She tried every position, hoping it would help with the pain. She perched on the edge of the bed in agony. The gas and air weren't helping. She was desperate to have this baby without an epidural but had reached the point where she no longer cared.

Looking at the midwife, Kirsten said, 'Just do it, stick it in.'

The anaesthesiologist arrived and asked Kirsten to stay where she was. Jack stood up so that Kirsten could lean on him. With her head on his shoulder, she waited for the large needle to be inserted. Jack looked down. He could see it heading towards her lower back.

'Bloody hell, it's like a spear.' He went white.

'Shut up, Jack. Or I'll ask them to stick it in you,' Kirsten said.

'Mr Stone, you could wait outside for a moment,' suggested the midwife.

Feeling lightheaded, Jack stepped back and, looking at the midwife, asked, 'Have you got her?'

'Are you going?'

He fell backwards, whacking his head on the door. He'd fainted for a second, but the whack on the head helped him wake up.

Looking up from the ground, he asked, 'Is she OK?'

Looking down at Jack, Kirsten asked, 'Is he OK?'

Jack had been outside in the corridor for an hour. Several midwives had walked past. Their comments about it happening to dads all the time didn't help Jack's pride. He knew he wouldn't be able to live this one down.

He was told to go back in. The baby was coming.

Holding Kirsten's hand, he used a cold flannel to wipe her brow. He'd never felt so proud of anyone in his life. Despite the epidural, he could see the pain she was still in, but she didn't complain once. She was a fighter.

Holding his son was the most magical feeling he'd ever experienced. Baby George gripped Jack's finger.

Kirsten was exhausted but desperate to call her parents. She put her phone on loudspeaker so that Jack could tell her parents, and maybe they'd hear George cry.

'His name? It's George Samuel Stone and he's perfect. He's just over eight pounds.'

'That's amazing. I can't wait to meet him. We can't wait. Your dad is so proud. And how are you, Kirsten?'

'I'm well too, Mum. Everything went perfectly. Jack's got a bump on his head but he's doing well.' She laughed as Jack kicked the bed.

'Oi, don't tell anyone.'

Jack's phone started to ring. He stood up and once Kirsten was ready to take George, he nervously passed him over. It said Dad on his phone screen.

'I better get this. They're gonna love his name.'

'Hi, Dad. I was going to ring you in a minute. You're a grandad. And mum's a granny. Kirsten is well. Baby is beautiful.'

'Oh, that's great, Jack.' Then there was silence.

'Dad, did you hear me? My son's been born. Your grandson, George Samuel Stone. I thought you'd be pleased.'

'Sorry, Jack. That's wonderful. I just wasn't expecting you to say that. I was calling for a different reason. Honestly, I'm over the moon. I can't wait to meet him. I'll get your mum.

She's going to be so happy.'

'What reason, Dad?' asked Jack.

'What?'

'You said you were ringing for a different reason. What is it?'

'It's Shawn. He's had an accident. We've been trying to contact you.'

'My phone's been off. I haven't long turned it back on. Is he all right?'

'I don't know, Jack.'

Chapter 28

'A real friend is one who walks in when the rest of the world walks out.'
Walter Winchell

After a few frantic phone calls, Jack found out that Shawn was in the same hospital. He was torn between seeing his best friend and staying with Kirsten and their new-born son.

'You have to go and see him, Jack. George is safe with me,' said Kirsten. 'We've got the rest of our lives to be together. Go and see Shawn.'

Jack kissed Kirsten and George and left the maternity ward.

Lee and Martin were already outside the ward entrance. No-one could go in apart from Shawn's parents. The three friends embraced.

'What happened? There must have been something wrong with his car. How else would he crash at that time of night? There are no bloody cars on the road at two in the morning,' Jack said.

'We don't know. We've spoken to his father. He doesn't believe what he's being told. The police said Shawn had been drinking. They're not sure how much alcohol he'd had.

There's a chance he did it on purpose,' said Lee.

'No, he wouldn't. No chance. He never said he was upset about anything. I didn't think he was depressed. He didn't act that way. He's always been the one smiling. Always nice to everyone. He wouldn't do that.' Jack looked for reassurance from his friends.

Martin swallowed hard, looked up, and then glanced at Lee.

Jack opened his arms out wide, desolation turning to irritation. 'If you know something, Martin, just tell me.'

'Jack, he didn't want to upset you. He hardly spoke about it to me, or anyone. He was struggling. We talked about it and he promised me it was under control. He was on antidepressants, strong ones,' Martin said.

With his hands on his head in despair, Jack was desperate for answers. 'I just don't get it. Why would he hold this back from me? Lee, did you know?'

Lee didn't need to reply. His lack of eye contact said it all. 'Jack, what could we do? He didn't want it put on you so he told us to keep quiet about it. And we didn't worry too much. Yes, he was a bit down. But he never said he would do this.'

Feeling dejected, Jack leaned against the wall. 'What did I do so wrong that he couldn't talk to me? He could have talked to me. We could have helped each other.'

'He felt you had enough going on, what with the fights coming up and then Kirsten being pregnant. Shawn felt he had it under control. He was talking to people. He told his doctor and all that, got the meds,' said Martin. 'When he last spoke to me about Sam, he said he couldn't get past the guilt. It was eating away at him, but he said he could handle it. I guess it just got too much and he snapped. I think we've all been close to snapping.'

They sat in silence in the corridor, Jack wishing he had done more to help Shawn and the other two. Wrapped up in his own memories and guilt he'd forgotten to check on his friends. He wished he'd asked them more often how they were coping.

Ken arrived, out of breath and anxious for answers. 'Jack, what's happening? How is he?'

'No idea, Dad. His parents are in with him. We've not been told anything.'

'Well, that means he's still with us. That's the main thing.' Putting his hand on Jack's shoulder, he asked, 'How are George and Kirsten?'

Lee and Martin both looked at Jack.

'George? Who's George?' asked Lee.

'That's my son. He's downstairs. So is Kirsten.'

'Why the fuck didn't you say? That's great news. Shit, Jack. Go back to them. We can call you if anything changes,' Martin said.

'I'll go in a minute.'

'George. I like it. George Stone. That's a strong name.' said Lee.

Jack looked at his friends and said, 'George Samuel Stone.'

'Even better. It had to be. That's perfect. Pleased for you, mate,' said Lee.

'Thanks. I'll pop back down with dad. Ring me if there's any news.'

'OK. Can't wait to meet George, and give our love to Kirsten,' Martin said.

'When the time is right, come down and meet him. You two are gonna be a big part of his life. You two and Shawn. So best you start getting to know him.'

At this wretched time, their smiles shone brightly. Martin clasped Jack's hand. 'Thanks, Jack, we won't let you down.'

Liz was holding her grandson when Jack and his dad returned.

'Well, Mum. What do you think?'

She kissed George's head. 'Just perfect. He's beautiful. He has his mother's eyes.'

Jack was proud. 'He does. He looks happy there with you, Mum.'

Liz beamed. 'I don't want to let him go. I'm keeping him.'

Kirsten smiled. 'He's a lucky boy. He's going to be so loved.' They were all silent, looking at George.

'How's Shawn? What's happening?' Kirsten wanted to know.

'We don't know anything. They won't let us in and won't tell us anything.'

'Jack, you don't need to protect me from the truth. Is he all right?'

Jack had to tell her. They didn't have secrets. 'He's not good. The police think he might have crashed on purpose.'

'Shawn? Why? He wouldn't do that.' Kirsten looked puzzled.

'Until he wakes up, we just don't know. Let's wait and see.' Saying it out loud, that Shawn had crashed on purpose, upset Jack.

'If you want to go back to him, just go. My parents will be here soon. I'll be fine and George won't want for cuddles. You should be there for Shawn.'

Martin and Lee were anxiously waiting for any sign of news from the ward. They would try and catch the eye of any doctor or nurse who walked past. They normally received a small smile back, but nothing else.

A nurse exited Shawn's room in a hurry. Martin went over for a closer look. He turned to Lee.

'Call Jack. I think something is happening.' Martin could see frantic movement from several of the nursing staff.

'I will in a minute. Let's see what happens first. Jack can wait.'

'What do you mean? He said to ring him if anything changes.'

Lee stood up, clearly agitated. 'Jack's not our boss. It's always the same, isn't it? Something bad happens to someone else but we have to all worry about Jack. Poor old Jack.'

Martin was confused. 'What are you on about, Lee? It's Jack. He's one of us. I'd do the same for you, or Shawn. You need to calm down, and bloody ring him.'

Pacing up and down the ward, Lee was holding back what he wanted to say. Instead, he composed himself and sat back down.

'You're right. This is about Shawn. Just ignore me.'

The door opened. Shawn's parents were hand in hand. They were both distraught. Martin and Lee looked at each other, fearing the worst.

'Thanks for calling, Martin. Can we go in and see him?' Jack said as he arrived back outside Shawn's room.

Martin and Lee didn't reply. They couldn't find the words.

'Well, what's going on? Just tell me.'

Martin broke down in front of Jack, dropping down on to the hard metal seat.

'He's lost too much blood. They don't know if he's going to make it. They're doing all they can. He's in an induced coma and receiving a blood transfusion. They've closed all his wounds, but he's banged up really bad. His car hit the wall on the driver's side. It caved in the engine.'

'Lee, what are you saying, mate. He's going to survive… right? He has to.'

'I'm saying they're not sure. He's in a real mess, mate.'

Jack sat with his friends in silence. He was picturing Shawn's life when he got through this, thinking about what he could do to help.

'I can help him get some treatment. Whatever he needs. I'll make it work.'

Martin nodded and patted Jack's leg. 'Yeah, we'll do all we can for him. He'll need help mentally as well.'

'I know where he can go for that, don't worry.' Jack stood and put his hands on to Martin and Lee's shoulders. 'It's gonna be OK. We are not losing him. We aren't going through that again.'

Although he'd said that out loud to his friends what he really meant was he couldn't go through it again.

Chapter 29

'Training to become champion is the toughest thing. The fight itself is just a test.'
Georges St-Pierre

Jack was now the European champion. His fight for the title was a second-round technical knockout. The fight for the British title against Carrick had been hard so to have a few easier ones was welcomed.

Jack had defended the British title several times before relinquishing the belt. He was now on his pursuit of the world title and to do that he had to start fighting world level fighters, not just British level. He'd been offered big money to fight Carrick several times but turned it down. He'd promised Carrick a re-match if he was world champ and he intended to stick to his word. The two fighters had kept in touch over the last few years, Carrick's career was going well. He'd won every fight since his return. They would phone each other after each win, sending congratulations and breaking down their fights. They'd even met up briefly one night for a drink, after they were both fighting on the same card. They had both got the win and celebrated together.

Jack was up early. He didn't have training. It was a rest day. He had to be at Chris's office for a meeting at 10 am, but before that he had a quick stop on the way to pick up his friend.

He pulled up, leaned over and opened the passenger door. 'Hurry up will ya.'

'Piss off,' Shawn replied with a smile.

Shawn got in Jack's Mercedes G Wagon.

'Can't you find something a little lower to the ground?' Shawn said as he winked at Jack.

Jack laughed and pulled away. They started discussing the day's business meeting. Chris hadn't mentioned why he wanted to see them, so they were guessing at what could be expected. It could be news about his next fight, a sponsorship deal or a TV appearance.

Shawn was dressed sharp as usual. His suits were now Armani, the shoes were hand-made by Loake, and the outfit was nicely finished off with a Cartier watch. They were making some good money together. Not just through the fight money but also through endorsements. Jack was being paid to take certain sports supplements, protein powders, and energy drinks. He'd be paid for simply posting pictures up on Instagram of him using the products. The rewards were high. His Nike tracksuit had his own JS logo on.

Their company was also managing new boxers. Fighters would see Jack doing well both in and out of the ring and wanted to sign up. Shawn would look after them alongside Jack. All the promotion was still carried out by Chris. They had a new member of staff. She was running it behind the scenes. She was intelligent and kept on top of the boys when they were taking it a bit too easy. It helped that she was Jack's girlfriend. With this new role Kirsten had reluctantly left her job as a midwife but vowed to return one day. She was a great mum to George. Jack would tell anyone who would listen that he was a fighter, but she was the strongest one in their family.

Life was good. It had been a long road back for Shawn. Once the NHS got him going physically, Jack had arranged some help for his mental state. He'd called Roisin and she recommended a fellow member of staff at The Priory for Shawn's therapy. He was still going once a week and had promised Jack he'd open up when things got hard. Jack agreed he would do the same. It also helped Shawn that the lads met up at least once a week. The friends would normally just hang out at Jack's house. Lee hardly came round despite being invited. He normally had the excuse of being at work late, but the lads didn't push him on this. As much as they missed him, it was his life.

Jack couldn't afford to be spotted out in public doing something silly after a few drinks, so he rarely went to pubs and bars. He'd moved properties in the last year to a large five-bedroomed house in Dorking. It had a big garden at the end of which Jack had built his own games room complete with gym equipment and a heavy bag. Little George would occasionally come out with them depending on what sort of night they were having. Martin and Shawn treated him like he was their own.

Once Jack's dad arrived, the meeting started. Jack watched as Chris got up from his chair and adjusted his trousers, so they covered his shoes evenly. He then took off his glasses and placed them on the table.

'We've got some exiting news. It's taken some working out, but we've got there. The WBC has said Jack is next in line to fight for the title and, after lengthy talks, Murray has agreed to the fight. I don't think he wanted it, but he had no choice. They threatened to take the belt off him. Jack, you are the number one contender.'

Jack had been waiting for this. This was the fight. He didn't care who it was against. To win a world title was the big dream for Jack, for most boxers. If he could win, Kirsten and George could be set for life financially.

'When?' Jack asked.

'July 25th. Five months from now,' Chris said.

'Where?'

Chris smiled and waited a few long seconds before answering. 'New York, Madison Square Garden.'

Jack beamed. Clenching his fist, he looked at his dad. 'We did it, Dad. Madison Square fucking Garden. It's what we talked about. Just like Ali and the greats.'

His dad put his hand on his heart and tapped twice. 'I'm proud of you, son. This is the one. Let's do it.'

'How much?' Shawn asked.

Jack hadn't thought about the money. He knew he and his dad wanted to sign there and then.

Chris sat back down and scanned his paperwork. 'Two point five million. Pounds that is, not dollars. If Murray had come to England to fight, he would have taken an even larger cut. Jack could have ended up with only one and a half. But to go to them, Jack is guaranteed two point five million, and more depending on pay per views in England. Tommy Murray, as champ walks away with four million plus add-ons. It's a fair deal.' He looked around the room at them.

Jack smiled. 'I'd have gone for less. It's Madison Square Garden. I'd have probably gone for free.'

Shawn scoffed. 'Think you've been punched too many times. No one's fighting for free. It's gonna cost us a few quid to take the team over. We'll need a training camp out there as well.'

'We will. I'd like Jack to spend at least the last four weeks of camp in America,' said Ken.

Chris and the team ironed out the details, signed the contracts, and it was back to the gym to discuss a training camp with Pete and David.

Driving back after the meeting, Jack couldn't hide his excitement, but Shawn was more reserved.

'Jack, have you thought about who you're fighting? Tommy Murray's no joke. He's a born killer. Out there they call him the new Tommy Hearns. Long arms, quick and powerful. I know we're fighting at The Garden, but we want to win the fight, not just be happy to take part.'

Jack frowned. 'I know who he is. I've wanted to fight him for a long time. He's a good fighter, probably the best, but I'm not going there to lose. I'm taking that belt. Just let me enjoy today. I'm happy today. Once camp starts, I'll be focused, and Pete and David will come up with a way for me to beat him. You'll see.'

'That's what I wanted to hear,' said Shawn.

'There is something I'd like to arrange but I'll need your help.'

'Yeah, anything.'

Jack looked back at the road then indicated and pulled over when it was safe. 'I'd like Martin and Lee to be involved. Maybe give them a job if they want it. This is the big one. I'd like everyone involved. Lee's being strange to me, not all the time, but enough for me to worry. He's OK now and then but he

199

doesn't come and see George. He hardly ever comes round to the house. If I ring him, he doesn't always answer. If I message him online, I know he's read it, but he doesn't reply and then a minute later I see he replies to you or Martin straight away. I'm just worried he feels left out. Maybe he expects more from me.'

'Lee's a funny bugger at times but he's OK. He just likes his own company, that's all. I think he hits the gear a bit as well, mostly coke. And he knows you can't, so he doesn't want it around you. You haven't upset him. And you don't owe him or anyone else anything. You're always offering to help the lads with money and all that. He needs a bloody girlfriend, a nice one, not one off an app. He's always putting it about on one-nighters. The rest of the time he's out on the piss pulling who knows what.' Shawn shrugged.

'Invite him to America, with Martin. I'll pay. Let's go out there in style, four little runts from Dorking taking over the Big Apple, eh! Not bad, is it?'

Shawn nodded, 'I like it. It's a great idea. I'll sort it.' He turned to look out of the window and Jack felt his mood change.

'What, what is it?'

'Sam. He'd have loved this. If he could see you now, he'd be proud of what you've become. You know that don't you? If he could see us now.'

Jack shifted in his seat. 'He'd be proud of us all.'

Jack looked in his rear-view mirror then down at his phone. He typed in George's birthdate to clear the security screen and went into iTunes. He typed *America* in the search. Neil Diamond, 'America'. It was perfect.

Shawn was twitching in the passenger seat. Jack could see

he looked nervous and wondered if it was because they were sitting on the side of a busy road.

'Shawn, today is for celebrating. Life is good now. Nothing is bringing us down. We're going to America, earning a shit ton of money and we're gonna have fun doing it. We did it. We only bloody did it.'

The friends hugged it out. 'Come on ya soft prick, let's enjoy it,' Jack said.

Shawn laughed. The tears showing were happy ones.

Jack un-paused the song. The orchestral opening to the song roared from Jack's Bose speakers.

He shouted over it.

'We're coming to America.'

'You really are nuts,' said Shawn but he joined in, singing along with Jack.

Chapter 30

'A champion is someone who gets up when he can't.'
Jack Dempsey

Liz moved in with Kirsten and George for the period Jack was in America with Ken and the team. It was the longest period Jack had been away from his son so far and he was dreading it, but it was all fuel to his fire when it came to fight night. He'd use this mental pain to train harder, reminding himself that Kirsten and George were the reason he was working so hard. He knew that one day he could retire from boxing and spend every minute with them.

The last week of fight camp included spending hours with the press to promote the fight. This was all part of the job, but it was the part that Jack dreaded. Getting punched in the head was far more appealing than answering the same question from fifty different reporters. Most were nice to him and he had a good relationship with them, but some would only ask questions about his private life. Jack had got used to switching off emotionally.

They asked about what he went through as a child. What it was like losing a brother in traumatic circumstances. He wanted to scream at them but didn't, he stayed composed and answered politely.

Eventually, Jack had taken one question too many and asked for a break. He respectfully made his excuse and walked off into an empty conference room within the hotel. Shawn could see he was upset and followed him.

'Jack, it's nearly over mate. Just a few more questions, then we can get back to the hotel room. You know what these reporters are like but it's their job. They need a headline. And in turn it helps sell the fight.'

Picking up a chair, Jack threw it across the room. 'The fight is sold, twice over. Fucking idiots, the lot of 'em. What do they think it was like losing Sam. Are they mental? And why did that one prick ask about the fight in the Cardiff hotel? That was years ago. Can't they just ask about the boxing? Fucking morons.'

Baring his teeth, he kicked another chair.

Shawn went towards him. 'Don't injure yourself. Just calm down. Get it together. Go back out there, answer their stupid questions and then we can go. They need to sell papers, sell the fight, that's all. You know that.'

Jack pushed his shoulder blades back. He heard the click he was waiting for. Some of the tension was released. 'Can't I just slap one of them? Just one, no black eyes or cuts. Just a tiny slap.'

Shawn nodded and held his arms out wide. 'I'd love you to. But, unfortunately, you can't. It's a bit shit, but it is what it is.'

'I know... I know you're right. Just give me five minutes.' Jack took five deep breaths.

'No problem.' Shawn said as he went to leave the conference

room. He then turned back as he got to the door.

'And pick those chairs up, you bloody hooligan. Typical West Ham fan.'

On fight night, it was full at Madison Square Garden. Over twenty thousand fans packed the arena. Over half were from Britain. British flags were being waved on the streets of New York. 'There's only one Jack Stone' was being chanted non-stop.

The whole team, including Martin and Lee, were all in matching T-shirts sporting Jack's name and sponsors. Black with gold writing. On the back of the shirts, one name, Sam. Jack's boxing shorts had a new name added - George - on the waistband at the back. Sam still at the front.

Jack had asked Shawn to change the walkout music. He wanted two songs mixed together. They got the call in the changing room, time to go. Jack was at the front, leading the team. Directly behind him were Pete and Ken. Behind them were Shawn, Martin, Lee, and David. Martin had one flag, The Union Jack. Lee had another, the stars and stripes of America. The two nations were close allies and Jack wanted to celebrate that. Shawn also thought it was a great idea when it came to good PR. The night was not America v Britain. It was just two fighters, at their peak, going toe to toe to see who was best.

Springing up and down on his toes, stretching his arms, Jack listened as his first song started. 'America' by Neil Diamond. Jack turned to see Shawn's reaction. He wasn't disappointed. His simple nod of appreciation meant everything. Jack could hear the crowd roar, the American fans loving this song choice. The Brits were going crazy as usual. The atmosphere in Madison Square Garden was incredible.

Jack let the opening instrumental sink in. He closed his eyes, ignoring the cameraman directly in front of him. The hairs on his arms stood up, goose-bumps covered his body.

The team took in the atmosphere. There was no shouting, no swearing. There was no need. Each of them felt that this was a special moment in their lives. They made their way through the crowd, security keeping fans back. Then Jack stopped. His team did the same. He was waiting for the next song to kick in. Two minutes and three seconds into the first song it stopped, and the next song began. It was mixed in seamlessly. 'Ill Manors (The Prodigy Remix)' by Plan B. Jack was now ready to walk to the ring. Expressionless, he dug deep into his thoughts. Sam was in there. Then he'd think of Kirsten and George. He climbed into the ring and stood motionless in his corner, waiting for the champ to enter.

Tommy 'Too Quick' Murray walked out to Time to Say Goodbye sung by Andrea Bocelli and Sarah Brightman. The crowd was taken aback. This wasn't the normal type of walkout music. There was something chilling about it. Jack's corner could feel it.

Unnerved, Ken came forward to Jack. 'Don't listen to it.'

'I'm OK. I like this song.' He went back to being deep in his thoughts. He was focused and didn't read anything into the song's lyrics. Maybe it was an intimidation tactic from his opponent's team, but he knew if they needed to try that, they must think he was a threat.

Before the fight Murray had said, 'The Brit will fall in two.'

As they met in the middle of the ring at the start of round one, Murray reminded Jack of this. 'This is over in two.'

Murray danced gracefully around Jack. He was light on his feet, throwing quick jabs, then moving effortlessly out of reach as Jack countered. Jack couldn't find his range. He needed to work out if Murray had any weaknesses he could exploit. He hadn't taken any serious damage, but the first round ended with Murray winning it.

'Be patient, Jack, it'll come. Once you tag him, he won't like it. He'll lose his confidence and make mistakes. And that's when you land,' Pete said.

Jack listened and went out for round two. He landed a jab. Murray smiled and then mouthed, 'Over in two.' His jabs were landing, peppering Jack's head, making it jerk back with each stinging shot. But Jack still came forward, waiting to land a power shot.

It was late in the round when he noticed something. Just before Murray threw the jab, he would raise slightly on his toes. This was his tell. It was split second, but it could be enough. Jack watched a few more jabs come at him. He was happy he was right. The next time Murray raised, Jack moved his head slightly to the right and delivered a peach of a body shot. Murray winced and backed off to recover.

They came back together, and Murray did it again. This time Jack moved his head to the left, slight bend of the knees and landed a left to the stomach. It was enough to back up the last shot, adding to Murray's pain.

The bell sounded the end of round two. Murray nodded at Jack, acknowledging the power in that first body shot. The nod was also a sign of respect to acknowledge that he didn't end the fight when he said he would. A small psychological win for Jack and one of many small percentages that were adding up in his favour.

David poured water into Jack's mouth while Pete did the talking. 'You spotted it too, the little raise before he throws those jabs. Well done. Carry on as you were. You're doing amazing.'

Round three and Jack's confidence was soaring. Murray was backing off more and more, alarmed that his jab was no longer effective. Jack landed a crushing hook which wobbled Murray. He covered up for the rest of the round, unsteady and lacking balance. As the round ended, Murray sat back down with his cornermen. Blood was trickling from his right ear.

As the ringside doctor came closer, Murray's head trainer covered the ear with a towel. He didn't want the ref seeing and he didn't let Murray know either. He didn't want his fighter worrying. If his eardrum was burst, the fight would need to be stopped as his balance would be seriously affected.

Round four started and Murray covered up straight away. As he moved around, all the elegance in his earlier movement was now eluding him. Murray had been rendered into a weak and fragile fighter by Jack's savage power. He had become a forlorn figure.

Still bleeding from his ear, he stumbled back to the stall at the end of round four. Murray's cut man spotted the bleeding ear and looked at the head coach. 'Stop the fight. His eardrum, it could be burst. He can't win like this. He'll take too much damage.'

Murray's head coach wiped the blood away and glared at the cut man. 'He's fine. We're not stopping this fight. Just do your job and shut your mouth with that talk.'

Murray wanted to carry on. Brave and fearless, he looked his trainer in the eye. 'I'm fine, wipe that shit off my ear. I'm going back out there. Don't dare stop it.'

He stood and headed back into the middle of the ring as the bell sounded. The first shot from Jack was a sickening right hand. And then made worse as he landed another hook to the affected ear. Murray slumped in the corner and tried to throw back. The ref looked closely, he was thinking of stopping the fight, but Murray was still punching back and defending himself.

'Finish it, Jack. Uppercut,' David shouted.

That's exactly what Jack threw. It landed, sending Murray to the ground. He was hurt and in pain, but he stood up raising his gloves in defiance. The ref asked him to walk towards him. He did so but he was a beaten man who needed saving from himself.

Jack could see something in the corner of his eye. He turned to see what it was. The white towel landed in between the ref and Murray. The ref and fighter both looked to Murray's corner. The cut man had thrown it in. His head coach was punching the canvas in anger.

The fight was over. Jack Stone was the WBC (World Boxing Council) middleweight champion of the world.

Jack's team stormed the ring, lifting Jack onto their shoulders.

Murray was distraught but full of class. He made his way to Jack. He wished him all the best going forward and asked for a re-match in the future. 'You're a great fighter, man. We'll do it again someday, yeah?'

'No problem, champ. No problem.' Jack said.

Once the pandemonium in the ring had eased, the ring announcer declared Jack the winner and *new* champion of the world.

Interviews were given and there were handshakes all round. It was taking ages and Jack wanted to speak with Kirsten.

Martin called her and handed his phone over.

'Did you see it? We did it. All the hard work was worth it. We bloody did it. I love you. Where's George?'

'I've just seen it. We couldn't wait any longer. We looked up the result, then your mum and I watched the replay. George is asleep. It's 5 am here. I'll show him when he wakes up. I'm so proud of you. Can't wait for you to get home.'

'I'll be back soon, a couple of days. I can't wait either. Got to go, bloody TV people are after me again. Tell mum, I love her.'

'I will. We love you too.'

As Jack left the ring, the English fans were all hanging around, trying to get a high five, or a selfie. Most of the American fans had left the arena. Jack noticed someone he recognised making their way through the crowd. He decided it couldn't be. More fans swamped him, more selfies. He looked back. She was closer this time. He could see her long red hair.

He shouted, 'Roisin.'

She gave Jack a huge smile. He asked his team to help clear the way for her so that she could get to him.

'I can't believe you came all this way to New York.' Jack was dumbfounded.

'A promise is a promise, Jack.'

He hugged Roisin but instantly let her go realising he was still sweaty and bleeding. She was dressed pristinely as usual.

'Oh, don't worry about that. Come here.' She hugged him properly before introducing him to her husband. Jack shook his hand and thanked him for coming.

'I thought Mike and I could turn it into a holiday. We'd always said we wanted to go to New York and now we're here, watching you become a champion. You said you would.'

Jack felt proud. Throughout most of his life he only ever wanted to make his parents proud. And then he met Roisin and felt the same with her. He wanted her to see he was doing well and that he was happy.

'Thank you so much. I'll never forget you came...that you did this. Thank you.'

'It's our pleasure. You must have so much you need to do. We'll let you get on. We are off for a posh meal, Mike's treat, and then we have an early start tomorrow sight-seeing. The Statue of Liberty and Empire State to start with. You go and celebrate. You deserve it.'

Again, they embraced, and Roisin whispered into Jack's ear, 'I told you...you deserve to be happy. Be happy, Jack.'

As he watched her leave, she turned and gave him the biggest smile.

Jack mouthed, 'Thank you.'

Back in the changing room, Jack was checking his phone. Hundreds of messages and missed calls. The first missed call was from James Carrick. Jack called him back.

Carrick answered the call within seconds. 'What's happening, Champ?'

Jack laughed. 'Oh, ya know, just chilling with my nice new shiny belt.'

Carrick cracked up laughing. 'You flash git. Well done, lad, you did it. I knew you would. Great performance as well. He couldn't take the power shots. He didn't like those did he?'

'It went well. I got a bit lucky with the ear problem. His balance went.'

'That's not luck. You caused that with a good shot. Enjoy

the victory, enjoy being the champ. Make that money while you can.'

'I will. Thanks, James.'

'We're still on, though, right? We are going to have that re-match?'

'I promised you, James. We'll do it. It's gonna be weird fighting you, now that I know you.'

Carrick came back quickly. 'It's just a sport. We'll still be friends after. It's what we do. We're fighters.'

'That's one way of looking at it. We'll make it happen.'

'And Jack, if you want an easy fight first to defend the title, I understand. I'd do the same. Make some money, enjoy the belt. And when our time comes, let us promote the shit out of it. Let's make this big. I need to get paid.'

'You're on, James. You take care, we'll speak soon.'

'We will, champ,' James said before hanging up.

Chapter 31

'I think self-awareness is probably the most important thing towards being a champion.'
Billie Jean King

Jack had not trained for two months, since winning the world title. He was due back into training soon but had made the most of his time with Kirsten and George. They hired a cottage overlooking the sea in the beautiful coastal town of Woolacombe, North Devon. Each day they would take George for walks on the beach. The sea air would tire him out and he would be in bed early. Jack could then spend quality time with Kirsten. They didn't watch television or go on their phones; they were just engrossed in each other and George. Jack would set up the open fire and they'd sit in front of it after dinner watching the flames curl and sway, listening to the crackling from the dry logs.

Kirsten backed into Jack and snuggled her head under his chin. 'I wish it could always be like this.'

'It can be whatever we want it to be.'

'It isn't though, is it? Once you're back fighting, George and I have to share you with everyone.'

'That's not forever. I won't be fighting forever. I just want enough money for us to be comfortable. Once I've done that we can go where we want, be what we want.'

Kirsten smiled. 'And have a sister for George?'

Jack laughed. 'Maybe. That would be lovely. Or a brother.'

Kirsten nodded. 'Or a brother.'

They sat in silence again, taking an occasional sip of wine.

'I'd never tell you when to stop fighting, you know that don't you?'

Jack kissed her cheek. 'I know. Pete has warned me over and over about knowing when to stop. He says the fighter is the last person to know. So maybe you should be the one who says when it's time.'

'I just want you to be OK. I've heard stories of fighters not knowing when to stop. They have one fight too many. If that happens, the money means nothing. I just want you. I don't care what you are or what you do for a living. We could move to somewhere like here. Be by the sea. I'll get a job in a hospital nearby and you could be with the kids. Whatever works, Jack.'

Jack held her tight. 'It'll be fine, I promise. One day I'll be around so much you'll want me out of the house. You'll be begging me to get out.'

Kirsten smiled. 'That would never happen. I'll never get tired of you.' She squeezed his hand.

'Mummy,' George called from upstairs.

Jack kissed Kirsten. 'I'll go.'

Being a family together on the coast was a welcome break from sweaty gyms and getting punched in the face. Jack would still get a daily run in each day. The beach was clear golden sand, three miles long. Each morning at six he'd run the full length and then walk back to the cottage with his head clear, ready for another day of fun with his boy.

Jack had been home from his break for a couple of days. He was on his way to catch up with Pete and decide what was next and was excited because he had a surprise for Pete. He had once made him a promise and today he would fulfil it.

He pulled into the gym car park, not in his G Wagon but in a 1960s, Jaguar Mk II, 2.4ltr. It had steel wheels and an Everflex vinyl roof. The car was a deep shade of red with a perfect leather interior.

He sounded the horn over and over until the gym door opened. David was standing there. He gave a wave and went back in to get his dad.

Pete made his way towards Jack and the car with a confused look. He was eyeing up every detail of this prestige vehicle. Jack stood there proudly, showing it off.

'Well, what do you think?' he asked.

'I think it's bloody lovely. Whose is it?'

'It's yours.' Jack smiled as he threw the keys at Pete.

'Paperwork is inside, just sign it in your name and send it off. You don't even need to tax it. It's so old you don't have to.'

Pete caught the keys. He was open mouthed but didn't speak.

'This is the right one? The one you always talk about. Like the one in that program with the old detective bloke. It's not the original but it is the same model and colour.'

Pete put his hand over his mouth, he was holding back tears. No words could express his gratitude.

'Get in,' urged Jack. 'It's yours. The leather and the wood on the interior smell amazing. No wonder you love old cars. It's been so well looked after. My dad helped me choose it. You're lucky you have it. He wanted it. I'll have to bloody buy him one now.'

Pete sat in the driver's seat. He ran his hands over the steering wheel and stroked the Jaguar badge in front of him. He touched the leather on the seats. Taking in the nostalgic odour, it reminded him of years gone by. The inside of his parents' car had smelled just the same.

'It's perfect, Jack. Truly perfect. You didn't have to do this. You've given me enough.'

'I told you I would. I promised I'd get you a car. It's just a small way of me thanking you. You helped change my life. I'll never forget that.'

'You helped change mine too, son. I've trained a world champ. No one can take that away from me. That was enough for me.'

'C'mon, let's go for a spin.'

David watched as they drove out of the car park. He closed the door and went back into the gym.

Chapter 32

'Be kind, for everyone you meet is fighting a battle you know nothing about.'

Kirsten knocked on the door and waited for Liz to answer.

'Hi Kirsten. Come in love. Where's my grandson? Is he hiding from me?' She laughed knowing he was there somewhere.

Kirsten smiled. 'He's at home alone, he didn't want to come.' It was George's cue to jump out from behind the wall.

'Hello Nanna.' He gave Liz a massive hug. She scooped him up and carried him indoors. Kirsten followed.

'Where are you guys off to?

'We're going to the park to see my friend,' George said.

'We're just popping down for a couple of hours. George has a play date. They love it down there.'

Liz made a cup of tea for her and Kirsten and found an iced lolly for George. Excited, he thanked his Nanna and ran out to the garden to play.

Kirsten sat down. 'Can I have a word, Liz?'

Liz sat down slowly. 'This sounds serious. Is everything all right? How's Jack?'

Kirsten touched Liz's hand. 'Oh no, there's nothing wrong. I just need to talk to you. Jack has asked me to. He says if he talks to you about this you might try and get out of it.'

'Does he now? Well, he's going to get a clip round the ear then when I see him.'

Kirsten grinned. 'He wants me to ask you if you are happy here, in this house?'

'I'm very happy.' Liz frowned.

'So, you wouldn't want to move? Jack said you wouldn't want to.'

'Jack's right. We love this house. It's not much but it's more than enough for Ken and me. And it has memories I don't want to forget.'

'I completely understand. So, that brings me to my next question.' Kirsten then spotted George kicking the football in to the flowers. 'George, be careful or Grandad Ken will be after you.'

George looked back and laughed. He knew full well Ken would never tell him off.

'Where was I...oh yeah, my next question. How much do you owe on the mortgage on the house? Jack reckons about fifty grand.'

Liz sat back in her seat. 'It's around that amount, maybe a bit less, but I'm not sure how he knows. Little bugger.'

'He's asked me to give you this.' Kirsten handed over a cheque for one hundred thousand pounds.

Liz covered her mouth with her hand. 'No, I can't take that. You have to take it back.'

Kirsten took Liz's hands and cupped them. 'Jack said you wouldn't take it which is why he's got me to do it. He knows I'll persuade you to take it. He said there's enough there to pay the house off, get dad a car and the rest is yours. Take a holiday, go shopping or whatever.'

Liz started to cry. 'I can't. It's too much.'

'Liz, it makes Jack happy when he can help you and Ken. He wants you to be worry free, with no mortgage. He was going to buy you a new house but knew you wouldn't move. Liz, you don't have a choice. You'll upset him if you don't take it.'

Liz's tears turned to laughter and she leant forward and kissed Kirsten just as George came running in. 'Nanna, why are you crying?'

Liz leaned down to hug George. 'I'm happy. Nanna's really happy. Your dad is a naughty boy, but he's made your Nanna very happy.'

George kissed her and ran back to the garden.

'Oh, and Jack also said to say this: if you don't take the money. One day the house will be his anyway, so just pay it off and shut up.' They both laughed.

'He's kicked that bloody ball in the flowers again, I'll go and stop him.' Kirsten went out to the garden. Liz picked up the cheque, written out by her boy, and clutched it into her chest.

III

Part Three

Chapter 33

'The man who smiles when things go wrong has thought of someone to blame it on.'
Robert Bloch

He looked in the mirror, smiled, and felt proud. He'd achieved so much. Today was a great day. Soundproofing the basement went exactly to plan. Up until now he had only used the basement for storage. There was no handle on the inside of the door and, once locked, there'd be no escape. There were no windows. No exit points. Just four dark walls. It was the perfect room for the job at hand. It was big, big enough, measuring in at twelve by eighteen feet. Ideal for a cinema room.

The single bed fitted perfectly in the corner of the room. He'd dragged it down there unconcerned about the dirt it had picked up along the way. The wall was damp, the bed would follow at some point, he knew that, but it wasn't his problem. A tiny bedside cabinet was home for the old-fashioned Roberts radio to sit on, tuned using traditional grooved dials.

His biggest challenge was a toilet. A bucket would have to do, as building a toilet with suitable drainage would take time and money. It would also draw attention to his house from nosy neighbours, especially Mrs Pounds next door. To him, she was an interfering pain in the arse. Locking her down there one day was an attractive option but she wasn't worth the prison time. He put up with her ways as she was old and would be dead soon anyway, hopefully. Silly old cow and dusty old bitch were just a couple of favourite names he used for her. When this was all over, he was happy that he wouldn't have to see her again.

There was a light in the basement. It shouldn't be in darkness. He wasn't a complete monster. Well, he didn't think he was.

Time to do the final checks. He turned the radio volume up to the max and walked back upstairs, closing the door. His soundproofing was exceptional. He smiled to himself, proud of his handiwork. He made his way back down the dusty wooden staircase and marvelled in his work. Cobwebs decorated the ceiling; a cluster of spiders were in their element down there. He decided to leave them.

He turned the radio off, made his way up the stairs and flicked the light switch. With one night left until the big day, he needed to think. He had to get this right. He was excited but reminded himself to calm down. Don't mess it up now, it had been months in the planning.

Chapter 34

'Courage is what it takes to stand up and speak. Courage is also what it takes to sit down and listen.'

Jack wished he could be with Kirsten and George in the park but, instead, he was at a meeting with Chris and Shawn to discuss their next move and have lunch together.

'Jack, I'm not sure Carrick is the right fight. That was a war last time. I don't think we need that again, not yet.'

Jack shrugged his shoulders. He'd noticed how Chris had looked at Shawn, hoping he would back him up. 'I made a promise. I'm happy to fight James. He deserves it. We have this fight, then I'll take a bit of time off and then we go after the other belts.'

Shawn picked up his coffee, took a sip, and placed it back down on the saucer. 'I don't like it, but I know you, Jack. You won't change your mind. Chris, if we make him fight anyone else, he won't be up for it. He told me all along that Carrick would get his re-match. Let's do it.'

Jack shifted in his seat. 'The money will be huge. We'd sell out a football stadium. The British fans want it. Let's give it to them. Two fighters in their prime, not ducking each other.

It's what boxing should be about. It pisses me off when other fighters avoid each other just so they can hold the belt longer than they should. I don't want to be like them. For me it's not about easy fights for easy money.'

Chris raised his eyebrows. 'I know what you're saying. And that's why the fans love you. It's the right thing for them but it's not them in the ring, is it? You're right on another thing. It'll bring in a lot of money. The gate at a football stadium will be big and the pay-per-views could break records, but my job, and Shawn's, is to protect you and give you a long career. A career where you walk away with plenty of money and your brain in one piece. We're thinking of you, Jack.'

'I know you are, and I appreciate it. I promise that after Carrick we'll go easy for a bit. Let's do it. Battle of Britain, in Liverpool. It'll be massive.'

Chris choked as he was sipping his coffee. 'Liverpool! No way. It's got to be in London.'

Jack patted Chris on the back. 'I've already promised. I told James it would be up north. Come on Chris, you'll make it work.'

Chris smiled. 'Fucking hell, you don't make my job easy, do you? Let's see what I can do.'

Jack called the waiter over. 'Now that's that sorted, I'm hungry. Let's eat. What do you boys want?'

Chris and Shawn nodded at each other. They knew they had some serious work to do.

Chapter 35

'Loving and losing, different only by one letter and a million degrees of pain.'
Jessica Katoff

The playground in the centre of town was always busy on a Saturday. Mums and dads would take their kids there and let them run riot for an hour or so while they did their best not to check their phones. Parents could get a well-deserved and much needed coffee from the soft play café. With the weather still sunny enough to sunbathe late into September, it was an ideal spot for local families to make the most of the British sun before it disappeared for another six months.

Kirsten was taking George for a playdate with his friend Bobby. The boys got on great and were happy to play together all day, with only the occasional disagreement over who had which toy first. Kirsten could see her friend, Emily approaching, hand in hand with Bobby. The minute he saw George he broke free and sprinted with his arms in the air calling George's name. They were the same age, both five years old. They'd originally met at school where they were in the same class. The boys were over excited and didn't know what to do first, go on the slides, run their feet through the sand, play on the swings or kick a football.

The sand won and soon their shoes were filled with it. George asked if he could take his off. Kirsten agreed but made it clear to him that he couldn't leave the sandpit area.

'Do you fancy a drink, Emily? Tea, coffee or something cold?'

'Yes please. I'd love a tea. If I give you the cash, can you get water as well?'

Kirsten picked up her bag. 'Of course, and don't worry about the money. You keep an eye on these little monkeys. There's no queue. I'll be back in a minute.'

Emily was in the sandpit with the boys. They were throwing sand everywhere, mostly at each other. 'Will you two please stop it. If that sand goes in your eyes, you'll know about it.' She needed to get a clean towel from her bag so that she could wipe the boys down when they finished in the sandpit. Her bag was on the bench a few feet away. As she walked towards it, she heard her phone ringing.

She turned to the two boys and made sure they were listening. 'Boys, I'm just grabbing my phone. Stay in the sand pit and don't move.' Emily missed the call because she couldn't make her phone work. There was too much sand on her hands. She searched her bag for wet wipes and, once she found them, wiped herself clean. The phone rang again, this time she answered.

Kirsten came back over and interrupted Emily's phone call. 'There's your coffee. I'll put the water in your bag.' Kirsten looked at the sandpit. There was only one boy in there, and it wasn't George. It was Bobby. He was singing to himself, building a sandcastle on his own.

'Where's George?'

Emily looked at the sandpit where she'd left him. Bobby was alone.

'Mummy, can we go now, I want to go home,' Bobby wailed.

Kirsten watched the colour drain from Emily's face. 'He was there two seconds ago. He was right there.' Emily pointed to where she last saw him. 'He must have gone on the slide. Bobby, where's George? Did you see where he went?'

'I don't know. He's gone.'

Kirsten dropped her coffee cup. The contents splashed up her leg. Despite the heat of it she felt no pain. Her heart raced as she called out, 'George...George, come on honey. Come on George. Come back to Mummy. If you're hiding, it's time to come out now.'

Worried parents asked Kirsten if they could help, one mum telling Kirsten, 'I hate it when they do this. It's happened to me several times. We'll find him, don't worry.' As the panic level grew other parents started gathering up their children, Emily included. She held her son tightly as she helped search for George.

George had wavy dark hair but so did plenty of other boys at the park that day. Kirsten started describing to anyone that would listen exactly what her son looked like. 'He had a light blue T-shirt on and cream-coloured shorts. The shirt...I think it was...plain. No, it had a union jack on the right shoulder, that's right, a big Union Jack on the shoulder. No shoes on, or socks, he's barefoot so he can't have gone far.'

Kirsten felt sick. She picked up George's shoes and held them to her chest. The shoes were shedding sand down Kirsten's front.

'I'm so sorry, Kirsten. I was only on my phone for a second.

I promise. I'm so sorry.'

Kirsten looked through Emily. She wasn't interested in her apologies. That's the last time she would trust her. How could she turn her back, even for a second?

'Let's just find him. Just find my George, then we're going home.'

Kirsten took her phone out and dialled 999. Lightheaded, crying uncontrollably, she tried to listen to the operator's questions.

'You're ringing the police?'

'Of course I bloody am. Can you see George? I can't.'

'Hello, emergency service operator, which service do you require? Fire, police or ambulance?'

'Police...it's my son.'

'Just connecting you.'

'Hello, where are you calling from?

'It's my son, he's gone... he's missing. He's only five years old. I'm in Dorking, Surrey. Meadowbank playground. Next to the football stadium.'

The phone operator kept a calm tone whilst they typed the information into their computer. 'And you say it's your son that is missing? What's the exact address please?'

Kirsten spoke louder. 'I don't know the exact address. It's Meadowbank, in Dorking. The children's playground. It's next to the stadium. Dorking Wanderers play there.'

'OK, no problem, I'll find it.'

'Please hurry. He's only five.'

'The police are on their way. Please tell me your son's name.'

'George. George Stone.'

'And your name, please.'

'Kirsten Kenward.'

'Thank you. And how long has your son been missing?'

'I'm not exactly sure, ten or fifteen minutes. Not long, I know, but something isn't right. He never goes off like this.'

Kirsten explained what George was wearing and what led up to him going missing. The operator stayed on the phone until Kirsten advised her the police had arrived.

Kirsten heard them first, then saw them pull into stadium car park. She ran towards them as they got out of their car. Kirsten carried on shouting, 'George...George.' She screamed his name over and over. More and more people were helping to search. Most locals knew who Kirsten was. Jack was famous in the sporting world and in a town like Dorking everyone knew each other. The locals looked at Jack as one of their own.

Kirsten knew she needed to ring Jack soon. It was probably already on social media, maybe even on the bloody news.

More police cars arrived. The sirens had stopped but they left the blue lights flashing. Kirsten felt like she was watching someone else go through this; it didn't feel real. It couldn't happen. Not to her and Jack. She could see some families in the background carrying on with their picnics or still playing ball games. How could they carry on as normal while her world was crumbling right in front of her? She started to scream George's name even louder.

A policeman approached her. He reached out to calm Kirsten down. 'Miss Kenward, we're here to help. I need to ask a few questions.'

Kirsten couldn't hear everything he was saying, everything around her was one noise. She couldn't concentrate. She felt light-headed.

'Miss Kenward. Please. I'm PC Curtis. I need to ask questions about your son.'

'Questions. OK. About George.'

'Yes. How old is George?'

'He's five.'

PC Curtis had a small pencil and notepad. He was noting Kirsten's answers. 'His clothing, what was he wearing?'

'Light blue T-shirt, with a union jack on the right shoulder. Cream shorts, knee-length. He'd taken his shoes and socks off. He's barefoot.'

'He's barefoot?'

Kirsten felt like she was being judged for letting her son take his shoes off. She snapped. 'Yes, he was barefoot. He was in the sand. Most kids do that in the sand pit.'

'That's all right, Miss Kenward. I'm sure he hasn't gone far. Not without shoes. We have officers going to all the exit points of the park. We've put a message out on police social media for any information. We must do all we can as soon as we can.'

'Social media, already. Oh God. My partner will see it. He doesn't know yet.' Kirsten was horrified at Jack finding out from someone else. She got her phone and dialled.

Jack was driving home with Shawn in the passenger seat. Both oblivious to the terrifying situation they would be walking back into. Jack's phone was in his pocket, still muted from earlier.

Shawn's phone rang. He answered.

'Shawn, don't say a word. Just listen. And don't look at Jack,' Kirsten said.

Shawn looked across to Jack, his eyes wide. He immediately looked back to the road in front. 'What's going on?'

'It's George. Something's happened. I need you to get back

home with Jack. Don't let Jack go on social media and don't stop anywhere. Just get home.'

Shawn couldn't help himself. Again, he looked across at Jack.

'What...what is it, Shawn?' Jack asked.

Shawn was caught in the middle. 'Kirsten, let me talk to Jack. I'll get him home. We're ten minutes away. Just tell me what's happened?'

Kirsten broke down. 'Oh, Shawn...George has run off. We can't find him.'

Shawn didn't expect it to be that bad. This was the worst scenario he could have imagined. 'I'll tell him, but...'

Kirsten interrupted. 'I need to go. I'm with the police. They need more information. Please, just get back.' She hung up.

Shawn put the phone in his lap and looked at Jack.

'Just tell me, Shawn. It's George, isn't it?'

'We need to get home now, Jack.'

Shawn had seen that haunted look on Jack's face before. Jack put his foot down on the accelerator. He wasn't listening to any more of what Shawn was saying. Instead, he was talking to himself. 'Not again. I'm not losing someone I love again. No fucking way.' He punched the steering wheel. 'If George has gone, so am I. We are not going through this again.'

Shawn couldn't talk to him. There was nothing he could say. He double-checked his seatbelt. Jack was driving dangerously fast, not stopping at roundabouts or junctions. Car horns were being sounded, aimed at Jack's reckless driving.

Chapter 36

'Anger doesn't solve anything. It builds nothing but can destroy everything.'
Lawrence Douglas Wilder

There was a fleet of vehicles blocking Jack from getting in. They included his dad's car, two police vehicles and a black BMW that belonged to the detective in charge. He abandoned his car. Before he reached the front door, his dad came running out. He put his hands up in front of him. 'Jack, keep calm. Everyone here is trying to help. Let's listen to them and do what they say.'

Jack held his palms up and headed for the door. 'I'm calm. I just want my fucking son found. I'm not going to do anything silly. Let me talk to the police and to Kirsten.'

'She's still at the park. Kirsten asked us to be here, just in case George turned up at home. Her parents are on their way here as well.'

Jack's face screwed up. 'He went missing at the park. How? Kirsten doesn't let him out of her sight.'

His dad sighed. 'It's not her fault. Her friend Emily was watching the kids while Kirsten was getting some drinks. Don't blame Kirsten. You need to be together on this.'

Hands on his head, Jack was holding back the fury he wanted to unleash. 'Fucking Emily. You can't trust her. She's got the attention span of a goldfish.' Jack clenched his fist and looked at the nearest car window, catching his reflection. He wanted to put his fist through it but didn't.

His mum was now by his dad's side. She stepped forward and stroked his arm. 'Jack, this isn't the time to blame anyone. Let's just concentrate on finding George. That's all that matters right now. Are you coming in to see the detective or going to Kirsten?'

Jack held his mum, kissed her on the forehead, then backed away. 'Does the detective know anything?'

'I don't think so, but he wants to ask you some questions.'

'Then I'm going to find my son.' He walked back to his car where Shawn was waiting for him.

'Shawn, please stay with him,' Jack's mum shouted. Shawn gave her a simple nod before jumping into the passenger seat.

They arrived at the playground to be greeted by a sea of people. Most were there helping with the search. They'd heard through social media what had happened and wanted to be there. Some were holding their phones up filming every move. One by one they would put it on to their Facebook, Instagram, or Twitter.

Jack ran to Kirsten once he spotted her. She saw him coming. The fear in her eyes was clear to see. She knew Jack would never hurt her, but she dreaded his reaction. The guilt was crippling.

Jack pulled Kirsten to him and held her tight. He kissed her and whispered, 'We'll find him. I promise we will find him.'

Kirsten needed this. She needed to know they were in this

together.

More camera phones came out, now pointing directly at them. Seeing these two parents at their most desperate would get them a lot of likes and views on Facebook.

Kirsten was crying and not all her words were coherent. They were high pitched, and she was speaking quickly. 'I'm so sorry. I thought she'd be OK with him for two minutes. She went on her sodding phone and turned her back. I shouldn't have got the bloody drinks.'

Jack pulled her in again. Inside he was raging but not with Kirsten. He was trying his best to keep calm. He had listened to his parents' earlier advice and said, 'Let's just find George.'

On the drive down to the park, Jack had decided once George was home safely, they would never let him out of their sight again.

Kirsten updated him. 'The police have covered all the exits. They've searched in and around the football stadium and checked the playground, the fields and the stream at the bottom of the park.'

Jack interrupted. 'What about the pond?' He pointed to his right. The pond was around a hundred metres from where they were standing.

'They haven't mentioned the pond. If George had got that far I'm sure he would have been seen. There are so many people down there.'

'But you're not sure, are you?'

Kirsten was scared to answer honestly but she had to. 'I'm not definite, Jack.' She looked towards the pond.

Jack now looked dead behind the eyes. There was no emotion in his voice. Kirsten was scared to ask what he was thinking.

'The police need to search in there. He's five years old. Do they realise how small he is? Anything could have happened. He won't stand a chance if he's gone in there.'

As Jack spoke a police helicopter was hovering above them. The same policeman Kirsten dealt with earlier came over once he realised Jack had arrived.

'I'm PC Curtis. You must be Jack. I'm sorry we have to meet like this. We're doing all we can.' The helicopter was quite low, and the PC started to shout as he pointed up. 'The helicopter has a camera that can see areas that we can't from the ground. Like inside the woodland areas, in alleyways and gardens.' Once the helicopter had passed, he lowered his voice. 'There are eight exits from this park. We have a policeman on every one of them.'

Jack was calm, listening but staring through the policeman. 'What about the pond?'

'We've searched all around the pond, but we haven't been in. I'll find out if we are going to request divers to start a search. I'll radio in.'

As the officer went for his radio, Jack heard, 'PC Curtis, are you with the family? Over.'

'This is PC Curtis. I'm with Mr and Mrs Stone. We're still in the park. Over.'

Kirsten looked at Jack. They weren't married yet. She wasn't Mrs Stone but right now it wasn't important.

'Please could you take the parents to their home. We have a new development. Over.'

'What does that mean?' Jack asked.

PC Curtis was a young officer. He'd had all the training, but he had not dealt with a situation as big as this so far in his career. He was hoping a senior officer would have arrived by now. It was starting to get to him. He stuttered his answer.

'I'm... not sure. They won't tell me on the radio. If... we could go back to your house... I think it would be for the best.'

'Can't they just tell us now? Please.'

Kirsten gabbed Jack's arm. 'Let's just get home.'

PC Curtis was grateful for Kirsten's help. 'I'll take you both. Please follow me to my car.'

They walked past Shawn who was waiting by Jack's Mercedes. Jack threw him the keys. 'Can you stay here and let me know if anything changes?'

'No problem. I'll ring Martin and Lee and get them to help.' Shawn smiled at Kirsten, but with tears in his eyes. The smile disappeared and he broke down, turning his head away, not wanting Kirsten to see.

Nothing further was said in the car. PC Curtis occasionally gave a nervous look in his rear-view mirror at the distraught parents.

Jack, Kirsten and PC Curtis entered the family home. Liz cuddled Kirsten and reassured her. 'Whatever they tell you, we'll deal with it. We'll get through this together.'

Jack's dad was motionless. His eyes were puffy and red. Jack had not seen him cry since Sam died. He noticed how his dad wouldn't have eye contact. Something drastic had changed since they spoke earlier.

A hard-looking, middle-aged man approached them. His appearance could easily have suited someone on the other side of the law. 'I'm Detective Holland. I'm part of the Criminal Investigations Department. Please could you join me in the front room.'

Again, Jack nervously looked at his dad, but he wouldn't look back at him, instead he sat down on a dining room chair and stared out of the window. He'd left the sofa clear for Kirsten and Jack.

'Is our son alive? Please just tell us,' Kirsten said as she sat down.

Jack stared at the detective. He was ready for the worst. He'd already decided that if George was dead, he would want to die too. He'd made that decision the moment the news of George's disappearance had reached him. Was this it, the news he had always dreaded? The news that he had lost another loved one in tragic circumstances.

'We've had some information from a member of the public. This isn't always reliable. It could be false, but we have to take it seriously. The details were very specific.'

Kirsten screamed out, 'Oh God, no. My boy, what's happened to my George?'

Jack didn't change. No shouting. No sign of exploding. He was stone-faced.

'Just say it,' Jack said. His knuckles turned white as he clenched his fists.

Detective Holland moved forward in his seat. 'Your son may have been seen walking hand in hand with someone leaving the park. The witness said he was with a man. We have a vague description of what the man was wearing and a rough idea of height, but that's all. They didn't see his face.'

Jack looked the detective in the eye. 'How do you know it was George?'

'The description of your son's clothes match. Also, they said the boy was barefoot and...' He paused as he tried to think of a way of making this less painful.

'And what?' Jack said.

'This will be hard to hear, I'm sorry. There was blood on

237

his toes. He was crying, saying that he didn't want to walk anymore and...that he wanted his mum.'

Chapter 37

'Hell is empty, and all the devils are here.'
William Shakespeare

'Would you like a piggyback?'

'No. I want my mum.'

This didn't go down well. 'Your mum isn't here, is she?'

George's parents were always patient around him. They were not strict and rarely shouted, let alone smacked him. This angry man towering over him was like no one he'd met before.

George's bottom lip started to quiver. He knew he had upset him but didn't understand what he had done wrong.

The man looked down at George, his teeth clamped together, and his eyes narrowed. 'You need to shut up.'

The man's tone of voice had changed drastically from when he invited George away from the park. He had become aggressive and mean. They were a safe distance from anybody now and the last person they saw was walking away in the other direction, but she was looking back regularly. The man was upset that George had caused her to notice them. Now she was out of earshot he could say what he liked. He no longer needed to keep up his act, that of a concerned and caring father.

Tears were running down George's puffy red cheeks. He looked down and noticed the blood between his toes. Now that he'd seen it, he felt the pain. He pulled his arm down, releasing his soft hand from the large rough one that was forcefully holding his.

The man stood in front of him and said, 'Don't.' Bending down on one knee he was now eye level with George and, just in case anyone was watching, he didn't shout or show his anger. He delivered his next sentence with a smile. 'You need to start doing as you are told. I told you earlier, your mum asked me to look after you. So that's what I'm going to do. There's no need for me to hurt you. I shouldn't have to do that. Or should I?'

George's eyes were stinging with sweat and the continuous tears. He was taking sharp intakes of breath as he spoke. 'You're... not... nice.'

The man smiled and spoke with sarcasm that George was too young to understand. 'Maybe I'm not. But then again, maybe I am. If you do as you are told, I'll be nice. If you continue to be naughty you will see I am not nice, not nice at all.'

The man thought about what he'd just said. He needed the boy calm. Maybe he was being a bit harsh. 'Tell me, George, what does your dad do if you are naughty?'

A mixture of tears and snot was running into George's mouth. As he cried a bubble appeared from his nose. He wiped it with his bare arm, all the way from his elbow down to the back of his hand. 'My dad isn't mean. You're mean. He doesn't grab my hand and he doesn't hurt me.'

The man grinned as he used his sleeve to wipe George's face.

From a distance he looked like any other parent caring for their upset child.

'So, your Dad, he's perfect, is he? That's about right. Mr Perfect doesn't hurt his kid.' He moved in closer to George, almost nose to nose. 'Perhaps he should hurt you. You'd do as you're bloody told then. Kids these days do what they like. There's no discipline at home. Well, I'll tell you now, I'm done being nice. I've been nice to lots of people and it's got me nowhere.' He grabbed George's tiny hand and grimaced as he felt the dampness from the mixture of tears and snot. He marched him towards the car and pressed the last of the three buttons on the key fob. The boot opened. George looked up at the man. Confused at why the boot was open. The man had nothing to put in there.

'In ya go.' He attempted to lift him, but George pulled his hand away and tried to run. He was caught straight away.

The man continued with his sarcastic tone. 'Don't cry. Girls cry. Are you a girl? You won't be in there long. I've put a torch in there for Christ's sake. Shout again and I'll have to tape up your mouth. And I don't want to do that. Can you be quiet for ten minutes?' He grinned at George as he laid him in the car boot. George's eyes were filled with horror.

George lay there pleading. 'I'll be good, I promise. I'm a good boy. Can I sit in the car like I do with mummy? She gives me her phone and I'm quiet.'

The man shook his head slowly side to side. 'That can't happen I'm afraid. That's not part of the game. If someone sees you, it's game over.' The man then made a noise like you'd hear on Family Fortunes when the family give a wrong answer. He continued. 'Think of it as an adventure and, if you're good, when we get to my house, I'll give you some chocolate. OK, Georgie?'

George thought carefully. 'But... but I've had chocolate today. One piece a day, or my teeth will fall out. That's what my mummy says. And... my name is George. Not Georgie.'

George could see that scowl again. He'd upset him.

The man bent down and hovered over George, close enough that George could smell his breath. The voice changed again, stern and cruel. 'I called you George. I know your bloody name, don't I? And as for chocolate, your mum has lied to you. She is a liar, liar pants on bloody fire. Your silly little teeth are going to fall out anyway so you might as well eat what you like, when you like.' He stood upright, nodded in disgust, and sighed. He started talking to himself in a childish voice. 'Shitty little know-it-all. I can't eat chocolate. My name is George. Blah blah blah.'

He put the torch on George's chest, pressed it on, and slammed the boot shut. He leaned down, knocked twice and put his mouth just above the boot. 'Not a word, boy. You hear me? You understand, don't you Georgie? Not a bloody word.'

George held back from crying out. He was petrified. He pressed his lips together and covered his mouth with both hands. After a few seconds he couldn't breathe, his nose was too bunged up. He moved his hands from his mouth, took a few deep breaths and whispered, 'My name is George, not Georgie. My name is George, not Georgie.'

The man started the engine and fiddled with his baseball cap, setting the peak straight with a slight bend in the middle. It was a fake replica cap he had found at home. It had NY on the front. He didn't remember buying it and had no interest in the New York Yankees or baseball. Today it was just a cap to help hide his face and hair.

Turning the stereo right up, he smiled at himself in the rear-view mirror. 'That was easier than we thought it would be. Nearly home and dry.'

He pulled away, confident that the road he parked in had no CCTV. He had carefully chosen Rothes road. It was full of old Victorian houses, not the sort to ruin the appearance by putting big ugly cameras up.

He got to the first junction and selected a different song before pulling away. 'Bad Guy' by Eminem. He looked back into his rear-view mirror. 'Hey Georgie Boy, your dad loves Eminem. He uses it to train to. I wonder how your dad is right now. He's going be a teensy-weensy bit upset when he finds out you're gone.' A huge grin filled his face and he chuckled. 'He's going kill me. He has got a temper on him, has your dad but he can't do anything because he's not here. Poor Jack.' His smile turned to a look of contentment. He gave a friendly thumbs up as a car gave way to him at the next junction. 'Today's a good day, Georgie. And wait until you see your room, Georgie. You'll love it.'

Chapter 38

'Tears come from the heart and not from the brain.'
Leonardo Da Vinci

Kirsten opened her eyes. She saw the clock at the bedside and jumped up. Her heart was racing, her stomach in knots as she remembered what was going on downstairs. Liz knocked and entered the bedroom.

'How are you, honey? You cried yourself to sleep. We decided to leave you for a bit.'

Kirsten pulled her shirt straight, then checked herself in the mirror. 'How long have I been out? Is there any news?'

'Not yet. Jack has gone back out. He's met with Martin and Shawn. Lee's joining them soon. Lots of local people are out searching and there are police everywhere.'

Kirsten sat back on the bed holding her stomach. The pain was awful. 'Where is he? I just want him home.'

Liz sat next to her. She pulled Kirsten into her chest. 'I know you do. We all do. Jack will find him. He won't stop until he does.'

'How could I have gone to sleep? I should be helping. I need to get out there.'

Liz stroked her head. 'It's probably best you're here, just in case George comes home. Stay here with me for now.'

Kirsten put her arms around Liz and sobbed.

Martin arrived at the park. He'd called Shawn to find out where they were. He was desperate to help with the search. Shawn was talking with the police and waved him over.

'Any word, Martin?' Shawn asked. He hoped Martin would have some inside information from within the police force.

He shook his head. 'I only know what you do. I'll keep asking though. Where's Jack?'

Shawn pointed towards the housing estate. 'He's going door to door. He asked me to cover down here and in the town centre. He's doing all right, but I feel he's going to blow at some point. This is too much. That boy is his life.'

After a brief silence Shawn asked, 'Where's Lee?'

'He told me he was going to help with the search. He may have even started elsewhere. I'll call him soon. Now, where are we searching and what can we do?'

'Let's go up to the town and ask about. Someone may have seen something.'

The police had advised Jack not to, but he was doing it anyway. He was knocking on every door, asking everyone if they'd seen his boy. He got the same answer at every house. Most of the time, they would ask Jack if they could help in any way or if they could join in the search.

Jack's phone rang non-stop, all friends and family concerned for George's welfare. The phone rang again. This time it was Pete.

'Jack, what's going on? What can I do?'

'There's not much you can do, other than search for him. I'm knocking on doors and the police are searching the local area.'

'I'm so sorry, son. You don't deserve this...we'll find him, Jack. We will find him. I'm picking David up soon and we'll help. You hang on in there.'

'Thanks, Pete.' Jack hung up and went to the next house on Park Way.

It was dark now. The police were still searching. Hundreds of locals were still helping. Torchlight lit up the park and local woodland. They were beating away heavy grass with sticks. George's name was being shouted all around Dorking. The police were looking at all the local CCTV that might help. Some shops were closed so they would need to check them when they re-opened in the morning.

Jack knocked on the last house in Park Way. The silver-haired lady was polite and concerned for Jack's son but had no information that could help. He thanked her, walked back down her path, and closed her gate, making sure it was safely shut. He looked around and could see volunteers knocking on the other doors. He didn't know where to go next.

His mind was playing out various scenarios of what might have happened to his son. The man. Did the man have George? What was he doing to him? Why would he want George? That vision of him making George walk with bloodied feet crippled him inside. His chest felt like someone was sitting on it. His breathing became short. He shook his head, but the thoughts were still there. He bent forward and put his hands on his knees. The orange streetlight was flickering above. A member of the public approached and asked if he was all right. He lied, saying he was fine. He stood up straight. He wanted to lash out. For years, lashing out was the way he'd dealt with difficult emotions. But he had to find George. He needed to dig in deep. He felt helpless and beaten but he wasn't going to stop.

Chapter 39

'Being evil is something that only humans are capable of.'
Jane Goodall

George could still hear the music, and he could also hear the man talking, but he couldn't hear what the man was saying. George was sobbing uncontrollably, desperately trying to cover up his own noise. Through his tears, he whispered to himself, 'Ten minutes. Ten minutes. I can get out in ten minutes.' He picked up the torch and aimed the light beam at his feet. His toes were hurting again. They were covered in dried blood. He quickly shone the torch away so that he didn't have to see it.

The car stopped. Seconds later so did the music. George covered his mouth. A door opened and then closed. The boy could hear a voice, a lady's voice. She sounded old but she must be too far away as he couldn't hear what she was saying, but he could hear the man.

'Yes, lovely day isn't it, Mrs Pounds.'

More muffled talking from the old lady.

'It has been a lovely summer, shame it has to end,' the man said in a funny posh voice. 'You have a good evening too. Good night, Mrs Pounds.'

There was a pause. The car door opened. The man was back in the car. He started talking to himself.

'Bloody woman. Lovely day, my arse. She don't care about the poxy weather. She's just a nosy bitch. It's about time she had a heart attack. She's about a hundred and ten. Just go and die already.'

George heard a loud knocking.

'What the f...' The man said a very bad word then there was a moment of silence,

then, 'Sorry, Mrs Pounds. I thought you'd gone in. You do move quick for an older lady.'

This time the lady was close enough for George to hear what she was saying.

'I just wanted to see if you were all right. You don't come outside much. We used to see you all the time,' she said.

'I'm very busy. I have to work. The bills won't pay themselves.' The man laughed. 'Anyway, I'd better carry on, got a busy day tomorrow. I need an early night. And I'm sure you have better things to do than look out for me. You take care.'

'Yes, I should get indoors. Norm needs his dinner. Got a nice piece of fish for him. Might do some mash with it. Chips are a bit heavy for Norm these days. Anyway, I'll let you go. Don't be a stranger.'

The lady must have gone. The man started talking again. 'She don't bloody stop. Bye-bye scary lady. Piss off indoors. I hope Norm chokes on a bone.'

The door opened, then closed. George heard a knock on the boot. 'Georgie, I'll be back soon. Don't make a sound. I'll get you out when that lady goes away. She's still watching. Once her curtains stop twitching, I'll be back.'

The sound of footsteps got weaker and then there was the sound of a door closing.

George thought about shouting, but what if the man was still out there. He would be mean to him again if he shouted. He covered his mouth and waited.

He was getting short of breath. It was so warm and humid. Sweat was running into his eyes and the stinging was becoming unbearable. The more he rubbed his eyes, the more they hurt. He blinked repeatedly, hoping it would help. He was desperate to get out, desperate to scream. He could hear the footsteps again. The boot opened. George was relieved. But then fear set in thinking about where he was going next.

The man was looking up and down the road whilst talking quietly. 'Leave the torch there. We're going to go in very quickly. Can you run fast, Georgie?'

He grabbed George by both arms and raised him out of the car. As George was set down his legs felt stiff, but he had to run. The man was pulling him. Once inside the house he slammed the door behind them.

'Stay there.'

George stood still, again looking down at his bloodied feet. He watched the man go to the window. He was looking across at Mrs Pound's house and muttering, 'That's right you silly old bag. Go to bed. And don't wake up. Ever.'

George looked at the man as he came back over to him. 'Are you talking to that lady that was out by your car?'

The man was surprised he'd heard him. 'Yes, I was, Georgie. I was just saying how I hope she gets a nice rest tonight. I'm just checking on my lovely neighbour. She's very old and she's always so busy.'

George stared up at the man. 'So... you are nice?'

He snapped back. 'Yes, of course I am. I'm not a monster.' He turned away from George and looked back out of the window. George could see enough to see the man was now smiling. He watched as he put the curtains straight. He then turned to George and clapped his hands together. 'Right, let's get you to your room.'

The man led George through the kitchen. The window blind was down. It was dark but he could see enough to know he didn't like this house. Lots of plates were stacked up on the work surface, dried old food stuck to them, some of which was a greeny-blue colour. George didn't like the smell, a mixture of wet dog and greasy food. He was then ushered back into the front room. It was stuffy and the furniture didn't match. There were trophies on a sideboard and photos on the wall, but George couldn't see who the people on the photos were from where he was. He thought he'd seen one of the pictures before. The man picked something up from the coffee table and turned back to George.

'Come on, nosy. Follow me.' He patted George's head.

George followed the man back to the kitchen. There was a door with a lock on it. As the man opened it, he gently pushed George forward. George looked down into pitch darkness. 'What's down there?' he asked as tried to back away.

The man stepped to the side, smiled and gestured for George to go on in, like he was welcoming him into a five -star hotel. 'It's your room. You'll like it. I've cleaned it for you. I've got a fan if you get hot. And I have a heater I can bring down if you are cold.'

'It's dark. I don't like it.'

The man's face went red and his eyes bulged. 'I'll turn the light on. You can leave it on if you like. But that sounds a bit babyish to me. Leaving a light on. Only a baby needs a light on.'

'I don't like the dark but I'm not a baby. I'm five.' He rubbed his eyes.

The man shrugged. 'If you say so. When I was five, I wasn't scared of the dark. Nothing scared me.'

George looked down at his feet. His bottom lip quivering, disappointed in himself that he wasn't as brave as the man.

The man moved on to the first step. 'I tell you what. I'll go down there first. You can follow me. How's that?'

'I'll try and do it.'

The man started walking down and George followed. He stepped on the first step, bent down for a better look. He didn't like it. He stepped back up.

'No, you don't.' The man reached up, took George's hand and led him down.

'Look at that. The bed is super comfy.'

George started crying. 'It's horrible. I don't like it. I want my mum.'

The man sucked in a huge breath. 'Your mum isn't here. It is not horrible. I think the problem is that you're a spoilt little brat. I bet your bedroom is massive, with toys everywhere and an owl flying round like you're Harry bloody Potter. Not all boys and girls have what you do. You need to be more grateful. I've gone to a lot of trouble making this room. I find your attitude very offensive.'

George was crying so hard his words wouldn't come out. His panicked breaths were getting worse. He ran but crashed straight into the man. 'No, you don't, Georgie.'

The man held him tight and bared his teeth. 'Don't do that again or you'll upset me.' He stared at George in silence.

'I've been nothing but nice to you. I haven't smacked you. I haven't really hurt you.' He pointed down at George's feet and continued, 'The blood on your toes is your mum's fault. If you had shoes on that wouldn't have happened. So, who is the bad guy? Me or your mummy?'

George didn't answer. He saw the bucket. He looked around his new surroundings but wherever he looked, his eyes went back to the bucket. The man noticed. 'Oh that. That's your toilet. Do whatever you need to in there. I'll empty it once a day.'

'No,' George said.

'No, not no. Yes. It's going to be yes.'

George pleaded with him. 'But I've never done that in a bucket. I use a toilet.'

'Well, it's all you have. You'll get used to it. If it smells, put the fan on. 'He pointed at the dusty old fan and walked over and pressed number three, the highest setting. It's powerful, isn't it? I like a fan. It helps me sleep. I have the same one in my bedroom.'

George backed up, inching away from the man. But there was nowhere to go. 'Not doing it. I won't,' he said.

'It's either in there or in your pants. You decide.' He pulled up his sleeves and shrugged. 'Now, no more talk of toilets. Right?' He walked over to the corner of the room and reached into a large black bin bag, pulling out a jumper. It was at least two sizes too big for George. 'Over here are some clothes, nothing fancy but they'll do. Charity shops don't sell much high-end stuff so it's this or nothing.' He threw the jumper back in the bag.

He clapped his hands together and gave George a thumbs up.

253

'You OK for a bit, Georgie? I'm going back upstairs. I'll get you some food later. Don't scream or shout. It'll do you no good. No one can hear outside. Plus, there are cameras in here. I can see everything you do.'

George looked around the ceiling. He couldn't see any video cameras, but he knew adults don't lie, so they must be up there somewhere.

The man went back up the stairs, two at a time, got to the top and slammed the door closed. George heard the key turn. He was alone with his own silence. He sat on the bed, pulled his knees up to his chest and buried his head. He cried uncontrollably and wished for his mum.

Chapter 40

'Do not pray for an easy life, pray for the strength to endure a difficult one.'
Bruce Lee

She had not used a public telephone in years. She would have been in her teens the last time and her memory of them was not a good one. Unhygienic and smelling of urine was what she expected but she was relieved that the one she chose was clean enough that she would not need her anti-bacterial wet wipes.

'Thank you for calling 101. We are connecting you to Surrey police. If you require an alternative force, press hash.' She then waited as her call rang again.

'Please note, calls are recorded for training and business monitoring purposes.'

Finally, a real-life person spoke. 'Good morning, you're through to Surrey police. How can I help?'

She took a deep breath. 'I'm calling regarding the disappearance of George Stone. I have some information that may help.'

The call handler was about to speak but she interrupted. 'I

don't want to give my name or talk to anyone else. I just want to give a name of someone the police should look into. David Huntley.'

'Madam, if you could just hold...'

'No. I don't want to hold. David Huntley. Have you got that written down?'

'Madam, the call is being recorded...'

'I'm sorry. I have to go.'

Roisin dropped the receiver as she tried to place it back in its rightful place. Grabbing two wet wipes, she then wiped everything she touched and ran back to her car.

Two weeks had passed. Two weeks of non-stop searching. The police were doing all they could. Thousands of man-hours had gone into finding George. Jack and Kirsten had attended a press conference which they both found an awful experience. The eyes of the world were upon them, some even wondering if they were involved. They were made aware that all too often the guilty party could be found within the very home the child lived in.

The police had questioned Jack and Kirsten, continuously asking the same questions but put differently. Did they know anyone who had any reason to hurt George? Could they think of anyone close to them that might hurt George? Where were they both when George went missing? The questions went on and on. Jack gave the police Roy Hardy's name as he was the only person he could think of who had anything against them. But he didn't believe Roy was capable of this.

The only other lead was an anonymous call about a David Huntley. One of the detectives visited him at his known address, a flat he shared with his father in Dorking. They asked him many questions and found out he was Jack's boxing trainer. But he had no criminal record and there was nothing on the premises to say he had anything to do with George's abduction. He was open and let them look around. He was extremely polite and offered to help in anyway the police needed him to. They didn't feel there was any more need to question him.

The press had the story on the front pages most days up until now. Some newspapers had moved the story to page four and five. Sky News and BBC News had seriously lowered the time they dedicated to it.

Jack and Kirsten were both being strong for one another, but in private they were breaking down and questioning if they could go on. They weren't going to bed. They would catch an hour here and there, scared they'd be asleep when any news came in. The support was still there from their parents and from Shawn and other close friends, but people's lives could not be put on hold forever.

The police provided a family liaison officer. They went through every detail, over and over. This was to allow the officer to establish the circumstances in which George went missing and how he and the family normally lived their day to day lives. They needed to gather all information on George. They asked so many questions. Was George on medication? Did he suffer with any mental health problems? Any behavioural issues? What was his lifestyle? His habits? Did he take anything with him when he went missing?

The police searched Jack's house from top to bottom and asked if they could take all the computers in the home, check all mobile phones, bank and credit card statements, and they wanted to see recent photos. They needed one in particular that most resembled George when he went missing. They also asked for George's toothbrush for DNA purposes. All of this was traumatic for the family. The police reminded them more than once that it was standard procedure.

Jack would walk for miles during the day, still searching locations he had already been to. As he walked through the town, he would watch people going about their normal lives. How could they? How could they still go to work, go to the gym or to the pub and enjoy themselves? His son was missing and there they were out socialising. He wanted to tear the world apart, scream in their faces.

Martin continued to ask within the police force if there was any information, the kind that could be held back from the parents and the press. But there was nothing. He rang Jack daily to let him know and promised him he would not stop until he found out more.

The boxing world had come together. They'd had a reward set up for any information that led to the arrest of anyone involved in George's disappearance. Jack's promoter, Chris, had helped start it. Fellow boxers couldn't wait to help. These men and women fought each other in the ring but away from the lights they were a family. Fifty thousand pounds had been put together so far.

The cellar door opened. George jumped up from his bed, sat upright, and waited.

The man came down the stairs, a big smile on his face, holding a newspaper. 'Morning Georgie. Fifty grand. That's what you're worth. What do you think of that? I could get me a nice car with that sort of money.'

George stayed silent.

'Well, what do you think?'

George did not look at him when he answered. 'I don't know.'

'Well, I do. I think you're worth more than that. Your dad has a lot more money than fifty Gs. Not very good, is it, Georgie? If you were my son, I'd give everything I had to get you back. Oh well, he's showing his true colours, isn't he?'

George didn't understand. His legs swung back and forth over the edge of the bed. He didn't feel very well, unsure if he was going to be sick. He didn't want to do it in front of the man. He knew he would get angry.

The man put his finger under George's chin and tipped it upwards. 'You're looking a bit peaky there, Georgie. You going to be sick?'

George shook his head to his left to escape the man's finger. 'No.'

'Well, if you are, do it in the bucket. You'll be OK. I'm going to make you some breakfast in a minute. That'll make you feel better.'

The man walked off, but after a few steps, he stopped and turned to face George. 'What was that, Georgie?'

'I didn't say anything.'

'Thank you, was what you were meant to say. Thank you for getting me some breakfast. So rude, I've told you before about that. And I know you don't want me to tell you like I did last time. I don't like hurting you. I'll make sure you change your manners before you leave here. Whatever it takes, I'll make sure.'

George's eyes shone with the onset of tears. A single tear fell on to his cheek and he bravely answered, 'Thank you.'

The man grinned. 'There you go. Not so hard.' Before he got to the top of the stairs, he stopped, bent down so he could see George and said, 'Crying is for babies and girls. I'll make a man of you as well. Right, coco pops it is. I'll be back in a minute.' He left the cellar and locked the door.

George lay back down and cried into his pillow.

That evening Shawn, Martin, and Lee arranged to get together and visit Jack at home.

Liz answered the door. She embraced them all and asked them to come through. Kirsten was sitting in the front room. She had one of George's blankets across her legs. It hadn't been washed since the day he went missing. She could still smell him and would regularly hold it to her nose. The TV was on Sky News. It was left on the news channels for most of the day, just in case there were any updates on George. Kirsten still had one eye on it as they walked in. She turned and said hello, accepted their hugs and thanked them for coming round. She did her best to be polite and pointed to the garden. 'He's in the games room. He hasn't said much today. I'm sure he would appreciate seeing you all.'

They approached the games room and could hear banging. Jack was hitting the punch bag. That wasn't all they could hear. As they got closer, they could hear him crying. They looked at each other, unsure if they should go in or leave him alone.

'I'll go in first,' Shawn said. He knocked, opened the door and showed his face. 'Jack, it's just us.'

Jack stopped. He didn't have boxing gloves on. He was hitting the bag bare-fisted. His back was to the door and Shawn could see blood on his knuckles. Jack didn't turn around when he replied, 'Give me a minute, yeah.'

'No problem, mate. When ya ready.' Shawn stepped back out and closed the door.

Jack wiped his hands on a towel and hid it, then wiped his face with his T-shirt and got a drink. Jack Daniels and Coke. He walked over to the door, pushed it open, then went to his chair and sat down.

The three friends went in. Jack noticed Shawn look at his drink and then raise his eyebrows at Martin. 'I haven't had much. You don't need to worry.'

'That's OK, mate. How ya doing? Silly question I know,' Lee said.

Jack stared at the floor. He didn't answer.

'Any updates? Have the police been around today?'

'The detective was here this morning. He didn't have anything new to tell us. He's been good. He's doing all he can. They all are. I told him about Roy. How we fell out and all that. They'd asked if anyone had anything against me or the family and he's the only one I could think of.'

'Something has to come up soon. Someone must know something,' Martin said.

Jack had heard the same comments from everyone around him. He would politely nod. 'Anyway, take a seat and get a drink if you want one.'

Shawn waved his keys. 'I'm driving, mate. Better not.'

Martin also declined.

'I'll have one with ya. I'll top yours up while I'm there,' Lee said, taking Jack's glass from him. He poured them both a drink and returned to his seat.

More silence for a minute, then Jack inched forward on his seat. 'What do you think he'll do to him?'

They all knew what Jack was asking and not one of them wanted to answer.

'Jack, we can't think of things of like that. Let's just find him.' Shawn patted Jack's knee.

'Don't bullshit me, Shawn. Not you, mate. I expect it from some people, but I need you to be honest with me.'

Shawn shrugged. 'Please, Jack, don't make me go there.'

'I'm not going to lash out. I'm not going to lose it. You can be honest. I've been thinking it over and over. Men take other people's kids for one reason, don't they?'

He looked up at Martin. 'C'mon Martin, you know. You must have some horrible cases to deal with. Paedophiles and all that. You can tell me. What happens to little boys?'

'Jack, don't.' Martin stood and put his arm around Jack's shoulder. 'Let's just find him. None of us are going to give up.'

Lee was watching Jack fall apart. He could see tears hitting the ground. 'We're with you, Jack. We'll make sure George comes back.'

Shawn got up and paced around the room, rubbing the back of his neck. 'I just wish we could do more. I feel so fucking helpless.'

Jack stood and went over to his mini bar. He downed his drink, poured another and stared out of the window.

'I'm going to kill him. You know that, don't you? Whoever he is. Whether George comes home or not, I'm going to kill him. I've been thinking about it.'

'No, Jack. Leave all this. Save all your energy, all your rage for finding George. You have to stay strong for Kirsten,' said Martin.

'I'll stay strong. I'll find my boy. I will. But I *will* kill whoever did this. Even if he goes to prison, you know I could make that happen. Do you know how many fans I have who would do it for me if I put the word out there?'

'I think Jack's right. I'm with him on this one,' said Lee. He held his drink up to Jack. 'But we find George first. Afterwards, we kill him. Whoever did this deserves to die.'

'Lee, don't say that. It's not helping,' said Shawn.

Jack shouted, 'Well, what fucking is?'

'I just... I just don't think now's the time to say all this. We don't know where George is...'

'Shawn, just stop. If he'd run off and got lost, we'd have found him. If he was dead, we'd have found him. We all fucking know some sick bastard has taken him. And if you don't want to say it, that's 'coz you're lying to yourself...and to me.'

'I'm not. I just want to focus on finding George. After we find him, we can talk about what we do next. I'm not saying no, I'm just saying... let's find your boy.' Shawn could feel himself about to cry. 'I'll ring you later, Jack. Maybe go indoors with Kirsten. She needs you.' He walked out, not looking at any of his friends.

Lee stood up. 'I'll go with him. See ya tomorrow.' He went over and hugged Jack, but he didn't move or return any affection.

Martin went to Jack and put his hand on his shoulder. 'Jack, I promise you I'll come to you first when I know something. I promise but I need you to do something for me.'

Jack looked up at Martin. 'What?'

'Don't mention any of what you said to anyone else. Don't talk to anyone else about killing anyone. Promise me?'

Jack nodded.

263

'I love you, mate. We're all with you, no matter what. We'll find him.' Martin walked outside, closing the door behind him. He managed to take a few steps before breaking down.

Chapter 41

'You cannot love a thing without wanting to fight for it.'
Gilbert K. Chesterton

'Hello Sir, I'd like to speak to Roy Hardy.'

Roy stood with no expression on his face. 'I'm Roy Hardy. How can I help?' He looked around to see if there was anyone watching.

'I'm detective Holland and this is detective Abbott. We'd like a chat. Can we come through? Is there a meeting room we can use?'

'You're not coming in this office full stop, I'm busy working, but I've got a few minutes. What's this about?' He folded his arms and moved so that he was blocking as much of the doorway as possible.

'Sir, it would be easier if we came in, or you can come down the station and have a chat. What would you prefer?' Detective Holland said.

'So, if I'm not under arrest, which I assume I'm not or you would have kicked my door down, then I don't have to do jack shit.' He unfolded his arms and stepped forward, pulling the door closed so that no one inside could hear them.

Sir, we're here to talk about George Stone. We're talking to everyone who knows or knew Jack and the family. We're just trying to...'

'Oh, I get it. Jack thinks I have his boy, does he? Yes, we fell out, but I haven't got his son. Tell him to accuse someone else. This is bullshit. I'm going back in.'

'Mr. Hardy, please. Jack hasn't accused you of anything. We're talking to everyone who knows Jack.'

'If you have a reason to arrest me, then do so. But if you haven't, then fuck off. I've got nothing to say to you.' Hardy's face was turning red. He went in and slammed the office door.

'Well, I thought that went rather well,' said Detective Holland.

Detective Abbot grinned. 'Me too. What a pleasant man.'

'Come on, let's go. We'll keep digging and the minute we get any evidence, I want him nicked.'

George knew he would be coming down soon. He could hear his footsteps upstairs in the kitchen. He couldn't wait for the bucket to be taken. It was horrible. George had learned to go at a certain time. If he went nearer to the time when the man was going to empty it, then he wouldn't have to put up with the smell for too long. The fan didn't help.

He heard the key in the lock. Natural light shone down as the door opened. 'Morning Georgie. It's a lovely day outside. Quite warm considering its mid-October. But I'm bringing that heater down, just in case. Night-time might get cold.'

'Thank you.' George was adapting fast. He knew he should say thank you to anything he was given. The man liked it.

'You're welcome, Georgie. Let me get rid of that bucket. It

266

smells a bit nasty down here.' He picked it up and headed back upstairs.

Five minutes later, he returned. He was whistling the tune from Snow White and The Seven Dwarfs, Whistle While You Work. He stopped when he got to the bottom step.

'Georgie, you've been here over a month now. You've been very good and become very polite. And you've stopped all that crying nonsense. How would you like to come upstairs sometimes? I don't mean all the time. I just mean to watch a bit of telly with me and use the big boy toilet before bedtime?'

'I'd like that... thank you.'

'You're welcome.' The man smiled. 'I knew you'd like it here, eventually. I'll take your clothes upstairs and wash them, give 'em a quick tumble dry and bring them back. Oh, you'll like that, I've got one of those nice smelling cloths you chuck in. Makes your clothes smell nice.' He grinned at George and waited for a smile in return, to show gratitude.

George had one more smile in him. He forced it out. The man went back up the stairs.

George waited for the door to close before collapsing in tears. He crawled under his bed covers and prayed for his mum and dad to find him. He thought about his Grandpa Ken and Nanny Liz and wondered why none of them were searching for him. They always gave him so much love. How could they leave him here with this man? What had he done that was so bad? He just didn't know. He desperately wanted to see his family so he could show them what a good boy he was and that he would never be naughty again.

The residents of Dorking had been holding candlelit vigils of hope once a week at the park, at the spot where George went missing. Thousands of concerned locals turned out. People were coming from all over the country to show their respect. There was another vigil planned that evening. Kirsten was getting ready to go. She knew Jack was in his games room. She would go and remind him soon. Liz and Ken were waiting for them in the front room.

She walked in unsure what Jack would be doing. She couldn't hear the heavy bag being hit. The TV wasn't on. She peered round the corner and could see him. He was sitting in his chair, asleep with a picture in his lap. An empty glass was resting in his hand, cushioned by his knee. Kirsten picked it up and took a sniff. She knew it was alcohol but was unsure which type, probably whiskey. Jack Daniels maybe. She placed the glass on the side and then went back to Jack and picked up the picture. Her stomach felt twisted inside. She was becoming breathless, her chest tight. The picture was from Jack's wallet. It was of Kirsten holding George in the hospital. He was about ten minutes old and had a grip on her finger, while she looked lovingly at Jack as he took the picture. She wanted to scream but instead she pressed her lips together and sat in silence next to Jack.

Jack moved but was still asleep. He had always suffered from bad dreams. Kirsten called them night terrors. He was becoming more agitated and speaking incoherently. She decided to watch him. She didn't wake him. In the past, she would normally rub his back or stroke his head until he woke. Not this time. She wanted to see his pain, to feel it. She didn't know why. Maybe she felt she deserved it. For days she had felt nothing, she just wanted to feel... something.

Jack never screamed out in his sleep. It was usually more of a painful high-pitched noise. She normally hated his discomfort. But not this time. His scream became loud. She knew she should wake him. He must be going through some version of hell in there, but she wanted to see more. She thought she did until the next frightening noise that bellowed out. His eyes opened. He looked crazed and dangerous. Kirsten was paralysed with fear. She couldn't stop it now. She felt like she might throw up. Jack's body shook with anger as he screamed out. Then silence. He sat, hands shaking, unable to make out what was going on.

Kirsten started to cry. She was trembling with fear at what had just happened. Moving in front of Jack, she knelt at his feet and held his hands. 'Jack, I'm sorry... I'm so sorry.'

He brushed the hair back from her face. It was wet from her tears. 'What's wrong? What's happened? Is it George?'

'I shouldn't have left him... I'm sorry.' She threw herself into his lap.

Jack held her tight. 'I don't blame you. I never will. Someone did this to us, to me.'

He kissed the top of her head. 'They would have found a way to get George on that day or another. They'd have found a way. They're to blame.'

'Jack, please can you promise me something.'

'Anything.'

'You won't hurt anyone. Even if you find who took George. Promise me.'

'You can't ask me that. That's not fair.' He gently moved Kirsten off his lap and walked away.

'Jack, we've lost George. I can't lose you as well. I want you back. I want my Jack back. Together we can do this. We love each other so much. You're everything to me.'

'I can't promise. I can't live knowing what someone has

done to my son.'

Kirsten screamed. 'He's our son. He's mine as well. Don't you think I'm angry, that I want revenge? Of course, I do. But if one of us goes to prison, that's our lives over. Me and you, over.'

Holding Kirsten by her arms, Jack shouted back at her. 'Our lives are over anyway without George.'

Kirsten stared at him. 'How dare you say that. Let go of me.'

'I'm sorry. Kirsten, I didn't mean it. Come here, please.'

'You did mean it, Jack.'

He pulled her into him, 'I'm sorry.'

Lost in each other they had forgotten about the vigil. Liz knocked on the door and walked in. She stopped when she saw Jack holding Kirsten. Jack looked at his mum and simply nodded. Liz knew to go without them. This was the first time they'd held each other in a long time. Jack leaned back, looked at Kirsten and realised the pain in her eyes mirrored his own.

Chapter 42

'You will not be punished for your anger; you will be punished by your anger.'

Fish fingers, chips, and beans. He put it on George's bed. 'Sorry I'm late with dinner tonight. I had to go out.'

George smiled. The man turned his head. He wasn't sure if George was really smiling or just keeping him happy by pretending.

'Aren't you curious where I've been. Would you like to know?'

George shrugged. He didn't know the right answer to give.

'I've been out holding a candle with all the others. They think you're dead. How does that make you feel?'

'But I'm not dead.'

The man laughed. 'I know. Imagine their faces when you go back.'

George's chest was pumping with excitement. 'Am I going back home?'

The man stopped laughing. 'Shit. OK, I can tell you. You will go back one day. Not yet. But soon.'

George smiled. This smile was real, and the man knew it.

'Thank you.'

'You've been very good, Georgie. You're a good boy – a real credit to your mum and dad. I'll take some credit too. You've got better while you've been here, more polite. You can now dress and wash, not perfect but you're improving. I'll tell you what, would you like to come upstairs and watch TV with me?'

George wasn't sure. Was he safer alone, or would it be nice to be out of the cellar? He answered the way he knew he should. 'Yes, please.'

'Right answer. Britain's Got Talent is on. My favourite. Do you like it?'

'I don't know it, 'George said.

'Who doesn't know Britain's Got Talent? Simon Cowell and the other ones. And they have all these stupid people doing stupid things. Some have got talent. Most don't. They're the ones I like. Britain's finest nutters, all under one roof.' He grinned. 'I'll set up the room and come and get you in ten minutes. This will be fun.' Another clap of the hands and he ran up the stairs with an extra skip.

Six weeks had passed. The media had moved on to other big stories – problems in the Royal family, Members of Parliament having affairs, overpaid footballers sleeping with prostitutes or the sex lives of B list celebrities were just some that were nearer to the front page than George being missing.

Chris had spoken with Sky Sports about Jack coming in for an interview. He thought it would be an excellent way to keep the story out there. He wanted to keep the public's attention, hoping if he did that it would keep the police interested. They would then carry on putting a lot of their resources into the search.

Jack agreed to the interview. The whole team agreed and those close to Jack wanted to go with him. They knew this would be a hard interview and Jack might find it too much. If they were there, they could step in if they needed to. Pete, David, Shawn, and Chris all went along.

Detective Holland agreed it was a good idea. He organised for someone to advise Jack on what to say. How to appeal for help and what information they could use on national television.

Jack agreed to do the interview live, straight after Sky Sports latest news. He sat in the studio, waiting nervously. He wasn't worried about how he looked. He didn't want any makeup or help in what he was wearing. He chose to wear his tracksuit; the usual one he'd wear with his name and his sponsors on the front.

The interviewer, Adam Bray, finished reading the latest news of the day, talking about which footballer was injured for Manchester City's big game, away at Liverpool that coming weekend. He then turned to the other camera and introduced Jack.

'Jack Stone, middleweight champion of the world, is with us. We always love Jack joining us here at Sky Sports but are extremely upset at the reason he is here with us today. The boxing world has been rocked by what's happened to one of their own. I'm so sorry to be meeting with Jack in these circumstances.' Adam turned to Jack. 'How are you, Jack?'

Jack looked straight down the camera. He'd been advised in the past that this was a big no-no in television, but he'd forgotten. He looked back at Adam. 'My life is on hold until I find my son.'

Adam nodded. 'Of course, and we all hope he's found soon. The whole country is praying for you and your family. You've bravely come in today and I know you want to ask the public for their on-going support and help.' Adam opened out his palm, pointing at camera two, it was time for Jack to talk to the camera and read out what he'd been told to say.

Jack froze. Pete was next to him. He put his arm on his shoulder. 'Go on, son. You've got this.'

Shawn was in the background behind the camera, with Chris and David.

Jack faced the camera. He had his notes in front of him. He looked down at the crumpled paper, then back up again.

'I'd like to thank everyone for their support. It means the world to my partner, Kirsten, and me. Without George, we are not a family. Five years ago, we were blessed with a beautiful son. He changed our lives for the better. We miss him so much. He's our world. His grandparents miss him so much. They want him home. We all do. If anyone out there has any information, it doesn't matter how small, please get in touch with the police.' Jack dropped his notes on to the desk.

Adam moved nervously. He could see Jack was getting upset. 'Jack, we understand there's a reward. We've been told all your friends and fellow fighters in boxing have been donating to this. I understand it currently stands at over one hundred thousand pounds. That's incredible. Truly great support. You're loved, Jack.'

Jack looked at Adam, then behind him where there was a big picture of himself with Kirsten and George on the screen. He faced forward. His shoulders felt heavy. He clicked his neck from side to side but couldn't release the tension.

Shawn touched Chris's shoulder. 'You might want to call

time on this. He's losing it.'

Chris waved Shawn off. 'He's doing well. Leave him a bit longer.'

David agreed. 'He's fine. The public will like this. It'll get their attention.'

'I know when he's losing it and I tell you, he's about to lose it,' Shawn said.

Jack scrunched up the piece of paper. He looked down the camera lens, then back at Adam. 'Are we still on camera two?'

'Yes. When you're ready, please continue. You're doing well. This must be so hard. Say what you want to say.'

Kirsten was home watching live with Liz and Ken. 'Go on, Jack, we love you.' Tears were falling as Liz held her hand. Ken shook his head in disbelief that his boy was having to go through this.

'He's getting angry, Liz. He's going to lose it,' Ken said.

'No, oh no, not on there,' cried Kirsten. 'This was an awful idea. Someone has to stop this. Call Shawn, now. I should have stopped him going. He's not ready.'

Jack gripped the table in front of him with one hand. The other made a fist. 'I've got one more thing to say. The reward is there. One hundred thousand pounds for any information that helps find my son. But...'

Pete interrupted. 'You've done a great job, Jack. Shall we go?'

Jack ignored him and stared hard at the camera, 'The police have been very honest with us. We know in these cases that not many children are found, not after this length of time. So, I'm prepared for the worst. The money stands for information that leads us to find George, but I'll also give whatever I have to find the man that took my boy. If you're watching, I promise

275

I will get to you one day. I'm going to kill you. Life without George is over for me anyway. I've nothing to lose.'

Adam tried to intervene. 'I'm sure this is desperately hard for you, and I know what you're saying is only out of anger. You might not mean it...'

Jack snapped. 'I mean it. Every word of it. I'm a man of my word, Adam. You know I am.'

Jack stared into the camera. 'You shouldn't have taken my boy. I watched my brother die. I didn't save him. I swore that no-one else I loved would die around me again. If George is gone, so am I, but before I go, I have to find whoever did this.'

'If George is still out there, I'm sure the public will do all they can to help,' Adam said.

Back at home, Kirsten screamed out at the television set. 'No, Jack. What have you done?'

Liz held her close. Ken put his head in his hands.

Jack was still looking directly into the camera. 'If my son is still alive, please, just let him go. I'll give you all the money, all my money, just take it, and you can go free. If it's money you want, you can have it. Leave George somewhere safe and I'll leave you alone. You have my word. But if you've already done something to my son, I'm going to kill you. I'll have to. I don't care how you die. I'll do it with these if I have to.' Jack lifted two fists to the camera. 'Or I'll pay someone else to do it. You're dead either way.'

Adam was angry that no one had taken the decision to take them off air. 'Enough, go to something else.' They listened and played in the adverts early.

Shawn stood in the background. 'What did I say? We should have bloody stopped him.'

Chris said nothing. There was nothing to say.

Jack sat in silence, staring down at the desk in front of him.

Pete stood up and put his hand on his shoulder. 'Come on, son. Let's go. Let's get you home to Kirsten. There's no more we can do here.'

Adam watched as Pete led Jack away.

Chapter 43

'If you want others to be happy, practice compassion. If you want to be happy, practice compassion.'

Dalai Lama

'Good morning Georgie, how are you today?' He stood over George, who was still in bed. He was awake and looking up at the man. The man was holding a handful of paper and colouring pens.

'I've bought these for you. I should have done this earlier. You've been with me for two months and I haven't let you do any schoolwork. I thought you could do some drawing and colouring. Does that sound fun?' The same vile grin appeared.

'Yes, please,' George said. If he didn't know what to say he knew please or thank you kept the man happy.

The man placed the paper and pens on the bedside table. 'Before I empty the bucket, I just want to check your temperature. You're very white, very pale, and I'm worried you have caught a bug.'

He sat on the edge of the bed, placed the digital device into George's ear and waited.

'39C. That's high, Georgie. I don't like that. You should

be under 38C. I'll get some medicine. Do you feel sick?' He stroked George's forehead.

'I just feel tired. Can I go back to sleep, please?' George rolled his body so that he was facing away from the man.

He didn't like George turning his back on him, but he held in his anger. 'You can sleep. But I want you to eat soon. I'll come back down with breakfast in an hour.' He stood up from the bed, picked up the bucket, and walked up the stairs. He stopped. 'Hey Georgie, you can come upstairs again tonight. I enjoy watching TV with you. It's nice to have a friend. You know what, I didn't know how we would get on, but I like you, Georgie. Your daddy was a silly boy yesterday. He got very, very angry at me. I knew he would. But I didn't know if he'd do it in public.' He laughed. 'It was very public. He did it live on TV. He went crazy in front of the whole world, offering money to anyone who would hurt me. What do you think about that, Georgie?'

George didn't answer.

The man carried on up the stairs but missed the final step. He stepped back to steady himself but fell backwards, landing on his back at the bottom of the stairs. The bucket tipped on him, covering him in urine and faeces. He was winded and panicked and couldn't get his breath. The back of his head had smashed against the concrete floor. He lay there dazed and semi-conscious. He tried to talk but couldn't.

George jumped up to the edge of the bed, frozen with fear. He fought back the tears. He didn't know what he should do. He looked at the man, writhing in pain, temporarily disabled and George made his decision. He could see the door was open, so he ran. He jumped over the man's legs and went straight up the stairs. The man watched George go but was unable to stop him. He blew air from his lips to get the urine away from going into his mouth. He knew it was over. It wasn't supposed to end like this. It wasn't the plan. He knew what he had to do next.

He lay there, dead still. He wasn't sure if he'd been unconscious or not. And, if he had been, he wasn't sure how long he'd been out of it. He was waiting until he felt he could move, first checking one leg at a time. He could move them both and was relieved he wasn't paralysed.

As he gave a huge sigh, a shadow appeared at the top of the stairs. He froze and focused his stare the best he could. He was shocked at what was in front of him.

George was walking back down the stairs holding the washing up bowl from the kitchen sink. The man watched in disbelief as George made his way carefully down the stairs. He stopped beside the man, placed the bowl on the floor, and took out the cloth. He rinsed it out into the bowl, then started wiping the man's face.

'I'm sorry you fell. I can clean you.' George said as he wiped his face. He then rinsed the cloth out again and wiped gently.

The man knew he could move by now, but he chose not to. Not since he was a boy, had he felt so looked after. Another human caring for him felt special. George wiped away the man's tears. The tears of a man crying, not from the pain of the fall but from the love he felt.

Chapter 44

*'There is a man who would give his life to keep a life you love
beside you.'*
Charles Dickens

Ten weeks had passed. For Jack and Kirsten, it felt like ten
years. Every day was the same. They'd get one or two hours of
sleep, rarely in the same bed. The rest of the time was spent
searching. They would talk to Detective Holland most days,
each day hoping for good news.

Jack's outburst on Sky Sports had not done too much
damage. Most of the public agreed with what he said. They
didn't blame a loving father showing that kind of anger. The
press spent another week making the most of the story but, in
the last few days, there had been hardly any reporting on it.

Chris and Shawn wanted to check on Jack. Most days, one
of Jack's friends would visit him. Today they needed to talk.

Kirsten let them in. Jack was in the dining room, waiting.
Lee was already there. He'd called in to check on the family.
They all talked about the search, asked how Jack was, and then
got down to why they were there.

'Jack, I know this sounds a bit insensitive, but the WBC has been in touch. They're not putting pressure on. They're fully behind you.'

Jack interrupted. 'But...'

Chris continued. 'They will need to arrange a fight for the title and know it's not going to be you, but they have to move on at some point. I'm sorry, Jack.'

Jack nodded. 'I understand. Tell them I'm retired anyway.'

Shawn and Chris looked at each other.

'You don't have to do that yet. Just say you're vacating the belt. There's no pressure to retire now, mate,' said Shawn.

'None of this means anything anymore. The belts, the money. Fuck it all. I'm out. What was it all for?'

'But they've said if and when you come back, you get a shot at the title. The WBC is on your side, Jack. They want to help you,' Chris said.

Lee had kept quiet. He sat upright to get Chris's attention. 'What if Jack did want to fight?'

'When? In the future?'

'No. Now. Soon. Jack's upset that the publicity is fading. He told me earlier. What if he fought, an easy one? Just so that it keeps George's name in the press?'

Shawn shook his head. 'No fucking way. He can't fight. He's out of shape and he won't want to train.' He looked across at Jack. 'You won't want to train, right?'

Jack shrugged his shoulders. 'I'd take a fight. Lee could be on to something. We could be in the press for over a month with the build-up to it. Fuck it, let's fight.'

Chris shook his head. 'No, Jack. The frame of mind you'll be in, you won't win.'

'I don't give a fuck about winning or losing. Fighting could help find George. Ring Pete and David and tell 'em we're fighting. I want to train.'

Lee smiled. He'd felt useless so far. It felt good having Jack agree with him.

Shawn looked at Lee with concern. 'This is your fault. Do you want him to lose? Lose what he's built?'

Jack snapped at Shawn. 'Don't blame Lee. It's the best idea I've heard in weeks. The media will love it. Just make the fight happen, please. Ring Carrick. He'll take it. I'll fight Carrick.'

Chris waved his hand. 'No, no, no. Not Carrick. You nearly killed each other last time. And you were in the form of your life. I can't let you do it.'

Jack placed his hand on Chris's shoulder. 'Chris, please. This is the way. It'll be a huge fight and I'll never ask you again for another favour. Please do this for me. And for George. And we need to make it happen soon.'

Shawn let out a sigh. 'Is this what you really want? Maybe speak to Kirsten first and see what she says.'

Kirsten had been listening from outside the room. She walked in and held Jack's hand. 'If Jack thinks this is the way, then I say yes. I trust him and know he's doing this for the right reasons.'

Chris walked over to the window, hands on his hips, weighing up what the right move was. Seconds passed before he turned around. 'I'll make it happen.' He left the room with his phone in his hand. He knew he was in for a busy few hours.

Later that evening, Jack's phone rang and vibrated on the table. He looked at the screen. It was James Carrick. He knew how James would feel about the fight. He needed to sell it to him.

'Jack, it's me, James. Is it a good time?'

'Yes, mate.'

What's going on, lad? We can't fight. I can't do it. I'll do anything but that to help you find your boy. Just tell me another way I can help. If you need more money, or press work, I'll do it. But I can't take this fight.'

'James, please. Please do this for me. If you don't fight me, the WBC will take the belt off me and who knows who they'll give it to? At least this way you get to fight for the title, and we get as much exposure for George as possible. It could be the difference between finding him and not.'

'Jack, I don't see how I can. You won't be up for it. Not like you were last time. I don't want you handing me the title. It's wrong. I just can't.'

'Please. It's just a fight. We've both had loads and this is one more. Twelve rounds and it's over. George could be out of my life forever. I can't face it. I just need to find him. I'll forever owe you.' Jack broke down and cried. He held the phone away, but his sobbing was loud enough for James to hear.

'And Kirsten? Is she OK with this?' Carrick asked.

'One hundred percent. She agrees it's the right move.'

'Then we'll do it. But it's got to be done right. Please fight me at your best. I can't take the title for free.'

'I promise, James. I'll give all I have.'

'And if there's anything I can do extra to promote the fight, I'm in. Let's find your boy. You take care. Hang on in there. I'm praying for George. We all are. I'll see you soon.'

Jack hung up and looked at Kirsten. 'He's in.'

Kirsten wrapped her arms around Jack, her head against his chest. 'You can't win this fight, can you? Be honest with me, please.'

Jack kissed the top of her head and replied. 'Not this one.'

Kirsten cried. 'I want to tell you not to take the fight, but I can't.'

Chapter 45

'We have two lives, and the second begins when we realise we only have one.'
Confucius

George sat on the sofa, his feet dangling over the edge. The man placed a tray of food on his lap.

'Be careful, Georgie, it's still a bit hot. Maybe let it cool down for five minutes.'

The curtains were pulled together and the only light was from the TV. The man smiled and sat down next to George who smiled too. His smiles were becoming real. He didn't need to force them out the way he once had.

The man placed his hand on George's forehead. 'Georgie, I'll check your temperature in the morning. You still feel warm to me. And you're very pale.' Since he'd first spotted George's high temperature, he had been giving him paracetamol, mixed in his drinks. He couldn't take him to see a doctor and was hoping it would pass.

'You've Been Framed. That'll do us nicely,' he said as he scrolled through the channels.

A toddler on a bike flew down a hill and crashed into a fence. The parents ran to pick him up. George and the man laughed out loud. The next clip was a fat lady sitting in a plastic seat, the legs gave out, and she hit the floor with a crash.

'I love this. People are so stupid, aren't they, Georgie?'

George was still laughing as he replied, 'Yes, they are.'

The man stopped laughing and put his knife and fork down. His eyes started to glisten. George could sense he wasn't happy. He wasn't nervous and didn't fear him anymore. Instead, he touched his arm and spoke. 'What's the matter?'

'I'm feeling a bit sad.'

'Why?'

'Because you have to go home soon. It's nearly over. I'm going to miss you. You're a special boy, Georgie. Don't ever let anyone tell you otherwise.'

'But when I go home, I can still see you, can't I?'

The man ruffled George's hair. 'I'm afraid that's not going to happen. I won't be here anymore.'

George became tearful. 'Why not? That's not fair.'

'The world isn't fair, Georgie. It's full of angry people. It's full of people who are sick in the head. They're not like us. Some people are full of hate. They can't control their temper.'

George sat there, thinking about what he was hearing. Another fat person just fell over, this time they were on a dance floor and they fell into a table knocking over all the food and drink. Laughter was coming from the TV but not from George, or the man.

'When will I go home?'

The man was watching the TV. He didn't look at George when he replied. 'When it's over. A few more weeks. It'll be over after your dad's next fight.'

George felt excited. He fidgeted about on the sofa. 'My dad is fighting again? Boxing?'

'He fights very soon. They've been talking about it on the news. Would you like to see it?'

George didn't hesitate. 'Yes, please.'

The man went through his planner for recorded programs. Lots of recorded fights were on there, all of Jack's. He found what he was looking for – the press conference for Stone v Carrick. He pressed play.

George shifted from side to side. 'There's my dad. There's my dad.'

The man watched the screen. 'He misses you. You know that, don't you?'

'I miss him too.' Despite George's excitement he had tears in his eyes.

'You'll see him soon. I promise.'

'Really? Thank you. And my mum?'

'Yes. You'll be back with them both soon. Georgie, there's something else I have to say. I want to say I'm sorry.'

George didn't reply. He didn't know why the man was sorry and didn't know what to say in case he upset him.

'I shouldn't have taken you the way I did. I was upset and I wanted him to pay. But now I feel different. It's too late to change what I did and too late to change how this will end. Whatever I do now, it has to end the same way. But I want you to know I'm sorry.'

George smiled but didn't understand. He wanted the man to stop talking so he pretended to be interested in the TV program. 'Look at the dog, he's dancing.'

'Georgie, I don't want you sleeping in the cellar anymore. You will still have to go in there when I go out and when I have to go to work, but at night, you can sleep in my room.'

George froze. He knew that sounded wrong. He looked down

at the ground, thinking about how to answer.

'Georgie, there was a time when I was a bad person. But I believe I've changed. I know what I was and that's not me anymore. You can have my bed on your own and I'll go on the floor. I tell you what, I'll sleep down here on the sofa.' He patted the cushion next to him. 'This is plenty good enough for me.'

The relief in George's expression was noticeable.

'I'm not strange, Georgie. I would never harm you. I'm your friend.'

They sat in silence, staring at the TV for a few minutes. A man cut a tree down with a chainsaw and it landed on his own house. His wife started shouting at him.

The man and George looked at each other and both laughed out loud.

Chapter 46

Six weeks to go until fight night and Jack had only been going
into the gym every other day. When he was there, he rarely
did more than an hour and never more than two. Pete and
David were becoming increasingly upset about his attitude.
They understood why, but they knew he couldn't beat Carrick
unless he was in top condition.

Today he was due in for some heavy sparring around midday.
It was 1pm before he arrived.

Pete looked at his watch as Jack got his sparring gear on.
'Jack, you need to be on time and start taking this seriously.
You can't do it this way. If you don't start training properly
soon, you'll get hurt in that ring. Carrick could kill you. You
know that, right?'

Jack carried on lacing up his boots. 'I'm doing my best, Pete.
I'm here, aren't I?'

'Yes, you're here, but you're not. Training like this will get
you killed on fight night. It's my job to protect you as well as

train you. I say we call it off. The fans will understand. Chris, Shawn, everyone involved, they won't blame you. We can do it another time. Come on, son, please. There has to be another way.'

Jack raised his voice. 'No, Pete. The fight is going ahead. I'll be fine. I'm here. Let's spar.' He jumped through the ropes and shouted at his opponent. 'C'mon, I'm here to fight. Start the timer, David. Three minutes, let's go,'

David shrugged. 'You're the boss.'

Jack came out like a bull with no guard up. His first punch thrown was a haymaker. It had bad intentions but fortunately missed his sparring partner, Mark.

'Come on, calm it down. It's just sparring,' Mark said as he circled Jack.

'Just fight,' Jack replied. He moved around, not throwing any punches for the next minute then he leaned back on the ropes and called Mark in closer. 'Come on, hit me. What you got?'

Mark came in and started hitting Jack but only at half power. He wasn't throwing anything hard, just jabs, and straight rights.

'Don't be a pussy. Fucking punch me properly,' Jack shouted. He unloaded on Mark hitting him with rights and lefts. Mark stumbled but wasn't giving up. He was getting angry. He let it all go. Fed up with Jack talking to him the way he was, he landed heavy blows, including uppercuts through the guard and body shots to the ribs. 'Fuck you, Jack,' he said as threw all he had.

'Time,' shouted David, waving his arms. 'This is over. Mark, get out of the ring. Jack, fuck off home. You can't come in here acting this way. We all know what you're going through but it's no excuse. Just go. They don't need to be around you when you're like this.' He indicated the other fighters in the gym. 'They all to look up to you, but you're a joke.'

'I'm a joke, am I?' Jack squared up to David. Their foreheads were touching.

David didn't back down. 'Gonna hit me again, are you? Like in Cardiff. Cheap shot me again like a coward. My dad doesn't deserve your shit. Come back when you want to train. In the meantime, fuck off out of my gym.'

Jack wanted a reason to hurt someone. He wanted an excuse to blow up. And here it was in front of him. He stepped back from David and took his gloves off, then his head guard. 'Your gym? This isn't yours. It's your dad's. You're nothing, David. You've achieved nothing and you never will without your dad.'

David's face went bright red. 'Maybe I haven't achieved much but I'll tell you something, Mr Bigtime. I wouldn't have lost a fucking son if I had one.'

No one said a word. Pete waited for Jack's reaction. 'Please don't touch him, Jack. Think of Kirsten, and of your boy. They need you.'

David smirked at Jack. 'Hurts coz it's true, isn't it?'

'Please don't, Jack. For me, don't do it. And, David, shut up,' Pete pleaded.

Jack felt something inside had changed. He didn't feel angry or violent. He didn't feel anything at all. His chin lowered to his chest. 'You win, David. I'm gonna go' He turned his back, climbed out of the ring and made his way to the exit.

Abruptly, he stopped, walked back to the ring and spoke to Mark. 'Sorry, Mark, I was out of order. You're a good lad. You don't deserve my bullshit.'

'No problem, Jack. I get it. I do,' Mark replied.

'Just go.' David shouted.

As Jack made his way out of the gym, Pete followed him. 'Please don't leave. Come and talk to me. I'll make us a drink. Come and sit down with me. I want to help you.'

Jack stared at him. 'You can't. I'm sorry. Sorry to all of you.' He gave one last look at the gym and at David and left.

Chapter 47

'My best dreams and worst nightmares have the same people in them.'
Philippos Syrigos

Media attention had grown in the build-up to the press conference and weigh in. Jack and his opponent, Carrick, had done all they could to keep the fight in the press. They'd also been in regular contact, meeting up on several occasions. More than once, James asked Jack if he wanted to go through with the fight. The answer was always the same. There was no way he would call the fight off. Only one reason would cause Jack to pull out: finding his boy.

Kirsten stayed at home in case there was any news about George. Liz moved in with her while Ken went with Jack and the team to Liverpool. The fight was in two days. The team travelled together, but David wasn't with them. Because of the fall out back at training, he'd chosen not to go to this fight. Pete told Jack he was happy with his son's decision. They didn't need any distractions. He knew Jack would be upset enough without David around antagonising him. This fight was going to be hard. Pete asked Mark to help out in the corner, alongside himself and Ken.

There was no party atmosphere on the way to Liverpool. Jack was sleeping. He'd hardly slept more than a couple of hours in a row in the twelve weeks George had been missing. Ken was at the back of the minibus talking fight plans with Pete.

'Pete, tell me honestly, can he win this fight?' Ken stared out of the window at the fields surrounding the M40 motorway. He already knew the answer.

'It's not going to happen, Ken. I watched Jack hit Carrick with everything last time and he wouldn't stop until he was nearly dead. Jack is half the fighter he was then. He hasn't trained properly, he's under-weight and he's tired. Jack at fifty percent would beat a decent average fighter but this is Carrick, Jack needed to be a hundred percent.'

Ken reached into his bag and got out his flask. Liz always sent him off with a flask of tea.

'I've got a spare cup. Fancy a brew?' He held the flask up to Pete.

Pete nodded.

They sat there holding their drinks, both deep in thought.

Ken blew on his tea to cool it down. 'It's not going to end well, is it? He took a sip and rested his head back on the seat. Again, he looked out of the window and asked another question he already knew the answer to. 'Can you pull him out?'

'I can't. He won't do it and he won't forgive me if I do. I've tried to convince him to postpone it... all we can do is save him from himself. I'm going to throw in the towel when it gets too much. That's the plan.'

'But we could say he has an injury or a sick bug. Tomorrow

morning, we could call it into Chris. No one would have to know.'

'Jack would know. He won't call it off. And if you or I do, I don't know what that would do to him. He wants the publicity to be huge from this. It's why he's doing it. He honestly believes this will find George. And he might be right. It's his son, his choice.'

Ken sipped his tea. 'But he's my son and I can't lose him.'

'I won't let that happen. I promise I'll stop the fight before it gets too bad.'

Ken put his hand on Pete's. 'I trust you. I just hope this works out the way Jack wants.'

Pete squeezed Ken's hand. 'I'll do everything I can. But after this fight, that'll be it. I'm not training Jack again. This will be our last. I won't put him through anymore of this and I won't watch him die. You're his Dad and I hope you don't mind me saying this, he's like a son to me. He changed my life, and I won't forget that.'

'I understand. I can't see Jack fighting again anyway. Without George he's empty. Even if George comes home, Jack isn't the same person he was. He'd never leave his boy's side again.'

They were silent for a few minutes, both in their own thoughts about how this would turn out.

Ken held the flask up again. 'Top-up?' He poured more tea for them both.

Jack woke after nearly three hours of sleep, the most he'd had in a long time. He sat upright and asked, 'Where are we?'

'M6, not long past Birmingham,' Shawn said. 'Under two hours to go, mate, unless we stop off. What do you reckon?'

'Nah, let's get there. Sort out the hotel and all that,' Jack said. He checked his phone in case there were any missed calls from Kirsten. Unfortunately, she had not called. All he could see was the picture on his phone screen of George, holding his WBC championship belt. He stared at it, his eyes filling with tears.

Shawn noticed his discomfort. 'I've spoken to Martin. He'll be heading to Liverpool tomorrow with Lee. They'll be there for the fight.'

'Thanks, mate.' Jack rubbed his eyes trying to clear any sign of tears.

'Have you thought about the weigh-in and all the interviews? Do you know what you are going to say?' Shawn asked.

Jack was still looking at the picture of George. Each time the phoned timed out, he would tap it to re-open. 'I'll just talk about George. There won't be any playing up to the cameras with Carrick. This fight is only about George.'

'You know the press are going to try and wind you up, right? They're going to criticise the fight going ahead. They'll say you're out of shape and shouldn't be there.'

'Fuck 'em.' Jack showed Shawn his phone. 'It's all about him. I don't care what they say. Good or bad, it makes the papers anyway. All I want is George's name in the press.'

Shawn looked at the picture. 'I miss him too, ya know. I love that boy. We'll find him. After the fight, we can get back to thinking of new ways to find him. He's still out there, I know it.'

Jack appreciated Shawn's kind words and nodded, but he wasn't so sure.

'You could win this fight. You know that don't you?'

'Shawn, we both know I can't. It doesn't matter. I'm happy

whatever happens. We've got the public's interest either way. Everyone is talking about George. The plan worked.'

'Your corner will throw in the towel if you're getting hurt, especially Pete. He's not going to let you suffer in there, and neither will I. I don't want you going mad at him. He cares about you. We all do.'

The driver braked hard. He'd been cut up by a white van. Jack and Shawn put their hands on the seat in front to steady themselves.

'Pete knows how I feel about that. I've asked him to remember that this is Carrick's night as well. He deserves this shot and he's been a good friend, true to his word. Carrick didn't have to take this fight. He's in a lose-lose situation. If he loses to me, people will say I wasn't fit, and he let me win. If he wins, they'll say he never beat the real me. I know that and so does he, but he took the fight anyway.'

'He's a good man. But this is a fight, a fight where you could get hurt.'

'Maybe, but it's my last one. After this one, it's over.'

Jack sat back. He wasn't interested in talking about it any further.

Shawn remembered the journey they'd been on together. Now it was nearly over. His chest hurt where there was a feeling of emptiness. Jack was making a decision that he understood and accepted, but by Jack making this decision, it affected them all.

Chapter 48

'Everything will be okay in the end. If it's not okay, it's not the end.'

The cellar door opened. George jumped up off his bed, wincing as he landed on his bad foot. He was dressed and ready. George only had to go down there if the man went out, that had been the rule for some time now. The door opening meant he was allowed upstairs, and he knew it. He liked it up there. He could eat and drink what he liked. He could use the bathroom, not the bucket. And he was excited because the man had promised he'd see his Mum and Dad soon, but only if he were good and didn't run away.

'Georgie, I've got it. You are going to love this.'

George smiled and tried to run up the stairs. His foot was hurting. He limped as fast as he could. 'Thank you. Can I have it now?'

'Before you do, can I check your foot? I'm still worried about the cut. You did that a long time ago and it should have healed by now.'

The man led George to the front room and examined the cut. There was green pus inside. He knew it was infected and it had spread but he couldn't take George to a hospital. He cleaned the wound and applied some cream.

'Keep your leg up on the stool, Georgie.'

'Can I have it now? Please,' George asked. He was excited.

The man ruffled his hair. 'Of course, you can. Close your eyes and hold your hands out.' The man gave George the gift. 'You can open your eyes now.'

A huge grin lit up George's face. 'That's the one. Just like in the book and on the film. I love it. Thank you.'

It was a Harry Potter Lego set. The Hogwarts Express Train set. It was made for eight-to-twelve-years-olds, but the man had promised to help him build it. They'd been reading Harry Potter recently and George loved it. Every night he asked the man to read it to him before bedtime. And if the man got tired, he would put the audio version on for George. The man would then drop off to sleep on the sofa.

George compared himself to Harry Potter in so many ways. He liked hearing the parts about Harry living under the stairs. It was like his life living in the cellar. He hoped one day he would have magic powers and that he could be a wizard and go to Hogwarts.

The man had purchased the toy locally from a little model shop in West Street, Dorking. He no longer cared for his original rules. If people noticed any unusual behaviour it did not bother him. He accepted that time was running out. It was all coming to an end soon. He wanted to make the most of the time he had left with George. And then, when the time was right, he could say his goodbyes. He no longer wanted anyone in pain, he had achieved what he wanted, and it hadn't given him what he thought it would. It was nearly time for him to end it.

Chapter 49

'We rise by lifting others.'
Robert Ingersoll

Most days, George was already waiting for the cellar door to open. He rarely fell asleep down there. At night-time, he had the comfort of a double bed. The man slept on the sofa downstairs and their nightly routine was that of most good parents and their child. George would have a bath after dinner at around 7 pm, then the man would read Harry Potter until George fell asleep.

The man opened the cellar door and waited excitedly for that sound of George as he ran up the stairs. But there was no sound. He poked his head in. 'Georgie, where are you? You need to come up here with me. Daddy's going to be on TV soon.'

He made his way down the stairs, crouching so he could see George's bed.

George was still asleep. 'Come on, Georgie, up you get.' George was facing the wall. The man walked over to the bed and sat down. He rocked George's shoulder gently. 'Come on, mate, wake up. Let's go and watch, Daddy.'

George stirred.

'Are you all right?' George's complexion worried the man.

Georgie rubbed his eyes. 'I'm tired. Can I stay asleep?'

The man placed his hand on George's forehead. 'What, down here! You're sweating loads.' He looked at the bedsheets. They were soaked. 'My God, Georgie, you're dripping wet.' He scooped him up. 'Come on, mate. Let's get you cleaned up and change your clothes. You can't stay like this.'

Once he was freshened up and in his clean clothes, the man laid George on the sofa. George was feeling weak. He didn't want to sit up.

'We can watch a Harry Potter film, any one of them you like, or we can carry on making the Lego train. What do you want to do Georgie?'

'Can I sleep a bit longer?'

The man stepped back and rubbed his forehead. He knew what he needed to do, and it would have to be soon. He pulled up the cover until it reached George's chest. 'You have a rest. I'll be here when you wake up.'

Once George was asleep, the man pulled the cover off as he wanted to check the injury. He knew all of George's symptoms were a result of the injured toe. The infection looked worse than before. George needed to see a doctor and he accepted that it had to be sooner rather than later. After putting the cover back, he stroked George's head and spoke softly. 'This will be over soon, Georgie. I've got to send you back. I've loved having you here. I'm glad we have become friends and I'll never forget you. I've never had a friend like you.' Tears were falling onto George's covers. 'I'm going to miss you. You're a special boy. Never let anyone tell you any different.'

Chapter 50

'Either I will find a way, or I will make one.'
Phillip Sidney

The final press conference was going to take place after the weigh in. James Carrick came out first. He wasn't waving his fist to the fans. He barely acknowledged them. He removed his tracksuit and trainers and stepped on to the scales. He weighed in at eleven stone five pounds. One pound under-weight. He stepped off the scales and put his clothes back on. He walked over to the side of the stage. It was now time for the champion to come out.

Jack entered the stage, stripped to his underwear, and weighed in. As he stood there, the crowd could see his physique had changed. The muscle definition wasn't the same. He was smaller around the shoulders and his face wasn't chiselled anymore, nothing like it should be on a normal fight weekend. Eleven stone dead. He was six-pounds under-weight. The crowd gasped when it was read out loud.

Carrick looked at his manager and nodded. 'For fuck's sake, look at him. This is wrong.' He left the stage, giving a small wave to the fans. They cheered but were disappointed. No hostility, no smack talk, and no face-off. They'd queued for hours to get in and this was their reward.

Backstage, Jack checked his phone. No call from home. 'Let's get these interviews knocked out quick,' he said to Shawn. The press was waiting, Sky Sports, BBC, ITV, Ring Magazine and Kugan Cassius from IFL TV. They all wanted to speak to him.

Jack did his best to convince the press that he was going to give his all in this fight. He wasn't lying. He was going to. But he couldn't admit to them that he was far from his best. He lied about his training and said he had a full camp as normal. He only told them what they needed to hear. He didn't talk about the fall out with David. When asked why David wasn't with them, Jack made an excuse that David was unwell and that the whole team missed him and, when asked for a prediction for the fight, he said he had no idea how it would end. He wasn't interested in making something up.

'C'mon Jack. You must have an idea. Will you knock him out?' The BBC reporter asked.

Jack stood up and raised his voice. 'Does it matter? It's going to be a fight. It'll end how it ends... and one of us will walk away with the belt. And then, after this fight...' he looked around the room, '...I'm done.'

On hearing this, reporters from all channels were shouting Jack's name, all shocked by his announcement.

'Wait, you're retiring after this fight?'

'Win or lose, I'm done.'

Shawn and Chris knew it was too late to stop the interview. This wasn't how they wanted Jack to announce his retirement.

The reporters continued with their questions. 'You're still relatively young. You're at your peak age and could have five or six more years at the top. A lot of fans will be disappointed today. Do you have a message for them?'

Jack thought for a moment before answering. 'I'd like to thank them all for following me on this journey. Without them, I wouldn't be here. I'm sorry if they're upset but they'll understand. We've had some amazing nights. The first Carrick fight and Madison Square Gardens were the highlight. I'm only doing this fight to help find my son, George. If they can continue to support me for one more night, I'll be forever grateful.'

Chapter 51

'Death is not the greatest loss in life. The greatest loss is what dies inside while still alive. Never Surrender.'

'Are you sure it's not anything more serious, sir? If his temperature's high, he should see the doctor,' said the assistant.

Moving in closer to the lady, he lowered his voice. 'He'll be OK. It's just a fever.' He looked behind him and then back at her. 'Hurry up.'

'Sir, if you'd like to go across to the reception at the doctors, they could book your son in for an appointment.'

His voice was rising as he hammered his fist on the counter. 'I don't need an appointment. This isn't my usual doctors' surgery. I just wanted to buy something from the chemist. I'll take some Calpol and go.'

'Sir, don't raise your voice at me. You can pay for the Calpol and go.'

He grabbed his purchase and left, bumping into an elderly lady. She turned and lifted her walking stick. 'You could say sorry.'

He didn't.

Chapter 52

'If you remember me. Then I don't care if everyone else forgets.'
Haruki Murakami

'Georgie, I've got some nice medicine. It'll help. And I'd like you to eat. I've got vegetable soup. My Mum used to make it for me when I felt unwell.'

George's eyes were barely open. He was pale but he managed to reply. 'Thank you. Your Mum sounds nice.'

The man looked across the room to a photo on the wall. 'She was lovely. I miss her every day.' He took down the photo to show George.

'Where is your Mum?'

'She died, Georgie.'

'That's sad. If my mummy died, I would be sad.'

'I get incredibly sad, Georgie. She was beautiful and I'm looking forward to being with her soon.'

George wasn't sure he'd heard the man correctly. He struggled but managed to raise his head from the pillow, wincing in pain as he sat up. 'But if your Mum is dead, you can't be with her.'

The man touched George's cheek. 'I will, Georgie. Far

away from here. Everybody ends up together one day. I once thought it would be a long time before I saw my Mum again, but things have changed. I'm happy with that. I'm ready.'

George poked his tongue into his cheek and looked at the man blankly. He lay back down. 'If you're happy, that's good. My nanny being happy is all that matters.'

The man stroked George's forehead. 'Not many people know when they are going to die. They don't have a choice. It's something most don't choose to know. I'm lucky. I know exactly when and I know how.'

George didn't answer. He was tired and closed his eyes.

'You go back to sleep, Georgie.'

The morning of the fight arrived. Jack had hardly slept. Kirsten had phoned several times during the night to tell him she needed him and was finding it hard not having him around.

He needed her more but didn't realise it.

It was 9 am and he was forcing down breakfast. He didn't want it but knew he needed fuel for the night. Pete had already insisted that Jack eat breakfast and lunch as, with no energy, it would be impossible to last a round against Carrick.

Jack sat in his hotel room with his head in his hands, wanting the day to be over so he could get back to Kirsten. He paced the room several times before sitting down in a chair in front of the window with a view out on to Victoria street. Shawn had chosen this hotel, The Shankly. Being a mad football fan, he wanted it the minute he saw the name. It honoured the memory of the legendary Liverpool FC manager, Bill Shankly. Jack had no interest in where he stayed. He wasn't here to build memories.

His phone rang. He jumped to it as normal but didn't recognise the number. He answered, praying it was good news about George.

'Hello, is that Jack?'

He recognised the voice immediately. 'Roisin.'

'I hope you don't mind me calling. I rang your home phone. Kirsten gave me your number.'

'Of course, I don't mind. How are you?'

Roisin didn't answer immediately, probably taken aback that he was asking how she was despite what he was going through. 'I'm sorry I haven't called before now. I didn't know if I should. Part of me hoped you would get in touch, that you might continue with our sessions. I'm worried about you.'

Jack peered out of the window. He noticed a few fight fans out on the street. They'd probably had a big night drinking in Liverpool and were looking for a hangover breakfast.

'Kirsten did ask me to call you, but I don't see anything changing how I feel. I don't think anything can make me feel better. I don't mean to be rude to you, Roisin. I just... I can't see how I can move on until George is found. Alive.'

'I understand that. I like to think I know you well enough for me to be honest.'

'You can be honest, of course, you can.'

'I know from our previous conversations that you think you don't have it in you to get through another loss. I'm scared you are going to give up on yourself.'

Jack stayed silent so Roisin continued. 'You don't have to give up, I can help you. We can do this and...'

Jack interrupted. 'Roisin, you're always honest with me. Can I be honest with you?'

'Yes, Jack. Always.'

'Roisin, I don't want to get through this if George is gone. It's over without him. I'm here all the time there's a chance George is alive.'

Roisin had never cried in front of a patient before. She tried to muffle the sound of her sniffing as the tears fell. 'Jack, please promise me you'll come and see me again, after the fight, once you are home. Please ring me and we can arrange an appointment. I can come to your house if you like. Kirsten could join us.'

Jack took another look out on to the street. 'Roisin, I'll never forget what you did for me. You saved my life. I wouldn't have met Kirsten; become a champion and I wouldn't have had George for a son. I don't regret having George. These last five years have been the best of my life. I'll always be grateful to you.'

'Jack, promise me, please.'

'Roisin, I can't...'

'Jack, Jack,' Roisin was pleading.

'Take care, Roisin.'

Jack ended the call. The picture of George holding Jack's WBC belt was there in front of him, again. Jack stared at it for a minute before the phone locked itself and George faded away.

Chapter 53

'The most dangerous creation of any society is the man who has nothing to lose.'
James Baldwin

The fight was taking place at Anfield, the home of Liverpool Football Club. Jack promised Carrick it would be there, and his promoter Chris had made it happen. There would be fifty thousand fans going crazy at this all-British world championship fight. Most would be from Liverpool hoping their man, Carrick, would become champion of the world. This would be the biggest fight in Liverpool since Tony Bellew won the World Cruiserweight title in 2016, at Goodison Park, the home of Everton football club.

Jack and his team arrived at the stadium at 7 pm. The undercard had started. Fans were piling in. The atmosphere was already electric, but there was tension in the air. The cameras were on Jack as he entered the stadium. This was being played to the crowd live on the big screens. His fans were cheering, and Carrick's fans were clapping respectfully. It was obvious they wanted Carrick to win but, because of Jack's situation and what he was going through, they were showing their respect. The people of Liverpool knew how it felt to grieve, to feel the loss and suffer at the hands of tragic events.

Jack was prepared for the cameras. It was all part of the event. He walked in alone, no thrills, just Jack in his tracksuit. His team, who had arrived in a separate vehicle, followed behind.

In the changing room, Jack was dressed, ready to go. With Pete's help he'd picked his gloves. The WBC allowed the fighters to choose from a selection of gloves. He chose the first two he held. Next, he'd need his wraps applied. Carrick's head trainer was allowed to sit in on this. He came in and watched. He spoke to Jack throughout. He was friendly and wished Jack luck. In the opposite changing room, Pete was witnessing Carrick's hands being wrapped. The same level of respect was being shown there. Before Pete left, he embraced Carrick and wished him well.

Carrick came out first. *You'll Never Walk Alone* started to play around the stadium. The whole crowd joined in singing the words. Jack could hear it from his dressing room and didn't react. It didn't affect the emotions he was feeling. He paced his changing room and decided against doing the normal pad work to warm up. Pete didn't push him. He knew tonight was all about Jack's mental state. He went along with what was right for tonight.

They got the nod to leave the dressing room. The stadium went into darkness. Carrick was in the ring, waiting with his team. The large screens within the stadium lit up. A picture of George Stone appeared, with a phone number at the bottom asking people to contact the police with any information of his whereabouts. The picture was the one Kirsten had taken in the park on the day George went missing. He was wearing his blue T-shirt with the Union Jack on it and was smiling at his mum.

The crowd was silent. Emotions were high. Some were crying. A ripple of a round of applause started. It grew louder and louder. The commentators for Sky Sports were speechless. They had never felt anything like this at a world title fight. It was special. It had sadness attached to the occasion, but the crowd came together, and the moment shared throughout the stadium would live in all their memories.

The cameraman was in front of Jack. Once the red light appeared on top of the camera, they should start walking out. Jack had decided, along with Shawn, that he didn't want his usual entrance music. He didn't want it alongside George's picture. The words would be inappropriate. They decided on something different. Something soft but powerful. Jack asked Pete to help choose because, with his knowledge of classical music, he trusted him to get it right. Pete had decided on a song within seconds, one he used to play at home with his wife. When she had passed away, he'd had this piece played at her funeral. *Spiegel im Speigel*, by Arvo Pärt performed by Tasmin Little and Martin Roscoe. The red light was on. The music started. Jack should have started walking. His eyes were closed. The whole stadium was watching him on one of the big screens. He didn't move. The other big screen still displayed George's photo. The beautiful, powerful piece of music was all that could be heard. The commentators were shaking their heads in disbelief. Tony Bellew was ringside as part of the commentary team. He leaned over to his fellow commentator and said, 'Jack shouldn't be here. He shouldn't have to fight under circumstances like this.'

A single tear ran down Jack's face. No-one behind the camera told him to hurry. They left him alone but continued to film. Jack still had his eyes closed and his chin against his chest. Behind him, Ken was in tears being consoled by Chris. In the ring, Carrick closed his eyes in solidarity with his opponent.

The song played for a full eight minutes and sixteen seconds. The crowd stayed silent throughout. The only sound was that of some fans crying.

The song finished and Jack raised his head, opened his eyes and walked towards the camera. There was no music. No noise. He walked into a silent stadium.

Suddenly, the fans started applauding. Everyone joined in. And, in true football fan style, a chant rang out. 'George, George, George.' The name echoed around the arena.

Jack gave a nod in appreciation.

He made it to the ring, climbed through the ropes and went to the four corners of the ring. In each he clapped his gloves together, thanking every person in the stadium for their support.

The man had the television paused. He was making their dinner and preparing George's medicine. He said George could stay up as it was a special night. His daddy was boxing, and they would stay up late to watch.

George was lying on the sofa. He was doing his best to stay awake, but he still felt weak. He'd tried to have a bath, but the water made his skin sting. He cried out loud, so the man allowed him to miss bath time.

The man came in with the tray of food, nuggets and chips and a large glass of cola. 'Here we go, Georgie, dinner is served.'

George didn't sit up. He felt too weak. 'Come on, Georgie. Look at this. It's your favourite. I'll put it next to you and then, when you're ready, you can jump in.' He placed the dinner down and stroked George's head.

'Right, I'll grab mine, then we can watch the fight. Come on, Jacky boy.' He skipped to the kitchen, picked up his food and returned to the sofa. He pressed play on the controller. 'This better be good, Jacky, boy. I've paid twenty quid for this.' The pay per view buys on the fight were huge and not just because of it being a big fight in British boxing history. It also had the added attention from non-boxing fans, watching because of what had happened to George.

The man watched Carrick come out. 'You're going to get hurt again, Carrick, just like last time,' he said, looking across at George, hoping he'd join in. But he was asleep.

Then the picture of him was on the screen. The man stared at it and was glad George was asleep. He didn't want him to see it.

Jack stood there with the music playing. The camera was panning from Jack to George, and then to fans in the crowd, the ones who were crying. The man put down his knife and fork. He moved the tray to one side. He started breathing heavily, his chest rising and falling. 'It wasn't supposed to be like this. I didn't want this.' He picked up his tray and threw it at the wall.

George woke with a start. 'What's happening?' he said.

'Nothing to worry about, Georgie. I dropped my food. You go back to sleep.'

George rolled over and faced the cushions. He was asleep immediately.

315

The man sat down, turning back to the screen. Jack was crying. The camera caught it all. 'Painful, isn't it, Jack? You've learned your lesson, that having someone take away what you love is wrong. You know that now. It's over. But your pain will end tomorrow.'

The ring announcer introduced the two fighters. The stadium all stood to listen respectfully to God Save The Queen.

The ref called the fighters to the middle of the ring. There was no staring each other out, no gamesmanship. Both fighters looked at the ground during the referee's instructions. They touched gloves and went back to their respective corners.

Pete gave his final instructions to Jack. 'Keep moving. Don't stand in front of Carrick. Spend the first round getting comfortable, finding your range.'

Jack nodded, then winked at his dad to reassure him all was well. He could see the concern on his father's face.

The bell rang and the fighters met in the middle once again. Carrick landed first, a double jab. Jack had his gloves up. He wasn't throwing yet. Carrick hit him with a good combination, left jab, right cross. Jack's nose started bleeding. He touched it several times as it was starting to bother him, but he moved around the ring trying to stay out of Carrick's range.

'Throw something, Jack. Use your jab.' Pete called out.

Jack ignored the instruction and carried on taking more punishment. The bell sounded for the end of the round.

Carrick went back to his corner. 'This isn't a fight. He doesn't want to be here,' he told his cornermen. He sipped some water and shook his head.

Pete sat Jack down on his stall. 'Have a drink. What's going on, son? You feel OK?'

Jack nodded.

'Then throw a punch, start with the jab. I'm not sitting back to watch you get beat up for twelve rounds. I'll call it off. Fight back or it's over.'

'Please, Jack. Listen to Pete,' pleaded Ken.

'Don't worry,' was Jack's reply.

Round two started. Carrick hit Jack with several jabs. He could have unloaded his power shot if he wanted to. Jack was there to be hit but Carrick's empathy for Jack wouldn't allow him to do so. Jack threw his first shot. It landed but had no effect. As Carrick came in, Jack covered up.

'Fight back,' Carrick shouted at him.

Jack didn't respond. He moved slowly around the ring. Carrick hit him hard with a body shot and an uppercut. Jack took it and stood still. It hurt but he didn't care. Carrick backed off. He looked at the ref, but the ref ordered him to fight on. Carrick unloaded in anger with six unanswered shots that landed on Jack. He was hurt but not going down. He wouldn't quit. Carrick backed off again. The bell sounded. As they parted, Carrick shouted at Jack, 'Fucking fight back.'

Carrick was crying in anger, shouting at his cornermen. 'I can't fucking do this. He's not fighting back. He doesn't want to be here and neither do I.'

It wasn't what his cornermen wanted to hear. 'Fuck that. Just put him away. This is the world title. *Your* world title. You deserve this. Finish the fight.'

Back in Jack's corner, Pete was begging. 'Son, I can't watch this. I won't see you get killed. One more round and I'm calling it.'

'Don't you do it. Don't stop this fight.'

'Then fight back, Jack.'

317

'You want me to fight. I'll fucking fight.' Jack took in the crowd and the giant screens still flashing George's picture up. Rage built up inside. His every muscle tensed as he prepared for round three. It wasn't Carrick opposite him. It was the bastard who took George.

He ran at Carrick throwing wild powerful shots. It was like a street fight, untidy, and violent. Carrick clung on to Jack and talked to him while in the clinch. 'Calm down. Just box.'

'Fuck you.' Jack pushed Carrick off and started throwing haymakers, wild hooks and overhand rights. And then shots to the body. Most of the punches were hitting Carrick's arms and gloves and Jack was now breathing hard. All he could see was George's face. Fuelled with rage, he threw punch after punch until he was unable to lift his arms any longer. He was so tired. The anger led to tears. The violence to despair. He was losing himself. The shots temporarily hurt Carrick, but he was not in trouble. He held on to Jack and talked to him again. 'Enough, Jack. Just box.'

The round ended. Jack went back exhausted, nothing left in him. He won the round but lost himself. His arms felt heavy, his chest rising and falling as he gasped for air. He collapsed on his stool and swallowed the water Pete poured into his mouth.

'Jack, I'm pulling you out. Your dad agrees. We can't watch this,' Pete said.

'Don't.' Jack had hardly enough breath to speak. 'Don't do it.'

Carrick's corner begged him to finish the fight. 'He's finished. Look at him. He can't breathe. Finish this fight and you're the new world champion.'

The bell sounded. Jack rose and Pete took away the stool.

Once Pete was out of the ring, he picked up the white towel. He wanted it there, ready to throw it in. Ken looked at him and nodded in agreement. 'Do it, Pete. Throw it.'

Carrick came forward and hit Jack with a right hand that sent him crashing to the floor. His gumshield came out. Jack was on his knees, trying to pick it up. The ref retrieved it for him and gave it to his corner to wash before he continued with his eight count.

At the count of six, Jack was on his feet. He saw Pete with the towel and shouted, 'Don't.' The ref called for the gumshield. Mark had washed it and handed it over. The ref put it back in Jack's mouth and asked him if he could go on. Jack said yes, and then demonstrated to the ref that he could walk unaided.

Carrick was in a neutral corner, shaking his head in disbelief that Jack was going to carry on. He raised his arms in the air questioning the ref's decision for the fight to continue.

Jack walked forward, gloves up, and looked out into the crowd. He could see George's picture again. He felt dizzy. White noise filled his head as he reached his arm out. He was reaching for the screens. For George. He stood still. His will to live had left him. He was drowning in his grief. His body felt leaden. He had nothing left to offer.

Carrick stayed where he was. The ref waved him on. 'Fight,' he ordered.

But Carrick wouldn't. 'No more,' he said. 'It's over.'

Jack dropped to his knees, broken but still reaching out with one arm towards George's picture. His other glove touched the canvas. The ref started to count. Carrick was about to become a world champion. The fight was over. All Carrick had to do was stay on his feet.

The ref was at four, then five, then six. Carrick walked over

319

to stand by Jack. He went down to his knee and touched the canvas with his glove just as the ref was at nine.

Carrick's corner were screaming at him. 'What the fuck are you doing?'

The ref didn't initially know what to do. He looked outside the ring for guidance. He'd never had this before. He had to make a decision. He waved his arms high above his head. The fight was over. He shouted. 'It's over. No contest.'

Carrick held Jack as he broke down. Resting his head on Carrick's chest, he repeated George's name over and over, while Carrick looked to Jack's corner in despair.

Chapter 54

'The battle between good and evil is endlessly fascinating because we are participants every day.'
Stephen King

George woke up. He was thirsty. He sat up. The man was waking up too.

'You OK, Georgie?' he asked.

'Can I have a drink, please?'

The man got to his feet. 'Of course. I'll get some water and orange juice. The vitamin C will give you some energy. We'll give you some medicine as well.'

He was in the kitchen preparing George's drinks when he heard George say something.

He went back into the room. 'What did you say, Georgie?'

George felt dizzy and weak. He rubbed his eyes. 'Did my dad win?'

The man didn't answer. He looked at the TV, which was off. He was buying time while he worked out what to say.

He smiled at George. 'Of course he did. He's still champion of the world. No one will beat your dad.'

George lay back down and closed his eyes. He looked happy.

Kirsten and Liz were in the front room drinking tea, both waiting by their phones. Neither had received a call from Jack. Kirsten looked again at the time on her phone. 'The fight should be finished, even if went twelve rounds. It should be over. Maybe they're having lots of interviews.'

Liz agreed. 'They could be. We could check. Would you like me to put Sky Sports on?'

'No, I want to hear from Jack.'

'I know,' said Liz. 'He'll call soon. And, if he hasn't won, it's all right. He knew this was going to be tough.'

'He couldn't win this one. He knew he wasn't going to. He took the fight for one reason. He's done that now.' Kirsten opened her phone and looked at her pictures.

Liz's phone rang. Kirsten jumped up. 'Who is it?'

'It's Ken,' Liz said, before she pressed her phone to answer.

Kirsten couldn't hear what was being said but she could see the effect of Ken's words as Liz slowly fell apart in front of her. 'Liz, tell me. Please.'

Liz sat down and let it sink in. She still had not said a word to Ken. She held her phone out to Kirsten. 'I can't. Sorry, Kirsten.'

Kirsten took the phone. Liz sat back in silence.

'Ken, tell me he's OK.'

'Physically, he's fine. The fight didn't go on long. But...'

'But what?' Kirsten asked.

'He's not well. Mentally he's struggling. Like he was years ago. He's hardly talking. We're not leaving his side. He won't go to the hospital, so we'll get him home. He needs you, Kirsten. Other than George, yours is the only other name he's saying.'

'Ken, I'll look after him. Please bring him home.'

'We're coming now. Should be home in four or five hours.'

Liz and Kirsten sat in silence. Moments later, Liz looked at Kirsten with a puzzled expression. 'Did he lose?'

'I didn't ask.'

Chapter 55

The fight and all its tragedy were worldwide news. It was shown on most news channels and made the front pages of the big newspapers. Due to the publicity, the police were expecting a spike in calls, hopefully giving vital information on George. They had the usual time-wasting calls coming in, people trying their luck, hoping to get a piece of the reward, or simply wanting a bit of attention. But they had one call in particular they wanted to follow up as soon as possible.

Detective Holland was advised of it and was keen to investigate but couldn't do anything until the shops were open the next day. Knowing Martin was a Dorking resident and close friends with Jack and his family, he contacted him and arranged to meet him at the chemist's the following morning at ten.

Martin didn't let Jack know. He wanted to find out if the new lead was something substantial first.

He arrived early, parked up and found the right amount of change for the parking meter, making sure to use up as many five pence coins as possible. He then waited for his superior. At 10am exactly, Detective Holland arrived.

'Good morning, Sir.'

'Good morning, Martin. Thank you for meeting me. I know it's your day off, but I thought with your local knowledge you might be able to help.'

'Of course, Sir. I'm pleased you asked. Do we know if the CCTV is any good?'

'No idea. It could just be another waste of time. We've been through hundreds of hours of it from around this town, none of it any good.'

Once inside the chemist's they asked to see Ms Lorraine Bates. It was she who had called the police, absolutely convinced she had found the man they all wanted.

She came out from the back of the premises, a prescription in hand for her customer. 'Mrs. Witts, can you please confirm your address for me.'

As Mrs. Witts left, Lorraine turned her attention to her next customers. 'Sorry to keep you waiting. How can I help?'

The detective knew he had the right person from her name badge. 'I'm Detective Holland. This is PC Parker. Thank you for calling in with your information. We have a few questions, and we'd like to check your CCTV if that's possible.'

She smiled awkwardly; nervous excitement clear in her voice. 'No problem at all. We can talk out the back in the storage room. The CCTV screen is in there.' She pointed behind the counter then called over a fellow member of staff to cover while she helped the officers.

She made three cups of tea and they sat, saying nothing, while the Detective got out his notebook and pen. Martin was chewing at his fingernails. He was possibly about to see the person who had some involvement with George going missing. He was also anxious to impress the Detective.

'Miss Bates, you said in your phone call that a man was acting strangely. Can you elaborate, please?' Holland asked.

She put her cup down and clasped her hands in her lap. 'Well, it was unusual from the start.' She took a sip of tea, placed the cup back on the table and continued. 'Normally, when someone is concerned about their child, they appreciate our advice. But this man, he was rude and desperate to get out. He just wouldn't listen.'

Detective Holland looked up from his notepad. He'd spoken to so many people over the last few months who had a feeling they knew who'd taken George. This sounded like it was just another. 'Rude? How was he rude?'

'Listen, I know when someone's up to no good. I've two grown-up sons and I've seen it all. The man raised his voice. He was aggressive and had that look, like he could turn nasty, just like that. 'She clicked her fingers. 'I was scared, and I wanted him out of here. The last time I felt that way was when I was married, and I kicked him out twenty years ago.'

Martin didn't want to grin, but he could feel it was coming. He swigged his tea instead.

She carried on. 'People don't realise how important my job is. I give medicine of all kinds to people of all ages. It would be serious if I got it wrong. Being a pharmacist is a complex job and I won't be told by anyone to give them something they shouldn't have. I told him to take his son to the doctor. But he wasn't interested.'

Holland made a note before replying. 'I'm sure your job is very important.'

She smiled in agreement. 'If someone comes in and tells

me their child has a high temperature, that they're not eating and they're tired all the time, it worries me. And that's what he told me. And it worries me more if they say the child has an injury. If they have an infected cut anywhere. It could be the cause. They could need antibiotics. It could be serious.'

Holland was all attention. 'Lorraine, did you say the child had a cut, an infected cut?'

'Yes. On his foot is what the man told me.'

Martin took another swig of tea and then glanced at Miss Bates.

'What else did he say about his son?' Holland asked.

'He told me to hurry up. He was rude and bossy. Several times I suggested that he take his son to the doctor, that he needed medical attention. He got all snappy with me. Stupid bloody man. Can I just say, even if he hasn't done this awful crime, I still think you guys should have a word with him.'

Martin and Holland nodded at the same time.

This time Martin spoke. 'I think you're right, Ms Bates. He sounds very unpleasant. If that is all that was said, please could we see the CCTV of that day.' He hoped he hadn't overstepped the mark by talking when he did.

Detective Holland put his pen and pad down. 'I think you're right. Let's have a look.'

'Of course,' said Lorraine. 'I've prepared it for you. It's set to where you can see him. He's got a cap on, a black one with initials on it, but you can still see his face.'

Martin remembered the reports of the man last seen with George. He had a cap on. A black one. A New York Yankees cap.

Lorraine pressed play. 'Here we go. I look so different on here. I'm sure I'm slimmer than that in real life.'

327

Martin stared at the screen. His hand went to his mouth. It couldn't be. His stomach knotted and he felt sick. He inched closer on his seat. So did Holland. They watched the man's every move. He hadn't yet looked directly at the camera, but Martin knew. They could see he was gesturing at Lorraine. He was very animated. And then three minutes in, there it was. He looked directly at the camera. Martin felt his stomach twist. He couldn't tell the Detective. He knew he should, but he didn't.

'Pause it there,' said Holland.

Lorraine pressed pause. 'You know him, don't you?' Holland asked Martin.

Martin gave his best poker expression but could feel his face burning. 'I'm not sure. He looks familiar but I wouldn't know his name.'

'PC Parker, if you know who that is you need to tell me his name.'

'Honestly, I don't know but he does look familiar. If it comes to me, I'll tell you.'

'Did I do good?' Lorraine asked. 'Has he got that boy? Little George? That's him, isn't it?'

'We're not sure, Miss Bates. You've been extremely helpful though. Please can I take a copy of the CCTV? We'll be back in touch if we need you further.'

The three of them exited the storage room. Holland and Martin turned to say thank you, but Lorraine spoke first. Her smile had disappeared. 'Listen. I don't want a penny of that reward. That's not why I'm talking to you. It's not why I called you. I have sons. I just want that bastard caught. I know that's him on that video. I saw your faces in there. You get him and get that boy back to his Mum and Dad.'

'Thank you, Ms Bates.' Holland shook her hand.

They walked in silence back to their cars. Martin's vehicle was the nearest. He opened the car door, but Holland closed it before he could get in.

'Martin, don't do anything stupid. Let's do this right. I'll arrange for this CCTV to be put out there. Someone will name him by the morning, but I need to plan this right and catch this bastard. I want George home, alive.'

Martin snapped back. 'What if George needs us now, tonight? He could die tonight. If we had a name, would you go in now, straight away?'

'We have to be sure the boy is where we think he is. We can't just storm in. If we do it wrong and George isn't there, he might never tell us where he is.'

Martin shook his head., 'You heard her in there. George is sick. Another day and he could be dead. Another day and that fucking monster might do God knows what to him.'

'You need to calm down. I've been doing this shit for twenty years. You've been a copper for twenty fucking minutes. Don't fuck me over on this. If you go against me, I'll have your job and put you away.'

Martin was not intimidated. 'I know you will. Now get out of my way.' He reached for the door handle of his car. Holland moved away.

There was no one to help Martin make his decision. He knew what was resting on how he played it. If he told Jack who was on that CCTV, it was over. Over in a way that was out of his control. He had to do what he thought was the right thing. This decision could end his career but if he played it safe and left it to the detective, it could boost his career. Holland would be grateful. But Jack came first.

No other cars were there when Martin pulled up outside Jack's house. No other family members, no police, no family liaison officers. It was clear to go in.

Kirsten answered the door. 'Hi Martin.' Her eyes, usually so beautiful and friendly, were bloodshot and tired. 'Jack's upstairs. He might be asleep. I'm not sure it's a good time. He's hardly said a word since he got back from Liverpool.'

'I understand. But... do you mind if I try? I want to ask him a few questions, run a few ideas by him, just in case we've overlooked something. It might help him open up.'

Kirsten did not want to offend Martin. Jack had told her many times she was too kind. A gift and a curse, he would say. She stepped back and opened the door wide. 'Please be careful what you say to him.'

'Of course. If he's not up to it I'll leave, I promise.' He hugged Kirsten, removed his shoes, and went upstairs. He left it a few seconds after he'd knocked Jack's bedroom door and then looked in. 'You OK, mate?'

No reply. Jack was lying on the bed, facing away from Martin.

'Jack, it's me, Martin. Can I have a word?'

Again, no answer. Martin walked around the bed and sat on the only seat available, Kirsten's make up chair.

He could see Jack's eyes were open. 'All right, mate. I wanted to know if you fancy coming out for a drive. And a bit of a chat. Might be good for you, I'm worried about you. We all are.'

Jack moved but still didn't speak.

'I've got some ideas but need to ask you some questions first. Would you come out with me?' Martin had no intention of giving up.

Jack rolled on to his back and stared at the ceiling. 'I can't.

There's nothing we can do. It's over.'

Martin leaned forward, his elbows on his knees. 'I think you should come with me. Trust me, Jack. I can't say too much yet. We need to go to Shawn's house. Trust me. You need to come. Now.'

Chapter 56

'Integrity is doing the right thing, even when no one is watching.'
Charles W. Marshall

Detective Holland called in his whole team. They had been on overtime for the last few months and would be until they had the suspect in custody. He told them he had organised for the CCTV to be put on tomorrow's prime-time news. He wanted every member of his team ready to go. He was positive a phone call would come in with a name. The CCTV footage was so clear that someone local must know who the man was. It worried him that the suspect was losing his temper with people. If he could lose it with a member of staff in a chemist's, what could he be doing with a five-year-old boy? Up until now he'd not put a foot wrong, so why was he going into a chemist and openly shouting at people? Was he near his end game? And what was that? There were many ways this could end, and the only outcome Detective Holland wanted was the one where George was alive.

The whole team watched the footage.

'I know him.'

'What did you say?' Holland asked.

Detective Abbot pointed at the picture. 'Him. I interviewed him weeks ago.'

'You're saying we fucking interviewed him?' Holland kicked a bin, sending wastepaper all over the floor. 'Give me his fucking name. Now.' For months he'd had sat in his office staring at George's picture. He felt he knew him. This boy was in his dreams at night and when he woke, the first face he saw was George's. Now he'd just found out they had the man's name all along. The guilt was crippling.

He turned his attention to Martin, realising now that he must have known the name. He was scared what the abductor would do if they turned up at his house. George's life was in their hands. He wanted the man apprehended but away from the boy. If George was still alive, and this man knew the police were coming, the suspect could end it his way because all the time he still had George, he was in control.

Chapter 57

'It's sad when someone you know becomes someone you knew.'

On the tray in front of him he had prepared orange juice, medicine, and soup. He picked it up and carried it to the bedroom.

'Georgie. Georgie, can you sit up for me?'

There was no reply, and no movement.

'C'mon, Georgie. You have to have this. It'll make you feel better.'

He placed the tray on the bedside table and sat on the edge of the bed. Touching George's forehead, he knew he was worse than yesterday. He shivered. The thought of losing his friend frightened him.

'One more day. Georgie. I'll get you to the hospital tomorrow. I promise. They'll give you what you need. I'll make sure your Mum and Dad are there. How about that?'

George stirred slightly but he didn't answer.

'I knew you'd like to hear that. Your Dad will be so happy to see you. He needs you home. He isn't very well either. I think if he had you, and you had him, it would all be OK. It's nearly over, Georgie.'

He adjusted the sheets on George's bed. 'I'm so sorry. This is all my fault. I didn't want this. I never wanted anyone hurt. I'll make it right though.'

George rolled slowly on to his back. He was frail and didn't speak but he did hold the man's hand. That was enough for the man to realise he had heard every word.

'Georgie, I'd like you to promise me something.'

George squeezed his hand.

'Promise me you won't forget me. Please remember I wasn't all bad. I've been good to you, right?'

He dropped to his knees, still holding George's hand. He put his head into the sheets to muffle his cry. 'I didn't want to hurt you Georgie.' Composing himself, he raised his head. 'After tomorrow, you won't see me again. All I want is for you to remember the good times we had. Could you do that for me?'

Another squeeze from George but weaker this time.

He helped George take his medicine, tucked him in and left him to sleep. He went downstairs and started preparing for the next day. He wanted his house to be clean. He knew the police and the press would be in there at some point. He didn't want them writing that he was some lonely loser who lived in his own filth. He had accepted that he was going to be portrayed as some sort of monster, which would be exacerbated by the public attention the story received, but hopefully he wouldn't be put in the same league as many others before him. The likes of the Moors Murderers who, to him, were child-murdering nonces. He reasoned to himself that what he did to George was different. He did what he did to upset one person. In his eyes it was fair at the time, but it had gone too far, and he knew it. Hurting that one person had been achieved. And now that he was going to let George go home, people would see he wasn't a monster.

He wrote a note explaining why he took George. He wanted people to understand. He was also going to write a letter to Jack and Kirsten but thought they wouldn't be interested, whatever he wrote.

He poured himself a coffee and sat in silence, wondering what he was going to miss after tomorrow. He knew he would miss George. He had loved their time together. George had taught him he could love someone without expecting anything in return. He sniggered as he thought of not missing Mrs Pounds from next door. After being with George this long he wished he'd had kids of his own but that was now an impossible dream.

The washing machine beeped; its cycle finished. He took out two items of clothing. A pair of boy's chino shorts, cream in colour, and a blue T-shirt, with a Union Jack on the sleeve. He wanted George to go home in the clothes his mother last saw him in. He held up the clean T-shirt. 'Kirsten will love this,' he said as he put the clothing into the tumble dryer. They would be ready for the morning. He had a new pair of children's trainers sitting on the kitchen table. Dorking didn't have a large sports shop. It wasn't that sort of town, too small for any large chain stores. But there was a shop called RuStar which sold high end rare trainers, the type sneakerheads would pay good money for. He'd gone in, ignored the staff and picked out the first pair he saw in a size that looked suitable for George. Nike Air Max 90s in a crisp white colour with blue tick, size one.

'Nice pair of Air Max they are, sir. Your boy will love them,' the shop owner said.

'His Dad will,' he had said as he left the shop.

The plan for the following day was a simple one. He was going to drive to the hospital and take George into accident and emergency. He would then leave him there in their capable hands. He had a note prepared to explain who George was and who his parents were. He was going to leave the note with the hospital staff, go home and then take care of himself. He was ready. One more day and it would be over.

Chapter 58

'True friendship is like sound health. The value of it is seldom known until it is lost.'

Martin told Kirsten they were going to Shawn's. She was pleased that Jack had agreed to go out and hoped he would open up to his friend. He was merely a shell of himself without George and she wanted him back so they could be a team again, putting all their energy into finding their son.

In the car, Jack didn't do any talking. Martin reassured him they wouldn't be out long, but they needed to see Shawn. Jack didn't ask why. They pulled up outside Shawn's house.

'Are you ready?' Martin asked,

Jack didn't answer but he got out of the car and headed for the door. Martin rang the doorbell and gave a double knock.

Shawn answered, short of breath. 'Jack, how are you, mate. What's wrong? What's happened?'

'I thought it would be good to get him out for a drive, come and see his mates. It's doing him no good being cooped up indoors,' Martin said, as he peered beyond Shawn into his house. 'Can we come in, or what?'

Shawn grinned. 'Yeah, of course. It's a bit of a mess. I wasn't expecting anyone. I'll get the kettle on.'

All three sat in silence sipping their coffee. Jack was slumped in his chair and rarely made eye contact with either of the others. Martin's attention was caught by photos of the friends together, and pictures of Jack winning his world title. 'Some amazing pictures here, mate. Great memories. I've never noticed them before.'

Shawn nodded. 'They've always been up there. I find myself taking them in more these days. Happier times.'

Martin downed what was left of his coffee and put his empty cup down. 'Do you think Lee is in? Let's go and see him.'

It was past 9pm. Shawn gave a slight shake of his head. 'I assume he will be but it's a bit late, isn't it? Shall I ring him first?'

'No,' Martin snapped.

'OK, mate, if you say so.'

'Shall we go now then? I've finished mine,' Martin said, putting his empty cup on the table.

Jack did the same.

'Give me a minute,' Shawn said. picking up the coffee cups, he took them out to the kitchen.

Martin and Jack waited in the car. Shawn got in the back and put his seatbelt on. Jack was sitting up front looking out of the window. Martin turned to Shawn. 'Let's go. You haven't rung him, have you?'

'No, why would I? You told me not to, so I didn't. What's up with you tonight? You're getting on my nerves. Is this all your police training turning you bossy?'

Martin didn't laugh.

After a few minutes uncomfortable silence Shawn stopped

339

shifting around in his seat. 'Any news, Martin? With all the new publicity I hoped the police would be overwhelmed with calls.'

Martin looked in his rear-view mirror. 'Nothing concrete, but there have been many calls coming in. It's a matter of picking out the right ones and getting rid of the crazies.'

The conversation had Jack's attention. 'The crazies? Who are they?'

'They want people talking about them. Lonely, sick bastards that want attention with nothing else in their pathetic little lives. They call the police, tell us some bullshit and hope we listen. And sometimes they're lucky enough to get a visit. That excites them. If it were up to me, I'd lock 'em up for a bit, see if they get excited about that. But that's never going to happen. Prisons are chocka. You have to do a lot wrong these days to get locked up.'

Jack took in what Martin said. 'And the right calls, any good ones you know about that can help us?'

Martin didn't take his eyes off the road. 'Nothing yet. I've spoken to Detective Holland. He's doing all he can. He's a good man. He won't quit until he finds George. I know that.'

Shawn was listening attentively from the back. He caught Martin's eyes in the rear-view mirror and knew he was holding something back.

When they arrived at Lee's house a light was on downstairs and one upstairs. Martin could see a neighbour peeping from behind the curtains. 'He's definitely in. Come on, let's give him a knock.'

He gave a proper policeman's knock.

'You really are a copper, aren't you?' said Shawn.

The door opened. 'Fucking hell. Are you trying to knock my

door down? What's wrong?'

'You busy?' Martin asked.

'Not really. What do you want?' Lee noticed Jack standing behind Martin and Shawn. 'Shit, Jack. I didn't expect to see you. Has something happened?'

Jack didn't answer. Martin and Shawn inched forward to enter Lee's house.

'What are you doing? Back up, you knobs. I'll come out to you. Go and wait in the car,'

Shawn moved even closer to Lee. 'Why can't we come in?'

'Yeah, why can't we come in, Lee?' asked Jack.

Lee frowned and pointed at his groin. 'I'm in my boxer shorts and the house is a shithole. I'd rather get dressed, then come outside. Is that alright with you lot?' He stared at Martin. 'You're starting to piss me off. Just wait in the car.'

Shawn was on edge, wanting to know what Lee was hiding. 'Let us in, ya soft prick. We don't care if it's a mess. And get some jeans on. You look a twat.' Shawn pointed at Lee's underwear. 'What are those? Bit tight, aren't they? I can see your piece.' He pushed past Lee, straight into the front room. Jack and Martin followed.

Lee held his arms out. 'Come on in. Make yourselves at fucking home.' He slammed the door and followed them.

'I suppose you want a drink? Coffee?' Lee asked.

'We've just had coffee at my gaff. Tea would be good though. Any biscuits?' Martin said.

'Yes, sir. No problem, sir. Would you like me to make some dinner as well?' Lee adjusted his shorts, worried something was poking out.

Shawn laughed. 'Tea will do fine.'

There was an uncomfortable silence between the four

friends with only an occasional slurp of tea being heard. Shawn scanned the room. There were more pictures of the friends. One of Lee and Jack when they were younger at a boxing event. There were also a few boxing trophies from Lee's victories in the amateurs.

'So, what are you boys up to tonight? I'm glad to see you out, Jack,' Lee said.

Shawn answered. 'I've no idea what we're doing. Martin turned up at my house and said he wanted us all together, so here we are.'

Just as Lee was going to reply they all heard a noise upstairs. Light footsteps moving across the floorboards. Lee groaned.

Chapter 59

'Returning violence for violence multiplies violence, adding deeper darkness to a night already devoid of stars.'
Martin Luther King

The home phone rarely rang. Her mum called her on it, but since George went missing, the only other people calling were the police. It was 9.30pm so if it was them, it must be important. She answered, praying it was good news.

'This is Detective Holland. How are you, Kirsten?'

'I'm OK. What's happened? Have you found him?'

'Sorry, Kirsten, not yet. But we might have a strong lead. I wanted to call you to let you and Jack know the latest. There will be some CCTV released tomorrow. It will be on most news channels. We have a possible suspect.'

'Is it him?'

'You know I'd never promise anything, but this is the best lead we've had so far. I won't go into why because we still don't know for sure.'

'Is it him? Is this going to be the man?' Kirsten started to cry. She was shaking. The idea of seeing the face of the man who took her son was scaring her.

'I think it is. Are you with Jack now? It would be best if you keep each other company through this,' the Detective said.

'I'll call my family. They will come round tomorrow. I'm alone at the moment. Jack's gone out.'

'Will he be back soon? Maybe I should talk to him as well.'

'I'm not sure. His friend, Martin, came and took him for a drive.'

'Martin Parker?'

'Yes, you know him, don't you? PC Martin Parker. He's been a good friend.'

'I know him. Did he say where they were going or what they were going to do?'

'He said they were going for a drive, probably to Shawn's. Shawn Dunmall. One of Jack's other close friends.'

'Do you have Shawn's address? I think it would be best if you called Jack and asked him to come home and then let him know about the CCTV.'

'I would but he didn't take his phone. I can see it in front of me. He's still not with it. He's hardly spoken since he got back from Liverpool. I'll get you Shawn's address. I'll text it over, I've got your number.'

'I think that would be best, and Shawn's phone number please.'

'Detective, you're starting to worry me. What's Martin done?'

'I just want to make sure no misinformation is coming to you and Jack. I only want you to hear the latest developments through me. I'm not sure what Martin thinks he knows, being in the police he may have heard rumours and he might be tempted to pass them on, that's all.'

'I'll ring him now and ask him to bring Jack home. And I'll

text over those details.'

'Thank you, Kirsten. Please call me if you need to talk. I'll be in touch tomorrow, after the release of the footage. Please don't be alone. This news might shake you up, seeing a potential suspect. Take care Kirsten.'

Chapter 60

'We live in a world where we have to hide to make love, while violence is practiced in broad daylight.'

Jack pointed to the ceiling. 'Who's up there?'

'It's no-one. Go out to the car and I'll be out in a minute,' Lee said.

Martin's phone started ringing. He looked and saw that it was Kirsten. He declined the call and put it on mute.

Shawn stood up and eyeballed Lee. 'Either you're being burgled, or you've got someone up there.' His phone rang.

'Turn it off,' Martin insisted.

Shawn was perplexed but did as he was asked without looking at who was calling.

The footsteps were coming down the stairs. The front room door opened and in walked a young lady, in her mid-twenties. She was beautifully delicate with perfect black skin. She smiled and batted her lashes in embarrassment. 'Hello, I'm Michelle.' With her bag in her hand, she was awkwardly trying to get her second shoe on. Lee got up to help her. 'You don't have to go.'

'Nice to meet you, Michelle,' said Shawn. 'Please stay. We'll go. I'm sorry we crashed in like this. I'm afraid Lee has no manners and didn't tell us you were here. We'll go, we can see him another time.'

As they all stood up, she reached her arm out to stop them going. 'No, don't. I've got to leave soon, anyway. My Mum's looking after my daughter. I need to get home.'

Michelle faced Jack. She clearly knew who he was. Lee must have told her everything. 'I'm so sorry about your son. I hope they find him soon. You must be going through hell. Lee's told me what a lovely boy George is.'

'Thank you, ' Jack said.

'Lee, I'll go. Call me later.' She kissed his cheek and then turned to the others. 'It was very nice to meet you all. Hopefully, I'll see you again.' She took Lee's hand. 'That's if this one ever takes me out.'

Jack sat back down, thinking of George, and Michelle's kind words.

Lee walked her to the front door and said goodbye. When he came back, he didn't speak.

'Well, who is she? And why is she with you? No wonder you didn't want us in your house,' Shawn said.

'And no wonder you were only in your tight, little boxers, dirty boy,' Martin joked.

'Yeah, yeah. It's not like that. It's early days. I didn't want to mess things up. I like her. I've never met anyone like her. I wanted to make sure, you know, that she was the one before I started introducing her to you guys. It's important to me that you like her. You've met her now, so it's all good,' Lee said.

'She's lovely, mate. You've done well. A bit too well, punching well above your weight there,' Martin said.

Lee laughed. 'Fuck off.'

Martin held up his hands. 'I haven't seen you with a girl in years. It's about time.'

Jack didn't join in their laughter. He walked over to a picture on Lee's wall. It was of all of them, with Sam.

Lee put a hand on Jack's shoulder. 'You don't mind, do you? I like having Sam's picture up. I talk to him sometimes. I know it's a bit mad, but it helps. He's only sixteen in that picture, but I still look up to him, like I always did.'

Jack touched Lee's hand. 'It's nice to see him.'

Lee changed the subject. 'Right, why are you boys here... honestly?'

Martin had a haunted look in his eyes. 'I've got something I need to talk about. I needed us all together. I don't want to say too much until I know for sure, so we need to go somewhere, and you all need to trust me. Lee, go and get some clothes on. We're going for a drive.'

Jack faced Martin. 'If it's about George, just tell me now. Please. I need to know.'

'Jack, trust me. If I tell you now and I'm wrong, I'll have upset you for no reason. It'll make things worse. Come with me, all of you. And when I know for sure, I'll say. I promise. I want us to do this together.'

Shawn dreaded what they were going to find out. 'Get ready, Lee,' he said. 'We'll be in the car.' As they headed out of the house, he saw Lee open a door under the staircase and pull out a baseball bat.

'Lee, put that fucking thing back.'

'Why? We might need it. You can go with your dick in your hand if you want, but I'm not. ' Lee said as he went to get his clothes on.

Martin started the engine. Jack was in the front, Shawn in the back. A few minutes later, Lee jumped in next to Shawn. He started mocking Martin. 'Had a busy night, driver? What time you on 'til?'

Martin's eyes were on him in his mirror. 'Fuck off. If this was a taxi, I'd throw you straight out.'

'How far now, driver? I need a piss. And stop the meter, you trying to rip me off?' Lee laughed again.

Martin's reply came with volume. 'Shawn, shut him up. The daft prick is doing my head in.' Lee nudged Shawn in the ribs.

They drove for another ten minutes and entered Lower Road, in Great Bookham, a charming and quiet village. Martin took a right on to Childs Hall Road. He was giving nothing away. He turned the headlights off as they pulled up outside a house. They could just make out the house name on the fence. Queensbury.

'I'll go and knock first,' Martin said.

'Whose fucking house is it?' Jack asked.

'Jack, just trust me, wait here.'

The three of them watched as Martin left the car.

Martin opened the gate and walked up the drive, looking around the whole time. He checked next door. Everything was quiet there. He carried on to the first window and peered inside. The curtains were drawn. He moved to the side of the house and peered through the kitchen window. Inside was tidy. On the kitchen table he could see some small Nike trainers.

A light came on. Martin hit the floor. From the car they could see everything. 'What the fuck is he doing? He's the worst copper I've ever seen,' Lee said as he pulled the baseball bat out from under his coat. 'Fuck it, I'm going in.'

The others followed him.

Martin waved frantically at them and mouthed, 'Get back. Fucking get back.' He crept towards them and took hold of Jack. Speaking quietly but with assertiveness, he said, 'Go back to the car. Do it my way, Jack, please.'

'Bollocks. Who's in there? We're going in.' Lee whispered.

'Lee, fuck off and do as you're told. Think of George and listen to me.'

They all went back to the car.

'Martin, who lives there, and what the fuck is going on?' Jack's voice was hoarse.

Martin sighed. 'Right, we'll go in. But this isn't where George is, so calm down. I'm just hoping he'll help. OK?'

'So, whoever lives in there can help? Really?'

'I don't know for definite, but maybe. If we do get in, please let me do the talking. Don't upset him, and don't touch him.'

'Let's just go,' Jack said.

As they left the car, Martin prodded Lee in the chest. 'Put that thing in the car. You won't need it.'

'Spoilsport,' Lee said but he did as he was asked.

Martin got to the front door, the other three behind him. 'You ready? Remember what I said and let me do the talking.'

Lee's attention was drawn to a light next door. The neighbour's curtain was part open. An elderly lady was watching them. He gave her a little wave and a wink. She closed the curtain quickly.

Martin rang the bell. They could hear footsteps. Someone was coming to answer the door.

Chapter 61

'An eye for an eye makes the whole world blind.'

Detective Holland knocked loudly. His team had every exit covered.

'Can I help you?' asked the man who answered the door.

Detective Holland recognised him. 'David Huntley, is he here?'

Pete opened the door fully and took a step back. His voice shook. 'What's he done?' 'Where is he, sir? Is he here? We're going to search anyway so don't lie to us.'

'He's not here. He's at my other place. All his post and that comes here but he sometimes stays in Bookham, our other house. Please tell me what he's done?'

Detective Holland turned to Detective Abbot. 'Did you check the other house when you interviewed him?'

Abbot looked at the ground. 'No. This is his registered address. I didn't know he had another place.'

Holland shook his head and looked back at Pete. 'What's your name, sir?'

'I'm Pete Huntley, his father.'

'I'm going to need your other address. Now.'

Pete clutched his throat. His breathing was fast and erratic.

Holland could see he was struggling to breathe and stepped forward to steady him.

Pete looked Holland in the eyes. 'He's got him... hasn't he? David... has Jack's... son. Little... George.' He slid slowly to the ground. His groan only lasted for a second before he grabbed again at his throat with both hands. His mouth was wide open, his eyes horror-stricken.

'Call an ambulance,' Holland shouted.

Detective Abbot pulled his phone from his pocket and made the call.

Holland loosened Pete's shirt, trying to alleviate pressure on his neck. As he watched, Pete's eyes slowly closed. He laid Pete flat on its back, then opened his airway with a tilt of his chin. Putting his ear to Pete's mouth he couldn't hear anything and shouted at Abbot. 'That fucking ambulance needs to get here now.'

Holland was on his knees. He placed one hand over the other and began working on Pete's chest. He pushed down with force. 'One, two, three, four...' After thirty chest compressions he gave two rescue breaths. He listened again for any noise from Pete's mouth but there was nothing.

'He's gone. I'm sure he has,' Holland said as he repeated the chest compressions.

'Let me have a go. Move back,' Abbot said.

Holland moved, his back now against the wall. He took huge deep breaths as he watched.

Abbot clamped his hands together and pushed down. There was a sickening crack. 'His bloody ribs are breaking.'

'Carry on until the ambulance gets here. Don't worry about his fucking ribs, just keep going.'

Abbot repeatedly gave mouth to mouth and chest compressions and listened and checked for any signs of breathing. 'There's nothing.'

Holland didn't take another turn, instead, he patted Abbot on the back and asked him to stop. 'It's over. He's gone.'

David answered the door. He didn't look surprised to see them there.

'Evening, gents, is everything OK?'

'Can we come in? We wanted to get Jack out for a drive, thought it would do him good to see his mates.'

'What do you want? How did you know I was here?' David asked.

'I did some digging about, found out your dad had another place,' Martin said.

'I thought you lived with your dad. Is he here?' Shawn asked.

'He stays in the flat in Dorking. This is the old family home. It's got too many painful memories of my mum. He couldn't handle it here.'

Martin was piecing things together. It made sense now. 'So, when the police interviewed you, it was at the flat?'

'I stay there a lot. I'm down as living there. It's closer to the gym.'

'Can we come in?' Lee asked.

'You can, but it's pretty late.'

'Come on mate, we won't stay long,' Martin said.

'Ok, come through. Don't worry about your shoes.' He directed them into the living room.

Jack felt uneasy. He couldn't work out why they were there and couldn't understand how he didn't know that Pete had

353

another house.

'Take a seat. Can I get you all a drink? Hot one? There might be some beers in the fridge.'

'Beer would be good,' said Lee.

'Beer all round please,' Shawn said.

David was only gone a minute and returned with five bottles of Peroni. 'It's Italian I think,' he said, as he looked at the label before handing one to each of his guests. Shawn took a quick swig. 'Not a bad size place you have here. You all alone?'

David ignored the question.

'I was telling the boys; a few new leads are coming in regarding George's disappearance. Some CCTV footage that might lead us to him.' Martin waited for David's reaction.

Jack gave him a frightened stare. 'You didn't say anything about any CCTV. Can I see it?'

'It might be nothing, but I've been told it's good footage. It was at the chemist in Dorking. Could be a lead, could be nothing.' David was bright red.

Martin put his bottle of beer on the coffee table. 'Do you mind if I use your toilet?'

'The place is a tip; do you really need the toilet?' David put his beer down.

'I wouldn't ask if I didn't need to go. Where is it?'

David pointed, 'through the kitchen. There's a toilet out the back. I can show you.'

'Nah, I'll find it. I'm a big boy.' Martin got up and gave David a gentle slap on the back before leaving the room and entering the kitchen. He closed the door behind him so they couldn't see what he was doing. He picked up the Nike Air Max from the table. Child size 1. Up until now, he'd prayed he had it wrong. He put the trainer down and quietly started going through the cupboards, then the fridge where he found Calpol medicine. As he closed the fridge, he noticed the door to the cellar. It had a padlock on it, but it wasn't locked. He took it off and pulled the door open. Inside was pitch black. He got out his phone and turned on the torch.

David was starting to sweat and a vein in his neck was visibly raised. He looked behind him worrying what Martin was up to. Lee noticed his discomfort and wanted his attention.

'Harry Potter fan, eh?' Lee said pointing at the television.

'Pardon?'

'The book over there, by the television. 'Goblet of Fire', is it?' Lee asked.

David took a closer look, 'Chamber of Secrets,' David replied.

'Nice. Prefer the films myself, not got time for the books. They do my head in.'

Jack felt dizzy. His hands were tingling, going numb. He started to clench his fists and open them repeatedly to bring some life back into them. His eyes remained on David.

'Are you OK, Jack?' David said.

Martin went down the steps slowly and used the light on his phone to search around the room. Near the bottom step was a sack of clothes. He shone the light inside. They were children's clothes. Boys. Martin was crumbling inside, his heart racing. There was no doubt now. But where was George? He walked slowly over to the empty bed. On the sideboard was a bundle of child's drawings. He looked at them, one by one. There was a picture of a man with big red hands. Martin realised they were boxing gloves. George had drawn his dad. He dropped to his knees, pain gripping his chest, his vision

355

blurred. 'No. No, God. Please no.'

They were too late. George was gone.

David stood up, he was visibly shaking, 'I can't do this... I know this looks bad but it's not what you think. He came to me a few months back and asked to rent my house. He knew I lived with my dad most of the time and said he needed a place nearby, for business and all that.'

'What the fuck are you talking about? Who are you talking about?' Lee asked.

David looked at Jack and held his palms out in self-defence, 'I had no idea until the other day, and the minute I knew I wanted to tell you, but he said if I said anything, he would say I was involved, he'd say that I took him. It's my bloody house, it looks like I'm involved... but I'm not. I tried to help. I went and got some medicine for him.'

'Medicine for who?' Jack asked. He then stood up and got in David's face.

'Jack, I promise I'm nothing to do with it. He'll be here in a minute, he's on his way.'

Shawn stood alongside Jack and poked David in his chest, 'Are you talking about George? Do you know who has him?'

Jack lunged forward and punched David, as David hit the ground, Jack leant over him. He pulled David's head up by his hair and with the other hand, he raised his fist. 'Tell me now or I'll fucking kill you. Where's George?'

They heard a key being turned in the front door.

'David, whose car is that outside?' the man shouted as he entered the house.

Shawn put his hand over David's mouth and whispered, 'Don't say a word.'

'I'll get him,' Lee said as he headed for the front door. Jack dropped David's head and followed.

Lee pulled the front room door open as hard and as fast as he could. There he was, standing with a stupid grin. A grin that disappeared once Jack went towards him punching him on the jaw, he hit the ground with a sickening thud and was instantly unconscious.

'Get his feet,' Jack said.

Lee grabbed the other leg to Jack, and they dragged him into the front room.

As they came in, Shawn let go of David.

'What the fuck is he doing here?' Shawn asked.

David got to his feet, 'That's what I was trying to tell you, he's been renting my house for months. I came round last week, and he wouldn't let me in. I returned the next day and when he was out, I let myself back in and... I found out what he'd done.'

'What do you mean, what he'd done?' Jack turned to Lee, 'Wake him up.'

Lee slapped the man's face, but nothing. 'Fuck this,' Lee said as he stepped back and then went forward kicking him in his groin.

His eyes opened and the man screamed out in pain.

Lee had a little grin on his face, 'That wakes up any man.'

Once his screaming stopped, he got to his knees, pulled his bow tie off, and undid his collar so he could breathe easier, 'You found Georgie yet, Jack?' Roy said.

Jack tilted his head slightly as he stared down at him. He wasn't sure he'd heard him right. 'What did you say? Georgie? His fucking name is George.'

'It's so painful when you lose someone you love, isn't it?'

357

Roy smiled.

David stepped forward, 'Roy. Stop talking, just tell him where George is. He'll kill you if you don't.'

But Roy didn't stop. His eyes were fixed on Jack. 'Rips your heart out, doesn't it? I lost my mum a while back, that hurt.'

Lee stepped to within an inch of Roy, 'I'm fucking warning you. Shut your disgusting mouth.' He turned to Shawn. 'You've got to shut him up.'

Shawn dropped his bottle of beer as it all sunk in.

'Shawn, you look a bit peaky; would you like some water?' Roy goaded him.

Shawn didn't reply.

David stepped forward, 'Roy, they will kill you, shut up or...'

Before David carried on, Shawn punched David in the stomach, 'Did you do it with him?'

Struggling for breath David replied, 'No, I promise. I didn't know. And when I found out he promised me he was giving George back.'

Holding his head in his hands and pulling on his hair Jack couldn't think straight, he couldn't work out what was happening. It was obvious but he didn't want to believe it.

'Shall I put some music on?' Roy said, he didn't wait for an answer. He got his phone out and selected a music app and pressed shuffle. The first random song wasn't to his liking. He pressed shuffle again. 'Coldplay? Nope, not good enough. Oh, I know.' Another grin. 'Jack you'll love this.' He selected 'Spiegel im Spiegel'. 'That'll do nicely, Jack. This was a lovely choice of song at your last fight. I find music helps, don't you?' Roy selected repeat. The music started playing through several speakers in the room. He closed his eyes and listened with a contented smile on his face as he sat on the chair.

'Turn that fucking thing off,' Shawn shouted.

'Jack, don't listen to it. Roy, turn it off.' Lee went to get up, but Shawn stopped him.

Jack sat up straight. 'Roy, where's George? You need to tell me.' Jack's eyes had a haunted, vacant look.

'Where's Martin?' Shawn shouted, 'Martin, get back in here.'

David was in tears, 'Don't do it, Jack.'

Jack turned his attention to David, 'You're involved, aren't you? He's your mate. I'm going to kill you both if you don't tell me where George is.'

David raised his hands and started crying, 'I'd never do that, I wouldn't hurt your lad, honest. I wanted to tell the police and tell you, but Roy said he was going to give George back the next day. I went and got some medicine for him to give to George coz he's ill and...'

Roy laughed. 'Too late, he's gone now,' Roy said.

Martin was still in the cellar. Frozen with fear, he knew what Jack was going to do. He'd wanted to find George before he told him, but that chance was gone. 'Shawn, don't let Jack near him, get him out of here, now,' he shouted. They all heard the muffled calling from the cellar.

Jack breathed hard. He felt weak and out of control of his body. 'Roy, what have you done?'

Roy ignored Jack and picked up his phone to turn up the volume. 'It's time, Jack. This is how it ends,' he said.

Lee jumped up. 'Outside, Jack. Let's get outside. Let's call the police. Don't do it. It's what he wants.'

Shawn didn't move. He'd always done the right thing in the past, he always tried to stop Jack from getting himself in trouble. He grabbed Lee and pulled him in close. 'Lee, leave him. Leave Jack to it. Roy deserves it.'

Jack had a feeling inside that was new. In all the fights he'd ever had, he'd never wanted to kill anyone. He'd fought angrily, he'd fought with violent intentions, but this thirst to kill was different. Everything in him was telling him to kill Roy. It felt right. He needed that release from the pain and grief inside.

Lee was frantically pushing Shawn. 'We've got to stop him. You know what Roy has done, right? Jack will kill him. We need to get him out. He's gonna fucking murder him.'

Shawn grabbed Lee and cupped his face. 'Not this time, mate. I'm not stopping him. And you're not either.' Shawn had tears in his eyes, but he was calm. He looked across at Jack and nodded. 'Do what you need to. Make him tell you where George is and then finish him.'

Lee screamed. 'No, Shawn. We can't.' Shawn grabbed him and pushed him until they were out of the room.

'Jack, please don't do it, it's what he wants,' David pleaded.

'David, unless you're involved in any way, you can go. Get out.'

'Jack, I'd never...'

Jack stood and screamed in David's face, 'just go.'

Only Jack and Roy remained in the front room as David left the house.

Roy didn't move. He wasn't going anywhere. He'd been waiting for this. This was his ending, the way he'd planned it. He was still smirking.

'Just tell me why?' Jack said as he rocked back and forth,

fighting his emotions. His anger was building. Kirsten was flashing in and out of his thoughts, but he could still feel his murderous rage inside needing to come out. He looked up and screamed, but not for help. It was him losing control. The pain within was ready to come out. The pain of old, losing Sam, watching him drown, the pain of losing George, imagining what Roy had done to him. He couldn't take any more.

Martin was sitting, crying, with his back to the cellar wall. He heard Jack's scream and knew what was happening upstairs but couldn't bring himself to stop it. It felt wrong and he was worried about the consequences for everyone, himself included.

As Roy moved to the edge of his seat, Jack unleashed his first blow. A straight punch to Roy's nose before screaming at him, 'Tell me why?'

Roy held his face with one hand, the other hand, palm up, was to indicate to Jack to not come closer. 'Jack, listen. When you sacked me, I was furious. I wanted revenge. I tried to get it legally, but my lawyer said I had no case. So, with my liking for boys, I thought I'd take yours. I knew how much it would hurt.' Roy wiped the blood from his nose. It was running into his mouth. He spat it out aiming at Jack's feet before continuing. 'David and I met years ago online. You see, we have similar interests. In kids that is. But he chose not to act on his impulse, he wanted help and he wanted to talk with other men like himself to see if they could help each other.'

'You two like kids? David likes kids?' Jack nodded in disbelief.

'Yeah, that's right, boys. But David chose to be good, his

dad made him get help. David wanted to change, he tried to help me in the beginning, said he had some shrink I could see, some Irish woman, he said she was really good and helped him fight his urges.'

'What?' Jack felt dizzy.

'You sick bastard.' With his left hand, Jack pulled Roy up by his neck, before firing his right fist into his forehead. Roy went down, his head bouncing off the floor as Jack punched him again. 'How could you hurt my George?' Another blow landed, this time a hammer fist to his forehead. Roy's face was covered in blood. There was a large laceration above his eyes and his nose was broken.

Outside, Shawn and Lee could hear the shouts from the house. 'He's gonna kill him. Please, we gotta go back in,' Lee pleaded.

'He's killed George. He's taken his boy from him, from all of us. We're not stopping Jack.'

Shawn switched attention to David, 'You need to go. Don't call anyone, just fuck off, this is your fault, bringing that sick bastard into Jack's life.'

David didn't argue. They watched as David walked into the distance.

Jack stepped back from Roy. It didn't make sense. He fell back onto the sofa, fighting the urge to kill. Thoughts of Kirsten came to mind, how she wanted them to still have a life together. She loved him as no one had before. He loved her.

Roy stood up, spat more blood out, and walked over to Jack. 'Do you realise how that made me feel? You, sacking me before I was about to make millions out of you, I knew you'd be a champion, I deserved some of that glory.' He choked on his blood and spat it again before he carried on. 'Georgie cried for you for so long... and then eventually, he didn't.' He prodded Jack's chest. 'He ended up liking me, I was his mate.'

Jack interrupted through shaky breaths. 'Tell me he's alive.'

Roy walked over to the window and had a quick look outside. 'I wanted to hurt you. I knew I couldn't beat you up physically. But mentally, you're weak. After what happened with your brother, I knew you couldn't handle losing anyone close again. Pete told me you suffered from depression and your brother dying messed you up. I knew I could seriously fuck with you. What was the worst thing I could do to you? Take your Georgie.'

Roy bent down to Jack's eye level and whispered, 'I took your boy. I'd always liked boys. Did you hear that, Jack?' He prodded Jack's chest twice as hard this time.

Jack knew what was coming. Slowly he looked Roy up and down. He could see the vein in his neck bulging as he spat out his hateful vile words. He could see the glass bottle on the table. Jack put his hands on his head and screamed out, 'Roy, shut up. Just shut up. Stop talking. Tell me, where is he?'

'Georgie's gone.' Roy closed his eyes and waited. 'It's time, Jack. Did you hear what I said? Little Georgie has gone. I did things to him first and then I killed your b...'

Jack grabbed him by the throat. With his free hand, he picked up the empty beer bottle and smashed it in half on the edge of the coffee table. He held it up to Roy's neck and begged him not to talk any further. Roy's bulging vein was inviting. It would take seconds to plunge the glass in and it would all be over.

Roy spat more blood at Jack. 'Do it. Finish it, Jack. You have to. I know it and so do you.'

Jack closed his eyes. Thoughts flashed through his mind, but now Kirsten's smile was all he could see. The love she had shown him since they'd been together was everything he wanted. He had a life. They could still have a future. Together they were one. They'd help each other cope with the loss of George.

Roy smiled, waiting for the glass to be plunged in.

Jack's final roar was deafening as he threw the glass across the room. He let go of Roy and backed away. The back of his legs hit the sofa and he fell back.

Outside, Lee had given up fighting to get past Shawn and was crying in his arms. Shawn held him tight as they heard Jack's scream.

Roy stood motionless, in disbelief. 'Jack, you have to.'

'I can't. I don't want to lose her.'

With a begging look in his eyes, Roy pleaded, 'But this is how this all ends.'

Jack was exhausted. 'Roy, I'm not a killer. Just tell me where George's body is. His mum deserves that. Do that for her, please.'

Roy stuttered. 'But... but I have to die. I c...can't go to prison. Not for what I've done.'

'Then do it yourself. I told you, I'm not a killer.'

Roy became frantic. 'I...I can't. I can't do it.'

Jack stood up. 'Where is he? Please, Roy, it's over, just tell me.'

'He's upstairs.'

Jack's head dropped and he exhaled. He had no idea what he would see when he got to his son's body. He started walking to the door.

'Jack.'

He turned to face Roy for what he knew would be the final time.

Roy had tears in his eyes. 'He's alive.'

Jack gasped. 'What did you say? I thought you'd...'

Roy interrupted, 'I'm not a killer either. He's alive, Jack.'

Jack took the stairs three at a time.

Roy shouted, 'he needs to go to the hospital. He's not well. Look after him.' He then whispered to himself, 'Look after my Georgie.'

Jack was afraid Roy was lying, but as he entered the room there was someone small in the bed. He looked closer. He was beautiful. His precious boy. On the bedside table was a Harry Potter Lego set perfectly displayed.

'George. George, come on, champ,' Jack fell onto the bed. He had Roy's blood on his hands, and this was transferred to the sheets as he lifted them off his son. George wasn't moving. 'Come on, George. Daddy's here now.' He rocked him gently. 'Let's go and see Mummy. She's lost without you. We both are.' He picked up his son and shouted, 'Shawn, call an ambulance. He's not moving.'

Shawn heard and ran back into the house. Lee followed. They stopped as they saw Jack walking down the stairs with his boy in his arms.

'Lee, call them, now,' Shawn said.

'Bring him outside, Jack. Don't take him in there.' Shawn gave a nod toward the living room.

They went out to the lawn where Jack laid George down. 'Is he breathing? I can't tell.'

Martin had regained his composure and came up from the cellar. He walked through the kitchen and opened the door to the front room. He saw Roy. The music was still playing. In anger, he pulled the wires out and threw the speakers across the room. Roy didn't flinch.

'Was it you all along? What about David?'

Roy sniggered, 'David couldn't do what I've done, he's too weak.'

Martin was in shock, 'Jack knows it's you, and he didn't kill you.'

Roy moved his head slowly and caught Martin's stare. 'He's not a killer. That's what he told me. I wanted him to, I can't go to prison.'

Martin scratched the back of his neck. He went back into the kitchen pulling open the drawers until he found the one with the cutlery. He took out the sharpest knife he could see. Picking up a small towel, he wiped the drawer handles before returning to the living room, He stood behind Roy.

Roy could feel his presence. 'At least someone's got some balls,' he said.

Martin wiped the handle to clean off his fingerprints and using the towel to hold the knife, he placed it down by Roy's side. 'Do it yourself, you sad little prick. You're right, prison's no place for someone like you.'

Roy shot Martin a look.

'It'll be hell. They'll do all sorts to you in there.'

Roy's malevolent smile had gone for good. He nodded in agreement and stared at the knife before picking it up.

As Martin left the house, he saw Jack and Shawn kneeling over George's body.

Shawn was listening to George's chest but all he could hear was Lee talking to the operator.

'They're on their way. Five minutes,' Lee said.

'Is he alive? Shawn, please tell me he's alive,' Jack pleaded.

Shawn looked at Jack in despair.

Lee was heading back to the house.

'Where are you going?' Martin asked.

'There's something I need to do,' Lee replied.

'Don't go back in there. It's done. Just leave it. Let's stay with Jack.'

'But we need to cover up what Jack's done before the police come.'

Martin put his hand on Lee's shoulder. 'Jack didn't kill him.'

Lee stared through Martin looking for answers.

'Don't worry about what happened to Roy, it's dealt with. We are all in the clear,' Martin said.

'Where's that ambulance?' Shawn shouted.

Jack felt George's hand move. 'George, come on, champ. It's Daddy. I'm here, son.' Jack spoke rapidly. 'He's OK. He just moved.'

They could hear sirens. The ambulance was close. 'About time,' Shawn said as he ran out to the road, waving his arms to let the driver know exactly where they were needed.

Jack held George in his arms and kissed his forehead.

'Lee, please ring Kirsten? Tell her we've found him, he's coming home.'

Lee smiled. 'No problem.'

The paramedics jumped out as soon as their vehicle stopped.

Jack walked towards them, cradling his boy. 'He's alive, but he needs help.'

One of the paramedics opened the back doors of the ambu-

367

lance. Jack took his son inside and placed him on the wheeled stretcher.

'Excuse me, sir,' the paramedic said as she slid in front of Jack and started to assess George. 'What's happened to him?'

'I'm not sure. His foot looks bad. I can't see anything else wrong.'

As she completed her initial assessment, she spoke to her colleague. 'I've got a pulse. Can you check him, please?' She pointed at Jack.

Jack ushered away any help. 'I'm fine. It's not my blood. Please help my son.'

George moved his head. He was desperately weak but managed to call out, 'Mummy.'

Shawn was at the back of the ambulance, tears rolling down his cheeks. 'Jack, we got him. We got your boy back.'

Jack smiled and kissed George again. 'It's all right, son. You rest up, champ. We're going to see mummy very soon.'

George opened his eyes and squinted in the bright light. He smiled.

'Dad, it's you.'

The End

For my brother Robert Cox
I miss you every day.

Acknowledgements

To my wife Claire, my four sons and Dobby, I would like to say thank you for allowing me to hide away in my man cave for many hours writing this book.

For her patience and guidance through my writing journey, I would like to thank Lynne Hackles. Her tutoring on the Writing Magazine home study course was a major part of my writing journey.

To my early readers, Leanne Ball for believing in me and pushing me to finish the book, to Janet Humphries for proofreading, to Peter Marsh, Mark Dunmall, Chris Joy, Justin Skinner, Alan Parker, Justin Flashman, Kenneth Macpherson, James Bray, Paul Abbott, Alexis Holland and Philip Garrard, thank you for all your valued feedback. Thank you Becka Coles and Ruth Ormsby-Ashworth at Eternal Tattoos for my logo design.
Finally, for my friends that were there on that day on June 11th, 1989, Shawn Butcher, Graham Kenward, Chris Joy, Paul Edwards and Robert Harding, friends for life.

About the Author

About the author:

Cassius Cox lives with his wife and four sons in Dorking, Surrey. This is his debut novel.

Instagram:
   Cassius Cox (@cassiuscoxauthor) · Instagram photos and videos

You can connect with me on:

 https://cassiuscox.com/coming-soon
 https://mobile.twitter.com/home
 https://www.facebook.com/cassius.cox.587

Subscribe to my newsletter:

 https://cassiuscox.com/coming-soon

Printed in Great Britain
by Amazon

59803535R00220